The Gym

Lawrence H. Sola

Black Rose Writing | Texas

ISBN: 978-1-68433-535-0 (Paperback); 978-1-944715-62-5 (Hardcover)
PUBLISHED BY BLACK ROSE WRITING
www.blackrosewriting.com

Library of Congress Control Number: 2020909165

Printed in the United States of America
Suggested Retail Price (SRP) $21.95 (Paperback); 26.95 (Hardcover)

The Gym is printed in Palatino Linotype

*As a planet-friendly publisher, Black Rose Writing does its best to eliminate
unnecessary waste to reduce paper usage and energy costs, while never compromising
the reading experience. As a result, the final word count vs. page count may not meet
common expectations.

To the little blond who made the second star to the right burn bright again.

Praise for
The Gym

"Sola flawlessly laces many memorable, timely, and poignant themes (love, jealously, betrayal, heartbreak, and many more) throughout this book!" 4 out of 4 stars!
–Online Book Club

"A humorous and thought-provoking foray into the author's Neverland and the search for his destiny."
–Sublime Book Review

"A fascinating look at life in a small beach town. A great beach read!"
–Author Bob Martin - Bronx Justice

"Well written, very easy to lose yourself in! The many dates one after another, ending with his final love. The characters are well developed. Many plot twists and great humor throughout!
–Author Emily Lynn Paulson

"I didn't read book one – The Show, but will now. But The Gym stands well on its own as I enjoyed the tale of a gym in Florida. Good characters and dialogue move a compelling plot along at a quick pace."
–Novelist Neil Perry Gordon

"Peter Pan Man attracts many women, many of whom are younger, who greatly inspire a story that will remind us that a morose past has no say in the life of those who will keep their eyes on the stars!"
–Alex Moore, an avid reader/member of The Gym

The Gym

The Gym

CONTENTS

PROLOGUE

THE AUTHOR WHO BOUGHT THE GYM

SEPTEMBER 2015 – DECEMBER 2016

It had been nearly five years since my darkness drove my illustrious career off a cliff. I still struggled to look forward as regret held me captive in its shadow. By now, I had come to refer to it as *The Dark One*. After many painful looks inwards, I would fly away in my mind while looking at the world with the eyes of a child. For as long as I could remember, things looked different to me than most people. I thought back to a time of inspiration, years before. Fighting bouts of depression, I was haunted by the recurring vision of a book cover, which galvanized unrelenting energy to pen the story of my rise and fall. Upon completing the manuscript, I felt a sense of accomplishment and closure, only to wake up one day, weeks later, exasperated and unsure.

The Dark One escorted me to the source of my angst.

With a pounding heart, I opened my laptop. My gaze shifted from empty wine bottles staggered about the table to the date on the screen: Tuesday, September 1st, 2015.

All at once, I struggled to breathe. *Did I waste two years of my life writing this story?* I questioned myself. The room darkened despite the morning hour as I sat motionless listening to the rain.

Minutes later, I wiped my teary eyes, determined to stop fighting with my thoughts. Then a crack of thunder sounded, and my iPhone rang as lightning illuminated the room. I blinked at the name.

It was the twenty-four-year-old grad student I passed my manuscript to on a blurry night; I could not recall fast enough but was anxious to answer. "This is Larry…" I held my breath.

"Hi Larry, it's Becky Morrison!" she cried triumphantly. "I'm emotionally drained and done!"

I frowned reflectively. "You and me both."

She laughed. "No, I finished your story." Papers shuffled, and she spoke methodically. "I have detailed notes for you," she seemed to be peering over them, "but I'm late for class and will email them."

I fidgeted in the chair. "A yea or nay will do."

"Calm down, ya silly goose! See, I'm already quoting you. I loved it. I'm starting to believe you are Peter Pan."

"The free-spirited boy bit is quite fictionalized."

"Save it for someone who hasn't met you. You let your inhibitions go like an unencumbered child."

I cleared my throat. "Well, I don't want you to be late for class, so…skip along now."

"Larry, stop. I happen to think it's a big reason you achieved the success you did."

"And drove it all off a cliff," I moaned and slid down in the chair.

"Yes, both. They are life lessons. Stop beating yourself up." She hesitated, then added coolly, "The story works. Trust me."

My mind raced forward. I had no idea how the call ended but sat with a sparkle of something in my eyes. I knew what was coming. Like magic, an email notification emerged from my darkness as another ray of light. It was more feedback for *The Show*, my aptly named manuscript. The lengthy message critiquing it ended with a recommendation to send it on to a small publisher who the woman knew. The very next day, my editor did the same. Within weeks, I received a publishing contract with a release date of March 24th, 2016. Without question, this bright spot in my life ushered in the new beginning I craved; however, it was a painful ending. After a poignant farewell call to Wendy Darlington—the leading lady of *The Show*—I began the divorce process and separated from my wife, something I fought for years. Being emotionally conflicted only heightened my creativity with the new notion or delusion; I would thrive with my own business. Often impetuous, I naturally ignored the risks involved and followed my heart with the belief that each day holds magic.

I walked into a grocery store with a hop to my step and was handed a booklet of businesses for sale by an older man in a red shirt and meticulously neat beard. Casually flipping through the pages, I noticed a beachside fitness club circled in red. It was the only business circled. When I turned to question the man, he was gone. Full of intrigue, I drove to the quiet seaside town across the river from where I lived to check it out.

Fascinated by Melbourne Beach's history and stories of Ponce De Leon landing there had me lowering my windows before I took a right into the fitness club's oddly quaint plaza. The ocean breeze energized me, although the faded wood signs did not appreciate the salt air as I did. They did not boast the Chinese restaurant, nail place, hair salon, or looming Publix supermarket, but it didn't matter.

It was the beach, after all.

A mysterious beach that Ponce De Leon's men, his conquistadors, had searched for gold and the iconic fountain of youth. Diaries discovered revealed that here the men found mosquitoes, small furry creatures, and not much else. It would take the invention of WWII era mosquito spray, air conditioning, and the founding of NASA to build the area up to the highly desirable locale it was now. The local fire department displayed, "Welcome to Paradise! Don't tell anyone!" on its marquis, and anyone who lived here would agree. I stepped out of my car to a clap of thunder as the spring sky suddenly darkened over the quaint club. It all seemed scripted, a similar feeling to the moment in my life that inspired *The Show*.

A myriad of bikes was scattered in front, and oddly enough, a very affable seeming smoker in workout clothes. He waved lazily at me as his tanned hand lifted for a long drag when I opened the door. The club's odd beach mural greeted me as a backdrop. Ocean caps and birds. 1990s? The haunting thought occurred that this mural, with its fuzzy edges, was very normal here. The members on the old treadmills looked at me with wide eyes and mysterious smiles. *What are they thinking?* I wondered. The journey that I would choose next was imminently unclear. Would I purchase a gym? Laughing to myself, I thought, I look the part and love the beach. But there was something else; synchronicity completely escaping the typical sense of reality that came to me in a random conversation that gifted me another vision.

Leaning against an odd wall of mirrors, I almost felt the salt spray on my face when two women wearing beachy yoga garb sashayed in. They looked keenly at me. Suspecting my interest in buying the club, they were eager to chat. After some small talk, they fired off an unsolicited warning about The Gym while gesturing to the high-spirited original owner, Bob Ripper. "Everyone calls him the Ripper. He lost part of his soul with this place," one said firmly, eyeing his workout. "He and his partner, Ivan Ignatius, were the first owners who had to sell this place. And now a third is rumored to be wanting out."

Her friend's eyes narrowed eerily at me. "It's not a wise business investment, yet there always seems to be a man and his ego that will try." Her pupils widened as her gaze shifted to a guy strutting by with a weight belt over his shoulder. "That muscle head was banned after a roid rage but allowed back because he's friends with the town's hotshot lawyer, Bill Reed. He's the shorter guy who keeps looking over." She turned back to her friend. "Who was that cute yogi Bill was engaged to?"

Her sidekick's eyebrows lifted. "Allison...Allison Tinke." My eyes curiously shifted back to her. "Bill moved Allison to Vero." A strange smile worked its way across her chin, then she quickly added, "But that didn't exactly work out." She made a head gesture to an older gentleman wearing a Georgia Bulldogs T-shirt. "That Bill is known as Bill 'Two a Day' Tidden. He comes in twice a day to ride that same recumbent bike. Such a sweet man." Her gaze shifted to two handsome young men. "And those hotties are Joey and Vinny, the social media famous Moretti brothers." She paused when her iPhone rang, giving me an out.

"Thank you both," I said with a smug smile as she answered it. *This is definitely a small town*, I mused to myself.

Walking by the Moretti brothers with their dark, copious hair, I felt a hankering for my youth. I slipped into the club's dimly lit bathroom with old green tile and splashed cold water on my face. *How can this feel so right?* I pondered, staring at myself in the mirror while surrendering to the moment. As I left the bathroom, new characters were forming in my mind. My thoughts sped up, only craving more as I noticed two teenage girls on eroding ellipticals ogling the Moretti brothers next to a girl who looked like a young Lady Gaga. Laughing inwardly, a voice caught my attention. "Hey, dude." I turned to a kid with big funny hair and bloodshot eyes. "Are you a member?"

With the slightest pause, I realized he worked there. "No. I'm just checking The Gym out."

He nodded, seemingly stoned. "So, how does everything look?"

I smirked. "Everything looks perfect."

He tilted his head with a look of bewilderment as I hurried by a random guy on a rowing machine with a cup of Frosted Flakes. I couldn't imagine the story there. No stranger to the strange or being open to a situation when one presented itself, I took in a deep breath and smiled.

Stepping outside to rumbles of thunder, I looked around the parking lot again. I noticed an older man who looked familiar. I could not place where I had seen him but knew I had. Approaching my car, I turned back to him. He smiled and said, "Ahoy-Mate!"

Driving home along the Indian River on Florida's great US1 spun memories of Tampa—my illustrious career—my family—Wendy—of everything that had brought out the "greatness" in me. And *The Dark One*, too. Staying home in this unique central Florida landscape where the Indian River meets the Atlantic Ocean suddenly felt right. There were pockets of culture and good schools and Snowbirds. Maybe it was not so crazy at all.

That night, when I finally dozed off, I dreamt I was flying high in a jet that landed at The Gym. I tossed and turned to flashes of wild nights with women and wine until I found myself at a crossroads. Still fighting my depressed states, *The Dark One* stood off to the left as a woman I was meant to meet magically appeared to the right in a trail of pixie light. It became a vision I could not shake.

Within weeks, spring turned to summer, and on July 8th, 2016, I purchased the gym. Or "The Gym" as you will come to know it.

• • •

Curiosity was at an all-time high. And as the summer heated up, so did the rumors. Now they were focused on me, the author who bought The Gym. With my book for sale at the check-in counter, I acted as if I was famous, ignoring the flames burning out of control from a late summer fling with my yoga teacher to hire a pretty, twenty-two-year-old Zumba instructor named Allie Valentine. As I continued to chase stars, I masked my pain, collecting these moments for a new book, unaware they shaped my destiny.

By December, I completed some chapters, yearning for a voice to make sense of it. At this point, I met Kristen Bircher, a fiery redhead with hazel eyes and a seductive smile. Just weeks later, I would see precisely what was behind it.

One January morning, she casually asked me when her membership expired before intently informing me, she will inspire a pivotal character in my next book. Nursing a hangover, I only nodded with a silly smile.

An hour later, she hopped off a spin bike and tried again. She peeked her flush face in my office. "Oh, and by the way," she said, breathing heavily from her workout. "I had another dream we had wine time, like in *The Show*. She paused briefly with a whimsical stare. "Weird, huh?"

I hesitated.

"In this dream, did the waitress think I was your father?"

She beamed. "No! And she didn't think that in my last one either." The hope in her voice was alluring, "I'm only four years younger than Wendy."

I jokingly sighed. "Ah, if only you were four years older."

"Seriously, Peter Pan...stop."

I appreciated her enthusiasm for my book and continued the fun. "The wine time part of the story is quite fictionalized." I pushed a wine bottle behind my laptop when she shot me an incredulous look that was unwavering. "Okay, you're scaring me. When do you want to do this?"

"Tonight!" she exclaimed. "It's Super Tuesday." Referencing *The Show* again, she smiled from ear to ear.

I shot her my well-worn smirk as the club's door opened with a curious gust of salt air on an otherwise tranquil day.

Suddenly, a woman in her early forties stood beside us. "Hi, I used to be a member here." She held out her right hand, and I shook it.

My eyebrows raised slightly at the word *KISMET* on her T-shirt. "Hi, I'm Larry."

The corners of her mouth curled deviously. "I recently moved back to the beach and found my old yoga class roster." She pulled it from her purse and handed it to me. "I lost touch with these ladies and was wondering if they still take classes here."

I didn't recognize the names and slowly shook my head, increasingly intrigued. "No, I'm sorry," I said and looked at her as if dumbfounded when I noticed the list was three years old.

She drummed her fingers on the counter and exhaled, thinking. "How about Allison Tinke?"

I looked at her calmly but felt strangely exhilarated. "Nope. No Tink here." I winked at Kristen.

Kristen's eyes lit up, and she mouthed, *We're gonna have fun tonight!* She suddenly appeared even younger than she was, so I quickly turned back to the forty-something. She tugged at her KISMET T-shirt and sputtered, "But...you know Allison?"

I shrugged curiously. "No."

The woman thanked me and pulled her purse off the counter to leave. She stopped at the door and turned to look back at me. She smiled a rare smile of reassurance that I would. And then she was gone.

ONE

JUST BE YOU...AND BELIEVE!

JANUARY 10, 2017

KRISTEN'S BEACH HOUSE

Standing on Kristen Bircher's balcony, I gazed up at the stars over the ocean. The moon was bright. My outlook was dark, yet this moment stirred something inside me. With my empty heart still pounding, I sensed a strange sensation that went beyond simple sexual pleasure. I leaned against the rail, imagining those waves caressing that shoreline on the book cover of a modern-day fairy tale.

But then it got dark again. *Our sequel is no fairy tale, Sport! The Dark One* whispered with a spine-chilling laugh. *These visions of book covers will end if you get mushy on me. Now get back to your women and wine...*

I winced, glancing over my shoulder as Kristen pranced back into the bedroom with an Evian. "Hey, sexy author," she chirped. "Are you romanticizing this night for your sequel?" Her mouth was half-open, and hazel eyes were squinting at me. I turned away, but not before her playful gaze had dimmed. After gradually acknowledging that she looked forward to coming to The Gym because it meant that she would see me, I turned back to her. "I didn't mean to mislead you," she said. "Long-distance relationships aren't easy. Are you upset?"

I contemplated that. "No."

Despite flirting the last month away, I knew this was not exactly a date. The fiery redhead was a twenty-eight-year-old event planner and avid reader fascinated with my book, wine, and a good time.

I took a calming breath. This was not a night to dread. On the contrary, it was one that I dreamt about after finding The Gym. I still questioned how I got here. But here I was. My dream became my reality. If only someone could explain why it was still so dark.

A moment later, Kristen's voice emerged directly behind me. "Come back inside and make me laugh, or I'm gonna tell everyone that the new owner of The Gym has no clue how to use any of the equipment."

My gaze shifted to her, wide-eyed, in reverie. "Why do I feel like I took a wrong turn and ended up at the right place?"

"A conflict or struggle the main character goes through, perhaps," she said with an odd smile that served to pique my curiosity. I stared at her indecisively as she told me that every good love story needs a relatable theme and a good plot. As Kristen baited me further, her voice was gentle and persuasive. "You are the character in your book." I glowered at her grinning face, unresponsive. "And it seems like you lost your shadow...Peter Pan." She paused for effect. "I'm wondering if Wendy has it." She smiled mischievously, referring to my novel.

I stared down at her for a long, quiet moment of morose reflection. "It's late," I said softly. "I should get going."

"You should start writing again."

"I tried." I closed my eyes, wondering when the woman in my dream would appear in a trail of pixie light. "It's not working, though."

She sighed heavily, making no effort to conceal her annoyance. "A woman wandered into your gym wearing a *KISMET* T-shirt inquiring about someone named Allison Tink(e). That is a sign calling to you!" My thoughts circled back to the vision of a book cover. "If you believed, again, you would see that."

"You're reaching," I replied, unable to contain my smile.

"If you were living life with the childlike joy you used to, you would believe in these signs again."

I needed a moment and gazed back at the ocean. "So, your mother lets you stay here when she travels?"

"Y-e-s," she said through clenched teeth. "Did you know Hemingway rewrote the first part of *A Farewell to Arms* over fifty times? I can help you, Larry."

I secretly craved her advice but was lost in the moment. When I turned to her, Kristen had vanished.

I blinked at her sudden, unexpected disappearance.

In the corner of my eye, I noticed her silhouette against the light in the next room. She picked up her cat Bella and screamed that she loved Ed Sheeran. *"Loving can hurt!"* she sang out as his song, "Photograph," blared through her mother's Bang & Olufsen speakers. *"Loving can hurt sometimes…"*

I grabbed my shirt off the bed and joined her in an enormous room with pricey artwork. Kristen sang loudly from an oversized couch with her red hair over her face. When I pulled my arm through my shirt sleeve, she shouted, "Wait! We have to take a picture." Wearing only her robe, which was open, she laughed at my facial expression of horrified surprise and snapped a selfie. We stared at the unsettling picture, with our hearts beating wildly.

I smirked. "Truly disturbing."

"I love it!" Kristen replied, startled by a text.

Her lips parted, glaring at it before she informed me it was her sister venting about another pretentious Facebook post from their mother. Kristen cried out, "My mother didn't have thirty-five-years of bliss in her marriage—who writes that? My dad took a job in another state because of their issues." She studied the post for a few more seconds and added, "And she tagged business owners she can't stand." Her eyes grew wide with a look of disgust. "Eww, she even tagged Jimmy Hook." I looked at her quizzically. "People call him Captain Hook." My eyes scanned the space for more wine. "I want to post this picture of us right now and have her shriek."

"Please, don't forget your boyfriend," I interjected. "That would be a tough one to explain."

"Yeah, well, I'd focus on everything that you have to figure out," Kristen barked back, marching away.

I let out a gentle laugh, gazed at her robe on the floor, and shooed Bella away. Twisting, a bit disoriented, I stumbled into an odd hallway and called out to Kristen. Within seconds, she texted me: *I am not done* (angry emoji) *with you!*

Although I was intrigued by it all, I could only focus on retracing my steps. *Which way is the Bircher's art gallery Bella?* I asked the cat as she then led the way.

A minute later, Kristen appeared wearing only a Grateful Dead T-shirt. She looked straight into my eyes. "I'm not going to apologize for tonight. I want to help you with your writer's block. This night had to happen." She was adamant.

I smiled spasmodically at her youthful exuberance. "A joyous night, indeed." My voice reeked of sarcasm as I collapsed on the oversized couch. "I can't write angry."

"Channel your rage, Larry. *The Show* worked." A small spark of hope ignited but dimmed quickly in my weariness.

I glanced over at the bottle of Meiomi Pinot Noir we had opened after dinner. "Thor at The Gym is ready to write a bestseller. Maybe you should help him—"

"No one wants to read about another roid head who sleeps with every woman he trains." Her mouth quirked in a derisive smile. "They'd rather read about an old school bad boy with a huge heart." She glared at me intensely. "Ask me why?"

I curled up in the fetal position. "Why?"

"Because they experience female emotion that inspires relevant, heartfelt storylines. Like you, ya silly goose!" With a tight grip on a couch pillow, I listened to her while searching the room for *The Dark One*. "May I be blunt?"

"Not unless you have more wine."

She rolled her eyes. "Part of your struggle has to do with how things recently ended with the yoga instructor you dated."

Memories of that late summer fling were swept away by sudden clarity. I took a breath and cleared my throat. "How many topics are we covering tonight?" My tone was peevish, though I would have refused to say why I was annoyed if asked.

Shaking her head, amused at how I squirmed on the couch, she kept talking. "You'll see, it's all tied to your writing." She smiled knowingly. "That said, how could you not realize hiring that little Zumba girl half her age wouldn't send her over the edge?"

"You're not helping."

"No, you're not listening." Angelic sincerity exuded from her smile. "You're a hopeless romantic with a special gift."

My gaze lifted to Kristen's eyes. "What gift?"

She flashed up my mirror shot. "The shirtless selfies you wrote about in *The Show* will help you," she said with a straight face.

I sank into the giant couch with the sensation it was quicksand. "I just want to be normal."

"I'm not sure that's possible. But on a positive note, these cute pics add to your Peter Pan mystic, you forty-nine-year-old boy!"

I frowned. "And you wonder why I'm struggling to write a continuation."

"Own it. It works. Your audience is growing, and your story is not complete." Kristen waved her mother's Facebook post in the air. Tenaciously, she continued. "I can't stand where this country is headed. I loathe watching the news and need your real, yet humorous, and vulnerable slant on life as you continue to figure it all out. So, Larry, stop pouting and start writing!"

I was shocked, bemused, and almost physically winded by her persistence. Under my breath, I said, "I just wish you'd tell me exactly how you feel."

The outspoken liberal put her red hair up in a ponytail while insisting I write on after she was gone. When I asked her where she was going, she gave me a half-laugh and said, "Steven, my boyfriend wants to look at different places to live outside the states."

"You are just full of surprises tonight."

Her cheeks were pink, but she seemed more miffed than embarrassed after this moment we shared. "Fate got you The Gym. If you get back to being you, I see another amazing love story. Only this one will grant you happiness and give that publisher of yours a crazy good sequel—one that I would call *The Gym*."

We were both strangely exhilarated.

Her iPhone pinged with another text, and I walked off to the bathroom. When I came back, Kristen smiled oddly. "Steven's leaving the airport Hyatt now." She paused, and my body tensed, buttoning my shirt. "I know this sounds crazy, but I do love him. And I don't sleep around, so please consider yourself a rare exception."

"That is touching. And quite disturbing. Until I sober up, I will pretend it's more touching," I choked out and with it the last trace of sarcasm I had left.

"Everything happens for a reason. Please capture it like I know you can." I nodded and smiled in silence. She smiled back at me. "Oh, and my friend texted me that there are cops up and down Ocean Avenue pulling cars over. You should stay at The Gym."

I wearily watched Kristen, reflecting that it was reasonable to assume she had a point. We walked out and hugged under a sky with no sign of my second star to the right. She smirked to drive her point home and said, "Only when you find her will your second star to the right burn bright again, Pan." She winked at me.

"Silly me for even looking up," I replied, staggering to my car.

The Dark One hopped in first.

Kristen tapped on my window. I lowered it, and she whispered, "It's gotta suck going from driving that Navigator in *The Show* to this little Kia Soul in *The Gym*."

"You do not give up."

"Neither do you. Open your eyes. This night is this first chapter of *The Gym*. I'll text you tomorrow when I can sneak off to Never Land for one last wine time."

"Will that be the second chapter?"

"Nah, Steven's taking me to Disney World this weekend." My eyes slowly closed. "Tomorrow will be the second. The dawn of a provocative plot..."

I took a sharp breath when *The Dark One* turned on the car stereo. "Okay. Please step off in the grass. Backing out is going to be a challenge." She laughed with her hands over her face. I smiled at her, turned up Disturbed's "The Sound of Silence," and quietly said, "Goodbye, Kristen."

"Don't say goodbye," she chirped. "Just be you...and believe!"

I backed out, clipped her mailbox, and shifted my gaze away from the mess I made in the red hue of my brake lights to the darkness ahead of me as I sped off into it, singing along.

Hello darkness, my old friend

I've come to talk to you again

TWO

THE DAWN OF A PROVOCATIVE PLOT

JANUARY 11, 2017
THE GYM
It was just hours later.

On an unseasonably warm winter morning, the Atlantic's calm waters glistened as the sun crept up over Melbourne Beach's dunes. I was passed out in my car across the street from that scenic shoreline, in front of The Gym I had purchased six blurry months before.

My eyes flickered open at the sound of Kristen's text: *This is the dawn of a provocative plot. Open your eyes and take it in. And then start writing. Talk soon.* Her compelling observation had me taking forty winks amused as the sea breeze blew through my open windows.

Minutes later, I heard a voice with a faint New York accent. It was one I recognized, and I believed I was dreaming but awoke when a hand shook my shoulder. My eyes opened slowly. I kept my face impassive, looking the man in the eye as if waiting for him to speak. When the man remained speechless, I blinked and realized it was the club's cagey castaway, Bob Tillie.

"You couldn't have parked behind The Gym? Day after day, all they do is watch you kill yourself."

I held his gaze as I pushed up out of my car. "I'm fine," I answered in a gruff and annoyed tone. I shut my car door, and we both stared at each other for a moment.

Bob was a fifty-year-old, divorced, Melbourne Beach resident who had moved to Beach Woods, a community just up the road from The Gym after he sold his Brooklyn Pizzeria in 2010. He had worked out at The Gym for years but still struggled with his weight. We began

7

speaking back in November when he heard I was dating our contentious yoga instructor. Certain members rolled their eyes when he would linger in my office, intrigued. Many had thought there was something deeply unsavory about him, but I didn't mind. I was humored by how contradictory he was of my impetuous actions; one minute, he would cheer on my antics, the next berate them—clearly torn—but typically humored.

At this moment, Bob emitted a long sigh, ready to rake me over the coals. "I heard that kid, Paul, had to open because you don't have a key to your own business?"

Now I spoke defensively. "I have one. I mean, I did," I said, opening my hatchback. "I need more water."

"What happened to your car?" Bob asked, clearly surprised.

"A mailbox jumped out at me." I paused when he shook his head in silence and grabbed deodorant from my knapsack. After two quick swipes, his eyes narrowed at me, and I added, "I'm hungover. Stop haranguing me."

"I figured you'd take a break after last week's date dropped your shoe off in a Chico's bag."

I gazed up at a few Laughing Gulls and whispered, "Please don't bring up Beth, the shoe girl. It was the most bizarre night of my life."

Bob's beady brown eyes grew wide. "What happened last night? Oh, wait, last night was Kristen Bircher and dinner at Djon's." He paused for a moment, read a text, and added, "You've apparently never seen Misery."

I chuckled. "Will you stop?"

"Stop?" he paused prudently. "The girl calls you Pan."

I winced. "Kristen's an avid reader," I said softly. "My book was next to The Underground Railroad on her nightstand—"

"What?"

"It ended up being a meaningful night."

"I knew that crazy redhead would be a good fuck," he snarled.

I took a deep breath and expelled it. "That's not what I meant," I said, hoping he would stop talking.

Bob watched me curiously rubbing his grey goatee. "You look like shit. If you had a key to get into The Gym, you could've slept on the massage table. Seriously, how do you not have a key?"

I groaned, "Didn't we have this conversation?"

"You never answered me."

"I lost one and gave the other one to Allie Girl."

Bob forced a laugh. "Allie Valentine. Another brilliant move on your part. Only you would hire a twenty-year-old fan of your book who plays hula hoop in front of The Gym. Don't you think it's time you stop chasing stars, Peter Pan Man?"

I took a long breath and, in a serious tone, said, "You should lighten up and open your heart." With the faint sound of waves caressing the shoreline, it dawned on me that Bob Tillie had been a delightfully disturbing character this entire time. I mused that Kristen might be onto something and smiled.

Bob's nostrils flared. "Why are you smiling? I think your second star to the right romantic rubbish has gone to your head."

I chuckled, amused. "I didn't think you read my book?"

"I didn't," he growled. "Some of the reviews are quite detailed."

"Seriously, you should try to laugh a little. It'll lower your blood pressure." I paused, fascinated at how uncomfortable he became as he scowled at me, thinking of a response to push me further.

"So, since Wendy was your last leading lady, who's next, Tinker Bell?" he said mockingly.

His jab tickled me. "If it is written in the stars, fate will find a way to bring her to me. Kristen reminded me of that—"

"It's wise to take advice from someone who calls you Pan."

I started walking to The Gym and passed him with his mouth agape. "Second star to the right and straight on till morning, Bob."

"Save it for your little mermaids." He took some quick steps to catch up to me. "How do you convince these people that The Gym will remain open while you party recklessly into the night and wake up out front in your car."

"Think happy thoughts, Bob." I picked up my pace and left the twinge of guilt Bob gifted me for him to trip over. "Is Allie here?" I turned back to him. "I don't see her car."

Bob grumbled that Allie's always late and blew out a frustrated breath reading another text. When he asked me if I knew Jimmy Hook, I winced. "Hook owns RH Marketing Solutions. They do your mailers."

I remembered Kristen mentioning his name during her tirade against her mother and was thoughtful for a moment. Then Hook's villainous face came through my foggy mind. "Yes, we met when he introduced me to his sales rep—"

"What's his name?" Bob said, testing me. "Hint, he's short and wears striped shirts that don't cover his belly."

I swallowed, parched, and then said, "Chris—Chris Smee."

Bob's eyes slowly closed. "Connor Lee is your advertising rep." He took a breath, reading a new text. "You should take Hook seriously."

I smiled bemusedly. "Captain Hook?"

Bob continued, "Hook knows that you're on dating sites."

"Why does he care?"

"Because he saw a shirtless screenshot of you throwing a football from one of the sites on his girl's phone."

I grinned as Bob shook off a look of confusion. "His girlfriend is on a dating site?"

"Apparently."

I asked Bob for her name, but he wasn't sure. Then he scrolled back through his texts, rubbed his goatee again, and said it might be Stephanie. He cocked his head to the side and mentioned that she also had my book on her iPad. I promised him I didn't know her while preoccupied with a text of my own. Bob snorted his doubt, and I read a message from a beautiful green-eyed thirty-three-year-old brunette named Maya McKinnon. After many lengthy chats, she suddenly seemed motivated to meet on Friday. When I went to reply, Bob cleared his throat. "Larry, Hook possesses influence with a ton of business connections. Stay away from his woman."

I never assumed Bob had my best interests and opened the door to The Gym. "Stephanie?" I asked, holding it open for him. "Yes, dad."

Bob's eyes widened and then narrowed. Although he felt that something dark had been lurking in the corners of my existence, he marveled at how I interacted with the members and often seemed envious of their affection for me. I surveyed the cardio area with the delicate task of reading the room and acting accordingly.

Cindy Eden, The Gym's fit, fifty-year-old early morning regular, looked silently out the window before waving me over like a little girl. The beautiful blond had many stalkers and informed me that one of them was in the parking lot by her car. Cindy's morning drama would typically create a buzz, and this Wednesday was no exception. Bob strolled over with a raised eyebrow as Bill "Two a Day" Tidden leaned into the mix, peddling his favorite recumbent bike in need of an update. Bob looked like he was ready to speak, then thought better of it. He knew Cindy viewed him as an intrusive man. Instead, he meandered off to the side after she shot him a cold stare and pulled up his Facebook app with a scowl.

And then, all at once, he held up a cozy picture of me and my recent hire, Allie Valentine, on the beach. Since many members thought we were dating, it seemed like a splendid opportunity to have a little fun with those rumors, which now came into focus as another incident of Drunkbooking. I quickly broke away from the conversation with Cindy when Bob pointed towards the door. "Here comes your Allie Girl!" he added in a sarcastic tone. The few who were not gawking now were. I took a slow, steadying breath and narrowed my eyes to her as she skipped through the door, holding her hula hoop, right on cue.

Allie's long brown hair flowed behind her, reminiscent of a sixty's hippie. The attractive young dancer was hired in November and immediately played a role in the dramatic demise of my infamous summer fling with the yoga instructor. Despite our twenty-seven-year-age gap, she called me Lawrence, not Larry, and with a voice that confused the situation even further. With all eyes on us, Allie blurted, "Oh, Lawrence!" I grabbed a bottle of water from the old cooler, and we scurried into the office. "You slept in your car?"

I forced a smile as Bob walked out. "My head is killing me," I replied and took a sip.

She dropped her hula hoop and collapsed in the office chair with her elbows hitting the desk as her face fell in her hands. "I heard a rumor Kristen is moving."

"Yes," I mumbled. "To an island with her boyfriend."

"Her boyfriend?" Allie rolled her eyes. "When is your next date?"

I took a deep breath as my shoulders slumped. "Kristen wants to have one last wine time before she leaves," I said. "But Friday the thirteenth for my next real date," I smirked. "I'm meeting that hot brunette I showed you."

She took a moment to compose herself and then snapped, "The one from the dating site?"

"Yes," I whispered, as Paul Faulk checked-in wearing one of his Baltimore Orioles T-shirts. The fifty-three-year-old Maryland native was a nice guy who knew precisely how daunting a challenge it was to run a business in this small beach town. His closed hardware store still sat vacant across the parking lot. I glanced over at his salty smirk. "Morning, Paul," I muttered to him while bracing myself.

"Morning, Larry and Allie." He paused for a moment with a raised eyebrow before taking a few quick steps to his favorite elliptical.

I turned back to Allie and opened my mouth to speak, but no words came out, so I tried again. "I need a bed. I'll call you later, Allie Girl." She let silence fill the space for a moment and stared at me before she shook her head and giggled.

All at once, I felt *The Dark One* nudge me forward. I turned and found myself face to face with the town's dashing, hotshot lawyer, Bill Reed. His piercing blue eyes under well-shaped eyebrows seemed amused. Since he was shorter than me, he immediately stood up straighter, then glancing at Allie, said to me, "I enjoy the vibe you've brought to The Gym. The music's improved, and the laughter is infectious." He gazed to the side of me, then back to Allie, who was now smiling, eavesdropping intrigued.

I nodded. "Thank you. I'm a firm believer that laughter is as important as a workout."

Bill's head tilted slightly as his eyes curiously narrowed at me. "That's interesting," he said. "So, when is your next book going to be ready?"

I smiled. "I was recently told this was a good time to start the story with The Gym as its backdrop."

Bill stared steadily at me, pursing his lips. "Well, then it shouldn't be long," he said and lowered his voice. "I've heard some colorful shit about you." He paused and looked behind him and then back to me. "Did a date drop your shoe off in a Chico's bag?"

My eyes popped forward in my aching head, and I shrugged with a slight nod. "Yes."

Bill laughed. "I've met someone I'm settling down with, so I will live through you, my friend. I'm already looking forward to reading it." My gaze shifted to his iPhone on the leg press when he grabbed a towel out of his bag. When he stood back up, one of his friends mentioned running into his girlfriend, Maya. It was then that I remembered I had to confirm my Friday date with Maya McKinnon. Everything seemed to be happening in slow motion. Bill leaned into his buddy and whispered, "I'm meeting her Friday night in Vero."

My eyes mysteriously shifted back to Bill's iPhone. Staring at it, he received a text. The name that flashed up was Allison Tinke. I froze unexpectedly and blinked when Bill snatched it up.

He seemed desperate to read it, then angered when he did.

"I'll let you go," I said, pondering another strange sensation. I was moved along by a member who enjoyed a bottle of wine I recommended.

Bill blinked away from the text with a statement that startled me. "I tried your wine diet," he explained. "It didn't work quite as well for me, though." He paused, wanting that statement back, as he then added tentatively, "I'm looking forward to the big game. Who do you like tonight, Alabama or Clemson?"

"I'm feeling Clemson," I said, turning away with another bout of nausea coming on. Before I could get to the door, another member placed a Trump shirt over my shoulder. The older republican was touring The Gym, boasting that "The Donald" was about to become our next President.

"Larry, wear it proudly," he sang, marching on. "And change that TV," he pointed to the second one, "to Fox News, please."

I looked over at Allie holding her hula hoop with bloodshot eyes, and shouted, "Allie Girl, please put Fox on for Conrad."

Conrad snuck up behind me. "I would change into that shirt now," he insisted. "You were seen in the same clothes last night at Djon's, and you weren't with your yoga girl."

I smiled outwardly, groaned inwardly, and then walked out.

THREE

A MORNING OF MISERY YIELDS MEANT-TO-BE MOMENTS

JANUARY 12, 2017
THE GYM

It was chilly, just before eight o'clock when I arrived at The Gym. A cold front had come through along with the elusive Connor Lee. I had not seen our stout thirty-something advertising rep since a text Allie sent prompted me to cut short an impromptu happy hour interview to rescue her.

It was roughly a month before—days after my so-called yoga girl stormed out of The Gym—when my imaginary cape appeared with the second bottle of Josh Cabernet. We only got this far because the yogini opened the interview, walking me through her "hot" yoga class, which I understood as shutting off the air. Musing a lower electric bill, I took a long sip pretending this could work while relishing the dark cherry and black plum flavors of my wine. As she rambled on, though, I wondered why she repeatedly referred to herself in the third person. "Hannah Haven continues to elicit breath using prana, to draw from within, to call for ujjayi breath like waves of the ocean—this is Hannah Haven yoga—"

"Okay, let's back up," I pleaded. "I had wine at lunch and want to be sure I'm following along." I paused when she pulled the straw out of her water glass and sipped her wine. "Aren't you Hannah Haven?"

She stuck the straw back in her water glass. "Of course, I'm Hannah Haven. How much wine did you consume at lunch, Larry?"

"Not enough," I moaned as my gaze shifted to Allie's text.

"If Hannah Haven could have a gong, would that be a problem?"

"I'm sorry, Hannah Haven," I said and flashed her Allie's text: *LAWRENCE SAVE ME!* "I'm needed back at The Gym—it's an emergency."

"Ooooh nooo," she breathed out gently; her light blue eyes seemed dazed. "With a gong and a crystal bowl, Hannah Haven can bring yoga baaaack to The Gym, baaack to where I can teach asana. I teach asana, Larry, but I also teach an extraordinary practice found in The Bhagavad Gita, the...the sutras?" She seemed to be confusing herself.

I grinned with the realization this was not a bad joke and placed cash down for the wine. "Your talents seem best suited for a yoga studio," I said. "Not a gym." I shook her hand and raced out.

Ten minutes later, I marched into The Gym with my imaginary cape flowing behind me. Allie had her ukulele in front of her as Connor Lee tossed his business cards at her.

"Allie doesn't make advertising decisions, Connor," I said sternly.

He nodded with bulging eyes as if he understood and slowly stood up with his heart thumping through his blue and white striped shirt. After checking his watch, we walked outside, and I shared my thoughts on their overpriced service. He listened intently and continued to nod, now to appease me, but inside he was dying. Finally, I paused, feeling sorry for him, while wishing I had taken the unfinished bottle of wine.

Just then, he said in a confused tone, "I'll call my boss. He'll fix this."

I cringed watching him quiver and murmured, "I'm half in the bag."

"What did you say?" he sputtered, pulling his blue and white striped shirt over his belly.

I cleared my throat. "I said good. Let us fix this. Please. Call the Captain..." my voice trailed off.

Captain Hook's voice reminded me of how dreadful he was. As Hook berated his sales representative, I realized why he looked like a man stripped of his dignity. Connor meandered out of earshot before he nodded a few more times and came back as if he was walking over coals. The expression etched on his face was of pain and sadness, but his new pricing made their outdated mailers seem somewhat appealing. During his sales pitch, Allie walked out with a bottle of water for me. His eyes drifted to the other end of the plaza when she hugged me. "Thank you, Lawrence," she whispered and walked back to the door. It was oddly quiet when it closed behind her. The short, stout man looked at me strangely. Then he gave me a shrug that meant I need a moment to find my voice.

Connor said, his voice shaky, "I know you're different, but the previous owners understood the importance of our advertising to the future success of The Gym."

My eyebrows raised slightly. "The previous owners who were desperate to sell it?"

Keenly aware that was true, he said, "Well, yes—but they all knew." His eyes averted mine.

This guy seems like a Mr. Smee, I thought, and at this point renamed him. It was apparent Captain Hook was pulling his strings, and it was only my optimism for this Snowbird season—and the bottles of wine—that had me cut him a check.

I had not seen him in the month since.

By seven o'clock on this crisp morning, he had already come through with the cold front, knowing I didn't typically show until eight. An hour later, I pulled two sticky-notes off the computer, questioning when I would hire a new yoga instructor, and opened the packet Mr. Smee dropped off.

A new point of view occurred to me.

Captain Hook was recouping his discounted rate while cutting the area of distribution on the mailers. I flipped back to the first page and let out a gentle laugh reading his note: *Contract Sign Here.*

An air of unreality permeated everything that happened next. My eyes lingered on a letter from the property management company that owned the plaza. I had been holding off sending the rent checks by a few days each month to protest the exorbitant lease. It took them six months, but they now requested a set date that it would automatically pull from my account. A relationship with them was imperative, but I chose to confirm plans to see Kristen one last time instead. With *The Dark One* cheering me on, I sighed deeply as voices reminded me it was time to sweep the yoga studio for Marlene Star's yoga class.

Grabbing the broom, I said a passing hello to Carl and Judy, our cute little yoga couple, and then goodbye to our retired President of FIT, Tony Campo, and his wife, Sarah. Sometimes branded as Florida Tech, so it wouldn't sound like it was trying to be MIT; the small engineering school had grown into a major university. Tony enjoyed chatting after his workouts and passed off a John Grisham novel on his way out.

No sooner had the door to The Gym close behind the Campo's did my thoughts turn darker. *When is Larry hiring a new Wednesday yoga instructor? Did you read his book? Why would he get involved with someone he worked with again?* Voices murmured in front of the yoga studio. That class's line stretched beyond the odd mirrored wall, which meant we were overcapacity. Refusing to refund any of them, I struck up a conversation with Maggie Biltmore, one of my favorite Snowbirds. Within seconds, those same voices whispered, *I love to hear Larry laugh.* After racing the broom around the studio, I shook a few hands and hauled ass back to the office.

The Dark One followed closely behind.

A moment later, Bob Tillie rushed in like a big tattletale late for recess at the schoolyard. "Hook told me your affair with Kristen isn't over," he bawled. His voice was so loud everyone in The Gym heard him.

I glared at him for a moment. "It is not an affair." Bob shrugged in silence as I shot him a wry grin. "I'm meeting her to say goodbye—"

"What are you going to do about the two classes your old yoga girl taught?" he demanded impetuously. "Everyone thinks you fired her."

I shook my head in frustration while shifting my attention to a slender man shuffling up to the check-in counter wearing an old Ron Jon T-shirt, worn jeans, and slippers. "How can I help you?"

"Yeah, do you play the Marshall Tucker Band here?" he asked with a raspy southern drawl.

If he didn't have that accent, I would've sworn he was Art Garfunkel. "Are you a fan?"

"You betcha," he said.

I placed the membership form in front of him. "You're in luck."

The man coughed a crusty smokers' cough. "Great! Thirty-seven bucks a month?"

"Thirty-five if you prepay for the year," I said and quickly shifted gears when he made a face. "Thirty-seven dollars is the auto-debit pricing," he shook his head, "but you can get that rate if you pay for six months."

He nodded. "Six months it is," he shook my hand, "I'm Stanley."

Bob collapsed in a chair, knowing the odds were slim he would make it past a month, and muttered, "Unfuckingbelievable."

"I'm Larry," I gestured to Bob, "and that's Billie Bob, but he goes by big Bob."

Bob groaned from behind me, "Please disregard anything Lucifer says. I am Bob. Bob Tillie."

The man squinted at me. "So, is it Larry or Lucifer?"

"Larry," I said, as Stanley smiled. He glanced at Bob and then back to me, curiously. "Fill this out and sign it, Stanley."

He leaned over the counter with an arched eyebrow. "Can I wear slippers on the treadmills?"

"How are you paying?"

"Discover."

"Yes, that is a Discover Card perk."

He laughed. "I like this place," said Stanley glancing back at the treadmills. With a tight grip on the clipboard, he added, "I'll getter done, boys," and shuffled to the door. "My credit card is in the car."

Within seconds another member complained about the canceled yoga classes. A pain throbbed in my head, turning to Bob. "After Wendy, how could you possibly get involved with someone at work?" The words nearly vomited out his mouth.

I rubbed my face. "It's different—"

"Why haven't you replaced her?"

With a slightly perplexed expression, I became angered. "I interviewed four instructors," I reminded him, craving a cold compress for my head. "And each one was wackier than the last."

Bob crossed his arms like a beaten bully. "You shouldn't have fired her when you guys stopped sleeping with each other."

I felt out of breath as if he were choking me. "You know the truth. You also know she was a handful."

"All women are. Especially the ones with killer bodies." He picked up a copy of Women's Health with Alison Brie on the cover and kissed it. "We're all animals looking for one thing. Sex. Think about that while

I drain the snake." I flinched as he patted my back on his way to the bathroom, hoping he did not return.

Meanwhile, I received another text from my Friday date, Maya McKinnon. After a curious call from her Wednesday night, she wanted my reaction to the bikini shots she texted me after sending her one of my infamous mirror shots. I say infamous because these juvenile pictures, better known as the "MS" written about in *The Show*, generated the book's most popular question on Goodreads. Ironically, even though I was now fast approaching fifty, they played more into this storyline than that one.

With all of this sexually charged energy swirling, I walked outside to call Maya and slow it down. Then two texts hit me. A Jennifer and Tab. No last names. They were fresh off one of the dating sites and eager to chat after yours truly downed a bottle of red and fired off a few of my latest and greatest MS's. We didn't know each other's last names, but they had half-naked pictures of me soaking wet in a towel. At the time, it made perfect sense. The real problem was that everything was moving too fast. The conversations were beginning to blend, and I needed a week to purge and refocus.

First, I needed to reschedule Maya.

I decided to text her and walked back into the office.

When Bob returned, I felt him hovering behind me and deleted it. "Bob, I need to take care of something," I said, anxious to correctly word the text.

I began typing another message to Maya but blinked away from it when he walked in front of me and stopped. His line of sight focused on my book with an eerie glare when he quietly said, "I heard about the newspaper interview for your shit show." He made a gesture to *The Show*. I shook my head, wishing this morning would end, and deleted that text too. I raised an eyebrow, clearly surprised he knew about the interview and questioned him about it.

A crooked grin spread across his face. "Hook is friends with the editor who is interviewing you. He went to lunch with her."

He had my attention.

With racing thoughts, Bob walked up next to me and then leaned forward to read my inbox. I followed his gaze to an email from her. It seemed he knew too much. *The Dark One* cozied up on the other side of me. I swallowed. My mouth was dry. I took a sip of water and told him this editor was also close with a mutual friend in the wine industry who recommended my book to her in November. She was quick to add me on Facebook and asked to interview me for a local author piece that they were running at the end of January.

"Did you fuck her?" Bob asked, his tone almost annoyed.

Slowly, and with some reluctance, I stood up and turned to him.

"No, Bob. She enjoyed *The Show*."

"And presto, you got an interview?"

"Well, yes. The newspaper was looking for a book released in 2016 by a local author with at least twenty-five reviews and a minimum rating of three and a half stars."

Bob was silent for a moment, chewing on his lip. "So, you gonna read her email?"

I took in a slow breath and opened it. Halfway through the first line, I collapsed in the chair: *Larry, I regret to inform you that my boss had filled the local author spot without my knowledge...*

"F-u-c-k..." I softly sputtered and rubbed my hands over my face.

Bob gently placed his hand on my left shoulder as *The Dark One* did the same on my right. "She canceled the interview she promised you?" he said. His tone was light, but he was not shocked. I blinked slowly, trying to control my anger.

I took a breath and calmed myself, but then Bob pointed out The Gym complaint box was full. I sounded tired and angry and frustrated, all at the same time. "I realize you have no interest in reading my book, but this is important should I continue writing. And I never received a key to that complaint box. So, if you would like to flip the thing upside down and pull out more good news, be my guest." He had the good sense to look contrite.

I stood up.

Since this editor had been communicating with me, mainly through Facebook, I decided to message her. I could not let it go, but now her name was gone.

I sat back down.

All the while, Bob looked at me, surprised. I rubbed my face again, baffled. *She not only unfriended me but blocked me*, I thought. *But why?* My emotions swung wildly. Part of my reaction was due to a bruised ego; the other part was that I had been sleep-deprived since I drove the illustrious career I wrote about off a cliff and was a bit punchy. Insomnia is nothing to joke about, though. It became difficult to even concentrate at times, never mind cope with a morning such as this one.

I took a deep breath and blew it out.

Finally, after a few members noticed the astonishment on my face, Bob said, "Larry, you got lucky with that book, but the run is done."

I typically laughed off his antagonizing remarks, but I was at my wits' end. Clear thinking was impossible. "What, Bob?" I said, trying to collect myself.

"The Show is over!" he scoffed. "And I wouldn't write anything else because your skin's not thick enough to handle the reality of this."

"*The Show* sold more copies in the last month than in the previous three." I pressed and then winced at a familiar high-pitched voice.

"Larry, the toilet in the women's locker room is about to overflow!" shrieked Kathy Mentor, another one of our adored Snowbirds who got a kick out of putting me in timeout. "Do I have to put you back in timeout?"

I slid down in the chair. "Let me pour a glass of wine first, Kathy."

"Oh, Laaaaaaary…"

I spun my chair to Bob with a scowl, mindful he recently replaced his toilet and could fix it. The bad news was, of course, wonderful news to Bob Tillie. He bit down on his smile and pretended to make a call. "I don't have a signal here," he said, rushing outside as the office line rang. Staring at the caller ID, I slid further down in the chair, acknowledging it was the property manager.

I took a shuddering breath watching it ring.

By this point, everyone in The Gym realized I was agitated, and as the call went to voicemail, a member rushed back to the broken toilet. "I'll fix it, Larry," Pete the Plumber yelled. Without even turning around, I thanked him. Quickly I checked the balances on my credit lines. *When did I use that?* I asked myself as Bob trudged back in.

I sighed deeply. "I need a grand…"

In the corner of my eye, I could see Bob's eyes widen. Without wasting a moment, he hurried back out. His panicked expression only meant he was worried I was going to hit him up for a loan. But I didn't have time to think about Bob Tillie just then. I gave him a few minutes to drive away and strolled back outside for some fresh air.

It was a beautiful, crisp sixty degrees after the front came through, and the sun felt good on my face. I looked up and closed my eyes, trying to slow my swirling thoughts, trying to calm my simmering emotions. The sound of the surf was soothing.

I could have dozed off standing there.

Then an angry voice abruptly interrupted that moment of Zen. "Allison, stop. We need to talk." My eyes shot open. "I'm going to be in Vero tomorrow, and I want to see you." I noticed Bill Reed off to the side of the bike rack on his iPhone. He breathed a dramatic sigh with his back to me and then started to speak again but stopped. He stammered a bit. I was confused by the typically smooth attorney's rambling tirade but didn't want to eavesdrop and walked back into The Gym.

Shortly after, Bill wandered up to the check-in counter. "Hey, Larry," he mumbled softly.

My head tilted slightly. "Morning, Bill."

His Dolphin's hat was backward on his head as he scanned The Gym with a scowl. It was plainly visible he was too distracted to workout. He took some slow steps by the spin bikes, reading a text, and stopped. He looked up, increasingly annoyed after his buddy said, "You should tell Maya when you're sneaking in a workout, so she doesn't bother you."

After a moment of uncomfortable silence, Bill said distractedly, "I have to go to the office, and I'll be in Vero tomorrow. Meet me here on Saturday morning." He paused and glanced back at the text. "It wasn't Maya texting me." Bill marched out, and I thought, *Shit, I still need to postpone Friday's date with Maya McKinnon.*

In the minutes that followed, she texted me again: *UM HELLO! SO, YOU DIDN'T LIKE THEM?* Maya referred to her bikini shots, which I scrolled up to revisit. The brunette had flawless skin, a curvy body, and crazy cat-like green eyes. I was excited and troubled. Part of that had to do with my vulnerable and vain state. Maya was not just attractive, she was strikingly beautiful, and that tapped my ego. But strangely, there was something else. And it had nothing to do with all this sexual banter. It was a similar feeling I had with Kristen.

The Dark One inched closer.

To calm my nerves, I began deleting the names in my contacts that I deemed too young but then stopped at Maya's. My hands shook uncontrollably, so I took that as a sign, I should justify her in far-reaching ways. *At least I know her last name. That is something,* I thought, and for that split second, pretended I was normal. Then I contemplated opening a Pinot Noir in my office wine cooler. But it wasn't even ten o'clock. Increasingly frustrated, I pretended my water was wine and polished off a bottle.

A moment later, I heard a gentle knock on the door frame of the office. It was from Maggie. "Carl wants you to know people are coughing and sneezing in the yoga room. He suggests you disinfect it because people are tearing up."

"I'm tearing up, too." I blinked and smiled. "I'll take care of it. Thanks, Maggie." I leaned back in the chair and closed my eyes for a moment. Then I heard another knock.

My eyes fluttered open to see Chet, an older member looking at me through his cataract-clouded eyes. "Hey Prince, when did Art Garfunkel join The Gym?"

"This morning," I said snippily.

"He's wearing slippers on the treadmill."

"Leave him alone."

"What's with the attitude?" he barked back. "Are you getting that flu bug going around?"

I sat up. "No, I'm sorry, Chet," I choked out as a thin crease of a smile spread across his face. "Just one of those mornings."

Chet nodded understandingly as Earl George, an outspoken, sixty-year-old staunch Republican who cut his own hair and worked out in flip-flops, then added, "Trump is going to help you, Larry. We just need those damn Democrats to stop stirring the pot with this nonsense about Russia interfering in the election. They lost. Fair and square."

"Is there such a thing in politics?" I inquired. My voice was cold.

Earl hesitated and unclenched his jaw. "After reading your book, I get why that's a sore subject. Let go of what was and have faith in what will be." His voice softened. "Start writing again. I enjoyed your book." He took on a guarded expression before both men walked out.

I took a sip of water and tried to relax, but the voicemail of another member cancellation stung my ear. No reason was left. I erased the message and held my breath to keep from hyperventilating, desperate for anything to snap me out of this funk.

Seconds later, I noticed my iPhone screen was full of notifications from Plenty of Fish's dating site. I hit the app, better known as POF, instantly relieved. It was difficult to explain, but that turned my frown upside down while ironically leading me further into the darkness. I scrolled through some of the more age-appropriate women on POF in hopes I would see the light.

But then *The Dark One* put his arm around me and laughed. *"News flash: The women your age will soon be arriving at menopause. That's HOT FLASHES – and all kinds of ugly shit you can't handle!"* He paused and looked over at me with a wink. *"Listen, Sport; you're forever a lost boy...a man-child! Stop fighting it. It's making you miserable. Get back to focusing on your fun wine times with the cute little ladies who enjoy your piggyback rides and pixie dust dreams—"*

My iPhone rang. It was Maya McKinnon.

I lunged for it like a lost boy. "Hey—"

"Were you going to text me back?" her voice sounded strained.

"Yes!" I chirped, sounding a bit too excited. I sat up straighter. "It's been a crazy morning."

After a long pause, she said, "Well, I had a crazy dream about a threesome. I was with you and this other older guy I was into."

My eyes widened, my mouth dropped open, and I said, "You've had threesomes?"

"Not double penetration."

I hesitated.

"Oh. Okay—"

"I'm blaming you and your mirror shot for that dream." She laughed. "And guess what?"

I blotted my head with a napkin. "Must there be more?"

"You were too big for my ass, but then you guys switched, and it was perfect. Weird, huh?"

I panicked, pondering too much. "Why would you say that?"

"I studied your pictures. Your chest—and then my imagination went down on you. Typically, I know the size of a man's penis by looking at his hands."

"Hands?"

"I'm never wrong."

Holy fuck. I am in over my head, I thought. After a long moment of silence, I sputtered, "I-I'll take your word for it—"

Quickly she screamed, "I love this!" and turned up Kelsea Ballerini's song, "Peter Pan." She sang loudly. And then there was silence.

"Maya?"

"The Chart House has a decent happy hour. Let's meet there tomorrow at four o'clock. We'll drink some wine and head back over the bridge. I've been craving Italian," she laughed, "soooo, maybe we can grab a quick slice at Bizzarro's, too."

I quietly said, "Sure."

She hesitated briefly and sighed. "Hey, do you open The Gym on Saturday?"

I sat there staring at my iPhone screen for a few seconds before I pulled it up to my mouth. "No..."

"Are you allergic to cats?"

I thought this over for a moment. Then I said, "What?" because I realized I needed more time.

"Do you have any cat allergies?"

I wiped the drool off my mouth. "Cats? Uh, no...no."

"Cool. Don't be late. I'd like to be ordering the second bottle by five..."

"That sounds magical."

"It will be. I promise."

Click.

I dropped my iPhone as if it were on fire. And just like that, I felt alive again.

Allie skipped in with her hula hoop and ukulele. She smiled at me slowly. "It looks like you have news," she was as suspicious, and I was exhausted. "What's going on now, Lawrence?"

I started to speak, my mouth opened to utter the words, nothing good, but stopped myself. Instead, I said, "Maya McKinnon is set for tomorrow night."

Allie sighed as if she was more concerned than disappointed that I didn't postpone her. "Oh, Lawrence," she said and stared into my eyes. "You're only masking your pain and fueling your darkness." She picked up her ukulele that she had placed down and lowered her voice. "Too much wine and too many women." She held her ukulele like a baby and just stared at me.

I was taken aback by her dire concern and shrugged like a boy. "It's only a happy hour date, Allie Girl," I insisted, determined to meet Maya.

Allie paused and took a deep breath, then looked me square in the eye. "Please listen," she implored. "Maya has no interest in dating a fifty-year-old. She's young, wild, sexual, and has her sights set on fucking you."

Reflecting on this with a frown, I slumped in the office chair. "Don't you think you're overly dramatic?" I asked the question but did not want the answer.

She cracked a sour grin. "No, not with you, Lawrence. Not at all."

FOUR

MAYA THE MERMAID

JANUARY 13, 2017
MAYA'S TOWNHOUSE

After too much wine, my Friday the thirteenth "happy hour" date ended precisely as Allie surmised it would. In her bed.

Maya McKinnon looked sideways at me when I pulled out of her. *You're good...you're good...just breath,* I repeated to myself, shifting slightly with the warmth of her vagina still causing me to see stars.

Her eyes widened. "Stop teasing me," she murmured lustily.

I'm not teasing you, you sexy little minx! I'm trying not to blow my load all over your belly button before the fat lady sings! my inner voice screamed as I whispered to her, "You love it..."

Agonizingly aware I had to keep moving, I reached under her ass and repositioned her curvy body on the bed for a bit more of a breather. Still improvising, I grabbed her breasts for a few more precious seconds. Luckily, it worked for both of us. She whined with pleasure. My hands slid over her body. Lower and lower. Her lips parted, and her legs trembled wide open. With my fingers all but sucked inside, I circled into her, setting off a shattering moan.

Suddenly, we were even.

The beautiful brunette arched her back, gathering up the bedsheets as I slid back into her. Slowly, her hands rose to my arms, and with a kung fu grip, she squeezed them tighter, and I thrust harder. "Mmmm," moaned the thirty-three-year-old. Her green eyes rolled pleasurably to the quickened pace. She gasped and shivered with the headboard banging against the wall. The sound cut through the air, amplified by the empty space she recently moved into as if gunshots were fired. *Pop*

– *Pop* – *Pop* - *Bang*. The headboard went through the drywall, and as I lurched back out of her, my fiery fluid flew.

"Oooh-sssh-shiiii-it!" I exhaled, stroking a ridiculous release that landed in her hair as I collapsed next to her.

Maya calmed her breathing and smiled blissfully at me. I wiped my forehead, attempting to contain my grin when her chin went against her chest. "Where did it go?" I had to turn my head as her hands searched for it. With no luck, she sat up hastily. "You didn't come inside me, did you?"

"No-no," I sputtered. "It landed in your hair," She patted her head, oddly amused, as a text hit her Android. When her demeanor changed, I sat up thinking about the hair gel scene in the movie There's Something About Mary. "I didn't mean for that to happen…"

Maya gazed at the text with a dour expression. "No, it's not that," she said. "I'm sorta seeing someone." I looked at her sharply to see if she was joking, but she was not. She informed me that he had business in Vero Beach and had planned on him staying the night.

The idea staggered me.

"Do all women in this town remain on dating sites while in a relationship?" I asked, not knowing what else to say.

With a deep breath, Maya said, "It's not like that." She laughed and shook her head erratically. "It's complicated." Her voice was so indifferent that I stood up, fascinated. Swaying a bit, I put on my boxers when she walked into her bathroom. "And don't worry," she added. "I never have unprotected sex."

"You just did," I said, grabbing my jeans.

She came back out and snatched a bottle of water off her dresser. "You've been married forever, and except for your recent gym flings, I could tell you don't sleep around."

My eyes narrowed at her. "Gym flings?" I crossed my arms across my chest. "I did date a yoga instructor."

Maya gulped water. "Well, I didn't expect to drink that much wine." She paused when I laughed as if she told a joke because of her detailed plans for happy hour and attempted to blame me. "Well, Peter Pan Man, all I can say is that what I've read seems accurate, so cheers to you!" She raised her water bottle to me as I fidgeted with my belt, taken aback that she was reading my book. When I opened my mouth to question her about it, she pointed to her nightstand. She pressed her lips together to keep from screaming. "You hit my nightstand, too." A smile sprouted on her face. "Still got a little something left in that power tool, huh old man?"

I shrugged, desperately needing a moment. "Can we back up?"

"No," she said quickly. "We only live once, and there was something about you. Okay?" She grabbed a towel. "Besides, you're only recently separated." I could tell she was avoiding something.

"This is not a trial separation," I insisted. "Unfortunately, my marriage is over. And that sucks. But it's been years." I paused, looking at her. Although she nodded, something in her expression made me swallow the rest of my statement. I blinked through troubling thoughts and realized it didn't matter.

Maya took a breath as if she were going to say something. Instead, she nervously pulled her hand through the stickiness in her hair and smiled. "You couldn't have hit me in the boobs?" I laughed briefly but remained muddled, so she hurled her bra at me. "Oh, come on, Larry, it was all fun and games when you sent me that mirror shot the other night."

"I thought you were single," I said with chagrin.

She held up my shirt, averting my glare. "My father's only five years older than you and couldn't get away with wearing this. Cheer up. You're a cute forty-nine-year-old boy."

I sighed. "Maya, what aren't you telling me?"

"Nothing all that important," she chirped. "You're overthinking." She threw my shirt at me, and I snagged it out of the air, discomforted. The wine and lack of sleep brought on dramatic mood swings. Suddenly I saw my life playing out like a reality show. I tried to relax, but her hair was now sticking up while she frantically yelled for her cat, who had fled the room when the headboard went through the drywall. "Jo Jo…Jo Jo…" She wiped her nightstand with a towel and tossed it in her bathroom. "Jo Jo, where are you?"

Fixated on the side of her head, I felt it necessary to find a humorous out. "Please work that in."

"I did!"

I smirked. "No. Your hair. I can't be as pissed off as I want to be with it sticking up like that."

Her middle finger rose as she kicked my shoes toward me. They slid across the hardwood floor and hit a box she hadn't unpacked from her recent move. "You can go out the front door, funny guy. Walk those Johnston & Murphy's around the path; it eventually leads to your car." I picked up my shoes with a puzzled look as she continued, "If he pulls in, it will look like you came from my neighbor's. You wouldn't want to upset one of your esteemed members of The Gym, would you?" She lifted her chin to me. I tried to swallow and scream at her, but I couldn't. And then she added, "I'm dating Bill Reed."

My stomach clenched. "The attorney?" I said, with a touch of panic. "Is that the newsflash you felt wasn't all that important?"

Maya laughed nervously before informing me that Bill was using her to get back the love of his life. When she mentioned her name was Allison, my heart pounded in my ears. I took a steadying breath and told her about Bill's phone conversation with her outside The Gym.

Maya's mind wandered off. "Allison was a member of The Gym a couple of years ago," she explained. "Before she moved to Vero…" her voice trailed off.

"How do you know she lives in Vero?"

"Because it was Bill who convinced her to move in with him when he lived there."

"Bill Reed lived in Vero?"

"Yes. He worked at the Vero office after a sexual harassment charge jeopardized his career." She took another gulp of water, waved her hand in the air as she swallowed it, and added, "Bill's father cleared him, but it was a mess. And since he was in Vero and Allison wanted to get out of Melbourne Beach, she rushed into a bad decision."

"What do you mean?"

"Well, from what I heard, Allison was seeing another guy on and off, undecided which direction to go. It was Bill's house that got her. She tried to make it work but couldn't," Maya said, shaking her head.

I cleared my throat. "So, what happened?"

"Months later, she called off the engagement and moved out." Maya paused, and a strained, unfamiliar look of embarrassment crossed her face. "That's when Bill moved back to Melbourne Beach and met me. On our first date, he told me I reminded him of Allison. My only response was that I wasn't a teacher. Because she is."

I was suspicious at how much Maya knew about Allison but stood motionless for a moment when she mentioned her last name was Tinke. Maya's eyes narrowed at me curiously when I admitted that I had heard her name. Then I realized Allison must have canceled Bill's plans with the text I saw on the leg press. I breathed out a long, slow breath, and with it, a small amount of my anxiety. It didn't help.

Within minutes I found out that Maya met Bill in November, was extremely cheap and didn't satisfy her in bed. Maya insisted that Bill wanted me to believe he was settling down with her because getting Allison back was a long shot. "His ego won't allow him to lose...anyone," she added as her gaze drifted to the open windows.

I waited for her to look at me. "Do you realize Bill asked me when my next book would be ready, and I told him it depends on the material that comes to me?" I said, looking bemused.

Maya nodded, showed no outward emotion, and finally said, "Isn't that ironic."

"Well, this has been fun." My voice reeked of sarcasm. "Thank you."

"Oh, calm down," she huffed, increasingly agitated. "I'm probably heading home, back to Long Island."

I exhaled. "So, you wanted to have a little fun before you left?"

She shrugged her shoulders. "And what's wrong with that?" Her voice seemed to ramble on from far away, although she was less than ten feet from me. She convinced herself that many women remain on dating sites after they've started dating someone to make sure it's right. She refused to be daunted by it and now seemed to be vaguely amused. She said coldly, "Besides, you shouldn't be throwing stones while living in that glass house you call The Gym." I caught my reflection in her giant framed mirror that rested against the bathroom wall, barely recognizing myself. I could feel her eyes cut through me as she stepped forward under the light on her ceiling fan to finish her thought. "Bill told me the fling with your yoga girl ended because you slept with your Zumba instructor." Maya's eyes were suddenly shimmering with excitement.

"And you believe that?"

She shook her head, humored. "No. But I do believe there is an overabundance of drama in your life, which I hear writers love. I called you Peter Pan Man because I'm reading your book." She grinned like a little girl. "Ironically, Bill's stories made me realize you were the older guy I was drawn to on POF. The author who bought The Gym."

"That's when you showed up there?"

"Yup. And saw your book for sale on the counter." She gazed at me, thinking. "What young woman wouldn't want to be a character in a bad boy author's book? So, what's my name going to be?"

I cleared my throat to give myself a second to think. Then I said, "How sick do you think I am?" Maya's head slumped, and eyebrows arched, scaring the shit out of me. I quickly tried again. "Well, typically, I use the same first name and change the last name—"

"McKinnon!" she shouted. "I want my last name to be McKinnon." Maya grinned mischievously, grabbed her Android, and pulled up an overplayed pop song of this time called "Starving." My eyes narrowed at her; fully aware the lyrics best describe that moment when you fall for someone new. I was captivated when I heard her voice. Sounding like the artist, Hailee Steinfeld, Maya sang beautifully in sync with the first line of the song: *You know just what to say – shit that scares me, I should just walk away.* Maya raised the volume, placed it on her bed, and seductively took off the T-shirt she had put on. My shirt dropped from my hand, fixated on the curves of her body, and unable to look away. She slowly bent over and sang, *"I didn't know I was starving till I tasted you."* Her feet spread apart, and her ass was in the air. *"Don't need no butterflies when you give me the whole damn zoo."*

A chill shot up my spine.

Holding her Android again, she spun to me, pointing at me.

I swallowed hard.

She turned back to her bed, grabbed her T-shirt, and sang on. *"By the way, you do things to my body – I didn't know I was starving till I tasted you—"*

I brushed my suddenly sweaty palms on my jeans and kicked my shirt to the side in anticipation of what came next: an exhilarating dance number. I was no stranger to these moments of witching wonderment.

I suddenly had a vision of my so-called yoga girl performing a tantalizing takeoff of Justin Timberlake's "Can't Stop the Feeling" in her apartment, two months before. Both women had stunning bodies that held me spellbound, but at this point, it was a coin toss on which song would haunt me longer.

Maya skillfully skipped over to me.

I drew a short breath.

She draped her shirt around my neck and slowly caressed my chest. Dancing around me, she gently brushed her breasts against my skin while staying entirely in sync with the song. *"You know just how to make my heart beat faster. Emotional earthquake—bring on disaster—"* At that moment, a car alarm sounded to lock the doors. She paused the song and looked up at me, her lips pursed with worry. "That was quick." She grabbed my shirt off the floor and tossed it to me. "He's here."

I exhaled. "The b-a-s-t-a-r-d!"

She let out a nervous chortle, hit me, and whispered, "Go out on the balcony and finish getting dressed."

"And then what…come back in and yell surprise?"

Maya shoved me to the glass slider, and the door alarm beeped. "No." She pushed me out. "Can't you fly, Larry? Or is it really Peter?" She smiled whimsically. "You looked like a little boy. No, jump. It's only storage below us. It's not a full floor." I turned to her, and she kissed me with a quick peck on the lips. "Bye." The door slid shut, and I heard a woman's voice as my iPhone rang. It was from Bob Tillie. Panicking, I answered quietly with too many thoughts hitting me at once. Bob had to repeat himself to snap me out of it.

"Larry? Why are you whispering?"

I tried to calm my voice. "I'm on Maya's balcony—"

With a short silence at the other end of the phone, I pulled my arm through my shirt. And then Bob asked, "Why?"

My breathing quickened. "She has a boyfriend." I peered over the rail. "And he's here."

"Wait. The hot brunette you showed me has a boyfriend, too?"

"Yes," I said and lowered my voice. "Bill Reed."

In another moment of silence, I took another peek over the rail.

"Please tell me you're kidding?" Bob pleaded.

"I wish I was."

"Larry, he's a lawyer in town—"

"I know—"

"And a member of The Gym!"

"I know who he is, Bob."

Bob continued, "Bill was engaged to a little blond who was a member of The Gym."

"Maya briefed me—"

Click.

Just then, the glass slider slid open. I almost jumped out of my skin, but it was Maya.

"Relax," she said. "It was my sister. She left." Maya playfully shoved me back inside. Before I could question her, the front door beeped again. We heard Bill's voice, but Maya shouted out her sister's name anyway. Then Bill yelled back upstairs that he was on the phone.

I whispered to Maya, "He has a key?" I paused as her eyes grew wide and added, "Silly me for thinking I had time to climb out the window after he rang the bell."

Through her gritted teeth, she said, "You're jumping off the balcony—"

Bill shouted, "Maya?"

Maya yelled to Bill, "Yes! Did you not hear me?"

"No," Bill replied. "I thought you said, Kristy? Did you not see your sister?"

"What—no," she sputtered. The color draining from her face.

"No?" he paused into an eerie silence. "How did you miss her?"

Maya rambled on that she took a shower and needed a small bag from her car. Bill assured her he would get it and mentioned her neighbor Teresa likely joined The Gym. Maya's eyes grew wide. With my heart thumping wildly, he explained that I parked my car in front of her place. Maya hit me again. "Why do you think it's his?" Her voice was flat as if it were a question, and she wasn't really seeking an answer.

"He has personalized plates." Maya's eyes slowly closed. "And Gary's out of town." Bill laughed. "I'm sure Larry's living out another chapter for his next book. He's a writer, you know?"

Her eyes narrowed eerily at me as she shouted, "I don't give a shit about that egomaniac, Bill. I need that bag." Maya lowered her voice as she said quietly to me, "You're fucking amazing." I suggested the egomaniac shout out was delivered with a bit too much emotion, and she again hit me. Then Bill asked her if she knew me. But his call ended, and he was walking up the stairs. Maya gripped my arm. "No. I've heard rumors, and I don't care, but I need my bag—"

"Are you on the phone?" Bob snapped, cutting her off.

"YES!" Maya barked, now thinking Bill undoubtedly busted us. "Can you get the fucking bag?"

"Hey, calm down," Bill retorted and then made his way back down. We blew out a deep breath, trying to keep it together. She pushed me back out but then stood there and shook her head while fanning her face with her hand. "Holy shit. I feel like I'm living out the pages of a book."

A smirk was my answer.

"Shut up." She laughed gently. "I'm not that fucked up. Say something—"

"No, it's good," I said convincingly. "No one wants to read about someone who isn't. Think about it."

"I know, right. Boring." She took a peek at the stairs. "Oh," she turned her head, "how's my hair?"

"Better. But don't forget the headboard went through the drywall."

Her eyes popped forward. "Please tell me it didn't." Maya sounded thoroughly distressed but smiled wickedly. "I love this," she whispered, slowly shutting the door. "I can't wait to read about our night together. Goodbye, Peter Pan Man."

I stood in the dark for a few seconds and then heard the ping of a text echo into the quietude of the night. I chuckled when I saw it was Allie. *How did it go with Maya the Mermaid? Was I right???*

I texted her back, *Yes. And I'm about to jump off her balcony. Hopefully, I can fill you in tomorrow.* I stared at the rail and then climbed over it.

I stood on the edge for a moment and then jumped. Deeper into the darkness.

FIVE

THE NOTEPAD

JANUARY 14, 2017
MY HOUSE/THE GYM

The morning came quickly, and my eyes opened slowly to the sound of a text. I rolled over inexplicably invigorated when I saw Maya's name, and in a flash, I read it: *That was some adventure.* (smiley face emoji) *And you touched me just right.* (winking emoji)

I could see her eyes. Deep green and devious.

I fired back: *An enchanting evening, indeed.* My ego took off before the air traffic controller on the left side of my brain could abort another ill-advised flight, which the right-side of my brain viewed as something else. Something essential. I took a slow breath as the morning light mysteriously brought on a soothing recollection of the rousing night we shared. One that felt fictional and led to further thoughts: Kristen had a point. I could see a prevailing narrative, one which develops the theme of *The Gym*.

I became entranced by Maya's response: *I woke up quite wet and tormented with desire.* Her romance novel tone passed and quickly. *Bill is so annoying. Thankfully, he's heading to The Gym so that I can get back to your MS.* (heart face emoji) *LOL!*

So, Bill stayed the night? I typed, restless for an answer.

Please don't judge. I know I should end it. But right now, I'd rather not talk to Bill. I feel like a girl again, and I just want to have fun, she replied.

My stomach did a flip-flop. Part of that was the wine consumed, the other part, Bill Reed. All at once, I wanted to talk to her, but just as much, to not even respond. I took in a slow breath, baffled yet increasingly intrigued. And then Allie called. I exhaled. "Hey, Allie Girl—"

"The Hanukkah bush that old man Whibbles put in the locker room is on fire!" she exclaimed.

Whibbles was another one of The Gym's colorful characters. He often did things to help "improve" our environment that went wayward. His diet consisted of the free Publix Apron meals, and I was pretty sure he got most of his T-shirts from company-sponsored events, as each time he came in, there was a different logo faded from too many washings. We had a good-natured sense of humor about his eccentricity around The Gym as he often called attention to himself with odd behaviors, such as walking backward on the treadmill.

I could feel my eyebrows crunch together with the strain of understanding and asked Allie to repeat herself. She did amid faint screams while explaining that it was dried out when he plugged it in. Then the call went cold. I sat up, unsteadily. "Allie Girl?"

"Yes, Paul rushed it out the back door in a yoga mat," she said over my huff of breath. Her voice was as impatient as mine. "It's still smoking…"

My mind raced on. "Hanukkah ended a month ago," I said with aggravation. "Why was it put in the locker room?"

"He told Paul it was a gift for you, the leader."

I sighed. "Where is he now?"

"He's walking backward on a treadmill while making his bird calls. Can you talk to him?"

"No. I'm hungover," I groaned, only wanting to make sure the fire was out. "Is the fire out?"

"Yes, but he's scaring the high school girls on the treadmills," Allie added. "Lawrence, you need to ask him to leave—"

"No!" I barked and then took a breath to calm down. "He just prepaid for the year—"

"Well, what the hell am I supposed to do?"

At that point, I needed to come up with something. "Okay," I took in a steadying breath, "tell Whibbles you'll play catch with that ball he loves and then mention there's a Publix Apron's meal next door."

She hesitated briefly and then laughed. "The free samples of food?"

"Yes."

"Jaasus, Lawrence," Allie cried out as Maya sent me a selfie after her orgasm.

I cleared my throat, staring at it. Amusement was overtaking frustration. "Allie Girl, trust me. It will work. I have to go."

"Wait. I want to hear about Maya the Mermaid."

Unable to look away from Maya's picture, I mumbled to Allie that she texted me. Then I wiped the drool off my mouth and wondered why I admitted that I had to jump off her balcony to leave her place. Impatience with this conversation overcame me. With a surge of angst, I could not deny Allie had a point: I should not have expected to hear from Maya. But I did. The eyes never lie. And hers were now haunting me. I sighed, overwhelmed. "Allie Girl, I'll call you later—"

"Lawrence!" she gasped, cutting me off. "Does she have a boyfriend too?"

My throat tightened. I couldn't utter a word, so I hit the little red iPhone dot.

Click.

By this point, I didn't need coffee. I was up and now questioning if this was all a dream. I then read Maya's next text: *Orgasm achieved, thanks!* (two heart face emojis) *Recalling your touch helped. It is soft yet masculine. LOL! If you'd like to have some more wine and another good time, let me know.*

I pushed myself up and staggered into the bathroom to splash cold water on my face. My brain needed a moment to recalibrate, but that was impossible because Bob Tillie called. I could see him driving his black convertible Corvette Stingray into The Gym's parking lot. Desperate to get rid of him, I abruptly answered, "I'm hungover. I'll call you later."

"No!" Bob snapped. "Bill Reed's having a heated conversation in his car. Do you think he found out you slept with his girl?"

Hesitating a fraction of a second, I patted my face dry. Bob's question scrambled my mind. "Who is Bill with?" I asked, wandering back to my bed. I grasped it was not Maya.

Bob lowered his voice. "He's on the phone. What's his girlfriend's name, again?"

"Maya—"

"I'm going to take a video."

"Of what?" My left foot inadvertently tapped the carpet when I sat down on the bed. "Bob?"

"Give me a second," he hissed. "You have to see his face."

I opened my mouth to answer quickly, then thought it over. "No...no, Bob, stop. I believe you." I jumped up and stumbled back to the bathroom.

"Relax," he said and stopped talking.

"Bob?"

Over the sound of my stream of urine hitting the water in the toilet, Bob whispered. "Hey, he's not talking to Maya. He's talking to Allison." He paused, and I missed my mark as Maya texted me again, now wanting to know if I liked her selfie.

I desperately attempted to collect my thoughts. "Last night, Maya told me Bill was engaged to a woman named Allison."

"I tried telling you that, but you hung up on me because you had to jump off Maya's balcony," Bob said slowly. "That little bond was something," he sighed, "this is bringing me back..."

"To what?"

"I'll call you later—"

Click.

A headache spiked behind my forehead when I received a text from an old wine industry acquaintance that I was supposed to meet up with and then another call from Allie. She informed me that old man Whibbles was heading to Publix and then moved on to a pressing issue about our new trainer. I visualized colorful characters again. This one referred to himself as Thor. His two distractedly different eye colors freaked me out, but I was envious of his flowing locks as mine had long disappeared. He had begun scheduling his time at The Gym when I wasn't there in hopes he wouldn't have to pay, which infuriated me. Allie handed her iPhone to him, and we agreed on an amount he owed me. After a moment of testosterone grunts, he ended the call with a plea to me that I needed him. "Larry, I know you're new to the fitness industry, but you should know the trainers here are charging different prices. I don't want to trash anybody, but—"

"But they pay The Gym," I said in a threatening tone.

"But I attract clients that none of them can," said Thor sharply.

I almost laughed before I answered. "If The Gym were a charity, that would be great, but it's not."

"I'm not understanding," he replied as if he had early-onset Alzheimer's with no recollection of my issue with him.

"The Gym's operating costs are exorbitant, and you have been caught on camera training clients without paying me."

"I planned on paying. I have to get back to my client," Thor said distractedly with the sound of more grunts around him. "I'll leave the money we discussed with Allie."

I noticed the notepad I recently pulled out of a box of promotional books from my publisher and scribbled characters at the top of the page and then Thor's name below it. "Thank you, Thor."

Click.

I collapsed back on the bed and realized Bob got his video, which, at this point, didn't faze me. There wasn't much Bob Tillie could do that would. I shook my head and hit play.

For eight seconds, I watched the back of Bill's head, unable to hear much. He was sitting in his convertible, and after Bob adjusted his angle, I could tell part of that was because Bill left many sentences unfinished. With an anxious breath, Bob walked right behind Bill when he said, "Allison, why did you cancel our plans?" he paused and added, "We need to talk." It was then it seemed that Allison urged him to end the call.

The video stopped, and I felt paralyzed, pondering it all.

Just minutes later, Bill worked his pecs on the bench press when he decided to add weight to the bar. Bob naturally sent me a string of texts, suddenly as intrigued as I was. When I read his latest text, I could see The Gym as it played out: Bill noticed Bob walking by and asked for a spot and, ironically, a video of it. Knowing what he knew, Bob quickly agreed to take the video when Joey Moretti offered to spot him.

Fifteen minutes later, I was watching it.

Bill said, "This is going to be a tough one at two hundred and fifty-five pounds, but I'm only doing one rep." After Bill positioned his athletic five-foot-nine-inch frame under the bar, he adjusted his hands and slowly pushed it up. He let it down and seemed fine, but Bill started to shake when he pushed it back up. My eyes were glued to the screen when beads of sweat erupted from his forehead. Within seconds, Joey went to grab the bar but stopped when Bill fought it up and dropped it back on the rack. "Yeah!" he bellowed. Bill took a moment to catch his breath as Bob shifted to Bill's duffel bag. A text from Allison Tinke flashed up on Bill's iPhone, and Bob ended the video. He would later confirm what she wrote: *I hope we can remain friends.*

When I went to watch it again, Kristen texted: *How is the storyline coming along?*

I blinked hard at her words, slightly spooked by this little redhead, and replied, *Well, I've opened my eyes, and plots are forming. Maybe our night together was meant to happen.*

It was. Be you and believe. Steven just walked in. Talk soon. (smiley face emoji) She texted back.

I restlessly rubbed my face and then texted Maya back to call me. After a few minutes and no response, I noticed she didn't receive it. Another text from Bob about Bill moved my thoughts along. I sighed bafflingly, recalling a few conversations about Bill when the notepad mysteriously fell off my nightstand. Suddenly, I felt compelled to jot these thoughts down.

With the notepad in tow, I started the coffee and grabbed a pen. After scrolling old texts, I wrote:

JANUARY 17, 2017

Bob was only a "gym acquaintance" of Bill's but confirmed his relocation rumors. In early 2015, Bill was advised by his father, who ran the firm, to work out of their Vero Beach office after the sexual harassment allegation Maya had mentioned threatened his career. Shortly after that, Bill found a perfect house near the beach and convinced Allison Tinke to move in. Bob was aware they'd been dating on and off and reiterated what Maya told me: Allison rushed into this decision because she ultimately wanted to move her young girls out of Melbourne Beach.

I placed the pen down when Bob sent another video.

Since Maya was never a gym member, Bob now looked to use Allison to stir the pot. He reached down to grab Bill's water bottle, hopeful of striking up a conversation.

I raised the volume on my iPhone.

The footage began with another unsteady shot of Bill's duffle bag, but I heard the conversation distinctly: "I haven't seen Allison around," Bob casually mentioned. "Did she not move back with you?"

Bob shifted to him, and I held my breath when Bill stared blankly into the parking lot. "No," he said. "She stayed in Vero. I'm now dating someone local."

Bob panned to the floor. "Do I know her?"

"No, she's not a member of The Gym."

Bob's an awful actor, I thought as he raised his voice. "Weren't you engaged?"

"Allison Tinke has issues. I had to end that months ago," Bill lied, as Bob also confirmed it was Allison who ended the engagement. "She won't come back to Melbourne Beach, her ex-husband's here, and her parents have a place in Vero."

As small talk persisted, the conversation shifted, and Bill asked if I was coming in. Bob snickered. "Doubtful, it's Saturday. Why?"

In a serious tone, Bill said, "I spoke to him the other day about a year membership I prepaid before I moved to Vero and didn't get to use a month of it." I shook my head as he amazingly added, "I'm now on auto-pay and need to get that back."

Bob also confirmed the rumors that Bill was stingy with his money by quickly replying, "A month? From two years ago?"

The smooth-talking attorney only nodded with a look of embarrassment. He awkwardly reached for his business card and asked Bob if he could send him the video of his Saturday morning bench-press heroics. With heads shaking around him, Bill retreated to my office, grabbed a sheet of paper, and wrote something down before he gazed over at the computer monitor. Bob confirmed that Allie's Facebook page was up with another picture of us, which I appeared to be more than her boss. I pulled up the video monitors and saw Bill standing by the check-in counter.

Within minutes, Allie texted, *Bill Reed wants to add me on Facebook. Call me!*

Before I could, Bob sent me a picture of Bill's note.

Larry, I wanted to follow up on our conversation about the month owed me. I hope you can resolve this before I'm charged for February. Thanks, Bill Reed.

Below that, Bob texted, *El Cheapo just left that! I think it was poetic justice you slept with Maya. And I found out some more information about Allison Tinke. Call me.*

Sunlight streamed through the window and onto the notepad.

I pushed my coffee to the side, pulled the notepad closer, and wrote Allison Tinke's name. Right after I did, I scribbled the words: *Pixie dust.* It felt surreal. It was as if the magical golden glitter was falling all around me. And at that precise moment, it occurred to me I was writing on the notepad I used for *The Show*.

Hastily, I flipped to the wine-stained page underneath and saw my thoughts from the emotionally draining, six-hour, and fifty-two-minute farewell call from Wendy Darlington. I drew in a slow breath, reflecting on our improbable dilemma in which life had led us beyond in a blur. Then I leaned over the notes with a flutter of anticipation.

My whole life was in flux, and this moment was screaming to me — memories rushing over me. I scanned over too many topics twice. *Wendy blames me for being jaded.* (wine stain) *I blame her for my ruined career.* (wine stain) *Wendy blames me for leaving her in a company she loathed.* (ink stain from the pen I pushed through the page) *I remind her that I was fired because of our relationship while sounding nuts, attempting to explain her to any law firm who examined my termination.* On the next page, I scribbled notes about her marriage — and my marriage to Marie, my ex, who technically was still my wife.

It was at that moment I realized I could more easily explain Wendy than Marie. I took a breath fighting the urge to tear the cork out of a bottle of Caymus — that with an uncontrollable twitch — I caught a glimpse of on the counter. I settled back over the stained mess with a deeper breath and read a passage that appeared peculiar. *And how shall you rise beyond your days and nights unless you break the chains which you at the dawn of your understanding have fastened around your noon hour?* After reading it two more times, I recalled jotting it down after I inexplicably picked up a dusty book by Kahlil Gibran while Wendy continued rewriting history. I pretended it made sense during the fifth hour of our call. Around the time, I had put Wendy on speakerphone to cork another bottle fearing I would sober up.

Reading on, I could not deny how marvelously idiotic I was. Sure, much of this was caused by the disconnect in my marriage, but this was about moving forward a little wiser. My remorse was deep and served as a kind of catharsis. Despite our marital discord, I regretted the pain I caused Marie. She had been a wonderful mother to our amazing kids, and I missed them. Splitting was painfully difficult, but something about this came with absolute clarity and closure. Part of me wished we had not been getting along since we separated. Another part of me was grateful we were. Frustration welled inside me, but I remained convinced I was on to something.

Then the house was eerily quiet.

It took me a couple of seconds to realize the cable had gone out as I peeked in the family room at a blue TV screen with my hands over the notepad, fearing it would self-destruct—you know, like the messages in the Mission Impossible movies. Spark, smoke, and poof. Spooked in my fragile state, I sensed my past, future, and present merging.

It was peaceful.

I was alone with my thoughts, which typically was scary in its own right. But this was different. Significant. As the content of this frayed entry of my life settled over me, I was conscious of the fourteen months passed since Wendy's call helped me process my emotions and see things in a more objective light. Although finding this notepad also signified the end of a stolen moment with Wendy, I couldn't deny she was the girl who made me smile in a way I hadn't since.

I thought perhaps it all came down to that.

Then I turned the page and glanced back at the name, *Allison Tinke*, determined to smile like that again.

SIX

CATCHING UP WITH THE KIDDOS

JANUARY 15, 2017
CARRABBA'S ITALIAN GRILL
On Sunday, my intuition had me curious to hear more about Allison Tinke. With her name stirring my imagination, I called Bob and scribbled bullet-points on my trusted notepad as he spoke.

Attractive blond - forty-two - divorced - teacher – well-liked - teaches yoga - dated Bill Reed on and off - wanted out of Melbourne Beach - moved to Vero with Bill – got engaged - realized her mistake – ended it.

At that point, I heard the voice of an older lady call out to Bob, and impatiently tapped my pen on the page until he whispered, "Fuck, I have to go. I'm taking my mom to brunch."

I tossed the pen on my pad. "S-h-i-t," I whimpered.

"You okay?"

"Yes. I just can't figure out why I'm on the edge of my seat—"

"What?"

"Nothing. Call me later."

"Yeah, sure."

Click.

Shaking my head, I walked away from my notepad and smiled when I pulled up my calendar: *Sunday, January 15 - dinner with the kids!*

I had made plans to meet my kiddos for an early dinner. Since Marie and I separated, we developed a routine of sorts. I would meet them at Carrabba's in Palm Bay, a city north of where I lived. It just so happened to be far enough away from the surf and sand and drama of The Gym to render the break I surely craved.

The sun was setting on the Italian grill's patio when I sat down. I blinked my eyes, and a decade passed. Memories rushed over me, and I only wanted to freeze time. Lauren was now a freshman in college, and our son, Jerry, was a junior at West Shore. He acted in all the high school plays while tweaking his plan to save the world.

I leaned back in my chair, sentimental as my six-foot-three-inch son's text straightened me upwards. *Daddaay* (Daddy), *we're here!* Sitting there in the shadow of our memories, I was startled by our waiter's voice. "Kids on the way?" he asked and placed my wine on the table.

I nodded with a smile. "They just pulled in."

"You have an hour left of happy hour," he said while pointing to my nine-ounce pour. "I'll check back with you in a minute."

"Thanks," I said. "Don't let me run dry."

The waiter flashed me a look as if he indeed knew the drill. I took a sip and noticed Lauren and Jerry arguing en route to the table. I stood up, and Jerry hugged me, while Lauren dropped in a chair, annoyed. "She's just like you, *Daddaay*," Jerry said, squeezing me tight. "Always texting."

I could tell Lauren was upset with her younger brother and said to her, "What's wrong? Did One Direction break up?"

Lauren whined, "I can't say a word when Jerry starts his drawn-out stories." Her thumbs were flying before she stopped suddenly and eyed my wine. "Dad, can I have some wine?"

A voice in my head was like: THIS IS GOING TO BE AN INSTANT CLASSIC. I nodded, grateful for a front-row seat, as Jerry shook his head at me, acting like the parent. Savoring each second, I watched him lecture Lauren about the dangers of alcohol. Even his mannerisms were humorous—until he turned to scold me. I put my hand up and said, "Jerry, relax. A little red wine is fine."

Jerry's hand went involuntarily to his head. "You don't even know what a little wine is. And she's nineteen. What the hell is wrong with you?"

I smiled, hoping the dumbfounded gaze he shot me was him flexing his acting muscles, but I quickly realized it was not. I suggested we walk back to our cars and come back in. They chuckled, and I brought up Trump's inauguration. That continued the fun as my liberal son sat up straighter in the chair, grumbling about Bernie Sanders getting the shaft by the DNC. When he insisted that this was a travesty of the 2016 presidential campaign, I explained how politics work and how corrupt much of it is. Of course, Jerry continued to argue his point until Lauren voiced her displeasure with the entire conversation. "Trump is about to be sworn in, and no one is even RSVPing to the inauguration. They'll all die stressed out and miserable for living a life of lies, and most of them won't even get it until they are on their deathbeds, so let it go," she huffed as a text flashed up. "Dad, who keeps texting you?"

I eyed the dating site names but only mentioned a text in the middle of them. "Some guy who read my book. We worked together back in the day, and he wants to meet up..." my voice trailed off.

Both kids chimed in simultaneously. "Have you started writing again?"

I inhaled, thinking about the notepad and Kristen and how crazy the past month had been, and said, "Well, when you want something hard enough, the entire universe conspires to help you."

Jerry's eyes lit up when Lauren rolled hers, turning to him. "Don't get any crazy ideas, Jerry. What dad's trying to say is that he met another girl at The Gym who blew smoke up his ass."

I adjusted myself in the chair. "No. Well, yes. But hold on."

Jerry turned to me. "My friends googled the book, and it still seems to be doing well."

"And I found the notepad I used for *The Show!*" I said excitedly. They both shot me blasé looks, so I quickly added, "And yes, I also met a girl at The Gym who is adamant I write the sequel."

Lauren laughed. "So, is this the girl in the Facebook posts with you at the beach?"

I cleared my throat. "No. Well, she enjoyed it too, but that's Allie Girl—" Jerry interrupted me.

"You call her Allie Girl? Dad, you're about to turn fifty." He paused, seemingly tongue-tied.

I cleared my throat. "Okay, where's the waiter?"

Lauren chuckled. "Mom and her friends think you're dating Allie Girl."

"No..." my mouth closed and then opened again. No words came out, so I gulped my wine and patted my forehead with the black cloth napkin.

Shaking her head, Lauren continued. "I'm surprised you're not on Snapchat. You need all your memories to be brief bursts—and then disappear."

I swallowed and changed the subject. "So, Jerry, what's your next play?"

Lauren spoke up. *To Kill a Mockingbird.*" She smiled. "We're glad you're our dad, though, and not just because you're the coolest. Being open about everything—your successes and failures have taught us a lot."

I nodded appreciatively. "Don't be afraid to dream big and fail. Our failures lead to a stronger foundation for success. Imagine it, believe it, and be it, and always be kind."

Lauren said, "Kind? Where did that fit in for you?"

"Since I'm at The Gym." I paused to ponder how true it was. "It's been a challenging six months. But I have seen how people struggle with all sorts of ailments, and being nice to them has gone a long way." I shrugged. "And in return, they've been patient with me. You both should believe in the magic of kindness."

"That's very cool," Lauren added.

I nodded. "It's the only thing I've figured out in the six months I've owned it."

"Please don't have another crash and burn," Lauren pleaded.

I again patted my head with the cloth napkin and motioned to the waiter. He rushed over. "The bartender has another glass ready at the bar," he said. "Give me a second."

I grinned. "Great, but we can also order." I glanced over at another text. This time it was Bob wanting to finish the conversation about Allison Tinke. *I'm with my kids. I'll see you at The Gym tomorrow;* I typed and watched each order their meals, cherishing the moment.

An hour flew by. When the laughter subsided, I muttered, "Time is a tricky thing—" I paused in mid-sentence when Allie called. "Hey, Allie Girl," I answered.

"Hey, Lawrence. We had more complaints about the new Zumba instructor today."

I sighed. "You're going to have to take over that class. That lady isn't working out—"

Allie interrupted, "Lawrence, they think she's on drugs."

"I know, but she's not." I paused and lowered my voice. "Which makes this an even more difficult situation to deal with."

Allie laughed. "Oh, and other members were asking what happened to your yoga girl."

I sighed deeply. "Are you saving the best for last?

"Like what?"

"Like maybe the place burned to the ground."

"Oh my God, stop."

"I'm kidding—but I am with my kids."

"Oh, how cute!" Allie chirped. "Okay, I'll see you tomorrow. Bye, Lawrence."

"Bye, Allie Girl."

Click.

Gazing across the table, I noticed Jerry seemed bothered. *Sometimes it's better to leave things as they are,* I thought to myself and forced a smile. I realized it had been six months since we all lived under the same roof and could tell he missed my voice and ear. He loved his mother dearly, but being a loving mother did not make her a father. I hugged him tight as we said our goodbyes, only planning to do it again soon.

When I got home, I was taken aback by it all.

The Dark One pushed a bottle of wine my way. After pouring a BIG GULP size glass, I turned on my Bose and winced as Justin Timberlake's "Can't Stop the Feeling" blared out of the speakers. *How long is this girl going to haunt me?* I thought as *The Dark One* yelled, *I LOVE THIS SONG! It reminds me of your yoga girl. You remember that little dance number she nailed naked in her apartment...don't you, Sport?*

I tossed the Bose remote on the couch and decided to call Maya. But then I wondered if she was with Bill. Not relishing the thought of explaining this, I dropped my iPhone next to the remote and stood there. Swaying a bit buzzed, I attempted to sort it out. Quickly, I realized it would be best to preserve this drunk musing on my trusted notepad.

After spilling wine on a page, I placed my glass down and wrote: *The summer seems like an eternity ago. My six months at The Gym often feels surreal. When I want to savor something, it will speed by in a blur. When I try to move on from something, it will drag on forever.*

SEVEN

EVERYONE HAS A STORY

JANUARY 16, 2017 (MORNING)
STARBUCKS/THE GYM

The next morning, I turned the shower on and peeked at another text, hoping it was Maya. A long sigh escaped me, as with increasing frustration, I realized it was not. We had not communicated since Saturday, and I raced out the door, convinced Bill Reed was the reason.

It was the third Monday of the month, and I was making a quick stop before heading to The Gym. My eyes were on my iPhone like it was a bomb, ready to explode. The names flashing up from the dating sites had me preoccupied enough to miss the turn for the Starbucks. This wasn't a caffeine fix, though. I had agreed to meet an old wine industry colleague who read my book. His name was Michael Oliver. The last time I had seen him, we used pagers and payphones. He connected with me on LinkedIn, hopeful to meet up as if we were on a dating site. Michael lived in Miami but frequently traveled for his winery. After a failed attempt to have lunch in Orlando, I agreed to a cup of coffee when I realized he was at his in-laws in West Melbourne. Checking the time, I circled back to Starbucks and noticed him on his iPhone. He wore glasses that I didn't recall and pulled his hand through his rapidly greying hair, looking stressed out in a suit that was too tight. *We're getting old*, I thought as he trod over to me.

"How do you stay so thin?" he yelled out with a look of amusement.

"I'm not really sure," I replied, walking into his limp handshake. "It's good to see you, Michael."

"Likewise. So, you torched your career and retired on the beach as a gym owner," he continued. "It sounds like another book is coming." He laughed, patting me on the back as if I were a child.

"I'm hoping." I paused and smiled. "How about that coffee?"

"You bet." He thrust the door open. "I've wanted to talk to you since I read your book. I hope that doesn't seem strange."

I shrugged. "It's been a super neat experience, and I'm grateful. Lead the way."

Without hesitation, he walked up to the counter and ordered a Mocha Frappuccino and a Grande Dark Roast for me. My eyes grew wide when he reminded me it was in *The Show*. He never admitted he enjoyed my book but was intrigued. After a few minutes of questions, there seemed to be something else, though. Michael could tell I was getting antsy waiting for it and handed me folded sheets of paper from his suit jacket. I blinked at a Prologue that looked just like *The Show*. "I'm a writer, too," he said and grinned. He was very pleased with himself.

And here it comes, I thought but said, "Oh, great, Michael."

"I sent my manuscript to a few publishers with no luck and wondered if you could give me some feedback," he said, thinking. "It's good." He hesitated, and I swayed with a feeling of vertigo. "Maybe you can send it to your publisher."

"Sure," I choked out and began reading. I waited for something to grab me and turned to the second page. When I began the third page, I said, "Has anyone else read this?"

"No. But my story has a longer set-up than yours," he said, slightly irritated. "I mean, I've never been fired and screeched out of a parking lot having to explain an affair to my wife. No offense."

"I never thought about publishing my story," I said, annoyed he was doing this for the wrong reason. "I write because of the creative release."

With a frustrated sigh, he snatched the pages from me. "I worked hard on this." He cleared his throat. "It's about my life. And a more relatable career than yours. Sorry, but it's true."

I nodded, startled by how defensive he was. "Okay," I said and took a sip of coffee as he stared at me in silence. "Let me read on."

He held it against his suit jacket as if it were his baby and then hit the pages with his hand to make a point like I should get this. "I write about my faith and my church and God," he said and sighed. "So, do you have any suggestions?"

I took a breath and feared I was rapidly entering troubled waters. "Maybe you skip a prologue and go straight to the first chapter." I paused as he looked intensely at me. "Is there a leading lady in this?"

His eyes narrowed at me. "Yes, Larry. My wife."

Oh fuck, forget it, I thought but said, "Of course. Good. Well, let's see. Did you have a dim protégé who fell in love with you and then snapped because he was jealous of the time you spent with her?" Michael's eyes slowly closed. "Or a chemically imbalanced admin like Mama Bear, who would growl when she called the office?" I paused as a small smile spun on his face. "Or a sales manager like Schultz, who claimed he saw nothing, heard nothing, and knew nothing having to do with you?"

He finally laughed gently. "I get your point, Larry. Everyone has a story, but not all are meant to be read." He gazed out the window for a moment, reflecting on it all. "Most men spend their energy trying to eliminate risk. Many know something is wrong and say nothing because they want the promotion. Years later, they suffocate in silence with high blood pressure. That will never be you. It's refreshing to see you never lost your sense of humor through this."

I nodded. "I'd rather laugh than cry. Keep writing, Michael." I jumped up, wondering how I got out of that but did not want to push my luck. "I do have to go, though." He pushed himself up and nodded appreciatively.

It was almost a relief now, realizing he understood. He just stood there for a moment, calm and sympathetic. I regarded him curiously. He went to speak but stopped. After a moment, he said, "I guess when I read *The Show*, I realized I couldn't stand the politics in my own company. It's not as bad as what you dealt with, but I want out, too. I can't at fifty, though." He paused, and his face showed that he had lost all hope.

"Believe me," I insisted. "I wish I had the stability of your career, Michael."

He sighed. "I don't know. What happened to all the years, Larry?" he said solemnly. Then, he smiled warmly at me. "It almost seems like you turned back the clock by living the way you do." He shook his head. "I believe this was all meant to happen to you."

I exhaled. "It is nerve-racking starting your life over at fifty while searching for so many answers at once, though."

Michael grinned at me. "Don't think so hard."

"Easier said than done."

"Life is really quite simple. Trust your instincts. And start writing now, so you capture it all." He laughed. "Now I'm giving you advice."

I nodded. So much hit me at once. I gazed at a text from Kristen. "Thank you, Michael," I said.

"You didn't have to respond to me, but you did," he replied. "I appreciate this, Larry."

We shook hands, and he trudged over to his Corolla.

I collapsed into my little Kia Soul, thinking about Jerry and the time I had been away from him. I wanted to call him but knew he was in school. My thoughts sped up, less rational because of it. With my quick fix being women and wine, I texted Kristen that I would meet her.

For the moment, I felt better.

Within minutes, I opened my windows and let any lingering remorse blow out as I raced over the Melbourne Causeway with Nickelback's "Rockstar" blaring out of the car's little speakers. The fifteen-minute drive from there didn't provide any clarity, either. I pulled into The Gym's parking lot, only hoping the Snowbirds migrating back had the cash for today's afternoon adventure. I could not put another wine time on my credit card but hopped out of my car optimistically.

Five potential cash customers were rushing in with Barbara Ross. Her popular Body Sculpt class was always full, and as I raced into the office, Barbara informed me she ordered *The Show* on Amazon. The attractive blond mom was a favorite instructor, and I thanked her graciously when Allie called. I walked back outside and answered. "Hey, did you get my text?"

"Yeah. I'll be there at twelve," Allie replied. "I know you have to say goodbye to the girl who rekindled your creative juices."

"I know it sounds crazy, but I felt something that night…"

Allie chuckled. "Just promise me we can re-open in Never Land when we go out of business in Melbourne Beach, Peter." She paused with a sigh. "And please, tell me Mr. Smee's not there."

"He's never here when I am. I think he runs out the back door when I pull in."

She laughed briefly. "Too bad Bob Tillie doesn't."

"Smile and keep laughing, Allie Girl."

She sighed deeply. "It's difficult when a few envious characters in this storyline also want you dead like in *The Show*. It's kinda scary."

"Don't be scared, ya silly goose. I'll see you soon."

"Bye, Lawrence."

"Bye, Allie Girl."

Click.

EIGHT

AN EMOTIONAL FAREWELL AND A MESSAGE FROM WALTER

JANUARY 16, 2017 (AFTERNOON)
MULLIGANS VERO BEACH/THE GYM

Three hours later, I raced out of The Gym to meet Kristen. She was flying out the next day and had manipulated her schedule to partake in one last wine time. She insisted that we meet in Vero Beach at Mulligan's Bar & Grill.

At first, I thought she chose the lunch spot because of the view, but I quickly realized it was far enough away from anyone who might recognize her in Melbourne Beach. Driving south on A1A, I ignored a call I should have taken from my banker while chatting with an attractive brunette named Sarah McMillen. Right after Sarah had reached out to me on POF, I had deleted the other dating sites pretending that I was getting somewhere, but it was mere pretense. "So, how about we meet on Friday for that glass of wine?" said Sarah as Maya's name flashed up on my caller ID. I sat stunned. "Larry?"

"Y-yes," I stammered. "That sounds great, but I have to call you back." I ended the call with Sarah and clicked over to Maya. "Hey—"

"I deleted your name from my contacts because I didn't want to keep texting you," Maya said. Her voice was soft and unrecognizable.

I glanced back at her name to make sure I read it right and then said, "Why?"

"I lost my best friend. I haven't been myself lately," she replied, sighing. "I called The Gym and got your number to let you know."

I hesitated.

"Strangely, meeting you feels right," I said gently, gripping the steering wheel tightly.

"I'm not dealing with emotions," said Maya. I wanted to respond but opened the windows instead. I lost her next words to the wind and the ocean as I raced along the shoreline.

After a moment of much needed fresh air, I closed them and interrupted her. "Your texts turned out to be meaningful for me."

"Why?"

"I found the notepad I used for *The Show*," I urged her. "And I see a storyline—"

"I'm glad I helped you with your sequel. Bye—"

"You're missing my point. I doubt I would've even noticed my notepad if you didn't text me on Saturday."

"I have to go—"

Click.

The vulnerability in her voice summed up my entire month on these dating sites, and I wished for that statement back. I realized Maya had more baggage than she led on, but there was something about her that I felt compassion for. I couldn't accurately pinpoint what that was, though. After another shot of fresh air, I called her back, overthinking everything and, at the same time, blocking out Bill Reed. When it went to voicemail, I didn't leave a message. And then Allie called me back. She quickly informed me that Bob gave my number to a woman who called The Gym. He had a habit of answering the office line, but this sent her over the edge, so I decided against telling her that it was Maya. Instead, I said, "Is The Gym crowded?" That was another mistake. It happened to be empty, and when she rambled on that members were leaving because of the drama with my so-called yoga girl, I was infuriated by Bob. After catching a glimpse of my speed, I slowed down, fully aware he was the main culprit who spread those rumors.

To make matters worse, Allie couldn't stand Bob and wondered why we were friends. With two more texts flashing up, I admitted that I tolerated his flippant remarks because he was a gym member, not a friend. She hesitantly confessed that a lady had left The Gym because he informed her that I thumb my nose at long-standing rules, drink in excess, and act recklessly with other men's women. Much of what Bob would say had just enough truth to keep a person from totally going off on him but left too many scratching their heads when they'd hear the full story. Allie insisted he deliberately spun everything negatively because he was hell-bent on seeing me fail. It was tough to argue her point, so I told her I would call her after lunch.

Fifteen minutes later, I was sitting under two coconut palms admiring Kristen's spirit. We held up our first glass of Oyster Bay Sauvignon Blanc and clinked glasses. Its pale straw green color displayed brilliant clarity against the beautiful turquoise waters of Vero Beach. Finally, I relaxed on what turned out to be a magnificent Monday. The high had reached seventy-eight degrees, and Kristen insisted we stick our toes in the sand. When I brought up my issues with Bob, she winced in distaste. "Bob spins the truth because he's a lonely and envious man," she insisted. "I never could stand him."

I nodded and suggested we change the subject. When she casually mentioned that I would hear from Maya again, I told her about the call. "It seems as if Maya refuses to get emotionally attached—"

"Because she already is," said Kristen, cutting me off.

Allie's name flashed up again. I took another sip of that delightful white and answered. "Mmm, what's up, Allie Girl?"

"Did anyone from The Gym see you and Maya on Friday?"

"Why?"

"People are talking."

I hesitated. "Bob called me when I was about to jump off Maya's balcony."

Allie sighed. "That explains a lot. Please call me when you're alone."

"Okay, Allie Girl."

"Bye, Lawrence."

Click.

Kristen took a sip and looked over at me. "And the plot thickens," she said, looking thoughtful. "Can't wait to see this all unfold on the pages of *The Gym*." She jumped up and added, "Oh, and make sure you give this story a full year." I thought about that, watching her walk off to the bathroom. With a reflective breath, I received another dating site "meet me" request.

My mind was in a fog. Within minutes the bottle of Sauvignon Blanc was empty, and even though the waitress was shocked, she didn't hesitate to ask if we'd like another. I eagerly nodded, and she rushed off to get it.

At four o'clock, Kristen's boyfriend called with dinner reservations for their last night in town. After we embraced in a long hug, goodbye, I stepped back and pondered her face. There was little doubt that Kristen Bircher came into my life for a reason. She lifted her chin. "You're going to find her. It might not be easy, but you will." She kissed my lips softly. "That was for the new book, *The Gym*." When I peered at her puzzled, she added, "We had to kiss goodbye." She gifted me one last glance of her seductive smile. "With the waves crashing against the shoreline. After one last wine time..." her voice trailed off. She pulled her fiery red hair back in one last ponytail as her hazel eyes glittered in the fading sunlight.

I smiled. And then, we went our separate ways.

When I got to my little Kia Soul, I listened to the surf, wanting to doze off right there. Instead, I turned on the car stereo, and "Starving" was playing. After raising the volume with Maya on my mind, I texted her to call me. She read the text, but I didn't hear back from her.

Twenty-five-minutes later, I pulled into The Gym parking lot, wondering how I missed the Wabasso Bridge. If I didn't have to take a piss so badly, I would've pulled back out. I took a breath and hurried in. Both original owners of The Gym, Bob Ripper, who everyone called the Ripper, and his partner, Ivan Ignatius, were by the free weights. The Ripper shook his head, amused. "Women and wine," said the handsome man. "You remind me of myself."

I held up my hand as I ran by them to the bathroom, about to burst. Ivan flexed his beautifully aging brown skin while blowing me a kiss. "Looking good, Ebony Prince!" I squealed to Ivan as a shout out to his days in the WWF.

When I came out, Allie called me over. I walked into the office, assuming she wanted to finish our conversation about Maya but noticed an older Snowbird with an uneasy expression. He stood at the check-in counter and looked her up and down. In a heavy Boston accent, he said, "Sweetheart, you are stunning!"

"Aw, thank you, I'm Allie," she said and smiled uncomfortably.

He took his credit card out and lowered his voice. "Sally, I forgot my number for this silly keypad you insist on using to get in this place."

Allie chirped, "What's your name?"

"Walter Clement," he shouted a little too loud. "Do I need a new picture?" he patted his white hair down and added, "Make sure you get my Pats shirt. They're going to win the Super Bowl this year." He took a step back and smiled wider. Allie could barely contain herself and informed him we had a picture on file. Since he didn't like it, he asked for a new one. With lingering vanity traits and a good sense of humor, he smoothed out his Patriots shirt with his hands and then placed them on his hips as if he was Superman.

Allie bit down on her lip and took the picture. "Very handsome, Walter."

Walter studied it. "Now that's a good one!" he boasted. "Where's Bob?"

"Which Bob?"

"The Ripper. And Ivan. The original owners of this place."

Allie smiled and pointed to them in the back of The Gym. "The Ripper rearranges the place as if he still owns it."

Walter waved at them and quietly said, "I was afraid of that." He paused and looked at me and then sighed. "My neighbor down here— Kathy...no Karen...anyway, she told me about the new owner's book." Allie, grinning like a girl, pointed to me. Walter smiled thinly and then gazed across The Gym for a long moment. I thought he was having a senior moment, but then he picked up one of my bookmarks and continued. "It's a battle that goes on inside all of us." He nodded solemnly.

Allie's head tilted slightly. "Excuse me, Walter," she said. "What battle?"

"Life's disappointments," he said to me. "Like a ruined career that was set for stardom. You can learn from it all, or it will torment you and prevent you from experiencing happiness and love. You are the only one who can conquer these demons. If not, they'll destroy you." He looked sure of what he was saying, even though he couldn't remember his neighbors' names, and called Allie Sally.

Allie's lips parted, and eyes narrowed at him. "So, you read *The Show*, Walter?"

I leaned forward, tense in anticipation of his answer.

He stood silent for a moment and said, "It was a recommended read." He nodded once at me, and with a shaky breath, added, "Hey, do you know what year the Melbourne Causeway was built?"

I looked behind us, expecting to see a hidden camera team, when Allie blurted out, "Wait—what?" She blinked at him with dubiety. "No."

"1921!" he barked at Allie. "You should know these things if you're working here." He pivoted slowly as Will Burleson strolled up to the counter. "Melbourne Beach was incorporated in 1923, and the Causeway was built in 1921. Do you know when the town was established?"

"Wow. Um, no, Walter," Allie said. "Please enlighten me." She ran Walter's credit card with a curious smile as he plowed on.

"The town was established in 1883. Pineapples were grown until 1895, but freezing temperatures wiped the crop out that year. I wasn't born yet, though." He smiled wide and added, "I'm a wise old man, Allie." He then turned back to me. "You can conquer your demons. I've been there. Many years ago, but it is the same dark lonely place, son. Please be careful."

I scrutinized him. I wanted to believe he was senile but knew he wasn't. "Thank you for reading my book," I said. "I understand."

Walter gave me a nod and signed the credit card receipt. The look on his face made it clear he didn't believe me. He drew his mouth into a tight line, looking back at two copies of *The Show* for sale on the counter before he walked by our other Kristen—Kristen Rylan. We always had fun with the fact she looked like Lady Gaga, so we called her Baby Gaga. Allie tried to joke with me about it, but my thoughts were dark. I craved a bed forgetting that Will wanted to train me. I turned to the twenty-three-year-old and said, "Next time, Will. I promise."

Will shook his head, humored. "You need to learn how to lift, Larry."

"How about we try next Wednesday?"

"Okay."

I grabbed a bottle of water and shuffled out. Refusing to turn on the car stereo, I sped up A1A and went to call Maya when my iPhone rang. I glanced at the caller ID, curious to see my new/old wine industry acquaintance that I met for coffee. I hit the accept button. "Hey, Michael."

"Hello Larry, I'm calling about your canceled newspaper interview."

I sat up straighter. "What about it?"

"I heard someone named Hook influenced the paper to switch authors," Michael said distractedly. "My buddy believes it was personal and that you know him."

I hesitated.

"Yes, I do," I muttered. "Captain Hook."

"Excuse me…"

I sighed. "Yes. I know him."

"I'm sorry, I can barely hear you. I'm walking into a meeting—"

"No problem. Thank you, Michael."

"Sure, Larry."

Click.

NINE

SHARKY'S SPIN BIKE

JANUARY 17, 2017
THE GYM/SAND ON THE BEACH

The following day, I finally conceded that the canceled newspaper interview had consumed me. Although this confirmed how important my writing was to me, I should have focused on my fitness center and heeded wise to Walter Clement's words, but I did neither.

I treaded through doors of The Gym to an onslaught of complaints before sitting down at a sales ledger that was short the money owed for December's sales tax. While I scrutinized the page, Cindy rushed into the office as Marlene's yoga class was filing out. "Larry, those bitchy witches are stuffing the complaint box."

I sighed. "Cindy, please stand there until they walk out."

Her eyes narrowed at me. "Why?"

"Because they'll think you're complaining, too, and might leave without adding to my misery."

She laughed. "Oh my God, this is hilarious."

By noon I was worn out. All I wanted to do was sleep. Unable to keep my eyes open, I leaned back in the office chair when our afternoon classic rock block transitioned from "Hey Joe" by Jimmy Hendrix to "The End" by The Doors. I yawned as the hypnotic instrumental played on and dozed off briefly until my eyes shot open when I heard a loud clinking sound by the spin bikes. I sighed when I realized another bike bit the dust. *This is the end.* Jim Morrison sang. *Beautiful friend...* A few seconds later, I groaned inwardly while walking out to the disturbance, wondering why the lady was still peddling. She shouted at me, "This bike sounds like it's going to blow!"

I pointed both index fingers to my ears, so she'd take out her EarPods and softly said, "Maybe you should stop pedaling."

Acting like I knew what was wrong with it, I then jiggled the wheel. "What's wrong?" the lady asked, hopping off it.

I shuffled around the bike. "Just a slight problem—right here—with this bar—and chain," I babbled and then banged the chain guard. When a rusted screw fell to the floor, I casually added, "This is common."

She sighed. "It isn't at my gym back home."

"It's common. Here. In the salt air..."

She wasn't entirely sure what to believe at this point but was willing to give me the benefit of the doubt. With only four working bikes left, I jumped on the one with the least amount of rust and peddled frantically as Jim Morrison sang on. *This is the end - My only friend, the end.* Indeed, it banged and clanged, signifying the end of that one too. By this point, the lady, who was vacationing with her husband at the Port d'Hiver Bed and Breakfast up the road, couldn't help but laugh. Her husband curiously wandered over from the free weights. Shaking his head, he watched me pedal the next one while I debated whether to cancel our Wednesday spin class.

"So?" said the lady, shifting to look at me from another bike in the line. "These all seem to have had too many miles logged on them."

"No...no, this one's fine," I replied, pedaling faster on the last bike in the row. "And those," I waved my hand at a few, "just need some WD-40."

After apologizing for the disruption in their workout, a few members rallied around this latest dilemma and tracked down a guy who had a spin bike, which happened to be in his pickup at a local bar. I muttered that I needed a drink and told myself not to question it.

Ten minutes later, I left The Gym fatigued by frustration from listening to Bob lecture me about Hook. "I warned you he would flex his political muscles, and now you lost an interview," he barked.

I exhaled. "What's this guy's problem?"

"His problem is that you didn't stay away from his girl," Bob said as I took a hard right into the parking lot of Sand on the Beach.

I zipped into a spot, second-guessing everything, and said, "I don't know Hook's girlfriend."

"You do. You just can't keep track of the women you're talking to."

"No. You're wrong, Bob," I replied as adamantly as I could when Sarah McMillen's name flashed up on my caller ID.

"How can you explain-BEEP-that Hook's girlfriend-BEEP-has your picture on her iPhone-BEEP-and your book on her iPad?"

I could not, so I clicked over. "Hey, Sarah."

"Hey, you. Did you get my text?"

"I might have," I said. "I was driving. What's up?"

"I wanted to know if you can meet at six on Friday instead of five?"

"Oh, sure," I said and sat up speechless. Peering into the rearview mirror, I caught Captain Hook marching across the parking lot with Mr. Smee stumbling up behind him. My mouth opened to question her about Hook, but I assumed she'd think I was nuts and only added, "That's not a problem."

"Are you sure?"

"Yes," I said and hesitated to watch them. "Can I call you back? I'm meeting a guy at Sand on the Beach to buy a spin bike."

"You're there now?" she asked. Her voice sounded startled.

"Yes," I said and peeked at my back seat for my jacket. "Why?"

"Nothing, I'll call you shortly."

"Okay—"

Click.

Seconds later, Hook took a call, and both men hopped into his Audi A8 and sped off. I threw my jacket on to ward off the crisp salt air and walked in looking for this guy. Everyone called him Sharky because a shark bit him surfing as a child. I remembered he looked like an older Justin Bieber and noticed him waving his tattooed arm in the air at me. I walked up to the table, and he stood up in long ripped shorts, an OP T-shirt, and flip-flops on a rapidly cooling evening in an open-air bar.

"I'm Sharky," he reminded me as we shook hands. After some small talk, Sharky told me he was grateful he had met me at The Gym after losing his job because of a DUI. "The bike in my truck came from my mother's, and you need it more than me. I picked it up this afternoon and then heard about your problem. It was meant to be."

I didn't quite understand and said, "Money is tight. How much are you looking for?"

He shook his head. "Nothing. I was down and out last summer when you extended my membership. The bike is yours."

"Thank you, Sharky," I said. "I'll reactivate your membership until you get back on your feet."

"That's very cool." He raised his Corona to me. "Is Patty Miller still teaching your spin class?"

"Yes, she's great."

All my instincts told me to make mental notes on everything that poured out of his mouth. "The DUI ruined me," said Sharky solemnly. "But Jimmy Hook gave me another chance." He made a funny face when he mentioned Hook's name but seemed excited to transition into his sales team. They held their meetings every Tuesday at Sand on the Beach—one I realized I just missed. As he rambled on, the waitress startled me with a glass of wine, and Sharky added, "Connor Lee told me you drink wine." We clinked glasses. "Cheers!"

"Are you friends with Smee?" I asked, taking a breath to calm down. *The Dark One* appeared, and my mind wandered back to the lost interview and then again to Walter's message at The Gym.

"He's a troubled acquaintance." Sharky's eyes narrowed at me. "You okay?"

I nodded yet struggled to look forward. "Yes."

"And you meant, Lee, right? Connor Lee?"

I managed to smile and wince at the same time. "I call him Smee. Mr. Smee."

Sharky laughed, gazed at another waitress who dropped off two Kamikazes, and said, "Mr. Smee has the hots for that little cheerleader you're dating. The girl who works for you."

We sat for a moment in awkward silence. "Allie?"

"Yeah, she wasn't there when I went to The Gym last summer."

"No, she wasn't, but we're not dating."

Sharky grinned mischievously as if he didn't believe me. "When did she start working for you?"

"November."

"Right before the yoga instructor with the hot body left." He smirked. "You were also friendly with her. Weren't you?"

I exhaled. "Yes. But it's not all that it seems, and a long story for another day…"

The Dark One inched closer and whispered in my ear, *This is getting good. Drink up, Sport!*

We slammed our empty shot glasses to the table, and a man hurried over in a shirt and tie. I was surprised to find out it was Sharky's brother. "We're leaving soon," he said sternly and marched off.

Sharky leaned over the table. "My brother thinks I've been drinking too much. And with the DUI, he insisted he drive."

I nodded and pushed myself up. "Well, good." Dark thoughts swirled around me. "I appreciate this, but I must get going, too."

He pointed to the waitress, rushing over. "I paid for that." The waitress dropped off another glass of wine. What came next was unexpected. "Hook dated that waitress," Sharky whispered. I watched her walk behind the bar and sat back down.

Leaning over my wine, I wanted to prove Bob wrong. "Is he dating her now?"

Sharky waved his hand in the air. "Nah. Hook likes beautiful women, kind of as an accessory, I suspect. I've never known any to last."

"Have you met Hook's current girlfriend?"

"Yeah." He shrugged. "She's no different from the others." I looked at him with confusion, and he quickly clarified. "Money. Women only date him for his money. Since Hook's loaded, there's always a new one." The sound of the rough surf pounding the shoreline caught our attention. "Shit, it's getting nasty out there—"

Impatiently I said, "Do you know her name?"

With a blank look on his face, Sharky sputtered, "I think Susan. They've been fighting." He glanced at his brother at the bar. "You didn't hear this from me, but Hook's paid his girlfriends for sex. Some kinky shit. Blow jobs with a bit extra if they swallow."

A few seconds of stunned silence passed. "How do you know this?" I asked, peering at him in disbelief.

"I run errands for Hook, too. They were arguing about it when I dropped their pizza off the other night. She unbuttoned his pants, and you know…"

I blinked. "Why would she do that?"

"Money. I heard a rumor she's still on POF. But she needs a guy with money." Sharky lowered his voice. "Honestly, Hook preys on vulnerable men, too." He paused and then laughed. "I get why you call Lee Smee. He's proof. Captain Hook and Mr. Smee, that's funny!"

"I'm hoping it will be," I said and stood up. "Let's go check out the bike."

After checking it out, he promised to deliver it before my Wednesday spin class. I thanked him again, and we both turned to a jeep screeching into the parking lot. A stripper who aspired to be a yoga instructor jumped out, reeking of weed. After Sharky introduced us, we ended up doing another shot, and everything was getting blurry again. I insisted it was time to go. Before I could, of course, Marie, my ex, who technically was still my wife and doing the books for the fitness center, called.

"Fuck," I sputtered and hurried past the stripper, who tipped back her Stella. "Hey," I answered Marie's call. "How are you?"

"Fine," Marie replied. "Your sales tax is due tomorrow. What are your plans to pay it?"

I cringed as inebriated shout-outs from the drunk stripper echoed over me. "LARRRRRY, I LOOOOVE YOGA. PLEASE HIRE ME!"

I walked further down the boardwalk and said, "When is the latest I can submit it?"

"So, you don't have the money to pay it even though it's your busy season?"

"I'll find it tomorrow."

Without hesitation, she added, "Because your back is against the wall, and it's suddenly a challenge."

I closed my eyes and took in a shuddering breath of the cold air. "I'll have it tomorrow."

Marie sighed almost sympathetically. "Make sure you do, and I'll pay it online. Next week you can meet me at my office and buy me a glass of wine at Pane Vino."

"Sounds good. Thank you."

Marie sighed deeper. "Be safe, Larry. I heard your drunk friends in the background."

Click.

For a moment, I stood with the angry surf. So many thoughts in an instant, overlapping and colliding, like the waves.

I fought my darkness.

Memories of Maya were moved along by back-to-back texts from two different "dating site" Jennifer's. These bursts of excitement allowed me to avoid facing this lingering regret and ire. And then, just as I got back to my car, Sarah called me back. I felt tense and sent the call to voicemail.

TEN

THE RIPPER'S RED FLAGS

JANUARY 18, 2017 (MORNING)

THE GYM

The next morning, with my bloodshot eyes hidden behind my sunglasses, I strolled into The Gym. After exchanging a glance with Patty Miller walking into her spin class, I somehow eluded a heated debate about Congress boycotting Donald Trump's inauguration and jumped in a chair next to Allie. I smirked. "Hey, Allie Girl."

"Those guys dropped off the spin bike," she said enthusiastically, scrolling her Instagram.

I grinned, amused. "I noticed Patty was relieved."

"Yup." She glanced at two new Snowbirds approaching the counter and lowered her voice. "I'll let you do your thing, Lawrence."

"Thanks, Allie Girl," I said, springing into action. *A four-month membership saves me;* I reminded myself and smiled at the adorable couple determined to sell them. "Good morning, folks..."

Fifteen minutes later, I informed Marie that I had the money for December's sales tax. I took a long breath, transfixed on another first name from the latest group of "dating site" profiles I had added to my contacts. By now, I was mindful that most would never be linked to a last name. This next step in the dating process would quickly reveal conspicuous concerns that had me deleting them soon after, like the following text. It was a thirty-nine-year-old bipolar woman who refused to drink alcohol the day before while suggesting we talk over a bottle of wine this afternoon. I sighed, baffled, reading another one. It was from Jennifer. Unfortunately, I had three teachers named Jennifer in my contacts who all loved the beach, yoga, romantic comedies, and CrossFit. There was a long, thoughtful silence on my end.

Allie was playing her ukulele with her eyes on my face, reading me. Finally, my head raised, and my eyes narrowed at her slightly.

"What?" I asked her distractedly.

She laughed. "You have no idea who is texting you." I smiled awkwardly, attempting to prove her wrong. I opened my mouth to speak and shut it. Then she curled her legs neatly under her, placed her ukulele on the desk, and leaned towards me. "Has Maya the Mermaid reached back out to you?"

I shook my head. "No," I said, anxious and eager and hopeful. "But I believe she will."

Allie seemed humored. "That seems about right."

"Tillie's been on these sites for years and says otherwise, though."

"Bob's not you. And you are not normal. When's your next date?"

I nodded in silence, read a new text, and like a little boy, chirped, "Hey, it's her!"

"Who?"

"Sarah McMillen."

"Wow, another last name," Allie said with a touch of sarcasm. "Who is she?"

I grinned. "My Friday date, and she's forty-two!"

"Forty-two is perfect for you," she insisted while immediately questioning me about her. After filling her in on our lengthy phone conversations, Allie added, "Oh my God." She hit my knee. "Sarah could be the one, Lawrence."

My eyes narrowed at her as she took a sip of water. "You said that about Beth, the shoe girl."

She dropped the bottle on the floor bright red with water coming out of her nose when I caught sight of an amused expression on Baby Gaga's face at the check-in counter. "When do I have to renew?" Baby Gaga asked. "It's today or tomorrow."

Allie wiped her face with her sleeve and read the screen. "Tomorrow," she sputtered.

Baby Gaga nodded as Will Burleson walked by her with a gleam in his eyes. He took a step into the office, and I winced. "Why aren't you ready to workout, Larry?" said Will with angry eyes.

Oh fuck, I thought but said, "Do you have a thing for Baby Gaga?"

Will snapped, "What?"

"You like Baby Gaga. The eyes never lie."

Will ignored me. "You told me you were lifting with me today—"

The Ripper's voice interrupted him from behind. "Larry's been partying like a rock star," he yelled out. "Let him sober up." The Ripper walked around Will, gave me a fist pump, and added, "I need to speak to you."

We had gotten closer to the New Year, so I gave him a nod and a brief smile, walking with him out to the parking lot. He scanned it through his silver-rimmed glasses and reminded me of his mistakes when he owned The Gym. When my iPhone continued to ping with inane texts, he looked me straight in the eyes. "It was the bullshit rumors that ruined me," he said. "They were the reason I had to sell The Gym."

I shot him a look of bewilderment and spoke before I could think. "Yes. I heard some rumors, some interesting stuff."

"Me, too." The Ripper gently pressed. "Now, about you."

It took a conscious effort to swallow and another to utter, "Really?"

"Yes," he said and sighed. "How did you come to hire Allie?"

I shrugged. "She enjoyed my book and was looking to become a Zumba instructor. Why?"

A look of surprise crossed his face. "I haven't read your book, but the rumors have you in a sequel heading off another cliff with an even younger woman," he said bluntly. "The red flags are obvious."

I heaved a long sigh. I barely had the energy to explain this. "I understand the concern, but it's nothing like that. As we've discussed, I'm separated and trying to figure out the next chapter of my life."

The Ripper hesitated before he turned to face me, his back to the hazy sunrise. "You're dating in a small beach town. You will continue to generate crazy stories, which could spin off false rumors that are more believable because of the crazy stories." He paused, and I could feel my face flush. "Do you remember back in September, when I'd come into The Gym to give you a break?"

The memory of that time instantly came back to me. It felt like an eternity ago, although only months had passed. I nodded slowly. And then muttered, "Yes, why?"

The Ripper leaned closer to me. "While you were taking a dip in the ocean, I took too many calls on the office line from your old yoga girl not to realize something was going on with you two."

"I never denied that."

"But you hired a twenty-two-year-old Zumba instructor, and it appeared that you went from one to the other."

I tried to look stern but laughed. "One situation is different than the other. I'm not going to change how I live because someone in The Gym decides to talk."

"It's outside The Gym, too. Your name came up at Squid Lips." He paused and lowered his voice. "The rumors of your ways with women have many believing you won't be in business by the summer."

"It's more the mess I inherited," I said. My voice was defensive.

Without hesitation, he said, "Yes, but you didn't board up the windows for a hurricane and wake up hungover in your car. Some think you have a passion for things you know can hurt you. Certain people have used that and this ongoing drama to make you look reckless."

Anger crept into my voice, but my expression remained guarded. "Who is saying this?"

He turned behind him and then back to me. "I would watch your advertising team, Jimmy Hook and Connor Lee. Lee is twisting all the shit about Allie and your old yoga girl. He talks to that pariah, Bob Tillie. Hook spoke as if he knew you because of Bob."

I squinted at him more than the sunlight required, wondering how much I was overlooking. But only said, "They don't know me."

"Yeah, well, Hook's going to cancel some deal he made with you on your direct mail flyers. I'll find out what I can on my end, but be careful," said the Ripper, exchanging a frown with me.

Bob's warning about Hook's girlfriend chatting with me on a dating site crossed my mind. I *knew* I hadn't met her. Instead, I asked him if Hook had any political ties to the newspaper. When he confirmed Hook did, I told him about my botched book interview. "That's exactly the kind of shit I'm talking about," The Ripper said, his eyes narrowing and flashing. "It could all come undone for you. Like what happened to your wine career." His eyes widened as his mouth did but immediately shut.

I hesitated.

At that moment, I had the clarity from years of pain. "I stopped laughing at the end of my career. I refuse to live like that. I take risks. I do what feels good." My voice slowed for a moment. "I won't apologize for the crazy stories my life generates while I figure it all out. People will see the truth. In the end, they always do," I said. My voice was soft and low but clear and certain.

The Ripper's frown deepened. "We'd all like to think that's true, but I know better. Just look at what I'm driving." He pointed to an old auctioned-off police car. "I gave my heart and soul to The Gym, and it turned into a financial nightmare because of these rumors. That is real life. Sometimes it sucks." He checked the time. "Shit—I have to go."

I drew back, uncomfortable. Taking in a slow breath, we both turned and noticed Barbara Ross. "Why can't everybody be like Body Sculpt Barbara? She's always smiling and happy and helpful."

"Hey, guys!" Barbara called to us.

We waved back at her, walking in The Gym. "Agreed," said the Ripper turning back to me. "But it only takes a few. I'm late for work. We can meet for a drink, though."

"Sure, anytime," I said when Allie reminded me Patty was waiting to be paid for her spin class. "I have to pay Patty Cakes."

I looked at the Ripper, and he looked at me, then smiled. "You remind me of myself, back in the day. Please don't ignore the red flags." He paused and reached into his pocket for his old iPhone. "I hope you didn't sign any long-term lease with this landlord; they don't negotiate. I tried for years. They made me cut the space," he pointed to the separate unit at the far end of The Gym, "that was where the front door used to be. It's been vacant for years," his gaze drifted out into the parking lot. With a wave of intense bitterness, he added, "They just don't care."

I swallowed hard. "Thanks for the heads up."

The Ripper gave me another fist pump and lumbered over to his old police car when another text flashed on my screen. I expected Sarah but was startled to see it was Maya.

Hey, she texted. *I'm sorry about the call the other day. Meet me at The Mansion for happy hour. They have a nice Syrah. My treat!*

I gazed out into the parking lot alone with my racing thoughts. Then I heard Allie's voice. "Lawrence, Patty Cakes is waiting."

I decided to meet Maya and nodded to Allie. "Can you close tonight?"

She smiled hesitantly. "Who are you meeting?"

"Maya." I shrugged a little too desperately.

"I knew it!" she snapped. "As did you—"

"Can you?"

"Yeah, I need the money and admire your determination to find the one!" Allie shouted and smiled.

I smiled back and let Maya know I would be there at six o'clock.

Cool, she immediately texted back. *I'll be at the bar on the roof.*

ELEVEN

THE STORMY NIGHT
THAT SPUN THE WEATHERVANE

JANUARY 18, 2017 (EVENING)
THE MANSION
It was nine hours later.

The sun was setting, and The Mansion's happy hour was ending. Maya didn't seem to mind, though. Sitting at the rooftop bar, she texted me a picture of two glasses of Stag's Leap Syrah with a caption: *Hurry up!*

Amused, I scampered up the steps and replied to a text behind the beguiling brunette when she startled me. "I thought that was your scent," Maya said and dropped off the barstool looking gorgeous.

I smiled a half-smile. "Hey, beautiful you," I said as we hugged. "How's that Syrah?"

Maya noticed I was distracted but resisted the urge to question me. She only handed me the wine, stared into my eyes, and smiled at a libidinous flashback of the night we shared. "To another adventure," she said softly, clinking my glass.

"Cheers," we both chirped gleefully.

Before we knew it, our glasses were empty, and we were nearly halfway through a bottle of Etude Pinot Noir on what began as a gorgeous evening. The slight breeze coming in off the Indian River made the seventy-degree temperature feel invigorating. The moon was high and beautiful—colored spooky white. Conversation flowed with memories of our hometowns back on Long Island until I received a text. With her eyes hot on my iPhone, Maya seemed like a jealous girlfriend, not someone casually hanging out. "So, what's her name, and when are you meeting her?" she asked and flashed a fake smile. "I might know her, and I don't want to run into you."

"Her name is Sarah McMillen. I'm meeting her on Friday at 302."

Maya's mouth opened a little when her gaze lifted to the waiter. "My shift's ending," he said, rushing by with an order of pretzel sticks.

"Order another bottle," exclaimed Maya. "I'll be right back." I nodded, and she walked off to the bathroom. Our waiter ogled her from the next table and eventually took the order. With a curious smile, he commented that Maya looked like Megan Fox.

When Maya returned, it was as if she were a movie star walking the red carpet. Her gaze casually scanned the other tables, smiling in response to the stares. She sat down and put her hair up in a ponytail. "I love ponytails," I said, acting as if she did it by chance.

Her lips curved slightly. "I love Etude Pinot Noir."

Our eyes locked. "It's good to see again." My pulse throbbed.

Finally, I blinked away to another text, and she said, "I want to join The Gym for a couple of weeks."

I smirked. "We do have a monthly membership if you're feeling super ambitious."

She turned her head, suppressing a smile, and said, "No, it's not that." She paused after I nodded absently, and her voice dropped. "Never mind. You're preoccupied tonight."

I apologized and began a one-sided conversation, which had me questioning if she was okay. She looked at me, a hint of hostility on her face, and huffed, "Bill's with Allison. The woman I told you about."

I lifted my chin. "Allison Tinke."

Maya was a little shocked, then momentarily suspicious. "You remember her name?"

I shrugged like a boy and felt oddly reflective before I explained, yet again that I had repeatedly heard her name. While she contemplated that, I played it all off with a line that worked. "Besides, I can't forget *Tink*," I exclaimed, figuring she would catch the reference to my Peter Pan inspired character in *The Show*.

She smiled wickedly. "I'm almost finished with your Never Land crash and burn." I winced, realizing she wasn't done, and took a breath and held it. Impulsively she added, "Can you see yourself with a little blond-haired, blue-eyed Tink?"

Much to my mystification, the breeze suddenly changed direction. For a moment, I swirled my wine glass on the table blissfully as if I knew someone who fit that description before I confessed that I did not. With a stronger gust, my gaze shifted to the metal roof.

The weathervane on the old restaurant spun.

Maya leaned forward, beaming brightly as this bantering persisted. "Okay, since Wendy was your leading lady in the first book, does the Tinker Bell coffee mug you drank from have any significance to a love interest in the sequel?"

I exhaled enchanted. "No. I did drink my coffee out of a Tink mug. I'm not sure why," I said, intrigued. "It is interesting, though, agreed."

"Well, yeah. I thought it was a brilliant tease because there's no other reference to a Tinker Bell character," she said, her sarcastic edge softening whimsically. Then she leaned over her wine, seeming to relish the moment. With a soft smile, she added, "I had a dream a petite Tinker Bell type pulled you out of your darkness and saved you." She made a distasteful face. "Bill was in it, too, and I'm not sure why. I had the dream after finishing a chapter of your book, but it's faded."

I stiffened slightly, unable to deny that all of this tickled me. I pushed my thoughts away from it, knowing I was solely responsible for how absurd it sounded. Quietly I said, "I've started writing again—on my notepad mostly—but there's no Tink in this storyline."

Her eyebrows arched. "It would be no fun if you met her in the first chapter," she breathed out with another gust of wind that had me resisting the urge to speak. Enthralled, I allowed her to finish her thought. "I believe that the Tinker Bell mug ended up in the story for a reason," her eyes narrowed at me, "and if it wasn't deliberate, it was meant to be." She gifted me a similar little head nod that, ironically, Wendy gave me in *The Show*.

I chuckled for a moment and received another text that made it hard to think straight. It was the fifth nude photo from a fit thirty-six-year-old nymphomaniac yoga instructor from Sanford. Maya noticed the picture and grabbed my iPhone. Studying it, she said, "Can you explain her?"

I patted my head with a cocktail napkin that blew on my lap and said, "No, but I can't explain you either."

She slid it back, increasingly irked, and picked up her Android. "It's Bill," she said distractedly and read his text to me. "I have a dinner meeting in Vero. I will call you tomorrow." Maya looked up at me. "It figures he convinced Allison to go."

Watching her thumbs fly, I asked, "Why not end it?"

She grinned mischievously. "Because I'm a bit jealous of that little Tinker Bell."

I spilled my wine as I squealed, "Tinker Bell?"

Heads turned to us.

"Bill told me they called her Tink at The Gym when Allison lived in Melbourne Beach."

"Was the woman in your dream Allison?" I asked, intrigued.

Her gaze drifted, thinking. "Maybe."

"That would explain why Bill was in it," I said curiously.

She grabbed her wine glass. "I might have blocked that out."

"Most dreams fade." I paused as she took a sip of wine and almost spat it out. She wiped her mouth and nailed my shin. "That's my shin!"

"Sorry, but can you imagine if Allison became your Tink?"

I shook my head. "Maya, I'm inspired by stuff that actually happens," I said with a sigh. "The story has to be believable."

"It's you who have to believe." She smiled devilishly. "Picture a modern-day fairy tale where Tinker Bell rescues Peter Pan Man from his darkness, and you fall in love!"

I hesitated.

That was it! The love story I dreamt about after I found The Gym. She magically appeared in a trail of pixie light. Wait, this is crazy...or is it? Maybe I should just believe, I thought. With my gaze fixated on the old weathervane, I whispered, "I did. In my dream..."

"What?"

I took a breath. "So, what part do you play in this fairy tale?"

"I don't do fairy tales," she pretended, pulling her napkin over her whimsical smile. "Okay. I'm the Mermaid who splashes water on Tink from your Mermaid Lagoon, like Molly the Mermaid splashed water on Wendy in *The Show*."

"Good, I've been referring to you as Maya the Mermaid," I confessed as if this were normal. Then I blinked and shook my head. "So, how do you know Bill is having dinner with Allison?"

"I've gotten close with Bill's admin," she said, and as she sat with an irritated expression, I recalled her having a falling out with her best friend. When I questioned her about it, I grasped that it had something to do with me. "Okay," she fidgeted in the chair, "Michelle Crowley was my old bestie." I looked blankly at her, and she added, "I thought you knew Michelle."

I shook my head. "No."

"Well, she knows about us. Anyway, we should keep a low profile."

My gaze shifted to a couple staring at us. "But meeting here is super discrete."

With her light, sexy laugh, Maya hid behind her wine. "It was Christina's idea."

"Christina?"

"Bill's admin, Christina Couples, my new bestie," Maya replied, climbing unsteadily to her feet. "You know her from The Gym."

I recalled Christina when Maya's face registered surprise. After she whispered that a man was watching us, he stumbled to the side of our table, intoxicated. I had seen him at The Gym with Bob and Mr. Smee but barely recognized him. He looked tired and disheveled as words formed on his lips. "The Gym will naever slay open," he muttered incoherently, swaying with disturbing energy.

"Move on to your Uber, you drunk!" Maya said bluntly.

I shrugged. "Now we know why they cut us off."

Maya was caught between a smile and laugh as the man took a few clumsy shuffle steps to the stairwell.

Our gazes shifted to the new waiter holding the second bottle. "Sorry for the delay. I'm Jimmy."

I said, "No worries. We're only glad you didn't cut us off."

The young waiter grinned. "I'm friends with Paul, who works at The Gym." He paused as my gaze lifted to him. With excitement in his voice, he added, "We met when you bought The Gym last summer." Jimmy shook my hand as if I was a celebrity.

"Yes, of course," I said. I remembered him being a big talker.

Within seconds, Jimmy brought up the man who stumbled by us. Of course, Maya craved the scoop, and our wordy waiter was ready and raring to give it to her. "He's a writer like you," he said. "He told me the number one question about your book on Goodreads was where to find a shirtless picture of you. He said you're just another Hank Moody."

Without another move, I forced a smile and sighed. "Thanks for all the fun, Jimmy." I raised my glass to him.

"Enjoy your wine," he said and hurried off.

Maya put her elbows on the table and folded her hands together, resting her chin on them. "Don't let that drunk get to you. My dad insists that you only have haters because you've achieved something that they can't."

Nodding, I hoped to change the subject. "On Friday, you mentioned going back to Long Island. So, what's next for Maya McKinnon?"

"I tried to tell you earlier, but you were preoccupied. The place I moved into was only for a couple of months. I put a down payment on a house for one last summer in the Hamptons."

I sat startled for a moment, with mixed emotions. "Did you get a transfer?"

"No, I might have an opportunity in the city with a web designer," she said. "I've been thinking a lot since I've been talking to you. And now it's time for a new version of me to be born."

"I didn't think you were serious about leaving."

Instead of answering, Maya smiled cryptically. "I enjoyed the other night. You are the oldest guy I've been with. But it worked."

I wanted to share the feelings I developed for her, but her walls shot up, and she shut down. I sat back, second-guessing how I should respond. "Again, I wasn't looking for a one-night stand the other night."

"I know." Maya smiled at me with her eyes. "I mean, I still think you're a bit of bad boy—but a good guy. And since I'm leaving...stop looking at me like that..."

With an effort, I suppressed my annoyance. "So, I really am your final Florida fling." I rubbed my suddenly sweaty palms on my jeans, wondering why I cared. But I did.

She averted my glare.

After a moment, she leaned back and crossed her legs. "Your pixie dust won't work on me." She laughed awkwardly. "I'm no Wendy. Not me." She took a much-needed breath and stared at the handsome bartender, seemingly searching for her next words. "He's hot. I flirted with him earlier."

I turned to the bar as Jimmy rushed over. "There's a storm coming," the waiter said. "We'll be closing the roof."

Maya's face became dangerously still for a moment. Then she shot me a look and turned to Jimmy. "Can we finish our wine?"

Jimmy glanced at her with curiosity, coupled with a polite smile. "Sure." He placed the check down. "It was a pleasure. I will be reading your book."

"Thank you, Jimmy," I said.

Maya rolled her eyes. "So, Christina mentioned that your book made some lists on Goodreads: *Bad Boys* and *Characters You Most Want to Sleep With*. Congratulations."

I slowly shook my head. "A character in *The Show* did," I said stiffly.

"Your character," she insisted. "One I enjoyed sleeping with." She paused as my mouth opened to speak but closed, and then she lowered her voice. "So, I figured since my vagina and your penis hit it off so...quickly, we shouldn't keep them apart." With lighting in the distance, she added, "No relationship. No emotion. Just sex!"

I stood up, letting her have her moment, and said, "Wasn't that a line in a movie?"

"Yes. Friends with Benefits, Justin Timberlake. LOVE HIM!"

"I have no desire to jump off any more balconies."

"Shut up!" she yelped. Then with a sigh, she amazingly maintained that Bill was in Vero with his love and would not interrupt us. I needed a moment.

He was with Allison Tinke.

I took in a slow breath and excused myself to go to the bathroom. As I raced down the steps, I received another text. I thought it was from my Friday date, Sarah, but it was Kristen. *I just poured a glass of Duckhorn and need an update! Who are you having sex with? I want the steamy details.*

That led to a string of texts.

Me: *It's more than just sex. The eyes never lie!*

Kristen: *You better explain!!* (punching emoji)

Me: *There has been another plot twist. Part of me wishes she were staying.*

Kristen: *Who is leaving???* (angry emoji) *Who are you with????*

Me: *Maya. The one who is dating Bill Reed, the attorney at The Gym who is obsessed with someone who supposedly looks like Tinker Bell!*

Kristen: *OMG, I LOVE IT! I'll call you tomorrow. Steven just walked in.*

I stumbled into the bathroom and almost pissed my pants. After relieving myself in record time, I realized everyone was leaving. Just then, Allie called. I turned to answer. "Hey, Allie Girl."

Her voice was frantic. "Lawrence, I hate Bob Tillie and Mr. Smee! Shit. Fuck. I'll call you back—"

Click.

I blinked hard and wandered over to a TV by the bar. There was a severe thunderstorm warning scrolling across the bottom of the screen. My head began to ache. I thought about everything that was happening and about to happen. With a slow breath, I called Allie back. "Okay," she said, trying to keep her voice calm. "Bob and Mr. Smee are spreading rumors that we're going out of business because you're reckless. They know about Maya, Kristen, and the crazy chick who dropped your shoe off in the Chico's bag, but did you stumble across Ocean Avenue with a twenty-five-year-old on your back?"

I cleared my throat. "She was a fan of my book and wanted a piggyback ride. Like Wendy. It was nothing." I waved my hand in an impatient sort of gesture to Maya when she held up her credit card before I angrily snapped to Allie, "I have to go."

Allie hesitated before she said, "I trust you. And I love working for you. It's just—sometimes, you're a lot."

I sighed. "I know. I'm working on that."

She sighed. "How's Maya the Mermaid?"

"She'll be leaving Mermaid Lagoon in a few weeks to go back to New York," trying to joke while fighting my emotions.

"Wait...what happened?"

I felt a chill, gazed across the empty restaurant, and said, "Aside from her having ties to an attorney who is a member of The Gym?"

Allie laughed. "Yes!"

"Maya's pretending she's not interested in a relationship. Or emotion. She just wants sex." My voice was shaky. "We like each other more than either of us will admit—"

"Wait! What did you say? Hold on—" voices were calling Allie.

I pinched the bridge of my nose and heard Maya's voice, now tinged with desperation. "Come back to my place. I'll open the Tignanello you saw in my wine cooler and show you my new fish in her cute little bowl."

"I heard her!" Allie blurted. "HOLY SHIT—"

Click.

Maya took a step forward. Her voice was now soft and sexy. "One glass." She looked up erotically at me, and her green eyes flashed with passion. "This stormy night was meant to touch our souls, and you know it."

My gaze shifted to the floor. *The Dark One* stared back up at me. *Go make her moan, Sport. You haven't done anything else right lately.*

Lighting lit up the storm clouds that were circling viciously. It was as if my darkness was taunting me. The thought flit through my mind that I was meant to go, and not solely for pleasurable pursuits alone. "Okay, one glass," I said ambiguously.

She smiled, quite buzzed. "Emotional earthquake bring on disaster. That was a line from the song."

I murmured, "The soundtrack of my life—"

Her finger pressed against my lips, and then she reached up for the back of my neck and kissed me as large raindrops fell from the ominous sky. We raced down the stairwell, and a gust of wind caught us at the bottom. She stuck her hand under my shirt and pushed her body against mine. Her heart was beating wildly as she could feel me poking through my jeans. Maya stared at me with her wicked smile. I could not deny she looked simultaneously very beautiful and very young.

"Follow me to my gate," she whispered. "Just like the last time."

"I remember."

We counted to three and ran into the pitch-black stormy night.

TWELVE

YOU ARE PAN!

JANUARY 19, 2017

MAYA'S TOWNHOUSE

The following morning, my eyes flickered open to the sound of a text. I took a few short breaths and painfully pushed myself up in a bed wrapped in a white sheet stained with blood. I was only wearing Hollister briefs and could tell the blood came from my hand, which was cut and bruised. I noticed a broken glass, bra, panties, and empty wine bottles through the hot steam from Maya's shower.

The night quickly came back to me.

Moaning quietly, I grabbed my iPhone while making a wheezing sound I could not control. I squinted at a text from Bob for a dizzying few seconds, wondering why he sent me a picture of a bearded man marching around puddles in front of Black Dog Bait & Tackle. When I scrolled up to his pancake breakfast, I realized he was at the Sunny Side Café directly across Ocean Avenue from the tackle shop and read his text. *Hey Pan, it looks like your archenemy, Captain Hook, is going fishing.* The photo did show Hook.

I rubbed my gritty eyes. Nauseous waves pulsed as I then heard Maya's gravelly voice. "My loft is trashed, and the wine and weed ruined me, but the sex was wonderful! Thanks, old man."

I remained impassive reading another text. This one was from Allie. *Who is Michelle Crowley? She bought a day pass and has been talking to Mr. Smee by the free weights.*

My head pounded, but I recognized the name and moaned to Maya, "Was it you who knew Michelle Crowley?"

In a startling voice, she stuck her head out of the bathroom. "Um, yeah. My ex-best friend. Remember?" She paused and stared at me until I nodded, the conversation coming back to me. Maya flashed me a look of worry when I told her Michelle was at The Gym. Nervously, she put on her Victoria Secret lavender lace undies, mumbling seemingly to herself that Michelle knew Connor Lee. I could tell she was concerned that she had told Michelle about our little fling. Her actions were erratic. Eyes bulging outward, she gripped her Android, desperate to find out what Michelle was up to.

I searched the room for her scary cat, Jo Jo, to make sure she didn't jump on me, and said, "So Michelle knows Mr. Smee?"

With an uneasy look on her face, Maya hissed, "I said, Connor Lee."

I smiled, shrugged, and said, "In my world, Connor Lee is Mr. Smee."

She responded that I have serious issues and wandered back into the bathroom. Seconds later, she marched out with a raised voice. Her lips curled into a smile. "Are you even capable of being serious? If Michelle is at The Gym, she's up to something. That's never good in this tiny town."

"Why are you so dramatic?" I said, realizing my voice was whiny.

Frustrated, Maya tossed up her hands. "Because Michelle is crazy and knows Hook and Smee." She paused and looked deep in thought. Then she raised a fist. "Damn you, Larry!" she blasted. "Lee—Connor Lee and Jimmy Hook and Bill all know Michelle." There were dots I was meant to connect. Captain Hook was a prelude to a plot twist I was not prepared for. The fact I was still legally drunk and bruised and bloody didn't help. Sitting up again, I rubbed a stabbing pain in my chest, captivated by how fast her thumbs flew, finishing a text. Abruptly Maya added, "Michelle dated Hook." She fell into a moment of strange silence. Returning to the bathroom, she looked at herself in the mirror and began explaining. "Hook created a position in one of his companies for her after they met at a party a couple of years ago. She only slept with him thinking his lifestyle would lessen the pain of being her. But it made it worse."

I looked at her, both amused and confused, and said, "Sounds like they deserve each other."

She remained in front of the mirror, sighing. "No one deserves Hook. Not even Michelle. She ended up filing a sexual harassment charge against him, which mysteriously ended everything."

Sunlight worked its way through her closed blinds as I squinted at her. "Mysteriously?"

"Yes," she said, walking out of the bathroom. "Michelle left the company and dropped the charges, refusing to talk about it."

I raised one eyebrow. "Sounds like the Captain paid her off?"

"I'm sure," Maya stated simply. "And now I'm certain Michelle is using Mr. Smee to get back into Captain Hook's wallet." I chuckled, looking away because she was now calling them by my Never Land nicknames. When I glanced back at her, she stopped pacing to read a new text. With an erratic blink, she faced me, angered. "Have you been talking to Hook's woman on a dating site?" Her voice was frantic.

I pondered Bob's warning about this and shrugged. "No." With tension in my jaw, I offered, "But I do need water."

Maya frowned. "Hook has proof you are. So, think of the women you're talking to. You can make a bad situation worse."

I felt dazed by it all but was so dehydrated my only focus was on her new fishbowl and the bathroom faucet. I chose the faucet and pushed myself up, stumbling by her to the sink. She thought I was avoiding the question, but I wasn't. I took a slurp from the running water, relieved I could at least swallow. "If I am, I had no idea," I said, passing her. Because I really didn't. It was more of a feeling than anything. It would be impossible to have this happen again. I was in so much pain, physically and mentally, I just wanted to leave. I cupped my good hand for a few more slurps as she pressed me for information about a woman who, like her, was on a dating site while in a relationship. Finally, I was able to swallow and finish my thoughts. "Maya, no one I'm currently talking to has admitted they are with Hook. You know, like you didn't mention dating Bill." It hurt to think about it. "I don't want to talk about it anymore. In fact, never again."

Her eyes dropped to another text. Her lips curled in frustration. "You cause chaos," she said. "Don't pout about it. Look in the mirror."

I didn't need to. "My dating site profile states that I'm separated. That's fucked up enough."

"Why? You are!" she said, cutting me off, her nose scrunching in thought and distraction.

"Technically married," I retorted. "It's not an ideal situation, but I was honest with you. You should have at least stated, *it's complicated* on your profile."

In a long, thoughtful breath, Maya contemplated, "Call it women's intuition, but I don't believe your wife wants to divorce you."

"No!" I yelped. "She does The Gym's books and wants to shoot me." I paused as her eyes popped forward in her head, wondering why I shared that.

"Wait, hold on," she muttered, intrigued. "She does your books?"

I awkwardly looked to the floor, realizing my knee was back and blue, too. "My knee is black and blue," I pointed to it, "stop putting words in my mouth. It's making it worse."

Maya took a big slurp of warm Red Bull and began swearing under her breath for a moment, and slowly her lips curved, eyes glittered. "Well, I feel bad for your wife and Wendy, the girl in your book." She shook her head. "The book you claim is fiction."

I stiffened slightly. "It is."

She let out a small belch and fanned the air in front of her mouth. "Barely."

I limped forward. "Don't try to get me riled because your crazy friend is at The Gym exposing you to Mr. Smee."

She furrowed her brow and gazed at me. Her lips pursed. "Michelle knows the details of us. So, if I am exposed, you are too. That is our reality. In the end, Hook will call Bill, which would suck for both of us and The Gym."

I held up my bruised and bloody hand like a crossing guard and told her that I understood. Unfortunately, it didn't calm her down. For a few more minutes, Maya rambled on about Michelle before suggesting that perhaps I slept with Hook's girl, too. Her lips quivering, she collapsed on her bed. When I staggered closer to her, a heavy bell seemed to boom in my head as I winced with a stern reminder that I didn't sleep around. A blurry flashback of the last two weeks made me cringe, concluding I could no longer say that. I gazed over at Maya and could tell this morning's news flash about Hook's girl had her doubting everything she initially thought about me. With a disapproving look, she then twisted a few lines from Kelsea Ballerini's song, "Peter Pan."

I swayed, enthralled.

She sang, *"The smile, the charm, the words, the spark, everything you had it – you kept pouring the wine – serving your lines – smelling so fine, I had to let you have it. You're just a player…w-h-o…seduces all the girls around you, you're just a player w-h-o—"* she paused with the ping of another text and looked at me with angry eyes. "Hook's girl knows you. So, think."

My eyebrows arched, and that even hurt. "Unless Beth, the shoe girl, is Captain Hook's girlfriend, I promise you; I haven't even met her."

Maya slowly shook her head and gritted her teeth. "Beth, the shoe girl? Your stories of women and wine are so fucking juvenile."

"Thankfully, I have our normal courtship to make my mother proud—"

"Shut up. You never had to leave my place with one shoe."

I nodded, only wishing she'd start singing again, and said, "True. I much prefer to jump off balconies."

"It's a little drop over a storage unit." Her gaze lifted and locked on mine. "How is it possible that a bald old man can tug at so many women's heartstrings?" Scowling, she put her dark hair up in a ponytail. "You are old and bald—you little fucking boy!"

The room suddenly spun.

I blinked, dizzy, and nauseous, attempting to clear the dots from my vision. "Did you just call me an old, bald little boy?"

Her expression reflected everything inside her—the fear, the intrigue, the girlish glee. "Yes! You, old, bald, metrosexual, little fucker," she barked and then smiled brilliantly.

The gleam in her eye made it impossible to suppress my growing grin. "Please don't say old and bald in the same sentence," I joked as she stared at my cut hand. "It puts me in a fragile state. And when I am parched like this, I could blackout and bump my bald head." Maya's eyes lit up like lightning strikes, so I continued. "I've repeatedly asked Dan Schultz for a helmet, but he only texts me back a disturbing picture of Richard Simmons in a Peter Pan costume."

She put her hands over her face, giggling like a girl. "Schultz, your Hogan's Hero, inspired sales manager from *The Show*?" Her giggle escalated into a deeper laughter as she rolled over on her elbows in her lavender lingerie. "The guy who had to pretend he knew nothing having to do with you?"

"So, you have been reading my book..."

Her eyes narrowed at me. "Don't take this the wrong way, but I'm curious why I sought you out when I'm hit on by a ton of much younger and hotter men." Again, more dots for me to connect. How should I know? "Answer me," she pressed, jumping off the bed.

I shrugged. "We both enjoy wine?" I drawled.

She took a step forward. I hopped back. Her chin lifted to me, and then she said, "No."

My eyes widened. "Can we revisit this after I hydrate—and throw back a cheeseburger?"

Maya spun to her nightstand. "Hint!" she hollered, yanking from her nightstand drawer *The Show*. "Your book!"

"Okay, just don't hit me with it," I sputtered. "The hardcover leaves black and blues—"

Maya drew a line across my cheek with her finger. "You are Pan!" She hit the hardcover. "Besides all the obvious, how else can you explain Ruth B's 'Lost Boy' song coming out with the release of the damn thing?"

I fought back nervous laughter and said, "Magic happens when it comes from the heart."

"I enjoy your imagination," she said, looking frazzled yet aroused at the same time. Her nipples hardened through her thin bra as she pressed my book against her chest. "Your story brought me back to my girlhood dreams," she shrugged, "lots of emotion—anyway, I'm done babbling." She buried my book under lingerie and shut the drawer, determined to tighten her lips against a smile. "I think I'm still drunk. I didn't think we could drink more than that first night, but we did."

"A drunk mind speaks a sober heart."

Her eyes dulled, and she coldly added, "I know you have your Friday date with Sarah, but if you can leave feelings out of this, I would like to hang out with you again before leaving for New York. Maybe, Saturday?"

She was not as tough as she pretended to be. Behind her walls was a sensitive thirty-three-year-old woman locked in her prison. How could her nipples be so hard and her lips so soft and sad? "What happened to you?" I felt compelled to ask.

"Stuff," she said.

"Okay," I replied. The generalization of it would do. I thought of my daughter and could kill a man that did what he probably did to her. I realized she didn't have a father like me. Her walls were well built, as sad as it was. Her melancholy eyes were the movie screen I needed to see her life.

"It happens to more women than you can imagine," she stated, almost matter-of-factly, ready to move on naturally. Reaching for her Android, she read another text with a frown. "Michelle told Smee everything. So... Pan, prepare to battle Hook."

I drew in a breath. "I'll alert the lost boys."

The beautiful brunette's gaze searched mine. Then she turned up The Chainsmokers' song, "Closer," and sang, "*Hey, I was doing fine before I met you. I drink too much. And that's an issue, but I'm okay...hey—*"

She sang on as her eyes followed me, deep green, direct, and now devious. The scent of her hair was alluring as she spun around in front of me. She hit her Facebook app and backed against me, typing in a name. Within seconds I felt strangely exhilarated. She frolicked around me, flashing a glimpse of an attractive woman. "Do you remember our conversation about the Tinker Bell mug in your book?"

"That I remember," I said, not pausing a moment.

Maya lowered the music and held up her Android to me. I grabbed it. I steadied my hand as my eyes narrowed at a petite blond with a twinge of excitement I had not felt in years. She was beautiful and adorable at the same time. And she had captured my utmost attention. "That's Allison Tinke," Maya said as I read her name. "I told you she looked like Tinker Bell. I guess Allison was the woman in my dream." Maya paused for effect. "So, what do you think, Pan?"

My heart skipped a beat. "S-h-e's beautiful..."

For reasons I could not understand, I was intrigued beyond her beauty. She possessed an intangible appeal as if I knew her from another time. I stared at her pictures, captivated when Maya decided to dance around me. "Fate has a strange way of twisting us all together," she decided. "I figured since you keep hearing her name, you should know what she looks like." I kept thinking and blinking. Maya disappeared into her closet. She seemed to dress for her own pleasure and at her own whim. But when she came out wearing a green camouflage print top, she seemed perversely satisfied she had pressed my buttons on so many levels. I tossed her Android on the bed when she sashayed by me and down to the kitchen. It all seemed surreal, and I laughed at the confusion.

I was late and called The Gym.

As it rang, I received a text from Kristen. Amazingly, I ended the call to read it. *I'm dying to know what happened last night*, she texted.

The aching in my skull ebbed and flowed like a cold tide, yet I chuckled, pondering it all. The vision of Allison Tinke, dancing in my head, now caused everything to swirl around me, figuratively and literally. The excitement fevered me, and I replied to Kristen with a spontaneous sophomoric text: *I ended up back in Maya's bed. We're still pretending this is all about sex. But I woke up to find out I'm also talking with Captain Hook's girl on a dating site while Maya's crazy friend is at The Gym selling the details of our little fling to Mr. Smee, who will tell Maya's boyfriend, who is still in love with his ex, Allison Tinke, who does look like Tinker Bell!!* Added to the text were thirteen awesome emojis.

Kristen deciphered it in seconds. *1. Maya is a hopeless romantic who refuses to admit it. 2. At another time, you guys might be perfect for each other, but I think she came into your life to get you to save Tinker Bell from whatshisname! Stay focused. I see flames engulfing the next few chapters!!*

With a frustrated breath, I replied, *What?? I don't even know, Tink!*

Kristen fired back: *Get her number and send her one of your MS's. Sign it: XO PAN. She'll be back at The Gym before you can say NO PAIN, NO GAIN! Be YOU, follow your HEART and WRITE ON!*

I suddenly felt like I was hit in the ass with Cupid's arrow. Averting her giant wall mirror, fearing I looked like that cartoon character whose eyes bulge hearts out of its head, I took a deep breath and made my way downstairs. Maya poured me a cup of coffee in her favorite mug. "Bring it with you on Saturday," she said quietly. "I want it back."

Maya smiled at me. A woman's kind smile is the best thing in the world.

THIRTEEN

I DIDN'T KNOW THAT I WAS STARVING 'TILL I TASTED YOU

JANUARY 20, 2017
MY HOUSE/THE GYM

The next day, I rolled over on my pillow to a glowing lightsaber. "Truly wonderful, the mind of a child is," I said to my $399 plus tax "collectible" Jedi Mickey Mouse standing on the nightstand.

Minutes later, I tripped over a pile of jeans en route to the bathroom, unable to deny the space looked more like a frat house than a bachelor pad. The rest of my Mickey collection was scattered on the living room floor in front of an odd chair you would only buy after consuming too much wine. Speaking of wine, a bottle typically sat empty on the kitchen table to the side of a cumbersome entertainment unit with an old box TV that took up the family room wall. It was what Marie left. And with a big yawn, I realized I was in no position to bitch. Instead, I turned on ESPN and started the coffee.

I had all intentions of checking some scores while the joe brewed but pined to pull up my POF app in search of Allison Tinke. I scoured the dating site, but there was no sign of Tink. Cursing Maya for showing me Allison's Facebook page, I laughed when her name flashed up with a text. *Turn on CNN. This march is incredible!* I flipped to the news channel. They were reporting on the Women's March on Washington. Quickly Maya sent a follow-up: *This is the largest demonstration in history for gender equality. Yay! Put that in your sequel.*

Walking back to the kitchen, I jotted the date and headline on my notepad when Maya texted me again. I blinked with surprise to read that she had an eleven o'clock Skype interview with the web design company in New York. She followed it up with a reminder that we were celebrating a foreseen job offer Saturday night.

I rubbed my face in a rush of emotions.

Now desperate for my caffeine fix, I thrust open the cabinet. With a burst of excitement, I noticed my old Tinker Bell mug. It was the mug Maya had curiously questioned me about.

This is too weird, I thought.

I filled it with coffee and wandered into the family room, quite nostalgic. Sitting on the couch, I closed my eyes, went inward, back six years. The memories of my long-lost career sparked varying emotions from the time I used the mug. It seemed like the last time I had seen it. But it wasn't the mug. It was me. It was as if my gaze, which was fixated on a closed door, shifted to one that opened. I felt that same sense of my past, future, and present all merging into one again.

Finally, I blinked away from the mug to read Maya's next text: *This quote was sent to me from Christina: You don't find love, it finds you. It's got a little to do with destiny, fate, and what's written in the stars.*

Before I could digest that, Cindy texted me from The Gym. *Larry, The Gym is open, but none of your employees are here, so I'm telling everyone to workout. LMFAO!*

I jumped up and called Allie.

Pacing the room, I checked the security cameras as it went to voicemail. Frantically, I opened each screen. The office was dark, the check-in screen was black, and one camera showed two police officers by the treadmills. I was alarmed and confused. Very briefly, I convinced myself this was some great mystery. Then I wandered by the dingy mirror in the hallway. I scowled at myself, mindful that I ran out to meet Maya on Wednesday evening while going straight home after leaving her place, Thursday morning, battered and bruised.

Seconds later, I received a text from Bob. *Are you alive? The police just arrived. LOL!*

I ached with helplessness studying the security cameras when Allie called me back. "Hey, where are you?" I asked sternly.

"In bed," she said groggily, as Bob continued razzing me with pictures of the police officers. "You never sent the work schedule."

"The police are there," I huffed.

"Did one of the old people die?"

"I don't know!" I said, my voice rising.

"Where are the boys?" she asked and then yelled at her cat, Kenny.

I shook my head. "Robbie went back to FSU, and Reid keeps shutting The Gym down thirty minutes before our scheduled closing time."

Allie yawned. "Where's Paul?"

"His mother will only allow him to work on Friday night."

Allie hesitated for a moment and then said, "I'll head over now."

I sighed, relieved. "Thanks, Allie Girl, I won't be far behind. I'm jumping in the shower—"

Click.

I gave my Tink mug a little warm-up and took a quick sip when the doorbell rang. Holding my iPhone and mug in the same hand, I opened the door to see a pleasant-looking lady standing there with a clipboard. "Hi, I'm Amanda Peters," she boasted with wide eyes, "I recently joined our HOA."

"Oh…hi," I gripped my iPhone with my free hand, "I'm Larry." My gaze shifted to another naked picture from the nymphomaniac in Sanford. "I'm sorry," I said apologetically. "I'm a little busy." I glanced at the nymphomaniac's next text; *I WANT TO FUCK YOU!* and cleared my throat. "What can I do for you?"

With a forced smile, the lady said, "Do you get our emails?"

I blinked. "I believe so, is there a problem?"

"Well, does your lawn service cut your palms?"

I glanced over her shoulder with the sun coming up on my overgrown landscape. "No. They spray the weeds and cut the grass."

Her eyebrows arched when her gaze shifted to my scabbed hand and Tinker Bell mug, and then down at my *I Heart Me* pajama pants. "When do you plan on trimming your palms, removing the dead trees, and replacing your broken mailbox?"

I casually pulled my scabbed hand behind my *I Heart Me* pajama pants and said, "Soon—a few weeks," I made a gesture to my overgrown and unsightly yard behind her, "it'll all be good. That's the plan."

She thanked me, and I abruptly shut the door when Bob called. I took a breath and answered, "Why are the police there?"

Bob laughed. "I figured the cop's wife blew you for breakfast, and they came to shoot you."

"Seriously, why are they at The Gym?"

"The alarm went off last night, and they came back this morning because the alarm company notified the old owner instead of you," he assured me. He was eating this up.

I sighed. "I need a shower." Bob laughed louder, and I hung up. *Click.*

I made my way to the bathroom, numb.

Thirty minutes later, I left for The Gym. *The Dark One* rode shotgun as I fought it all, pushing my thoughts away from Maya to a much-anticipated first date with a woman who was closer to my age. I needed something, and that is what I settled on.

When I pulled into The Gym's parking lot, I noticed our fit little Matty Merlin. She was a long-time trainer at the club who acted like my mother. I took in a deep breath. "Morning, mom."

Matty marched at me, looking like Mighty Mouse on a mission. On this day, her motherly lecture came with a sterner tone. "Larry, we're losing members." She paused and tried again as my expression flashed her an annoyed look. "Listen, I know you know how to make money," a brief smile curled on her face, "but think about how much you could make if you were focused on The Gym and not hungover every morning. You should reread *The Show* because you are heading off another cliff."

I started walking towards The Gym. "The book is fictionalized."

She pressed on. "I understand you have to say that to sleep at night."

I sighed and turned back to her. "I wish I slept at night, ma!"

She looked up at me. "Cut down on the women and wine, and you will." Her eyes grew wide with an animated expression that only meant she was attempting to push my buttons. "I wonder how our yoga girl is doing. You still haven't replaced her. Should I call her?"

My eyes narrowed at her as I spoke slowly. "Matty, please stop."

"Listen, people like you, but honestly, that's the only thing saving you. The Gym is filthy, the equipment is old, there's no toilet paper in the bathrooms, and that office is awful."

I groaned, "Points taken. Give me a couple of months."

"You said that two months ago." She sighed. "I hope your princess Allie isn't working today."

We both turned back to Allie's car in the parking lot. "Don't forget to use your nice voice to say good morning to my princess," I said, opening the door.

With a scowl, Matty marched through it, and Allie ran over to me. "I'm going to give you the good news first," she chirped.

"Thank you," I replied as she pushed me over to the treadmills.

"Both Misha and sweet little Wilma are signing back up for the year."

I exhaled. "Wonderful...and..."

She paused and lowered her voice. "This crazy lady at the check-in counter came in with an ancient punch card and is scaring me."

"Excuse me," said the crazy lady cutting in. Her eyes strained backward at the corners. "This was paid for." I only looked away from her grossly artificial appearance when she waved her old punch card in the air. "Why is this a problem?" she rudely added.

The nip and tucked lady could pass for Captain Hook's mother. "Our three-day punch cards expire after sixty days," I explained. "Allie can show you the new rates." I walked around her and into the office. Through gritted teeth, Allie informed me she already had.

The lady snarled, "The old owners used to advertise, but I see things have changed."

This meanie is Captain Hook's mother! I thought and turned to her. "They are old owners for a reason. And yes, things have and will continue to change. There is much to be improved on."

The lady ignored me. "That's a shame; I was going to become a member again."

"What is a shame?" I said, my voice was a bit too intense. "I'll credit you the day on your ten-year-old punch card, and Allie will put you in the system. It's quite simple."

The lady stood speechless for a long moment and then contradicted herself by refusing to sign anything. When I told her to pay the difference for a day pass, she finally agreed. I shook my head when she handed Allie a fifty-dollar bill while complaining that the music was too loud. After bitching under her breath, she stuffed her forty-five dollars back in her purse and marched over to the paper towel dispenser to yank out enough paper to dry herself after a shower. I decided I would phase the paper towels out of The Gym. Nothing happens overnight, but I had done too little after taking mental notes on too much that was wrong for too long.

Within minutes, I settled at my desk to cut a check for our crowd-pleasing Friday yoga instructor, Diane. I winced when I heard Allie's voice behind me. "The woman's toilet is leaking again."

Still looking at my check ledger, I said, "Is Pete the Plumber here?"

"No, his wife had an affair, and he moved to West Melbourne."

I turned to Allie. "Can you get Mr. Smee to fix it?"

"He left. But he's desperate to find out where you're going tonight." She shook her head. "So, I'd rather not."

"I'll put a sign on the bathroom door," I replied. My mind was elsewhere. "So, you'll come back for the hour before Paul comes in? I have a big date tonight."

Allie nodded. "I'll be here." She smiled, walking out. "Every experience makes you grow, Peter. Second star to the right and straight on til morning..."

By noon, The Gym was empty. With hours of dead time in the middle of the day, I had to incorporate a membership specifically for the afternoon. I worked up some pricing and dozed off when my eyes flickered open to a voicemail from Maya. With a sigh, I listened to her message: *"Hey, I didn't understand your text earlier, so I wanted to call. I'll be going back to New York with a job. That web design company hired me! Anyway, I hope your date with Sarah is everything you want. Maybe we should cancel tomorrow night."* She turned up Ellie Goulding's, On My Mind, and after a long moment, quickly added, *"Call me."*

Before I could, Sarah called. She seemed jittery and desperate to confirm six o'clock still worked. When I assured my more age-appropriate match that I was eager to meet her, Sarah seemed relieved and pleased.

I took that as a sign to open a bottle of Josh Cabernet from my wine cooler. The blackberry and blackcurrant flavors never disappointed. After a long sip, I strolled by the old spin bikes. I took a longer sip, unable to deny I'd been getting by with quick fixes, and knew I had to put some permanent changes in motion. Strangely though, I wasn't panicked. This evolving storyline preoccupied me. I jotted some notes to capture the moment as it was. Even after the night with Kristen and my time with Maya and all her Tink talk, I wasn't sure of what I had, but I knew I had something. There was a stirring in my soul.

I walked back into the office and pulled up my calendar:

Tuesday, January 10—wine time with Kristen.

Friday, January 13—wine time with Maya.

Sunday, January 15—dinner with the kiddos.

Monday, January 16—coffee with Michael.

Monday, January 16—wine time with Kristen.

Wednesday, January 18—wine time with Maya.

Friday, January 20—wine time with Sarah.

These ten days changed so much, I said to myself and shifted my focus forward with wild anticipation. Then a familiar brunette startled me upright. "Hey!" she chirped. "I had no idea you knew Maya. I saw you guys at The Mansion on Wednesday." I forced a smile as she handed me her credit card. "I haven't been here since—shit, September."

I checked her name on the card. "Welcome back, Alexa."

"Thanks," she said. "So…is Bill Reed still a member of The Gym?"

I shrugged. "Sure."

"Well, tell Maya I miss her. I texted her, but she hasn't responded."

I sputtered, "I-I will."

The thirty-something threw a flirty glance over her shoulder, walking away. "Oh, and I forgot my earbuds. No classic rock, please."

I changed the station and then winced as "Starving" came on. With the remote in my hand, I turned up the volume and heard the ping of a text. It was Maya.

I was a bit unnerved.

Ever since our first night together, I think of you when I hear the song Starving, she texted.

With sudden chills, I replied, *The feeling's mutual. I'll call you tomorrow.* I took in a slow breath and exhaled. The lyrics made it impossible not to muse about Maya.

You know just what to say
Shit that scares me, I should just walk away, but I can't move my feet
The more that I know you, the more I want to
Something inside me's changed
I was so much younger yesterday...

Maya then replied with the next line just as Hailee Steinfeld sang it: *I didn't know that I was starving 'till I tasted you...LOL!* (winking emoji) *Enjoy your date with Sarah.*

FOURTEEN

HOOKED

JANUARY 20, 2017 (EVENING)
OCEAN 302 BAR & GRILL

At ten minutes to six, I was seated in a booth at Ocean 302, feeling energized. After ordering a bottle of wine, Allie Face Timed me to see how I was doing. I answered with a silly smile, and she quickly said, "I was thinking, this is probably your most anticipated date yet."

I laughed uneasily. "I'm not sure how to rate this dating experience—"

"But it's best you move past Maya." Her eyes widened as she lowered her voice. "Rumors are being spread that you stole Bill's girl."

I sighed. "I better pull up Sarah's pictures, so I recognize her."

"I'm sorry. Just…focus on tonight, Lawrence."

"Bye, Allie Girl."

Click.

Sarah McMillen was a forty-two-year-old mother of a thirteen-year-old daughter from her first marriage and a nine-year-old daughter from her second marriage. Although she had been divorced twice, we had enough pleasant conversations to roll the dice. I glanced away from Sarah's profile to taste the Malbec. "That's fine," I said to the waiter.

He smiled curiously. "Would you like me to pour the other glass?"

I smiled absently. "Yes."

"And you're not having dinner," he said, pouring Sarah's glass. "But you are having another bottle of wine?"

"Yes," I said impatiently as if this request was normal. "Once this bottle is finished, please bring another with the check."

"A bottle for each glass." His eyes narrowed at me with a look of amusement. "Got it."

After he grabbed the menus, I received a call from Bob. I sighed, apprehensively, but answered. "Hey, I'm at the restaurant."

Bob's voice was thick and hesitant. "I know. I just left The Gym. Is she there?"

"No."

"So, you want me to meet you?" Bob scoffed.

"Why?" I asked curtly.

"Because she probably won't show," Bob sneered. "Honestly, I thought Maya was a Nigerian dating site scam. You've been lucky."

"Lucky?" I said when I finally managed to swallow. "Everyone thinks I stole Bill's girl."

"Yeah, but Bill's girl still fucked you." His voice cracked. "So, you had to jump off her balcony to escape the first night. And almost bleed out the second. No big deal." I fidgeted in the booth, wishing someone would save me from *The Dark One*, when Bob screamed, "Learn how to drive, asshole!" I checked the time as he added, "Typically, they cancel at the last minute."

"You're wrong," I said but took a sip from Sarah's glass.

Bob continued, "I've been on these dating sites for years. The women are stuck endlessly shopping for someone who doesn't exist because they're scared of getting hurt again." I turned to the door, panicky. A group walked in, and I grabbed my wallet to see if I had cash to leave for the wine. At this point, I planned to sneak out past them, but Bob yelled, "Larry?"

"Yes," I said. "I'm listening." But I wasn't. I was counting my cash. My palms became sweaty when I came up short, and the tiny breaths I took made it worse.

When I went to end the call, I heard. "Online dating sucks." The ambiguities of these dating sites left me discomforted. However, the conversations I had with Sarah had me again doubting Bob. As he rambled on, I noticed the waiter pointing to the hostess. My gaze shifted to Sarah standing there.

I shot up and softly said, "She's here." I shoved the cash back in my wallet and only heard Johnny Cash's Ring of Fire on his car stereo. "Bob?"

"Yeah," he snarled. "Are you fucking kidding me?"

"No—"

Click.

Sarah swayed in place until the hostess pointed to me. She waved, appearing heavier than her pictures but just as attractive. Dark shoulder-length hair framed her full lips and hazel eyes, which were ablaze. I stood up, intrigued.

"Well, hello, Larry," said Sarah, as she looked me up and down.

"Hi, Sarah," I said warmly. "It's nice to meet you finally."

After hugging me, she stepped on my toe and asked me if raided my son's closet. I thought my mouth might have been hanging open and made a head gesture to our booth while staring down at my shirt abashed. She only snorted, and I cringed. "I'm sorry." She lowered her voice. "You have me snorting already. Is it obvious I had drinks with friends?"

I shook my head. "Not at all," I said. "I'm not sure why everyone's staring." She turned a brighter shade of red, thankfully unable to speak. I seized the moment and tried to make my voice sound as authoritative as possible. "This isn't a dinner show crowd. We should sit down."

Sarah let out a guffaw and fell into the booth. "I need water," she said, eyeing her wine. "I can't stop laughing." She picked up her wine, taking three huge sips as if it were water, and she had to choke down a pill. Placing the glass back down, she glanced over at me.

I smiled. "The water is in the other glass."

"Stop! My temples hurt." Her gaze shifted to the restrooms. "You'll have to excuse me. I have to go to the little girl's room." Sarah stood up but reached for her wine glass. "Whoa, that last shot got me." She tipped the glass back and emptied it. "Sit tight." She squeezed my arm, and as she walked away, she called back, "Love those little muscles. So cute. I'll be right back."

Perhaps it was the unexpected pleasure of being out on a warm winter night or the fact that, at this very moment, I noticed the tables around me still peeking over, but regardless of the reason, I couldn't wipe the smile off my face.

A few minutes later, Sarah inelegantly staggered back.

When the waiter refilled our glasses, she read a text, and her demeanor changed, which only further intrigued me. I watched her intently. Her eyes surveyed the restaurant before she walked outside without any explanation. I thought that was inexplicably bizarre but sat captivated. Minutes later, Sarah returned. It appeared she had been crying. She wiped the mascara smudges from under her eyes, palmed her wine, and polished it off.

"Is everything okay?" I asked.

"Yes. I needed this," she said with a fresh smile. It was apparent the alcohol she had consumed removed all filters. "After our last conversation—and what I read—I knew you'd make me laugh." I lifted my gaze to her, realizing she googled my name and seen my book. Sarah's hands briefly shot over her face, and then they dropped to the table, revealing a reluctant grin. She quickly changed the subject. "So, were you on your dating apps?"

"What do you mean?" I asked guilelessly. The waiter passed the table, and I flashed him two fingers, motioning to our nearly empty bottle. He stopped with a disapproving expression, so in a rather stern tone, I said, "We're ready for another bottle."

A faint smile relieved Sarah's lips of their tension. "Did you see his face?" She wiped the dribble of wine off her chin. "I'm sorry, I'm a mess. I also took a hit of weed."

I could feel my eyebrows arch. "When you went outside?"

Sarah shook her head. "No. With my friends before I met you." She smiled. "You're new to these dating sites, but it's rare people ever meet." She paused, and her facial expression soured. "Typically, they endlessly message each other."

I sighed. "So, I've heard," I said and glanced over at her with one raised eyebrow as if I was the Dos Equis man, the most interesting man in the world. "But here we sit." I put one arm on the back of the booth while grabbing my wine glass with the other hand. "Cheers," I chirped. Looking ridiculous, I leaned over my wine, waiting for her to say something.

Sarah became uncomfortable, far from relaxed. "Whatever," she snapped. "Love sucks." She hesitated uneasily, averting my eyes. "I won't be hurt again." Her arms crossed as her voice turned defensive. "You know I have trust issues. We spoke for hours. Don't ruin my Friday—"

I held up my hand. "Okay."

For the next few minutes, Sarah revisited her horrible marriages, refusing to take the blame for anything. In her mind, she was the victim and let me know every chance she got. "I kept the texts from the last ass." Sarah's tone was peevish. "Only now do I realize that neither of them was all that attractive."

Interestingly, she never brought up her girls or Lauren and Jerry, and I was mindful of the obvious. I swirled my wine and said, "Slightly jaded?"

"I'm forty-two," she barked back. "I have been burned enough. Most guys just want to stick their dicks in a wet hole."

I withdrew my hand from the wine glass, and in a soft tone, said, "Sarah, you have to believe you'll find happiness to find it."

She impaled me with a cold stare. "You really do live in fantasyland." Her frown lines eased a bit.

"It's Never Land, Sarah." I smiled, hoping to lighten the mood.

She turned her head, suppressing a smile, and brought her napkin over her mouth. "So why didn't you share your gym fling with me?" she asked and inched forward when the waiter returned with the second bottle. "Your yoga instructor, perhaps?" Her voice was loud and theatrical. "It's a small beach town, Larry…"

The waiter turned to me, humored. "We might be needing a third bottle," I said to him. "Stay sharp."

The waiter smiled, turning away. "I was a member of The Gym during the Ripper days," she continued, eyeing me. "I heard the rumors are flying again."

My eyes narrowed at her. "Why did you stop going?"

"Because the friends I took classes with moved," she replied. My mind wandered until I heard the name Allison Tinke. I perked up, and she had noticed. "Did you date Allison?"

"No. I keep hearing her name, though. It's weird. I'm sorry, go on."

She raised her brows and shook her head. "You looked like a little boy for a second." She hesitated and smiled. "So, was this yoga instructor just good sex?" She took her straw out and flicked water at me. "Or was she more?" She stared at me long enough to realize I wasn't going to elaborate and whined, "Just answer the question."

I drew in a sharp breath and huffed. "It doesn't matter; I couldn't mend that broken wing." Sarah kicked me under the table with a slight grin. "Okay. When her walls were down, and she wasn't consumed with some of the same shit you are, she was more." I took another sip because I needed it and added, "And when I checked my ego and wasn't an idiot, yes. We had our moments."

Sarah's eyebrows raised skeptically. "And how often did all of that happen?"

I sighed. "Four days out of the four months, we hung out, but it was a blissful ninety-six hours."

Sarah chuckled, looking away, before then facing me. "You seriously believe you're going to meet some princess and live happily ever after, in Never Land?"

I smiled. "Yes. I do."

"Good luck with that, Peter Pan," she said with a falsely jovial smile before she leaned over the table and swatted the air inches from my nose. "I love your eyes." Hers instantly widened, desperately wanting that line back. "I love them when I freak you out. I can learn so much from them."

I took another sip, wondering why I needed more of this, but certainly did. "Like what?"

A few fleeting thoughts flickered across Sarah's face. "Like, it's all ego. We end up the victims—" I placed the bottle down hard enough to get her attention.

"You do realize we're all flawed to some degree? Honestly, I'm scared shitless. I have no idea what I'm doing in the dating world at forty-nine."

"But you're determined to find her." She rolled her eyes. "You are definitely a better salesman than I'm used to. But go on."

"I'm not selling anything. I'm searching for answers, but it's obvious that life is full of misunderstandings. Think about it. Stupid shit that blows up because of our insecurities. We all make those mistakes." I paused as she looked away. "It's never one person's fault."

Smiling with her eyes, Sarah told me about a night she blacked out and woke up with a guy sucking her toes. I blinked to regain my senses, and she began speaking again. Her voice was uncharacteristically calm. "I can see myself ending up with you." I winced internally, thinking I had to have misunderstood her. Flashing her a panicked look on my face that she instantly mirrored, she changed her tune. "Well. I'm officially drunk."

I smirked. "And terrifically touched."

"Yeah, and you love a bit of crazy…that's obvious, too."

I tried to swallow and speak but could not.

Sarah smiled with an alluring lust laden stare. I glanced at the waiter walking up. When I turned back to her, she stretched her arm across the table to hold my hand. The waiter froze briefly before filling our water glasses. "Are you scared to hold my hand?"

I opened my mouth and closed it when Allie texted me that Captain Hook walked into The Gym when she left. Seconds later, I received a call from the kid who took over for Allie.

"Hey, Paul, what's up?"

"Hey Larry, Jimmy," he paused as if he was reading his business card. "Jimmy Hook, the guy who does our advertising, came in and dropped your check off. They didn't cash it because they missed the deadline. He kept asking me where you were."

"That's bizarre," I said softly. "What else did Captain Hook say?"

Paul laughed. "Captain Hook blamed that guy, Connor. The guy who hits on Allie."

I noticed a curious look on Sarah's face. "Anything else?"

"The older lady who complains about the bathrooms is now complaining that the treadmill is too loud."

"We're getting new ones…someday. For now, tell her to use another one."

"She likes that one."

I blew out a frustrated breath, with Captain Hook and Mr. Smee on my mind. "Okay, turn it off and turn it back on. Act as if that fixes it.

Then go back to the office, and slowly raise the volume on the stereo." Sarah's head slumped forward with arched eyebrows.

"You got it, Larry!" said Paul excitedly.

Click.

"I enjoy you." Sarah smiled. "You really are," she lowered her voice, "something else. What's wrong?"

Her gaze was steady, daring me to say something, so as the waiter filled our wine glasses, I did. "Why does Captain Hook loathe me?"

Sarah's eyes popped forward. "Who? Who is Captain Hook?"

"I was joking. My advertising company screwed me." It was apparent she was hiding something. "Do you know Hook?"

"No," she said, frantic to change the subject. "I can't believe you agreed to see M-a-y-a after her first shit show." Sarah spoke about Maya as if she knew her. "Oh, and by the way, who plays every sport shirtless and throws the pictures up on their dating site profiles?"

"I'm not well," I muttered.

Although Sarah chuckled, I could no longer deny my expectations for her were unrealistic. She was not the one. As my smile flatlined, Sarah shook her head, looking me flush in the eye. "Let's go next door to the Oasis for one."

I hesitated.

"Don't you have to meet your girls?"

Reading a text, she said, "Let's just have another quick one here." Her eyes seemed to be full of pain. She adjusted herself in the booth and knocked her napkin on the floor. When I jumped up to get it, she noticed I was wearing American Eagle boxer briefs, which tickled her so that she screamed it out. Then, the manager checked on us. I assured him we were fine. With a look of indignation, he gave me a single nod and walked on.

Sarah made a face at him before abruptly turning to me. "Oh, and I don't believe for a second that you didn't sleep with Wendy."

My eyes narrowed at her in confusion. "You mean, Maya?"

"No. The girl in your book, Peter Pan Man."

I leaned back in the booth, startled as gleeful realization dawned upon me. "You bought *The Show*?"

"Yes, right after we first started talking, I googled your name. I didn't want to tell you I was reading it, but that's how I knew you were funny." Sarah cocked her head and bit her lower lip suggestively. When she kicked off her shoe, I winced, and her foot rode up my inner thigh. I braced myself right before she pressed it against my nuts.

The waiter rushed back over. Even though she was now a brighter shade of red, he refused to look at her, giggling uncontrollably. Sarah noticed the check and spouted, "No. Wine time doesn't end with two bottles. Just ask Wendy!" Her eyes were bloodshot, but she looked ten years younger. "It's in his book." She hiccupped.

The look on the waiter's face was priceless. "You're an author?"

Sarah hiccupped again. "Yep," she gushed. "And owns The Gym."

The waiter looked blankly at me when Sarah received another text. Her face was alarmingly still. She read it, and I slid out to go to the bathroom. Sarah's eyes popped forward, suddenly panicked. "Wait," she said but then stared at me with a sad smile. "I had fun." She hiccupped yet again. "Thank you."

I peered at her. "Well, good. I'll be right back."

When I walked back to the table, I assumed Sarah went to the bathroom. Then I caught the waiter looking over at me from another table and received a text from Bob: *You're with Hook's girl!*

With a knot in my stomach, I tuned everything out until the waiter came up to me, looking sympathetic. "She handed me cash for the bill and asked for a cocktail napkin," he explained quietly. I blinked at him, and he pointed to it behind her glass. It had her lipstick smudged kiss and a smiley face. "If I didn't see it, I wouldn't have believed it either."

I laughed uneasily. "Okay, well, thanks." The waiter nodded and hurried off.

After a long moment, I swallowed the negative emotions building inside of me, glanced at the cocktail napkin with her lipstick kiss, and scampered out.

• • •

The next day, I woke up to Sarah's text: *Hi, I hate goodbyes. Anyway, you should spend some time alone. I would delete your POF profile. I hope one day, you understand. If you do, you will make some woman happy. PS I am enjoying your book* (heart emoji), *Sarah.*

I heard her voice in my ear and fell back on my bed, hungover and punchy. I still couldn't fathom Sarah with Hook. I just couldn't. Desperate for answers, I listened to Bob's voicemail: *Hey, people are talking. You're going to lose more than members if you keep fucking these women. Call me.*

Increasingly leery of Bob, I fell back asleep irritable and lonely.

At six o'clock that night, as planned, I met up with Maya. We decided on a Saturday bar hop around downtown Melbourne and met at Meg O'Malley's. After her first sip of wine, she grilled me about Sarah. When the convoluted conversation turned ugly, I reminded Maya that she only wanted to have fun before leaving for New York. Although the heated moment passed, I could not deny we were on a slippery slope.

An hour later, we looked like a couple walking across the street to Matt's Casbah. Maya's eyes spoke volumes that her words refused to. Age gap aside, we had much in common and raised our glasses to our special friendship. "Spend the night with me," she said softly. "Maybe with a little emotion—" a call interrupted her. She excused herself under the pretense Bill wanted a shirt at her place. With an effort, I managed to restrain my incredulous laughter. The truth was he wanted to know if she was with me. When Maya sat back down, I agreed that Bill was using her. I should have expressed my feelings for her, but my insecurities got the best of me. Instead, I played the character that everyone imagined I was, and the night went up in flames.

At ten o'clock on Sunday morning, I received a text from Sarah: *I'm on chapter thirty-one and have some questions. Can you meet me at the Tavern at 2? We can have a Sunday Funday Q & A session about The Show.*

Craving any distraction to Maya, I replied, *Sarah, I would, but I don't date women in relationships.* I sighed while deleting that and tried again. *Sarah, I would, but I know you're dating Hook.*

I figured so. She shot back. *But it's not a date. He's fishing, and I have questions about your book.*

I took a slow breath, and *The Dark One* whispered, *I'm dying to see what happens in the next chapter next, Sport! Please tell her you will!*

I typed: *See at 2, ya silly goose!* And hit send as quickly as I could. Then I scribbled on my notepad: *Hooked!*

FIFTEEN

JUST ANOTHER MANIC MONDAY
WITH MIMOSAS

JANUARY 23, 2017
MY HOUSE/THE GYM

My iPhone rang the next morning just before seven o'clock, and I rolled over from my Sunday Funday with Sarah to see it was her. I yawned, and in a groggy voice, moaned, "Good morning." She coughed twice, and I raised a questioning brow. "You okay?" I hit the speaker button.

"Not really." Her voice quivered. "I forgot to pick up my antidepressant prescription before I met you, and then Jimmy showed up at my place drunk. I hate my life…"

I breathed in and out, cognizant there would be no small talk ensuing. None at all, in fact. Within seconds, Sarah divulged details that Hook verbally abused her after his fishing excursion, grabbed a Bud Light from her fridge, and proceeded to surprise an old friend with a call that had him inquiring how well he knew me. When Sarah confirmed it was Bill, I realized Maya was right. Although Sarah talked in circles, I surmised Bill and Hook were close but had a falling out.

My mind raced on. "How did my name come up?"

"Jimmy told Bill you prefer sleeping with women in relationships."

I took a steadying breath and said, "You didn't think that was strange?"

"Yes," she yelled. "I'm freaked out. None of it made sense—"

"Sarah!" I gasped. "Hook knows you're on dating sites."

"What? How? I need my crazy pills," said Sarah quickly. Her voice edged with tension. "Please explain."

I let out a weary sigh. "A guy at The Gym warned me that Hook saw my shirtless football photo on your iPhone and *The Show* on your iPad."

"OH MY GOD!" she shrieked. Her dog barked, followed by a thud and an ominous silence. "When?" I let out a long breath that I hadn't quite realized I'd been holding. Then I expected her to confess she snapped because she didn't take her crazy pills and whacked her dog unconscious with a frying pan, but instead only added, "Larry, I need my fucking pills. When did this guy say that?"

I exhaled when the dog barked again. "A couple of weeks ago, maybe a week after we started talking. But he thought your name was Stephanie, and honestly, I never thought it could be you." I cleared my throat. "What else did Hook say to Bill?"

There was a moment of silence before she quietly said, "He was sorry to hear that Bill's engagement was broken off. But Jimmy couldn't be happier to hear that it ended."

I asked her what she meant. After a long moment, she explained that Hook still held animosity towards Bill because of Allison Tinke. I paced my bedroom fascinated before dropping back on the bed when Sarah confessed that she had thought I dated Allison after mentioning her name Friday night. "I was worried because when Allison finally got divorced, many men were interested in her, including Jimmy."

Suddenly parched, I knocked the water bottle on my nightstand into my Jedi Mickey, sending it to the floor. "Noooo," I groaned.

She sighed deeply. "What?"

"So, Hook had the hots for Tink, too?"

"Yes," she said and coughed again. "You've weakened my immune system. My body can't handle you."

I blew out a frustrated breath. "You're only saying that because you're reading my book."

"Well, it seems pretty accurate." Her voice sounded increasingly hoarse. "Why would Jimmy call Bill out of the blue and ask about you?"

Unfortunately, it all came together, and it was time to enlighten her on the reason Hook called Bill. I took a slow breath. And then said, "Bill is dating Maya, and Hook knows that Maya hung out with me. So, if Hook is still harboring animosity towards Bill because of Allison

Tinke—while being upset about us—he's probably riling Bill up, as a sort of payback—"

"Wait!" Sarah cried out. "Maya? Your whore from the dating site is with Bill Reed?"

"Maya is not a whore."

"How could you not have told me this?"

I reminded her that this topic came up after we finished our first bottle of Sunday Funday Fume Blanc but ended abruptly when her bare foot rode up my inner thigh to massage my nuts again. It only took her a second to purge that and get back to what irked her. "So, Jimmy's right," she said knowingly. "You do prefer sleeping with women in relationships."

With a rush of adrenaline, I stood up. "No!" I huffed. "I had no idea that Maya was with Bill. Like I had no idea you're dating Hook—"

Sarah interrupted me, furious. "Don't mention me. I didn't fuck you."

"No, but you reached out to me on a dating site," I said with an edge to my voice I could no longer suppress. "And I do not sleep with other men's women."

"You mean, purposely?" she said, her voice shrill. I dropped my iPhone on the bed, dizzy, but it was still on speaker, so the pain persisted. "Because you do."

How can this be happening? I thought and ripped a pillow from under *The Dark One's* head when he blew me a kiss. And then I screamed into it, "F-U-C-K!"

She snorted. "What? Talk into your phone."

I snatched it off the bed. "Why? You're not listening." My voice was impatient.

She let out a shaky breath. "Oh, but I am. You're saying that you accidentally ended up in the vagina of...hmm, let's see, from our conversations, I know of three women in three weeks."

That sounded impossible. I swore it did. So, I breathed out. "What?" and counted in my head.

Sarah finished first. "There's Beth, the shoe girl, the twenty-something who's moving to an island with her boyfriend because of Trump, and Maya—the slut!"

Jeez, how drunk was I to share that, I thought. Although quite impressed, Sarah remembered the details of the shoe, island, and Trump. "Sarah, I can assure you none of them shared their relationship status until after the act."

She paused for a couple of seconds to inhale a touch of sarcasm and exhaled angrily. "Would it be a stretch to suggest they might've if you hadn't closed the deal so quickly after the second bottle, Lucifer?"

I gazed at my iPhone, feeling tattered. "None of you were looking for a bowling partner, so, stop," I said. "I'm now late—and you need your pills. Was anything else said?"

After a long moment, Sarah whined, "Jimmy's calling Bill to finalize a time and place to meet." She paused and sighed.

"Sarah?"

The call mysteriously ended.

Twenty minutes later, Maya texted me: *I'm sorry about Saturday night, but we need to talk. I heard about a call on Bill's speakerphone from Captain Hook.* Looking down at my iPhone, I realized it must have been Christina, Bill's admin, who eavesdrops and gets all the dirt.

I took a deep breath and called Maya. When she answered passionately, I exhaled slowly, envisioning an old Kardashians episode. "Hook told Bill he has proof we chatted on a dating site, met up, and had sex!"

"So much for not arousing suspicion."

Quickly Maya reminded me her nut-job-ex-bestie Michelle Crowley knew Hook would pay for this information and received two tickets to the Bruno Mars show in Miami for the proof. Regardless of how insane this sounded, Maya confirmed what Sarah stated: Bill was meeting Hook. They decided on Sands on The Beach, the bar up the road from The Gym, and it wasn't to rekindle any long-lost friendship. It was to examine the screenshots of our messages. I tried to calm my nerves by lying back on the bed, but Maya screamed, "Shit! Michelle also has your mirror shot."

I jumped up.

It was a knee jerk reaction. But then laughter bubbled up in the back of my throat as I visualized Hook passing Bill pictures of me soaking wet in a towel. I blew out a breath, and in my best authoritative voice, said, "Now, Maya, why would you send her that?"

"Michelle didn't read your book and couldn't believe it."

I bit down on my cheek and then, through my gritted teeth, attempted to hiss, "Oh, Maya." I pulled it off but almost burst out laughing, so I held my breath.

Forgetting Maya was a true Scorpio, she refused to apologize, and the call went cold. Since there was nothing funny about turning blue, I took a few breaths while snatching the water bottle off the floor, desperate for a quick sip, hoping she had hung up. When I heard her sigh again, I braced myself. "This has more to do with Allison Tinke blowing Bill off than anything else, so I don't want to hear it."

It was like I was running in a fog while repeatedly hitting a wall. I shook my head and said, "But you admitted this is only an ongoing issue because you refused to officially end it with Bill because you were jealous of Tink." My voice was full of wonder. When Maya sighed deeply into the phone, I eyed a text from Allie: *CALL ME!!*

"It really doesn't matter," Maya continued. "Bill got what he deserved. I'm not going to apologize for what happened. I met you. I had fun. And I'll be going home soon. No, big deal."

For the moment, I considered everything and craved a shower. "Kinda sleazy, though," I mumbled, suddenly clammy.

"Stop getting EMO (emotional)!" she shouted, now referencing Wendy in *The Show.* Her voice softened. "I haven't had sex with Bill since I've been with you. So, don't make me out to be that woman."

I exhaled. "I'll call you from my car."

"You are a little boy. You drive me CRAZY!" Then there was nothing on the other end but heavy breathing.

Click.

Meanwhile, Allie sent another text: *Um, Bill Reed just came in wearing a suit and went straight to the locker room. He didn't say hello, checking in. Lot's to talk about. CALL ME!!*

Thirty-five minutes later, I treaded into The Gym, tense. My eyes scanned the space, and I noticed Bill by the free weights. He was talking with our beloved ex-NFL—CFL football legend, Doug Flattery. I continued into my office when Cindy rushed over. "Did you know Bill

Reed is leaving The Gym?" she asked archly. Her glance darted anxiously from me to Allie. "Bill told Joey and Vinny that he's done at the end of the month and that you'd be out of business by the summer."

My body stiffened. "Funny, a couple of weeks ago, Bill told me the music's improved and thought the laughter was infectious."

Cindy gave me a suspicious stare. "I heard you're sleeping with his girlfriend, Larry."

My gaze erratically shifted back to Bill; his full head of greyish brown hair seemed even thicker as if anger had shocked it. "That's not exactly true—"

"What part?"

I cleared my throat. "I'll find out what's going on."

Cindy shook her head. "Perhaps you better, before any crazy rumors circulate," she said, a hint of challenge in her voice.

"Bye, Cindy."

"Bye, guys," said Cindy walking out.

I waited a moment and then turned to Allie. She jumped into an office chair, holding her pom-poms, dying to fill me in. Her panicked voice had me collapsing in the other chair as she began with what I'd already heard: Hook was aware I was with Sarah on Friday night at Ocean 302 and again, yesterday, at the Copperhead Tavern. Allie's green eyes flashed wildly, recapping it all before enlightening me on a fascinating piece of this puzzle I wasn't privy to. "I found out that Hook advised Bill's father to have Bill work out of their Vero office after his old admin filed a sexual harassment charge against him when Hook and Bill were friends. Mr. Smee told me their friendship ended, months later, over a woman who used to go to The Gym. Someone that Bill later moved to Vero."

I exhaled loudly. "Allison Tinke."

Allie's eyes widened. "Yes. Do you know her?"

I leaned back in the chair. "No." Shaking my head, I gestured to Allie to keep going.

She tossed her pom-poms on the desk to get comfier. "Well, after Allison got divorced, Hook hit on her when they were both members of The Gym, only she wasn't interested in him. However, she began dating Bill."

I blinked hard. "I had no idea Hook was a member of The Gym."

"Mr. Smee believes that Allison was the reason Hook left," Allie insisted. "When he found out that Allison had begun dating Bill, he left The Gym, jealous and determined to get even. Apparently, Hook thought he could buy her?" She paused as I nodded and then added, "So, fast forward to today, and you can see that Hook paid for the dirt on you because you were not only sleeping with Bill's girl but his girl, too."

"Please lower your voice," I said, my voice tense. "I did not sleep with Sarah."

Allie pushed herself back in the chair with a look of puzzlement, which I decided meant it didn't matter, a realization that was more disorienting than liberating. "Okay, Lawrence," she said, "Sooo, let's just say the play-dates with Sarah at your Mermaid Lagoon have caused him to have the same desire to kill you as Captain Hook did Peter Pan," she tilted her head slightly, "while getting a dig in at Bill for what happened with Allison—because everyone knows that you're sleeping with Maya." She smiled. "Get it?"

I leaned forward, nauseous, as *The Dark One* whispered in my ear, *Just nod, you are a fucking legend!* I sighed and nodded, but unfortunately, Allie continued.

Then, with a nervous eye on Bill, I noticed him walking towards the office with an inscrutable expression. I made a gesture to Allie to stop talking. I assumed he would stop in the office, but his eyes averted mine strolling around to the check-in counter. I stood up warily when Bill informed me this would be his last month at The Gym. "Is everything okay?" I said, sharing a glance, knowing without a doubt that he had been fully aware of what happened with Maya.

He dropped his duffel bag on the counter. "It will be," he said, his face thoughtful. "I have to take this." He paused suddenly to take a call. "Make sure my membership is canceled."

After he walked out, the office line rang. I collapsed in the chair, eyeing my Josh Cabernet, when Allie handed the phone to me, rolling her eyes. I had no idea who it was. Cautiously I said, "This is Larry—"

A woman enthusiastically chirped, "Hey! It's Christina Couples."

It crossed my mind that this call was not a coincidence, and I struggled to find my voice. "Oh, hi."

Quickly she added, "I'm still laughing about that spin bike seat you couldn't adjust for me last week, and then Joey popped it up like it was nothing."

Allie lunged for her iPhone, thumbs flying. My eyes widened. "Yes, that was…stuck or something," I babbled. "How can I help you?"

"Oh, I need to talk to my boss. Is Bill Reed there?"

"He just left."

"Okay. I'll be going to The Gym after work, so I'll see you later."

"I'll have your spin bike ready."

"Please don't hurt yourself." She gave a short laugh. "A handyman, you're not." She laughed louder. "See ya soon—"

Click.

Allie picked up her pom-poms and stared at me for a moment. Her face softened in a contemplative look; I was becoming familiar with. "Let's go get breakfast on the beach. Have a mimosa…or three…and laugh like we used to," she said wistfully.

I paused for a second, immediately dismissing how incomprehensible that would be, and shot her an approving smirk. "That sounds magical, Allie Girl. Text one of the boys and see if they can cover for you—" She interrupted me excitedly.

"I did—YAY—YAY—he's on the way!" Allie cheered, shaking her pom-poms gleefully while sending her foot over her head, which ended with an exhilarating hip gyration.

When her poms-poms fell to her side, Matty shook her head at me. I sank in the chair. But then *The Dark One* put his arm around me and whispered, *Allie Girl is cheering for you, Sport. Stay focused on her pom-poms and that mimosa…*

• • • •

The next day I pretended I was over Maya and shifted my focus to a fifty-year-old woman who lived in Vero Beach. Just saying her age sounded strange at this point. Her pictures were alluring, and after a couple of spritely conversations, I was excited to meet her away from the peril of this escalating drama. Although my excitement about her was slightly tempered when Captain Hook listed The Gym as a CLOSED business on Yelp, I looked towards February, hopeful it would be a fresh start. Perhaps that was the alcohol talking.

In any case, it was not. Sarah disappeared without a trace, while Maya quietly packed for New York, torn. On the first Saturday in February, I awoke to her scathing text: *You were right. You are a forty-nine-year-old child!* (angry emoji) *How could you possibly allow Christina to Snapchat you drunk on the beach in front of your business? Grow up!*

I blew out a frustrated breath. And then feverishly typed: *We were talking about you!* I stopped fully aware Maya was upset with Christina, too, and tried again. *Regardless of how we met, there is something about you, Maya. The truth is that I miss you. I don't want to wake up hungover and haunted by another road not taken...* With a deep sigh, I deleted that as well.

In the minutes that followed, I stared at my ceiling fan until I fell back asleep exhausted.

SIXTEEN

CONVERSATIONS WITH CHRISTINA

FEBRUARY 2017
THE GYM

Just days after the Patriots won Super Bowl LI, I schlepped into The Gym drained and dehydrated. When I stopped for a bottle of water at the old cooler, my weary eyes caught Christina leap off a spin bike. I winced and braced myself eyeing her hurry over to me. "Are you ready for the latest?" Christina asked in a breathless voice.

I shook my head at her. "Not really," I murmured as Matty yelled out that we were out of paper towels.

My eyes closed and then shot open when Christina shoved me into the office. "Seriously, you have to hear this."

I was curious as to why she was wearing eyeliner and not at work. "If this has anything to do with Hook...or Maya, I don't want to hear it," I said wearily. "I'm in a fragile state."

Christina gazed at me from under her perfectly plucked eyebrows and informed me it was about Hook's girlfriend. Then she leaned into me and whispered, "The one you recently went out with."

There was a short silence. "Sarah?"

Christina flashed me a look as if assessing whether I cared. "Yes." She paused and took a quick peek behind her. "Sarah was in the hospital. That's why you haven't heard from her."

A muscle tightened in my jaw. "Why?"

Her eyebrows arched. "Depression." Our eyes locked. "She contemplated suicide."

I was so stunned I could barely speak.

"What?" I asked. My voice was thin and rising with emotion. "When did this happen?"

"Right after everything blew up last week," she said, grimly. "Both Bill and Hook are blaming you."

I shakily placed the water bottle on the desk in my exhausted state and rubbed my temples. After reading a text, Christina informed me that Sarah had moved in with her mother and was okay. When she sounded surprised, my eyes narrowed at her. "How do you know this?" I asked, sitting down in one of the office chairs.

She spun the other chair to her but remained standing. "Bill was cleaning out his desk early this morning and got it all from Hook himself. They both agreed you seduce women for dramatic purposes to inspire your writing."

I looked straight ahead and let out a long breath. "Karma will kill those two." My voice was just above a whisper.

"What?"

"Nothing," I replied, still startled. I took another breath, feeling suspicious. "Do you tap Bill's calls?"

Christina shrugged. "No, he still takes them on speakerphone." She paused for a moment to read a text before continuing. "And since Bill is back in Vero, Maya's having second thoughts about leaving."

I was silent for a second. "I'm not happy about her seeing our Snapchat shenanigans on the beach—"

"Maya knows it was harmless fun." My mind was spinning when Christina waved her text at me. "See?"

"When was that from?"

"Last night," she said. "We cleared the air, had too much wine, and I got an earful." She hesitated and then shockingly added, "Maya wants a little Larry."

My eyes rolled into hers. "What?"

Christina laughed. "Maya's biological clock is ticking, and she had a dream she had a baby with you."

I needed more than a moment. "Maya has lots of dreams—"

"Women don't have those dreams unless they really like you."

"How much wine did you have?" I asked. My tone was jokey, but she sensed I was emotional.

Her head tilted slightly. "In a weird way, she meant it."

"I might act like I'm sixteen, but let's remember I'm almost fifty." I straightened up slowly, taking a moment to catch my breath. "Besides, we both know Maya enjoys getting lost in imaginary places—"

"She enjoyed your book."

"Right," I insisted. "She got lost in a silly book."

"You can pretend it's just that, but you know it's not," Christina said and smiled, a half-smile, but it didn't reach her eyes. "Maybe you should call her."

For one brief, tense moment, we looked steadily at each other, and I could see Christina was assessing where I stood. "I do care about Maya," I said, increasingly annoyed. "But she refuses to say what her eyes have been saying for weeks. Besides, she should be excited about her job opportunity in New York." I spoke too quickly and took a breath. "Why aren't you at work?"

She inhaled, sitting down. "They eliminated my position after I refused to go with Bill to the Vero office." She shrugged. "They know I can't stand him. I'm actually relieved." I looked at her quizzically and asked her what she was going to do. Christina needed a moment to regain her composure. Then she insisted she was going to the beach before she did anything. She believed the waves wipe away worries, and the seashells would bring her good luck.

I sighed. "What did you tell your boyfriend?"

She shook her head. "Nothing yet. Come with me to the beach."

"I can't." I paused, reflecting with my head to one side, lightheaded. Sarah and Maya and the issues of The Gym had me on edge. My mind raced on, and I let my head fall slightly between my knees. *Just breathe,* I told myself. I thought I had a panic attack.

Seconds later, Christina chirped, "So, Maya also told me you keep hearing Bill's ex's name—"

Christina saw the surprise in my eyes, and I blinked with a sudden image of Allison Tinke. For a moment, they took my breath away. "Yes," Allison Tinke," I choked out. I felt excitement prickle at my neck. Christina stared at me, searching my eyes, perhaps, for a scoop. Or something. Unfortunately, I had nothing but this unusual feeling for someone I'd never met. Strangely though, I felt better and added, "It's been weird."

She shook her head. "It's not weird. Our lives are filled with meaningful coincidences or synchronicity. There might be a reason it's happening." Christina kicked my Converse. "Did you ever think to reach out to her?"

"And say what? Hi Tink, you don't know me, but people call me Pan. Would you like to come to Never Land?"

"Why not?" she said quietly, smiling. "You believe in fairy tales."

Fighting this darkly surreal notion that I sold myself this belief, I said, "You should go to the beach, Christina." Still dehydrated, I took another sip of water.

"You should come with me."

"I desperately need to sell memberships," I said as my iPhone pinged with a text. I dropped the water bottle next to me, unnerved. It was Marie reminding me that my January sales tax was due. *I just paid December,* I thought. My gaze shifted back to Christina. "I've been on these dating sites for a month and have nothing but insane stories and a business spiraling into the red."

Christina reminded me I had been looking at the glass half full but now seemed full of doubt. With a whimsical smile, she said, "Why didn't you tell me Bill's ex looks like Tinker Bell?"

My eyes widened. "Please lower your voice—"

"No. Come pick up some shells with me and stick your toes in the sand to ground your soul, Pan. It seems like it flew away from you."

With members peering in at us, I cleared my throat and crossed my arms. "Nothing flew away."

She shook her head. "Your darkness is causing you to doubt what you know to be true. So, beat that fucker back and be you!"

I leaned forward with my arms on my knees, gripping the water bottle with both hands, hopeful and supremely uncomfortable. "Christina, I'd rather not get hauled off in a straight-jacket before I kill another career." I paused and then sighed deeply when she beamed brightly. "I'm sorry I ever wrote that book."

Christina kicked me again. "Oh, bullshit! You were meant to write it, so stop pouting."

For the next few moments, I faded in and out. I felt her eyes on me but didn't raise mine from the floor. "Enough. I'm now hanging out with a woman who is eight months older than I am. No pixie dust or imaginary backdrops with this one."

There was a short silence.

"Are you talking about that Linda chick on Facebook?" she said snidely while pulling up a post with Linda faster than I thought was humanly possible. "The woman you renamed Lucy. Is that right, RICKY?" *Those nicknames seemed so adorable when we were wasted*, I thought, only now wishing she'd call me Pan. "News flash! You are not Ricky. You are Peter; so, you stop it, Pan!"

Ah, much better, I pretended. Then I blinked hard, wondering why all my friends were twenty-five-years younger than me. I snatched the copies of *The Show* I was selling off the counter, only wishing I could normalize my life. "I don't want to talk about anything having to do with that. Or this," I waved *The Show* at her, "it's fiction—"

"You keep telling yourself that," she said, rolling her eyes. "It's you. Hence the reason you had writer's block—and the reason you can't escape it. Didn't you tell me that one girl who used to go to The Gym finally convinced you to be you and write on?"

"Yes." I sputtered. "Kristen Bircher."

Christina raised her eyebrows while casually informing me that Kristen knew people in Michelle Crowley's circle. Thinking that was odd, I asked her how well she knew Michelle. She shook her head and became flustered. "It's a small beach town," she said breezily. "And Kristen was right, just keep taking your notes, and one day that sequel will come together. The first story worked."

I took a slow breath glaring at her for a moment, and then tossed the books under my desk. "Well," I said. "Right now, I would have to call the sequel wine, women, and song. That's not the story I envisioned." My voice was distinctly uneasy.

"Your dates in January are all symbolic of the times. So, relax."

I anxiously threw my bookmarks in the garbage as if that would help. "I'm not concerned about any storylines. I have a business to run," I shooed her away, "go be unemployed someplace else."

For the rest of the week, Christina showed up at The Gym between two and three o'clock every afternoon. Then on a dreary winter day in late February, Christina informed me she was moving back to Miami. I expected this news but was still taken aback by it.

I could not deny how close we had gotten and suddenly wondered why I didn't call Maya when Christina suggested to. Maya had texted me the week before when I was on a date. There were moments I wished to have back. After a few minutes of small talk about the move, Christina was passionate about missing my laugh. She stared at me for a moment, and in a serious tone, said, "I'm fascinated by people who form special connections with such ease. Magnetism is a definite force, and your very presence emanated an indefinable power the first time I met you."

"Whoa…big words…"

Christina continued, "It was the reason you nailed the connection you had with Wendy." She hesitated thoughtfully. "Unfortunate, but perfect. A love that could not be stopped. Any regrets?"

I smiled and paused for a second. "Regrets? I was married."

"And couldn't make that work," she insisted. "So, I'll ask again. Any regrets?"

"It was life's bad timing," I muttered. "So, please stop."

"I'll take that as a yes," Christina said to lighten the mood. "So, how's Facebook Lucy?"

I explained that we had fun together but couldn't figure out where it was going. Christina quickly admitted it was evident from the pictures that we liked each other but thought it was weird that she'd never invited me to her house. When she questioned me about Lucy's other guy, I realized I had shared too much with her. "You told me his name is Sheldon. You told me she met him first, and I am telling you Lucy is torn," Christina said as her mind raced on. "I guess that goes back to your point about life's timing. Sometimes it sucks." She paused and lowered her voice. "Have you slept with her yet?"

I shook my head. "No."

"Seriously?"

I nodded. "Yes. After two bottles of wine, we race each other to her car to play kissy-face while listening to the song she dedicated to me." I stopped and glanced at her apprehensively.

Christina stared at me, motionless for a moment. She shook her head and sputtered, "You seriously were put on this planet to entertain us." She mock fanned herself. "What's the song?"

I slowly slid down in the chair. "Savage Garden's, Truly, Madly, Deeply," I whispered, hopeful she didn't hear me.

When her eyes closed, I realized she did. "I'm going to miss you and this crazy little gym." She beamed brightly like a beacon.

I sat up. "When is your last day?"

She hesitated. "Tomorrow." Her eyes averted mine.

The next day, her last, we hugged each other tight enough to acknowledge our magical bond. After some small talk about Beyoncé having twins and the Oscar mix up with "La La Land" and "Moonlight," Christina changed the music to the pop station she used to listen to when she worked out at The Gym.

At that point, she chirped, "Wow, it's Kelsea Ballerini's, Peter Pan. It's magical!" and started singing along.

There was silence.

Like I was in an airtight glass box. I could see Christina's mouth moving but heard nothing. With a thumping in my chest, *The Dark One* appeared behind her and yelled, *I LOVE THAT SONG!*

The next day, both Christina and Maya moved out of Melbourne Beach for good.

On the first day of March, Maya texted me for the first time in weeks: *I don't regret sharing that moment with you, but I unfriended you on Facebook. Good luck with Lucy. You're always going to fly away, just because you can.* (broken heart emoji) *You're never gonna learn there's no such place as Never Land* (broken heart emoji) *Peter Pan...*

SEVENTEEN

LUCILLE BALL

MARCH 2017

THE GYM

I should've closed the chapter on February with three little words that would've guided me forward: "From now on..."

But I didn't.

In the first few days of March, I asked myself a hundred times exactly what I was doing. Doubt clouded my judgment, and I began making knee jerk business decisions in a desperate attempt to sort out my personal melodrama. I kicked off the month by blowing the payroll savings Rick Morris bestowed on me when he agreed to open The Gym at the ungodly hour he worked out. At the very least, I should have used it to help pay my current payroll, but I did not. I used it on wine time with Linda Maher, the woman I renamed Lucy. As in Lucille Ball.

My life became a sitcom, stuck in reruns. It was episode after episode of endless shenanigans. Ricky and Lucy stumbling through the Vero Beach bar scene, drinking too much wine, laughing too loud, and then making out in her car to "Truly, Madly, Deeply" replayed too many times.

Focused on our drollery, I sold myself this notion that our happy hour high jinks would magically transcend into a healthy relationship. However, after six weeks of this, we still had not had sex, and our Facebook posts made us seem more like callow youth gone wild than two adults looking for love. Nevertheless, after January's string of one-night stands, I didn't mind taking it slow.

At least that's the story I was sticking to.

By mid-month, right around the time, FBI Director James Comey confirmed they were investigating President Trump's ties to Russia, Allie was suspicious of Lucy. At first, I would jokingly spin her concerns, yearning for normalcy. But with each rerun, I'd become increasingly irritated driving home alone—past the red flags—in an alcohol-induced fog that only sparked negative feelings of fear and worry.

On the Wednesday before St. Patrick's Day, after Patty's spin class, Allie marched into The Gym on a mission. "What?" I muttered. "I don't like that look." I took a sip of water slumped over in an office chair.

She stared at me, standing in the office doorway, holding her hula hoop. "Lawrence," she said, with perceptible reluctance. "I figured out what's going on with Lucy."

I crossed my arms and said, "Thank goodness someone has."

Allie sat down in the other chair. "Sheldon is her real boyfriend. You're not invited to Lucy's house because he's waiting there for her to eat dinner. Remember Wendy and Jessie? Think about it."

I waved at her mess on the desk. "Can you move this shit? I have to lie down—"

"I'm sorry, Lawrence, but Sheldon's more than Lucy is leading you to believe he is."

I hesitated while I thought. "No, no. Sheldon hangs her ceiling fans," I said, shaking my head. "She's not that into him—"

"With you, she doesn't have to be. Sheldon's the stable handyman, and you're the reckless bad boy she can't stay away from," said Allie excitedly. "Lucille Ball has the best of both worlds—" I interrupted her.

"Her real name is Linda Maher."

"Lawrence, she's not going to stop this charade."

"How can you explain what she does on social media with us then?"

Allie sat baffled for a moment. "That's the only part of this that doesn't make sense," her voice rose, "but I'm telling you, I am right about the rest of it."

My emotions caused extreme procrastination. It was like I was in quicksand sinking. I was confused and increasingly irritated. There was a connection with Linda, but Allie's assessment of the matter had me doubting everything. Something was wrong. Listening intently, I scrolled through old texts from Maya fighting yesterday. And as Allie rambled on, I had to stop her in need of some fresh air. I wandered out to the bench and called Linda. When she answered as Lucy, the sun disappeared. Then as the wind picked up, she became angered with Allie's accusations. The sky darkened. An early spring storm was on the way. I exhaled, unable to deny the two women despised each other when Linda lashed out. "I'm done with Allie! She's extremely immature."

"Linda, she has valid points—"

"No, she fills your head with lies. Tell her to go home to her mother." She paused to scream at one of her fluffy cats. "Let's meet at Mulligan's. I want to see you."

My mood lifted a little as I exhaled a deeper breath. "We need to finish this conversation," I insisted.

"Fine," she huffed. "Let's meet and talk."

"Once this storm passes, I'll head over."

Click.

I walked back into The Gym tense. "Allie Girl, I'm meeting Lucy— Linda. I'll clear up everything." I held my breath.

Allie shook her head and grabbed her hula hoop with a sour expression. "Lawrence, I'm sorry, but you know where I stand. Lucille Ball belongs with Sheldon or a real Ricky." She sighed deeply with a whimsical look. "You're not Ricky Ricardo. You are Peter Pan."

I blinked at the thought of that statement and then blinked harder, recalling Christina saying the same thing. I gazed at my books, still under the office desk in a basket. *I'm responsible for this insanity, and it must stop,* I pretended. I fought the smile curling on my face, quite content with it all. "Allie Girl," I said. "Thanks for the talk. I'll see you tomorrow."

Away I went.

Thirty minutes later, when I arrived at the restaurant, Matty texted me: *We're out of toilet paper, and your princess has been playing hula hoop outside The Gym since you left. Please hurry back!*

I took in a deep breath and gazed over Linda's shoulder at the table I sat at with Kristen. Two months had passed, and the memories rushed over me. Indecision has a way of not moving forward. I swallowed, wired to hear Linda out, and sat down across from her with a forced smile.

She smiled back with her blond hair shining in the late daylight. "What's wrong?" she moaned.

Going over how to word this, I took a breath and said, "What is Sheldon to you?"

She rolled her eyes. "He's the other guy I'm hanging out with—"

"Meaning what? How long do you plan on staying on the fence? What is this?" I fumbled with a series of beginnings. "What is he to you?" I opened my mouth and closed it when Marie texted me: *Your February sales tax is due, and our son needs to talk to you. Priorities, Larry. What the hell are you doing?*

I took a peek behind me to make sure she wasn't at the next table and started typing. *I'm about to get hammered with Lucille Ball.* I stopped. With a deeper breath, I frantically hit the backspace button. Then I sighed, staring at a blank text, and typed: *I'll have the money for the sales tax tomorrow and will call Jerry in a few hours.*

Linda was resolved to move us along. "Ricky, red or white?" With a long pause, she turned up her Lucy voice and repeated herself. "Red or White?" I placed my iPhone down. The waitress hustled up to us, and Lucy impolitely informed her we weren't ready. When the waitress scampered away, she added, "A year ago, I was in a miserable marriage and can't make any mistakes. Okay?"

I hesitated.

"A year ago, I had first seen The Gym," I said. "Later that night, I had a dream I was flying high above it. There were wild nights with women and wine, and then she appeared. Magically—"

"Stop dreaming about fairy tales," she said, cutting me off.

"Dreams do come true, if only we wish hard enough..." my voice trailed off as my gaze shifted to the shoreline, unsettled.

"Yeah. When you grow up, we can continue this conversation."

"Your feelings for Sheldon are stronger than you've led me to believe."

"No, I met him first," Lucy pleaded. "But I keep coming back to you." She sighed. "Can you please be patient with me?" She threw a crumpled-up napkin at me to regain my attention. "I need to hear your laugh. So, stop pouting." She paused, waiting for me to speak, but when I didn't, she added, "Let's play the eyelash game!"

She scooted her chair up to me like a little girl while referencing the idiotic game I played with Wendy and wrote about in *The Show*. Lucy was face to face with me poised to win, so I leaned into her, flicked my lashes at hers, and she fell back, laughing hysterically. "I win again," I yelped, as heads turned to our table with concerned curiosity.

That never fazed Lucy, though. "No, Ricky! Two out of three."

It was the end of any serious conversations for that episode.

The following Thursday, Allie called to ask me if I'd be in on Friday. My author friend, Bob Martin, was leaving that day, and she reminded me he wanted to share his thoughts on *The Show*.

It would be the last day of March. I made sure I was there in the morning, aware that many of the Snowbirds were leaving with Bob. He and his lovely wife, Marg, were seasonal members who had stayed at resorts up and down A1A for years. Bob wasn't on social media but had heard about my book. He had emailed me in December that he would enjoy a chat when he arrived for the winter. We quickly became friends who agreed on how taxing the writing process was. I felt his pride and pain when he handed me an autographed copy of his book. It was a gripping crime story that took place in New York called *Bronx Justice*. After thanking him, we said our goodbyes.

I struggled through the rest of the day exhausted.

When I got home, I dozed off. I woke up to a lengthy text from Kristen: *OMG, I've been dying to talk to you! We'll be moving to Antigua the second week of April. I read your texts. It sounds like you're moving into the ugly chapters. On a positive note, I had lunch with an old friend who knows Allison Tinke. Small world, huh. FYI: Tink is single and living in Vero Beach with her two young girls. I showed my friend your picture, and she said you're her type. Just be YOU and BELIEVE! Talk soon.*

I stared at the ceiling with racing thoughts that were interrupted by the ping of another text. This time it was Linda who was still acting like Lucy. *Ricky, I miss you! Please be patient with me. It'll be worth it.* (heart face emoji) *I can't talk now, but I'll call you tomorrow morning when you get to The Gym.*

I shook my head, unable to respond to either of them. Then I went to call Jerry but was so drained of energy I texted him that I'd do so in the morning. It was easier to stay in bed and doze back off.

Hours later, I heard Maya call to me. She walked out of my bathroom with watery eyes. *"The tears I shed are tears of sadness, of the things that could have been…"*

The room darkened.

Maya was gone.

Then a flash of pixie light flew by my bedroom window.

I turned to a glowing lightsaber on my nightstand. *Fear is the path to the dark side,* said my Jedi Mickey. *Fear leads to anger. Anger leads to hate. Hate leads to suffering.*

I awoke on my damp pillow and propped myself up on my elbows, next to my Jedi Mickey. *Another dream,* I thought. I was bleary-eyed and alone and fearful.

EIGHTEEN

TRULY MADLY DEEPLY

APRIL 2017
THE GYM
It was four days later.

With muddled thoughts, I pushed myself up to start the coffee. After a big yawn, I turned on ESPN. My gaze shifted from the March Madness highlights of UNC's win over Gonzaga to Linda's first text of the day. *Are you at The Gym?*

I rubbed my face and then replied, *No, I'm sleepwalking around my kitchen. I'll call you after I shower.*

Twenty minutes later, I walked out to a lovely spring morning but drove off surly, suspecting that she was looking to cancel our afternoon plans. I chuckled when I went to call her back, unsure why but relieved that the tension shooting up my back subsided. I turned left on US1 to head up the river and tried again. On the third ring, she answered in her exaggerated Lucille Ball voice, "Ooooh Ricky, this new house of mine is making me cray-cray."

I exhaled. "Go ahead and blame the house; just don't cancel our Super Tuesday plans for another trip to Pier One."

Predictably, she ignored my dig at her and then listed forty things she had to do—overwhelmed by all of it—but slow to admit anything. For the next few minutes, we tested each other's patience. When I mentioned that I would like to see her house before spring turned to summer, she lost it. "Ricky, dammit, I'm trying!"

"Lucy, we met in February," I replied. "Should I pencil us in for christening that new bed of yours on Easter?"

She snapped, "You're not compassionate!"

Driving on, lightheaded, she swore I would see her decorating prowess soon. When she screamed at one of her two fluffy cats, I swerved back onto the road. I cleared my throat. "Lucy, say goodbye to Ricky before I drive into the river."

"Ricky, I hate it when you get like this!"

"Lucy, we should talk when I'm at The Gym—and able to lie down on the bench outside it. I handle these conversations better when my head is below my heart."

"R-I-C—"

Click.

Fifteen minutes later, I pulled into The Gym, and she texted me a picture of the giant fluffy cat, which caused her minor melt-down with a caption: *I WILL KILL THIS CAT!*

Then Allie texted me, *OMG, I hate working mornings! And how have I never met Chuck?*

Craving the invigorating salt air blowing in off the ocean, I jumped out of the car and took a deep breath. Allie was heading my way. "Lawrence, everyone is begging me to open the doors to blow out the stale air, but that guy, Chuck, is throwing a fit," she quickly got down to business.

Being a bit groggy, I turned to The Gym. "We have three Chuck's and a Chuck who goes by CC," I said and glanced at Allie. "Who are we talking about?"

Her hands went to her sides. "The older trainer who gets dropped off by his wife, Jean." She shook her head. "Jane's twin sister."

I sighed. "Oh, the trainer, Chuck—"

"Yes, he's in there throwing back cans of Monster Energy."

I pinched the bridge of my nose, glancing at my shadow thrown westward from the morning sun. "He leaves The Gym by eight every morning," I checked the time, "I'm surprised he's still there. Moving forward, he'll be helping Rick open," I took another deep breath. "I love it when you can smell the sand."

Allie's nose scrunched. She insisted I take a bigger whiff and hold it. Then walking in, Allie didn't flinch when I told her Linda canceled our afternoon plans. She scrolled her Instagram, unfazed, before she finally said, "Is Lucy supervising Sheldon paint another room or hang another fan?"

Before I could answer, Fern Farrow, another trainer, opened the door for us. The stale air was full of discernable tension. Holding it open, Fern said, "Cindy needs to talk to you, and Joey wants the light bulbs changed out over the squat rack so he can see himself in the mirror." She lowered her voice. "And Chuck is in rare form. They're all waiting for you to open the doors to air this place out."

"Allie briefed me." I felt tense but kept my voice light. "Let me put my knapsack down."

With members glued to the various news reports on the escalating tensions between the United States and North Korea, Fern replied, "I'll be training Susan, who is probably passed out by the free weights if you need me."

A voice startled me from behind. "Larry, thank God you're here," one of the Mike's said. "Chuck won't open the doors!" I nodded at my morning regular, and he smiled back at me behind his dark sunglasses and Italia baseball hat. I walked into the office, and Allie whispered, "Oh, I forgot to tell you, our night members miss you. They all mentioned they hadn't seen you since December."

I replied with a faint groan.

"It's cool they miss you, though." She was trying to keep it positive.

I was silent for a moment. "I miss those days...I never thought I'd say that..." my voice trailed off as Linda texted me again: *Ricky, I'm heading to Sam's and Pier One. I'll call you when I get back.*

Three hours later, she did. But something was wrong. I hung up, fearful I wasted two months, and I knew Linda heard it in my voice. What I did not realize was that the feeling was mutual.

Two blurry weeks went by without seeing her, and after barely speaking the week of Easter, Allie insisted Sheldon was being introduced to her family. That thought increased my peevishness and irritability just as our sales halted with the departure of the last Snowbirds. I was sleeping less and increasingly fearful of the future.

Then on Tax Day, as thousands demanded President Trump release his tax returns, I sat in front of a stack of bills in a state of absolute disbelief and muttered, "I thought I paid this?" I tossed the statement on the desk and turned to Allie, who was strumming her ukulele. "Allie Girl, how about a little wine?"

"Sure," said the twenty-two-year-old cheerleader. "Is Lucy still MIA?"

I shrugged. "Yes."

"Well, it's been a shitty week for me, too. Wine time sounds wonderful..." and off we went.

Ten days later, on the last Thursday in April, Linda tagged me in a Facebook post. On Friday she called me. I let out a shaky breath wanting to send her to my voicemail, but on the fourth ring, I answered, "Hey..."

"Hi," she said softly. "I miss you." Her serious tone caught me off guard. "I miss your laugh." Today, she wasn't mimicking Lucille Ball, and it was refreshing. I was desperate to have a serious conversation with her and felt relieved she was determined to have one, too. "I need to talk to you. Meet me at the Friday's next to the Indian River Mall."

I agreed but refused to tell Allie. Feeling a wide range of emotions, I remained quiet for a few hours and then breezed out of The Gym, hopeful to have an enlightening chat that was long overdue.

An hour later, I was at the restaurant; however, Linda was running late. At this point, I referred to her as Linda, not Lucy, because she sounded so different. I sighed, frustrated when she texted me again. *Order the wine! But DO NOT GET SAVANNAH!* Linda was referring to the waitress she loathed, who suddenly appeared next to me.

"I picked up your table," said Savannah, opening the Josh Cabernet we always ordered.

Just my fucking luck, I thought but said, "Well done, Savannah."

Savannah beamed. "I got ya, Larry..." and filled my glass to the rim.

I smiled and carefully took a sip. With beads of sweat forming on my forehead, I only wanted to move her along, but she dropped into the chair across from me to confirm that I was meeting Linda. After I nodded at her disapproving stare, she asked if we were a couple. She crossed her hands on the table as if she were a talk show host waiting for my candid answer.

I took a deep breath, suppressing my emotions. "The jury is still out on that."

Savannah waved her hand dismissively as I only wished for Scottie to beam me up. "You should come over to my house and meet my mother-in-law," she continued. "I told her about your book."

I spilled my wine. "Mm, shit. You want me to meet your husband's mother?"

"Yeah, she's my bestie. We'd have so much fun." She paused and grabbed her iPhone off the table to read a text with a mischievous smile. "So, how do you know Michelle Crowley?"

I hesitated.

"I don't. I've only seen her a couple of times at The Gym," I said, stunned.

"Michelle is a member?"

"No, she uses punch cards. How do you know her?"

Redoing her ponytail, Savannah said, "I worked with her at the Fridays in Melbourne a few years ago. She reached out to me after I posted that picture of us at your book signing." She glanced behind me into the restaurant. "Michelle told me you broke her best friend's heart." She snickered. "And nearly caused her boyfriend's ex to commit suicide."

I shook my head. "Wow, she is something."

"I know. So, what's the truth?"

"Back in January, I hung out with both women. We had fun for a brief time, but it was complicated because they were in relationships. Then, I found out about Sarah's depression."

Savannah smiled. "You should watch yourself at that gym of yours. Michelle seemed like she had a plan to burn you."

I quickly texted Allie to find out if Michelle was at The Gym, but she wasn't. Then I gazed at Savannah and said, "Who is Michelle dating?"

She laughed. "Jimmy Hook."

"She's back with Captain Hook," I muttered quietly.

She nodded. "I've been to parties with them. It was a love-hate thing. He's even more fucked up than she is—"

A gruff voice cut her off. "Savannah!" I pulled back in the chair as words seemed to get caught in her manager's throat. "Your tables— inside," he took a step forward and glanced over at me, "they all want to order—"

"I know!" she snapped. His eyes grew wide at the brassy blond and then took a wobbly step back when she hopped up. They stared at each other for a moment before he marched off in a huff. My heart was pumping a mile a minute when Savannah sashayed by me. "I'll be back with more wine, so drink up."

There was no choice, I decided. I held the wine glass up, admiring its vibrant red hues against a beautiful late afternoon sky. With alluring cherry and cedar aroma, I took a long sip of the seductive red and pulled up the new trailer for *The Last Jedi*. Just as it ended, Linda came through the little patio gate. I placed the wine glass down under my own personal black cloud and clambered to my feet. She put her Coach bag down, the one in a previous episode I doused in wine, and we hugged tight. I could tell she had words on the tip of her tongue and filled her wine glass, expecting Savannah to burst through the door.

"This is weird," Linda said, looking slightly woebegone. She took a couple of sips to catch up. Her eyes softened. "The past month has been difficult for me."

With a sudden pain behind my left eyebrow, I rubbed it with two fingers. "I know the feeling."

She looked at me questionably. "I'm not hiding anything," she insisted. "I'm trying not to make a mistake."

"By not making a choice?" I asked.

She shook her head and spoke about the fun times we had while harping on the wine we had consumed. It was then I realized that was the cusp of her problem. Linda's reservations about me were also what drew her to me. After anxiously reading a text, she said, "Sheldon thinks I can't stay away from you. It's been tough on him." She paused as I smiled, as if I understood, although even the mention of Sheldon's name made me feel oddly unbalanced. I felt remorseful that he had met her first while now desperate to lighten her mood. "He has an author friend," she continued as I fidgeted in the chair. "I mentioned her—you probably forgot—"

"The one who told Sheldon I'm a reckless drunk?"

"Yes," she said, raising her wine glass over her smile.

With a sigh, I leaned forward over my wine. "Well, let's focus on the positive." I paused, hopeful something would hit me. "I don't do meth," I cleared my throat as she shook her head, "or steroids…"

Her eyes narrowed at me, and her words left her lips at a frantic rate. "You don't lift weights. You get muscle definition by walking by weight machines that you have no idea how to use—you freak."

I shushed her. "I don't like your tone."

"Don't give me your puppy dog eyes," she said, amused. "Sometimes, I just want to kiss you while listening to our song."

"Truly, Madly, Deeply…"

We both chuckled, but the tension was palpable. Thoughts ticked across Linda's face, and I knew she was not done questioning me about Sheldon's author friends' innuendos. Quickly I realized they were reading my book reviews. She reached into her Coach bag for one from the book website, Goodreads. "So, can you explain these reviews?" she unfolded the paper. "Here's a classic one from October." My stomach tightened in a knot while reading the first line of the review from a reader who ironically went by *The Truth*.

Goodreads Review

The Truth October 11, 2016

The premise of this story has a talented self-destructive guy driving his career and life off a cliff. The protagonist is Peter Pan Man, a forty-two-year-old executive who refused to grow up while being exalted to the sales director position for a new sales division, which he was hand-picked to run as he partied like a frat boy.

The antics detailed are borderline slapstick and left me unsettled yet unable to stop laughing. To give a tiny taste of this debauchery, Peter Pan Man sent poems and MS's (mirror shots dripping wet in his towel) to a coworker, very aware she fell in love with him while blaming it all on his pixie dust because he can't admit he's Lucifer.

I'll now confess I'm also a slightly jealous writer and pissed off that my wife even checked out his MS's. So, I'll conclude by raising my glass and middle finger. Cheers and FUCK YOU, PETER PAN MAN!

I handed it back to her, not sure if I should laugh or cry. "That's—"

"That's the truth," said Linda cutting me off.

"I'm not Lucifer—"

"Why would old colleagues say you nailed the business side of the story while questioning your feelings for Wendy? A few wrote you had many Wendy's, implying you slept around."

She had this way of looking at me. I shook my head. My temper flared. "You know me," I said with an angered gaze. "I'm here because of our connection—"

She took a deep breath and softly said, "I'm listening."

I inhaled sharply but calmly said, "I didn't sleep around." A thin smile crossed my lips. "I promise you there was only one Wendy—"

"I really don't want to hear about Wendy."

"Many of the reviews are from people who met me once, at wine tastings twenty years ago." I drew in a frustrated breath and exhaled. "And Sheldon's friend doesn't know me at all. Okay?"

Without the slightest hesitation, she replied, "When we first met, you admitted that you slept with too many women."

My glare intensified. "Since I am separated," I said. "I was just an idiot back then." I paused, fighting back this unrelenting anger. I wished I could hit the reset button.

Linda's eyes widened, her thick fake lashes at attention. "So, how about now?"

"I just told you!" I exclaimed.

"Well, you're a lot, so tell me again," she said, nearly out of breath. "About you now."

"Now…" I was gifted a humorous out as lyrics rushed to my mind. And then I sang, "I'm just a gigolo, and everywhere I go, people know the part I'm playing." Linda smiled, looking away. When she turned back to me, I continued, "I made mistakes in January, as I told you, but strangely, I feel it was all necessary as was writing *The Show*. I struggle with admitting that sometimes but it's true."

Linda looked at me for several seconds longer than was comfortable for either of us. Eventually, she said, "Why would you say that?"

I sighed, a little more shakily than I'd expected. "It's been a double-edged sword. I told you about Mr. Smee's writer friend at The Mansion and Captain Hook canceling my newspaper interview and—"

"Yes, and that's life!" she shouted. "Grow up. Or just focus on the Savannah's of your world—she keeps looking over. I think she wants another autographed copy."

I wasn't entirely sure what drove me to keep going. Perhaps it was the anger bubbling back up. Maybe I was just feeling sorry for myself. Mostly though, I wanted Linda to understand everything. After a long sip of wine, I refocused on something I shouldn't have: a so-called friend and his wife who trashed me shortly after *The Show* made a few listopia lists on Goodreads. Linda listened with a shocked glare as I continued, "They created a fake profile to leave scathing comments about the book under a fictitious name. When Facebook sent me a notification that it was her—my so-called friend's wife—I screenshot it, and they scrambled to spin everything. That's when he slammed the closet door on his skeletons and had his wife attempt to rile up Marie." I paused. Gazing out into the parking lot, I whispered, "Is that life?"

She lifted her chin thoughtfully. "Unfortunately, it is. So, what happened?"

"The guy spread rumors my affair with Wendy was sexual. Then I lied to him and told him it was."

Linda, whose cheeks were red from the wine and conversation, said, "Did that end it?"

I nodded in silence.

I was lost in thought—somewhere in that place I feared and had promised myself I would never go again but did. "Everyone in the wine industry wanted to read that story when they thought I was printing out copies at Kinko's to stuff in their mailboxes."

She looked sideways at me. "Like Jerry McGuire?"

"Exactly. Everything changed when I received the publishing contract."

Linda connected the dots. "Little lost boy, you drove a career—that many were envious of—off a cliff, then wrote the story, which was published with your likeness on the cover holding a wine glass up that might as well have been your middle finger." Her voice became light, yet also awe-filled. "You achieved something quite impressive. If you hadn't, the envious would not have gone to such extremes to trash you."

I let out a breath I didn't realize I was holding. "Well, it sucks because I enjoy writing."

Linda laughed gently. "And you will continue writing. But the real world is not Never Land. It is often dark and troubling with individuals who are jealous cancers. You should be used to that by now."

I shook my head. "It doesn't have to be, though. I created a culture that celebrated life and success, and everyone loved it."

"Everyone can't just live, love, and laugh."

I stared at her for a long moment. "Well, we all should—"

"There will always be fucked up individuals who ruin that," Linda continued. "You can't change it. So, relax—"

Savannah interrupted Linda with immaculate timing. "I liked your Facebook author page, Larry!" she shouted from behind me as I winced. "Did you get my friend request?" Savannah snatched the empty wine bottle off the table when I shifted my gaze across it.

Linda slowly shook her head at me. "Oh, I'm sure I did," I sputtered. "Thanks."

When Savannah glanced at Linda, I gripped the chair and counted down in my head, three—two—one. And then Savannah said, "I love your hair. It makes you look a bit younger." At that moment, Linda shot Savannah a bogus smile as they exchanged subtle jabs. Savannah disappeared, gripping the empty bottle with an assurance to bring another. I exhaled, relieved, but then counted down again, three—two—one...

"I'm going to end up killing that little bitch," Linda seethed through gritted teeth. "Ricky, let's play the eyelash game! Turn your chair to me."

I blinked.

It was as if the heart with the words I LOVE LUCY flashed up in front of me as another rerun aired of us as Lucy & Ricky. I fell back in the chair tipsy enough to be tickled and laughed when I should've cried.

An hour later, Linda was back to being Lucy and slurred, "Riiicky, we're adorable tonight. Let's post a picture of us." I threw back the rest of my favored red, baring my purple teeth to the flash.

Ten minutes after that, as Lucy fervently responded to it, I asked her Sheldon's take on our delightfully disturbing posts. She looked up slowly and made a face. "He doesn't see these," she rolled her eyes at me, "I unfriended him on Facebook two months ago."

With raised eyebrows, I said, "You unfriended your boyfriend?"

She ignored me. "Ooooh Ricky, in a month, it'll be Memorial Day and the beginning of us. And the best summer ever!"

I blinker harder.

Then, as Savannah watched us from the door, she thrust it open when I flashed her three fingers. She shouted, "A third bottle coming up!" She spun on a dime and was gone, like the Road Runner...BEEP-BEEP.

Lucy looked up. "What did that midget bitch say?"

I smiled at her. "She loves your hair. She thinks your new do makes you look younger."

Lucy smiled back at me. "Um...I KNOW." Her head dropped back to the Facebook post. "AND MY FRIENDS LOVE US, RICKY! Look at how cute we are." She waved her iPhone in the air with one hand while lunging for her wine with the other.

By nine-thirty, we were hammered in Lucy's car. Our hands were all over each other, whispering words punctuated by sighs of erotic pleasure when the mall cop slowly drove by her fogged-up windows as "Truly, Madly, Deeply" started over for the seventh time...

I'll be your dream; I'll be your wish I'll be your fantasy.

I'll be your hope; I'll be your love be everything that you need.

I love you more with every breath truly madly deeply do...

NINETEEN

MAY MAYHEM

MAY 2017
THE GYM

A week later, I was caught behind a school bus flipping briskly through my notepad. *You're living in the thought of tomorrow, waiting for a fairy tale that will never come, Sport! The Dark One* whispered. I tossed the pad on the floor and sighed as the last kid boarded the bus. It took the rest of the drive to calm down.

Then, much to my dismay, I noticed Bob Tillie's black Corvette Stingray in front of The Gym. He'd been out with hernia surgery complications. Although I couldn't recall the last time we spoke, I knew the morning vibe would not help my simmering emotions.

My thoughts turned darker.

I strolled into The Gym trying to see the good in this man, but then Bob broke an office chair and shrilled, "These chairs suck!" Turning up his New York accent, he pointed at Allie's Facebook page on our computer monitor. "And this Lucy and Ricky shit is getting old."

I said a terse hello, not even trying to hide my annoyance, and Bob belched, plopping down in the other chair. "Come on," he barked. "We have some catching up to do." I faded in and out of the conversation until he mentioned a woman I went out with once, back in February.

I turned to him. "Well, it wasn't exactly the world series of love."

Bob laughed, a little unhinged. "Seriously, what happened to her?"

My throat tightened. "We had one too many at The Tavern," I said, recalling her. "And she asked me to go with her to pick her kid up at Gemini Elementary aftercare."

He shook his head and then rubbed his goatee for a moment. "This shit only happens to you," he said, looking the slightest trace appalled.

"You've missed a lot, Bob."

"Not from the looks of your Facebook page, Ricky."

We exchanged glares. I opened my mouth to tell Bob that I was as lonely as he was but closed it when he leveled an accusing finger at me. "So, you lied to me," he insisted. "Hook told me you slept with Sarah."

"I had wine with her...back in January," I said. My voice was measured and low, but inside I was enraged.

A heavyset middle-aged lady dropped her elbows on the check-in counter with a thud. "Excuse me," said the lady, sweating profusely.

"Yes."

"I can't exercise with the scent of fried chicken wafting in from the grocery store next door." She paused, wiping her face with a wad of paper towels. "Can I get my money back?" I motioned Bob out of the office when he began to chuckle.

"Yes, of course," I said, realizing Allie left the door open when she took the garbage out after her Zumba class at the precise time Publix cooks their fried chicken. After refunding the lady her day pass, the music stopped. Before long, I had three credit cards I couldn't process. Oddly, it took me a moment to realize the internet had gone out. Only then did it hit me that they were connected. I wiped my forehead with my shirt. It was warmer than usual.

My pulse quickened when Fern scampered up to me. "Larry, my clients are complaining that the air conditioner is not working," she whispered desperately.

Hours later, I stared at an invoice to replace the old ten-ton unit.

The next day, Bob yelled out that President Trump's tweets sparked as much chaos as my life. I wanted to throw him out of The Gym but sadly needed his thirty-seven dollars, so I took a breath instead.

He pointed at a treadmill. "Your treadmill is smoking!" cried Bob.

I ran over and unplugged it after a hotel guest jumped off. The treadmill had stopped, but Bob proceeded to pound the stop key anyway. "And you wonder why these have issues?" I groaned.

"Don't blame me," Bob replied snippily. "You were sold old shit."

"Stop whacking the buttons!" I demanded insistently. "Please." I turned to another member who divulged the nasty details of a clogged toilet and running urinal, on the verge of tears.

On Monday, the fire marshal fined me because my staff neglected to inform me that we had failed our inspection. Livid, I called Allie. She finally answered before it went to voicemail, "Lawrence, I'm so hungover. I can't hang out with you anymore. You're too much—"

"Allie Girl, sober up!" I snapped. "Did you speak to the fire marshal who left a report to replace all the exit signs and floodlights?"

"No, I left when he came in. The stoner who stole the fifty bucks from our register dealt with him."

"Why didn't you call me?"

"I did. You were playing the eyelash game with Lucille Ball and told me you'd call me back…"

I wanted to throw my iPhone through our cheesy beach scene mural but pulled it back to my face. "I have to go—"

"So, do I! I need to throw up—"

Click.

The remaining days of that week were a living nightmare. In my true ignore-the-issue style, I texted Linda to meet up. On my way out, I heard whispers that the long hot summer ahead would be the last for The Gym.

On the third Tuesday of May, I counted five people in Marlene's popular yoga class. I turned to Allie hysterical. "She only has five people. Where are Carl and Judy?" I asked. My voice sounded increasingly strained. "Have you seen the Ripper? I glared around The Gym. "Or Ivan or Keagan?"

There was a long silence, long enough that Allie thought perhaps I was on the verge of a breakdown. "Yes, please calm down," she finally said. "Keegan was just in and told me his mom…" she paused, thinking of her name as I contemplated opening a bottle in my cooler.

I turned to her instead, "Dawn, her name is Dawn."

"Yes, Dawn will re-up when they get back in town next week."

I took a slow breath and exhaled. "Good, I miss her—"

"Oh, yeah," Allie continued. "That kid," she glanced at his resume, "Wilson called back to see if you're going to hire him."

I shook my head. "The kid partied too hard his freshman year at FSU and thinks this is the place to work to continue that lifestyle."

Allie chuckled. "Um, can you blame him?"

"No. Tell him to hurry."

"Why?"

"So, he gets a few shifts in before we go out of business," I whined.

Before she could respond, Matty marched into the office. She had this look on her face that she had to break up whatever this was. "Son," she said, forcing a smile. "Go to the bank." She looked at Allie. "And have your princess start cleaning. Something. Anything."

Allie rolled her eyes, and I staggered out to my car.

Later that evening, after aimlessly wandering around Lauren and Jerry's empty rooms, I dozed off watching a Yankees game.

At just after nine, I awoke to a text from Linda. *Your whore waitress, Savannah, is now working at Mulligan's. She followed us. Check your Facebook. Now we can't go there tomorrow. You cause nothing but chaos!*

I giggled uncontrollably. After a long string of exhausting texts, I ensured her that I would handle it.

The next day I arrived at the restaurant before Linda and casually walked up to the hostess stand. The bubbly hostess smiled wide and chirped, "Hey, it's great to see you again."

"Likewise," I said. "Is Savannah working today?"

Her eyes widened. "Her shift just ended."

"Table for two, please."

The hostess hesitated.

"Oh, okay." She narrowed her eyes, confused. "Follow me."

Seconds later, I stood at the table we typically sat at overlooking the turquoise waters of Vero Beach. Today the view didn't seem as relaxing, though. I called Linda when I sat down. She answered abruptly, "You better not tell me we have to go back to Friday's—"

"We don't."

"How are you so sure?"

"I told you I'd handle it. And we got our table, hurry up."

"I'm hurrying!"

Click.

An hour later, Linda confessed that she *had* introduced Sheldon to her family over Easter. I opened my mouth to call her a liar and then shut it when I gazed into her eyes. She was torn and tense. After pushing her hair behind her one ear, she then reached across the table for my hand. When I pulled back like a pouty little boy, Linda sighed deeply. "Stop. You know what you mean to me. We're even closer since you clarified that shit about your book. That's called making progress. So, be patient with me." I took a deep breath when my iPhone pinged. "Someone keeps texting you."

I noticed it was Bob. With a sigh, I read it: *Everyone thinks The Gym is closing. Why would you invest in a business that has failed for years?* I rubbed my face and asked for the check. Then Bob sent me another text. *Where are you?*

I rubbed my face harder and typed: *Lost in the abyss.*

On the following Monday, the week before Memorial Day, I met Linda at the Italian Grill in Vero. This wasn't one of our typical planned evenings out, though. It came about after she admitted to being in a sexual relationship with Sheldon. Predictably, he'd been distraught over the last four months and only tolerated it because she told him she wasn't going to stop seeing me. In her mind, she'd hoped he'd leave her. Anguish settled over me. But when she explained everything, she made it clear she was ready to move forward with me. Hence this impromptu wine time.

Feeling relieved, we followed the waiter to an outdoor table. We sat down, and she took a call. By the expression on her face, I guessed it was Sheldon. Linda anxiously walked out to the parking lot. During the five-minute conversation with him, I continued to have doubts. I asked myself what I was thinking while reading a text from Christina. *My boyfriend made me unfriend you on Facebook. I can't talk now but will call you tomorrow.* I leaned back in the chair.

Linda walked up on the verge of tears. We sat in silence for a few torturous seconds before she said, "I want to make love to you." She paused and looked at me with clear, steadfast eyes. But then added, "But Sheldon told when we do, it's over." She seemed sure of what she was saying, even though she sounded certifiable.

When my eyes narrowed at her, doubt filled my heart. "Linda, do you want him, or do you want me?"

She folded her arms across her chest and took a deep breath. "I wish I'd met you first, okay."

I paused, deep in thought. "Just answer me—"

"What's your mother's name?" she frantically cut me off.

I tried not to sound chronically frustrated. "What?" I said, dipping the cloth napkin in my ice water. "My equilibrium is going again." I patted my face with it. "Did you ask me for my mother's name?"

She nodded. "I want to prove to you what you mean to me," she said, looking down at her Facebook app before glancing back at me. "I'm sending her a Facebook friend request."

With the cloth napkin on my head, I peered at her for a moment, tongue-tied. After muttering my mother's name under my breath, I said, "You told me you weren't even into Sheldon when you first met him."

The waiter approached the table, only to then hurry on to the next.

"I wasn't," Linda huffed, increasingly irritated. "I ended up going back out with him because I had an awful experience with a lawyer I went out with at the same time." She paused, frowning as my mind raced on. "I ended up more comfortable with Sheldon because of it. So, blame the cheap-ass lawyer that spooked me—you rude fucker."

"Wait." I swallowed, took a breath, and tried to calm down. "What was the lawyer's name?"

Linda looked at me for several long seconds and then said, "Bill Reed."

TWENTY

A LITTLE LAUGHTER
GOES A LONG WAY

JUNE 2, 2017
THE GYM
It was eleven days later.

I collapsed on the bench outside The Gym. It was my tenth or so "break" when I made a mental note not to text Christina on a night that would yield a morning call from her hungover. "You slay me!" she said, a little too exuberantly, "I cannot believe Lucy also dated Bill Reed!"

"Her real name is Linda Maher—"

"Whatever," Christina hollered. "This storyline of yours is officially going through the ugly chapters."

Musing that for a moment, I yawned and laid down on the bench. "How long do these ugly chapters last?"

"As long the protagonist takes to figure out everything they've been doing wrong. It's life." She chuckled. "And why didn't you call me when Linda told you the Bill Reed scoop?"

"Because it took ten days for the shock to wear off," I explained timidly.

Christina snorted. "I'll bet."

Over and over, I tried to comprehend how this could happen again. A victim of sanctioned déjà vu, I listened to Christina piece together the timeline of it all. "Think about the timing of Bill creeping out, Linda." She paused and laughed. "That shit head was still attempting to get Allison Tinke back while telling you he was in love with Maya, who you were fucking."

"You're not helping."

She continued excitedly, "How ironic is it that Bill was the reason Linda got with Sheldon, which caused this never-ending stalemate with you."

"I have to go," I muttered.

"NO!" she shouted.

I sat up with an awkward smile as Matty marched up to the door. "Hold on, Christina."

Matty shook her head. "Priorities, son. Did the hand sanitizer come in yet?"

"No, ma," I grumbled at Matty. She opened the door, cursing me under her breath.

When it closed, I laid back down and moaned to Christina, "The sun is cooking my hangover, and my life is spiraling into the abyss."

"Ugly chapters!" She laughed louder. "How have you and Linda been since she told you about Bill?"

"We've gotten closer."

Christina answered with a loud sigh.

Increasingly flustered, Christina asked me if Linda ended it with Sheldon, knowing she had not. I swallowed hard, momentarily speechless before I choked out, "She will, soon—"

"Soon? You looked like a happy couple on Facebook back in February. Tell her to choose!" Christina implored me.

Suddenly testy, I began rambling on about our sorry plight when the door to The Gym flew open. It was an irritated yogi from Diane's class rushing out of Savasana to report a kid shaking the studio with deadlifts. I sat up. "Hold on," I said to Christina walking into The Gym. "Keagan!" I yelled at the kid. "There's a yoga class in there." I pointed to the studio. "Don't shake the building until they leave."

The handsome dark-haired twenty-year-old smiled proudly. "Sure, Larry," he shouted back. "Can you get a video of me?"

I nodded and shuffled back to the bench. "I'm back, so after Linda had issues with my book—"

"Larry, it's June!" Christina snapped. "Linda has issues. Period."

I exhaled. "Well, this has been nice. Thanks for your support."

"Breathe, darling. This is just a chapter necessary to get to the ending you desire. I will only remind you to get it all on that notepad of your." Christina paused and then whispered, "I have to show an office space. I'll call you later. But don't forget, I'm coming up at the end of the month. So, plan for wine time."

I sighed exasperatedly. "I remember."

Click.

As a direct result of that conversation, I sent Linda's scheduled morning call to voicemail and schlepped back into The Gym. The atmosphere was undeniably depressing. Without knowing it, it was why I had spent fifty-eight minutes of the hour I'd been at The Gym on the bench outside it. I blinked away from that thought when Cindy stuck her head in the office. "Larry," she whispered. "What happened to the laughter?"

With a stress knot in my back, I muttered, "Ten-grand for a new air conditioner tends to be a bit of buzzkill." I glanced around the office. "Doesn't this office look like it was furnished from a yard sale?"

Cindy laughed loudly, walking out. "Yes. Gut it, Larry. It's the first thing people see when they walk in."

I took a quick mental note on that and read two post-it-notes stuck to the camera monitor: *The laughter is gone. Is the fat lady about to sing?* I frowned, checking my emails. I was looking for a response from the landlord about my rent reduction plea. When the air conditioner had died, I opened lines of communication with them that had been long overdue yet surprisingly productive. We took steps forward, but then doubt crept in when they had not countered my latest proposal.

The room began to spin.

Bob wandered in with salt for my wounds. "So, did the landlord get back to you?" I ignored him and took a calming breath attempting to reset the faulty check-in screen. "You didn't really think they would help you? They made the Ripper cut the space." Bob raised his voice. "You have a better chance of winning the lottery."

I ended up back on the bench, reading a text from Linda. Halfway through it, I was startled by the raspy voice of an older man. "History has a way of repeating itself if we allow it to." A chill ran up my spine when I looked up at Walter Clement. "Do you have a minute?"

During a few seconds of stunned silence, I thought he appeared sickly. "Sure, Walter," I said and sat up straighter. He took a few slow steps towards me, then told me that he had sold his condo. He seemed choked up.

When I asked him if he'd plan on braving the Massachusetts winters again, he shared his plans to move to Arizona with his kids and grandchildren. He took another steadying breath, and I sensed something was wrong. The road Walter took in from Massachusetts seemed to be paved with good intentions, and I respectfully reached out to shake his hand to say goodbye. But he said, "I overheard your conversation with the landlord last week. You have a gift, but your potential needs your attention today." He patted my arm once and sighed when I received another text. His somber face startled me as his gaze shifted to it. "You certainly are determined to find the one." He shook his head. "I wasn't quite as driven. I've been alone since my career faux pas."

I could only utter, "I'm sorry."

Walter took a shaky breath. "Do you feel like you did right before your wine career came undone?" He paused, and I couldn't deny that I did. "Start laughing again. Life is simple unless you make it difficult. Save this special place. And then the girl might appear right where you weren't looking. Work hard comes before play hard."

"Sure—"

"Son, sometimes life presents a better storyline than your imagination," he replied. "Have faith. But use your talents before it's too late." Walter smiled thinly with sad eyes and walked back to his white BMW with his initials on the license plate. I'd seen him drive out a few times and never noticed it. Today I did.

My eyes were wide open. I sat back on the bench, staring out at the sky with moments of clarity, like the sun breaking through the clouds. I was determined to keep it simple. I needed to find the laughter again. Rubbing my tired eyes, I realized I couldn't live without it.

Then, exhausted and frayed, I received back-to-back texts. One was from Linda. But the second was from a sweet forty-six-year-old teacher I had met on POF named Kim Johnson. She wanted to confirm plans to meet up, so I called Linda first. She could tell I was stressed out about our situation. She knew I was talking to Kim but had no idea how bleak my outlook on all fronts had gotten. Thinking it would help my mood, she recapped our last wine time adventure until it triggered my temper. "Wine time isn't giving us a chance to see what we can be together, and you know it."

In her serious Linda voice, she said, "I do." She sighed. "Do you still plan on meeting that teacher next Saturday?"

I replied hastily, "How can I not?"

She became angered. "If you want to cancel tonight, that's fine, too."

I sighed. "Must you get defensive?"

"I'm stressed out with this and need to hear your laugh. Sheldon's driving me crazy—"

"I don't want to hear his name," I said sternly.

"I'm sorry," she said and sighed louder. "I didn't mean for this to happen. I'll see you soon."

I took a breath. "Okay."

"Bye."

Click.

It was five o'clock when we began the evening in Vero Beach at Gloria Estefan's resort, Costa d' Este. We were fond of its elegant atmosphere and seemingly wired to kick off the fun with a bottle of Sauvignon Blanc. On this night, it was Chalk Hill. Creamy and lush on the palate and beguiling on the nose, I placed the taste down and nodded to the waitress. With the waves caressing the golden treasure coast shoreline, she filled our glasses, and I took a moment to consider Walter's wisdom.

"This morning, an older member confessed that he'd never found that special someone." Linda's eyes widened as I spoke. "Looking back on this year, it's crazy how much has changed and the number of people that have left my life and entered it." I exhaled. "It's too much."

Her eyes met mine. "You'll find her," said Linda, as if conceding it was not her. We sat back in our chairs in a moment of reflective silence.

Eventually, I said, "I had this vision of finding the girl and then having everything else fall in place. It hasn't worked out that way."

Her eyes rolled into mine. "I told you that real life isn't a fairy tale."

I shrugged. "It can be," I said just above a whisper. "The truth is that The Gym is spiraling into the red, and my quick fixes are no longer enough."

She shifted to grimace at me. "Oh, come on, how many wine times have I sat across from you and listened to you work your magic and save the day?"

I blew out a frustrated breath and looked Linda in the eyes, pondering her earlier words irritated. "It's beyond that," I muttered under my breath and sat perfectly still, thinking. "Am I wasting my time here? What did you mean by you'll find her?"

Linda's gaze shifted to the beach, and the breeze blew her hair in her face. She pulled it behind her ear. "Maybe I'll always be single," she said softly. "But you won't." She took a sip of wine and turned back to me. Her face was overcast with an expression of anxiety and unease. "I'm trying harder than you know. I don't know what else I can do?"

"You can make a decision—"

She interrupted me. "Can we just laugh tonight?"

"You've been saying that for months. And now I'm about to meet this teacher—"

"Kim!" she snapped, cutting me off angrily.

"Yes," I said and shook my head. "With nothing resolved between us—"

"Bullshit. We've come a long way in a few weeks. Now I need a break from the stress, so stop." Linda demanded with a much-needed breath. "I'm sorry about The Gym." She reached her hand across the table to soothe me. "Tonight's on me. Just please, make me laugh."

We were silent for a moment. I took in a breath, trying to quell the tension riding up my back, and finally nodded. "Fine."

Linda smiled a smile of relief, and we clinked glasses. Although I realized she might never make "that" decision, my spirits lifted. I did enjoy her company and knew we would laugh together. After she paid the check, I didn't want her to spend any more money, so we strolled up the beach talking. The conversation was time well spent as I understood her a little more. Although it was all basically shit, we realized we needed to relax and let life happen while being our silly selves.

She cozied up against me. "See, Ricky?" Lucy whispered. "We're much better as Lucy & Ricky..."

Twenty minutes later, we found ourselves in front of the Kimpton Hotel & Spa. "Lucy, let's check it out!" I chirped excitedly as we playfully bumped into each other to the delight of the gawking bellhop. We walked in as if we were staying there, and that turned out to be key because the staff was serving resort guests wine for their complimentary happy hour.

Our gaze shifted to it in the back of the lobby, and our eyes lit up. "Ricky, we can't," Lucy said a little too loudly while giggling like a little girl.

I squeezed her hand. "Lucy, this was meant to be. Let's have fun." Lucy's face was fixed with a silly smile. She insisted they knew we weren't staying there with her eyes never leaving the floor. Since she refused to look up, I knelt to tie my right Converse and glanced up at her with a quick wink. "Just believe." She burst out laughing when two resort guests walked up, so I stood up and smiled at them. It appeared that we were waiting for them, and as the lady smiled back, we all strolled merrily over to the freebies. Lucy pulled up behind me and was fanning herself when I turned to her. "Lucille, try this cheese," I pointed to the lavish spread, "it's delicious!" The lady's husband tugged at her Lilly Pulitzer shirt sleeve. He seemed quite uptight and unable to embrace our good-natured humor, so I meandered around Mr. Meanie, remarking on the beautiful artwork.

His wife nodded at me with a warm smile. "Oh, it's beautiful. We just love this resort."

"It's one of our favorites, too," I said, putting my arm around Lucy. "Isn't that right, Lucille Ball?"

The lady blinked as Lucy winced. One of the staff members said, "Red or white?"

Without the slightest hesitation, I said, "Red."

Lucy breathed out a snickering breath, and our glasses were filled. After clinking them, we found a fancy couch and sank into it. "Lucille, watch your wine. We can't even afford to clean this bad boy." I sniffed the wine exaggeratedly when Lucy took a sip. With wine nearly coming out of her nose, I eyed them, opening a new bottle, and added, "I think we can polish that off before they shut this thing down." By this point, she was bright red, swatting at me with a limp hand.

Fifteen minutes later, we noticed everyone heading back to the elevators. Lucy took another sip, giggling uncontrollably. I leaned into her, intrigued by the shade of purple she turned. "In all our episodes, I've never seen you turn that color," I whispered. "It's turning me on." Her cheeks blew out, and her hands shot over her mouth. "This isn't Mulligan's. You can't spit it in your hand, Lucille." At that point, I noticed Mr. Meanie was staring at Lucy, probably marveling at how much she looked like one of Wonka's Oompa Loompas. After a moment, he mumbled "rudeness" under his breath. His jaw was set in indignation when they placed their glasses down and marched to the elevator.

Lucy began to perspire while choking the swill down. She took some erratic breaths to regain enough strength to hit me again before she choked out, "Oh my God—I almost spat that everywhere!" I smiled, relieved of the tension my body had stored, and turned to her as she added, "Everyone is heading back to their room. We have to act like we're going back to ours."

"Please, don't excite me," I said and stood up to adjust my jeans. And with that, Lucy abruptly staggered away. Seconds later, after dropping her iPhone, she hid behind a potted palm across the lobby for some much-needed alone time. Finally, she texted me. *If I come back over there, you have to promise that you'll stop talking.*

No, stay there, I texted back. *We can play charades. Ladies first, but let me put on my magical glasses so I can see you better.* I made the eyeglasses' circles with my index fingers touching my thumbs and flipped my hands over my eyes. And then yelled across to her, "GO AHEAD, LUCILLE!"

Lucy let out a guffaw and then turned her back to me, texting again. *Be serious! What the hell are we going to do?*

She peeked unsteadily at me between the palms and grinned while pointing to her iPhone as if I didn't realize she texted me. Then I typed: *Head around the corner to the mop room. I'll mount you in there!*

Once I hit send, one of the staff members bit down on a smile and collected my wine glass. When I noticed Lucy bumping into people en route to the elevator, I hurried over to pour gasoline on the flames.

Heads turned to us.

Finally, the elevator doors opened, and we walked in. By this point, Lucy refused to look at me, so I threw up a peace sign behind her head that she caught in the mirror. Her eyes slowly closed, and as she bit down on her cheek, the elevator man said, "Good evening, folks. What floor are you on?"

"Six," I said and glanced at the buttons to see there were only five floors. "Five."

With Lucy now wheezing, the elevator man peered at us eerily. I thought about telling him we decided to visit friends on two but feared his eyebrow would freeze in that awkward upright position, so I just squeezed Lucy's arm tight. "Hold on, dear," I whispered. "Almost there."

When the elevator doors opened, we stumbled to another custom couch, cracking up. This evening didn't permanently solve any problems, but the laughter we shared put us in a frame of mind where we could more easily cope with it all. In truth, it was the reason we were still pretending one day we'd have a room of our own as we made out on that couch with our song playing out of her iPhone.

I'll be your dream—I'll be your wish—I'll be your fantasy…

The following morning Kristen texted me. *I had a dream you laughed your way out of the ugly chapters and saw the light. Everything suddenly made sense. Don't overthink the setbacks. I'll check in soon. To thinking happy thoughts again, Cheers!*

I rubbed my face, yawned, and typed; *Well, I don't—* The revelation came to me before I could complete the sentence.

TWENTY-ONE

I WILL SURVIVE

JUNE 11, 2017
THE GYM

It was nine days later.

In the dark days of May, I had seen the light. And then, on the first Friday in June, I scribbled on my notepad: *Mistakes are doorways. The more I open, the more I understand.*

Through all the problems were flickers of optimism and opportunity. Encouragement was a tricky thing, though. Just days after a terror attack in London, I opened yet another doorway and only saw flames. Typically, I was most focused under these circumstances, but this was different. There was no hope of saving The Gym without relief from the landlord. I tried to stay hopeful, but my grief was versatile. It manifested into moments of raging anger and overt sadness.

To celebrate this return flight into my darkness, I downed a glass of Rodney Strong Pinot Noir waiting for Linda at The Patio in Vero. I looked to share these troubling feelings with her, but she was late again. With tension shooting up my back, I read her latest text: *Ricky sit on the big couch near the bar. I'm almost ready.* I pushed myself up from the "patio" table we typically sat at and schlepped into the bar. Five minutes later, I texted her back. *I needed you to be on time tonight.* After ordering another glass, she replied, *Ricky, I'll be there soon.* With a deep sigh, I watched the minutes pass. Thirty-three minutes later, I was slumped on that big couch chatting with a lovely lady name Martha when Linda finally strolled in. I only wanted to laugh to defuse the tension, but the look on Linda's face caused contempt. Heated words flew, and I almost flipped my little Kia on the ride home.

On the following Saturday, I didn't just open another doorway; I got thrown through one. The next morning, *The Dark One* whispered in my ear, *That was one hell of a night, Sport!*

I awoke in my bed, gently nursing wounds from a skirmish at a local bar when Allie called. I spilled my water bottle, unable to stop my hand from shaking. When she called back, I hesitated and moaned. In my groggy voice, I answered, "Sorry, I missed your call. I wet my bed."

Allie ignored me, distracted. "Fuck," she said slowly. "L.A. Fitness wants me to sub a Zumba class this morning." She sighed. "Where were you last night?"

I rolled over and choked out, "The Oasis."

Sounding incredulous, Allie went on, "What happened with Kim?"

"She canceled," I groaned, swallowing hard.

"What?" Allie said. Her voice startled. "Why?"

I shared my thoughts about mistakes being like doorways until I heard her panting. Then I exclaimed, "I woke up Saturday still drunk from our Friday night fiasco at Jake's (Crab Shack)!" I took a breath and lowered my voice. "Then I agreed to meet Linda at Gloria Estefan's place in Vero—"

She gasped, "I thought you were done with her?"

I fidgeted in the wet bed. "Well, we had a date at The Patio the week before that didn't exactly go as planned, and she wanted to apologize for accusing me of sleeping with an eighty-year-old—"

"What?"

"Nothing. I met Linda early Saturday."

"So that picture on Facebook was from yesterday afternoon?"

"Yes."

"How could you possibly do that when you had a date with Kim Saturday night?"

Since I didn't want to answer her, I held my iPhone out and whispered, "I don't know." Allie screamed Lucy's name with a surge of indignation, so I quickly continued, "I forgot Kim was on Facebook with me—"

"So, she saw that ridiculous post in your matching outfits and hauled ass," Allie exclaimed, cutting me off. "Imagine that."

I sighed, and even doing that hurt. I explained that after Kim canceled, I went by The Gym when a member found another Popov vodka bottle by the men's showers. Allie began chuckling deliriously. "Why doesn't Wilson throw his empties in the dumpster?"

"There's more," I sputtered. It felt like needles were being stuck in my leg around bruises, scrapes, and lacerations. Allie asked me if there was another bottle. "No." I sighed. "There's more from last night."

"Oh God," Allie's voice squealed through my speaker. "I can't!"

I shuddered. "Fine. I have to find Bob Tillie."

"Talk about mistakes. Why do you want to talk to him?"

I murmured, "I've ignored too much." I paused as the night continued to come back to me. After an awkward moment of silence, I told her Bob was with me at The Oasis when a conversation with a surfer became heated after he brought up Sarah McMillen.

Allie hesitated and then said, "Wait. Captain Hook's old girlfriend?"

I tried again to quench my thirst and steadied my shaky hand long enough for a sip. "Mm, shit. Yes. He insisted that I fucked her and left her."

"But you-you didn't sleep with Sarah," she stammered.

"Correct." I took another sip. "But it didn't matter. He blamed me for Sarah's attempted suicide, and a fight broke out."

"No!" she bellowed. "Are you kidding me?"

I paused when she sighed deeply and then continued when I heard her chuckling deliriously. "After I was thrown through the doorway, it ended on Ocean Avenue with the police. I was bloody and bruised from the pavement." I took a peek at my arm and leg. "It's scabbing."

"Lawrence, you're fifty! How old was this idiot?"

"Your age," I replied. Allie let out a chortle as I held my iPhone out when Wilson's name flashed up. "Allie Girl, Wilson's calling from The Gym. Call me after your class—"

Click.

"Wilson?" I called out.

"Boss, man!" Wilson shouted over The Trammps "Disco Inferno," blaring in the background. "That dancer dude came back."

"Gary?" I asked, referring to our dance instructor.

"No," Wilson shouted. "The guy that rocks Rihanna's red afro—"

The music got louder. "Wilson lower that." After a long solo of someone singing, *Burn Baby Burn...Disco Inferno...Burn Baby Burn...* I raised my voice. "Wilson, walk outside."

The "dancer dude," Wilson described as rocking Rihanna's memorable red afro, was Cosmo: an effeminate sixty-something dance instructor from New York with a wealthy Melbourne Beach client who wanted to dance to some time-honored disco. We agreed on a price and date on April Fool's Day when Cosmo showed me his website with glittering disco balls and drag queens. I wasn't interested in Wilson's convoluted explanation of the date change but perked up when he walked back in The Gym to confirm Cosmo was paying cash to rent the space. Over the *Burn Baby Burn*, I mustered the energy to yell, "Wilson, put the money in the register. I'll be there soon..."

...when the boogie started to explode – I heard someone say – disco inferno – BURN BABY BURN...

Click.

Twenty minutes later, I took one last sip from my Tink mug while speculating why I hadn't heard from Bob. When my call went to voicemail, my thoughts were consumed by this dubious night.

Thirty minutes after that, I crossed the Melbourne Causeway, and my next call went to voicemail. I wondered if it was only by sheer coincidence we ended up at The Oasis. I couldn't recall seeing Bob after the conversation with the surfer became heated. If not for a gym member, it could've ended with me in the hospital or worse. I had temporarily waved this member's fees when she lost her job, and her friend was appreciative. "So, ya da the old bald writer who helped Mary when she lost her job?" her large friend asked as I nervously nodded. "I'll faacking kill that caacksucker if he comes back to haraass you."

I pulled into The Gym, consumed by it all. My body ached when I stepped out of the car. Squinting my bloodshot eyes in the bright sunlight, I limped to the door and noticed Sharky, the Justin Bieber look-alike who gifted me the spin bike. He ended a call and struggled to push himself off the bench. I hadn't seen him since January, and he appeared as tattered as I was. But with words on the tips of his tongue, I seized this opportunity to be enlightened.

Minutes later, I realized I had been set up.

Sharky informed me that Captain Hook got to Bob. Even though Bob had repeatedly warned me about Hook, his words seemed to be scripted. Now knowing Hook preyed on the weak, I wasn't shocked when Bob took Hook's bait: Yankee tickets against the Marlins and a weekend in Key Biscayne. "All Bob had to do was get you to The Oasis," Sharky explained. "Hook had his flunky surfer boy waiting there to pick a fight with you in hopes you'd get arrested. This goes beyond any female drama." His face fell as soon as the words came out.

I shook my head, piecing it all together. "I don't hang out with Bob. This happened when he called me about a bottle of vodka at The Gym."

"I know," he said. "Hook's back with Michelle Crowley. They planned this at lunch before Bob called you. But how..." Sharky's mouth gradually closed. Shaking his head, he tried again, "How did the police break up this shit show and not arrest you?"

"Ironically, they had gotten to know me because of the false alarms at The Gym." I cleared my throat. "So, they let me go."

"Seriously?" he gently pressed. "They let you drive?"

"No, a gym member was there. Her friend drove my car home, and another friend followed in a pick-up."

He gave me a surprised look. "Well, don't trust Bob Tillie," he murmured in disbelief. "Hook's making him a partner of a pizzeria he's opening downtown. Bob is a lonely, jealous man. He can't believe you've been able to keep The Gym open and seems envious of you. He referred to you as kite dancing in a hurricane."

My pulse quickened. "Bob's the villain I was looking for, after all."

Sharky pressed on. "You were looking for a villain?" His eyebrows raised. "I'm not following."

"I'm still taking notes to write that sequel and thought he was the perfect pariah." I paused when he dropped his Mountain Dew, then bent over to pick it up for him. "But anyway, thank you, Sharky."

We shook hands, and I hobbled into The Gym. While watching Netflix, Wilson pointed at another post-it-note. I snatched it off the desk. *You overpaid for this dump. And now you're going to lose everything.*

"Who left this?" I asked angrily.

Wilson shrugged. "I have no idea."

Just then, I received a text from Marie: *The good news is that your May sales tax isn't much. The bad news is that your sales can no longer pay the bills. Is it time to raise the membership fees? Your operating costs keep going up. I am concerned.*

My insides buckled when I sat down on the chair, Bob broke. After Wilson informed me the note was stuck to the desk when he opened The Gym, I eased myself off the chair to shuffle outside. There were only three cars in the parking lot, including mine, and I struggled for a breath. The air was thick and moist as the summer clouds drifted across the sky lazily. My gaze shifted to them almost hypnotically. I saw a face laughing. It appeared to be framed, and then another face form next to it. With the vision of a picture wall—like the one I had in *The Show*—I found myself back in the office with no recollection of walking through the doorway. Standing there with a newfound purpose, I said, "Wilson, we're gutting the office. Throw all of this shit in the dumpster."

Wilson's head tilted slightly. "Really, boss?"

"Yes, once we do that, we're painting the walls fire engine red before the pictures go up."

He gave me a blank look. "Pictures?" he said. "Did the landlord send us some good news?"

"Not yet. But they will," I insisted, pointing to the rusted file cabinet. "Let's empty that first."

For a moment, he just glared at me. Then yelled, "Are you still drunk from last night?"

I clapped once, feeling energized. "Probably," I rubbed my hands together, "but let's focus on the goal."

Wilson opened the top drawer of the file cabinet. He pulled out old folders with an eye on me, wandering around the empty space. The only people in The Gym were Cosmo and his client doing disco in the yoga studio. Walking towards it, I froze when the door flew open. Gloria Gaynor's "I Will Survive" blared out of it along with Cosmo and a little old lady who looked like Andy Warhol. Cosmo sashayed up to me singing the lyrics, *"Oh no, not I—I will survive – Oh, as long as I know how to love, I know I'll stay alive – I've got all my life to live – And I've got all my love to give, and I'll survive – I WILL SURVIVE!"* He hugged me and then took a step back. He looked me up and down and shouted over the music, "Larry, you're a mess. What happened?"

I shrugged. "Another rough night, Cosmo."

With his jazz hands waving in the air, he exclaimed, "YOU WILL SURVIVE!" He whispered in my ear, "Do you feel it?"

Reminiscent of a Twilight Zone episode, I smiled through the strange mix of drama, comedy, and sorrow. They rushed out, laughing at the confusion. I felt better, albeit sensing something else I could not quite grasp. Hastily, I returned to the office and opened the second drawer of the rusted file cabinet as if it would provide some clue. And it did. I blinked at our instructor's folders and handed a bunch of them to Wilson. When I went to grab the next one, it slowly sank in the file revealing the folder behind it: my so-called-yoga girl's. A shiver shot up my spine. I hadn't seen it since last summer but remembered, all too vividly, how it played into our late summer fling.

One that settled in my mind as unanticipatedly significant.

My first Wednesday shift at The Gym was when the little brunette strutted through the door and caught my eye. With immaculate timing, Matty leaned into me and whispered, "That's Shannon." She paused for dramatic effect. "Your Wednesday yoga instructor."

The scene played out like a romantic comedy.

We exchanged glances, and I introduced myself. She seemed to have prepared for this. "I know who you are," interrupted Shannon with haughty impatience. "Your bookmark is on my dresser; I wrote someone's number on it last week." After catching my breath, I asked her if she had read my book, but she only rolled her eyes and—with perfect posture—marched ridiculously upright into the yoga studio.

Like a hit and run victim, I staggered to the bathroom to splash cold water on my face. Looking at myself in the mirror, *The Dark One* appeared over my shoulder. *So, Sport, do you want to kill her…or kiss her?* Splashing more water on my face, I found I was curious to find out. Seconds later, I smiled at Carl and Judy, holding their yoga mats, and then sighed, catching sight of Shannon strutting around the room with a broom.

With biting sarcasm, she said, "I got it. You didn't strike me as someone who pushes a broom." Marching on, she then shot me another look, as if to say, *now get the fuck out!*

So, I did, tickled.

After her class, she dawdled in the office for a bit before occupying the chair next to me. I smirked, unable to look away from her yoga bed head. "Thanks for getting your hair done before coming to see me," I said with a slow nod. "I appreciate you doing your homework."

Her green eyes lit up, looking away. With a sharp breath, she turned back to me. "Listen," she said through clenched teeth. "I didn't do anything to prepare to meet you."

I smiled and spun my chair to the office computer. "Huh, maybe it's a sign then."

She kicked my chair. "What?"

"Tousled bed hair turns me on," I confessed.

"You seriously should come with a warning label across your forehead..." her voice trailed off.

I shifted my gaze from the computer monitor. "I'm having computer problems," I narrowed my eyes at her, "are you one of those sexy...crazy bed head IT girls?"

She bolted up. "I know computers," she said unconvincingly, leaning over me.

"You're extremely talented." I looked up at her as she palmed the mouse. "Can I tell you something else?"

Her eyes shut tight before she abruptly rolled my chair back. "No!" Her left hand balled into a fist, but her face broke into a smile, looking at me. She sighed. "You're not my type..."

I inhaled softly with a triumphant grin. "I can tell," I said, quietly holding my hand out to her. "Please, pull me back over. I believe I can grow on you." The sparks ignited. Then, as the witty banter persisted, we fanned the flames with all intentions of turning whatever this was to ash.

Meanwhile, members stared at us, mouths open and eyes wide as we frolicked around The Gym with a new shipment of paper towels. She could tell I had no idea how to change them out and ripped a roll out of my hand, increasingly amused. "Do you do anything besides make people laugh?"

I shrugged my shoulders. "No."

She shoved me to the side with a flirtatious smile. "You obviously need me."

"More with each passing moment." My voice was just above a whisper as she bit down on her cheek. After that janitorial feat, we skipped out for some fresh air, toured Publix, and realized two hours had passed.

"I'm late," she said with a whimsical smile. "You have my number if you need me."

Shortly after settling back in the office chair, it hit me that she referred to her personal information in the folder I was holding, now ten months later.

It felt like déjà vu when that flashback was interrupted by Wilson. "Larry, why are you smiling?"

I paused for a moment, smiling wider. "Life, it's an amazing journey full of lessons." I hit the folder, feeling exhilarated. "Don't lack compassion, and keep an open mind to their needs, Wilson."

Wilson looked at me. "Who are we talking about?"

"The women you meet on your journey," I said with a little grin.

"Whose folder are you holding?"

"My yoga girl's." I waved it in the air. "It all started with her."

With his arms around another stack of folders, he looked closely at me—he was so deadpan I was worried he was having a stroke. But when his lips finally curled, I realized it just dawned on him where he stashed his new bottle of Popov. He nodded once and marched out.

I blinked.

Everything suddenly seemed brighter. I solaced in breaking free of that gray sheen filter I'd been looking through and shifted my perspective on so much I had so wrong. Since my notepad was on my nightstand, I scribbled my thoughts on scrap paper: *I feel younger when I find the humor in everything dark. And a little wiser when I allow myself to tweak my misperceptions. Today is the day I see my glass as half full again. I will get through this. I WILL SURVIVE…*

Allie scampered in, stressed out.

I placed the pen down with a grin. She dropped her giant hippie bag on the floor, holding her Dunkin Donuts iced coffee. Eying my fight-night wounds, she pleaded with me to go to Surfside Urgent Care. I took a deep breath. "It's okay. I heal quickly," I insisted, briefly fanning my fucked-up leg with my hand to make her feel better. "Did you sub that Zumba class at L.A. Fitness?"

She shook her gaze away from my wounds. "Oh my God, yes!" she gasped. "So, are you ready?"

I quickly massaged the bridge of my nose with my thumb and index finger. "I'm having one of those aha moments. Please don't ruin it—"

"Bob Tillie joined L.A. Fitness," she seethed. "And I also saw our old trainer, Thor." She paused, smiled, and took a sip of her iced coffee. "And are you ready for the best?"

"How do you top that?" I asked, peering eagerly at her.

She beamed excitedly. "I ran right into your old yoga girl, Shannon!"

"I had my doubts, but you delivered. Well done, Allie Girl."

She laughed, placing her iced coffee down. "Why are you emptying the file cabinets?"

I collected my scrap paper. "Oh, and we're gutting the office. A new day has dawned."

Without hesitation, she asked if we got relief from the landlord. Wilson walked back in with a red solo cup and answered for me. "Not yet, but we will," he sang. His voice reeked of sarcasm, and his hazel eyes grew wide to Allie before he slowly shook his head.

Momentarily silenced, Allie looked at me and grimaced. "Lawrence, what's going on?" she asked with exasperation in her voice. "Are we okay?"

I was distracted by texts from Kim and Christina and placed my iPhone back on the desk. "Think happy thoughts, and we will be," I urged her. "We've gotten away from doing that for too long now." I pointed to the bottom drawer. "Wilson, did you get to that one yet?"

"Not yet. But the dumpsters are full," he lied, wanting to close early and take our party to the beach. "Can we enjoy this gorgeous beach day and do this on Monday?"

"Nope," I said and opened it. I avoided an old jockstrap and a box of condoms and pulled out a folder with the word: CLASSES. Inside it was an old schedule and three faded pictures. I froze transfixed on the third — four ladies in their late thirties holding yoga mats. I immediately recognized the little blond was Allison Tinke. She still possessed this intangible appeal as if I knew her from another time. I couldn't get over that. Staring at the picture, I recalled Maya insisting that fate had a strange way of twisting us all together.

I pondered that thought.

Then Allie's voice shook me free. "Lawrence, you're grinning like a little boy," she said. The sour little smirk on her pink lips flatlined. "Who is that?"

I exhaled. "Tink..." Allie grabbed it from me.

Wilson raised his eyebrows. "You have a Yoga Girl, an Allie Girl, a Lucille Ball, and a Tinker Bell?"

Allie swung around to him. "Don't be ridiculous," she huffed. "There is no Tinker Bell. But Lawrence did have a Mermaid named Maya. So, if you're gonna work here, you'd better stay current."

Wilson smiled back at her but looked a little offended. "And you wonder why I drink on this job—" Allie interrupted him.

"Lawrence," she held the picture in the air, "seriously, who is this?"

I grinned sheepishly. "It's Allison Tinke."

Wilson nodded. His mouth curled into something between a smirk and a smile as he raised his red solo cup to me. "Cheers, Peter Pan Man..."

• • •

That evening, I slid into bed gingerly. Although my thoughts drifted from writing any sequel, the rambling impressions on my notepad inspired me. Suddenly, my views of a happily-ever-after included the harsh reality of finally finding that special someone with a shit load of baggage. Baggage I'd better find the compassion to help her unpack.

With the ping of a text, I placed my notepad on the nightstand and read that Kim had a change of heart. I said to Jedi Mickey, "Kim's giving me another chance. She wants to meet me. She might not be the one, but this experience is changing everything, Mickey..."

I turned off the light.

Another trail of pixie light flashed by my window. And then Jedi Mickey said, *"In a dark place we find ourselves, and a little more knowledge lights our way."*

TWENTY-TWO

CRUELLA CROWLEY

JUNE 12, 2017
MY HOUSE/THE GYM

Although the next day dawned brighter, I found myself tempted by a text. It was Christina's version of my MS: a towel wrapped around her waist and nothing else. I winced away from it when *The Dark One* whispered, *I don't see Linda doing anything about your blue balls, Sport.*

I turned on the news, increasingly uncomfortable. MSNBC was mocking Trump's tweets, CNN was still reporting on the suicide bomber at the Ariana Grande concert, and FOX was retracing the timeline of a terror attack in London. *The Dark One* continued, *Shut that shit off and call Christina!*

I checked my emails instead. With nothing from the landlord, I glanced back at Christina's picture and then took a breath. *It's Monday. They'll get back to me on Tuesday,* I said to myself, with the ping of another text.

I peeked at it.

It was Christina's follow-up: *That was payback for your MS from last week!*

The Dark One howled, *Ooops, you did it again, Sport!* I swallowed hard and read on. *I'm staying at a friend's in Beach Woods on Friday, so make sure you're available by 1 pm.* (flame emoji)

I glanced at my calendar:

Wednesday, June 14 – wine time with Linda.

Friday, June 16 – wine time with Christina.

Sunday, June 18 – brunch with Kim.

After a few slow breaths, I began typing a response but stopped. I exhaled, thinking I had an out because Allie had a cheer tryout.

But then *The Dark One* added, *You can wait at home for Linda to make a decision or call Wilson to make sure he can work Allie's shift and write this vixen into the next chapter.* My eyes narrowed at my notepad without even realizing I dialed Wilson. But then I almost dropped my iPhone. "I can't talk!" he answered frantically. "One of Hook's salesmen committed suicide—"

Click

I raced out the door.

Thirty minutes after that, I hurried into The Gym and received a text from Linda. *YOU'RE NOT GOING TO BELIEVE THIS. CALL ME!*

Since Wilson was on the phone, I called Linda, on edge. She answered: "That ass sent me another message on POF!"

I tried to sound insouciant. "Who?"

She continued hastily, "Bill Reed!"

"I can't talk about him now," I insisted. "There was a suicide."

"Will you cut the shit and listen to me—"

"Shush!"

"You shush—"

I forced a smile at Matty, marching up to the door. "Priorities, son," she said, yet again, as it hit me, I was nineteen years older than her real son. Not wanting to cry in front of The Gym, I pushed off the bench and schlepped over to Publix. After Linda explained that Bill had been through all the single women in Vero, she casually added, "So, have you heard from Kim?" she was breathless for an answer.

"Yes," I said with a nervous laugh. "She agreed to meet me again."

Of course, Linda acted like she was happy for me but certainly was not. By this point, Kim knew of Linda, and not only because of the Facebook post in our matching outfits. Linda reached out to Kim on messenger while then swearing the message was meant for someone else. Kim maintained Linda had deep-rooted issues that she could not properly process. Ten minutes later, back on the bench, I could barely concentrate on anything and ended the call when Wilson waved me back inside.

His eyes grew wide.

"It was Smee who killed himself," Wilson muttered. We stopped in front of the office, and he gave my forearm a quick pat. "And Michelle is waiting for you."

I hesitated. "Michelle, who?"

He pointed to a woman by the free weights staring at us and said, "Crowley. I thought you knew her. She came in when you went to Publix." He lowered his voice. "She wants to speak to you."

A lump rose suddenly to my throat, and I motioned him into the office. She looked different. "I've only seen her a few times," I confessed. "She knew someone I hung out with." Wilson nodded knowingly before our gazes shifted back to the plagued thirty-something in her chic Alo Yoga apparel. "I can't believe Smee is dead," I said, pondering too much. "And Michelle." I took a breath. "She dated Hook. Has she mentioned getting back with him?"

Wilson pulled his hand through his hair. "No, she told me she lost her best friend because she slept with you while dating Bill Reed, though."

"Michelle used what happened between us for her own selfish needs," I protested.

Wilson stared at me, mouth open, eyes wide. "She said you also dated Hook's girl—"

"We had wine time together. That's it."

An odd smile curled on his face. "I now know why that Schultz guy in your book claimed he saw nothing." Wilson paused, looking like he was going to faint.

"Grab some water," I said, fanning him with my hand. "I'll go see what this witch wants."

At that point, I went over to introduce myself to Michelle. It became quickly evident that she had new boobs, a fresh Botox treatment, and was not the slightest bit remorseful Mr. Smee had taken his life. "Melbourne Beach is notorious for suicides," she insisted, reeking of Hook's money. "I have no respect for anyone who takes their life." Her spine stiffened, and her voice softened. "I need to talk to you about something else." Perhaps registering my sudden rigidity, she asked to go outside. I followed her out to a black Porsche Cayenne parked on an angle in the first two spots. Recalling Maya tell me she despised her old beat-up Honda, I only smiled when she turned to me. "James Hook wants a fitness center to add to our business portfolio," she said. "He's willing to relieve you of your nightmare." Michelle gestured to The Gym with gumption.

I waited a moment and then queried with exaggerated impudence: "Hook wants to buy The Gym?"

Michelle glanced at her slim gold watch. "We have resources that will turn it into a real fitness center," she said with sarcasm. "We can cut your losses before you lose everything." When she paused, too anxious to breathe, I visualized a young Cruella de Vil. *Cruella Crowley,* I thought, *perfect.* With an erratic breath, she finally sighed loudly. "Say something! James is waiting for my call." She looked up at me, narrowing her eerie cat-like eyes.

My gaze hardened. "I'm not selling The Gym to Captain Hook."

She smoothed her straightened hair with her free hand while gripping her iPhone tightly with the other. "You should take this seriously," she demanded. I remained silent. Face flaming: she then came unglued. "You can't afford the rent. Go back to Tampa. Or wherever your book left you destitute. Your ego took you off one cliff. No one wants to read about anyone who goes off two—"

"Then I better not go off that second cliff," I said with a grin.

I took a few steps towards The Gym, and she snapped, "Wait!" I glanced back at her, and she had a look of panic. She slumped against the Porsche and erratically scanned a text. When Cruella lifted her head, her fair skin was flushed. It seemed as if Hook provided her enough drugs to believe I would just hand the keys to her and disappear. I walked back to her undeterred yet inspired to capture this "Cruella Crowley" plot twist on my notepad. Her hands began to shake. "You cannot survive this." Cruella dropped her iPhone as her sad life showed in her eyes. "Save your fucking dignity."

I picked her iPhone up and handed it to her. "My job is to save The Gym."

TWENTY-THREE

CHRISTINA, KRISTEN, CRUELLA, AND A BOTTLE OF KIM

JUNE 16, 2017
MY HOUSE/THE MANSION
It was four days later.

I was in bed, scrolling my Instagram, when Christina texted me. *I got my Starbucks and am hopping on 95* (smiley face emoji) *looking forward to a little wine and a good time!* I sat up, crossed my arms, and turned to Jedi Mickey perched on my nightstand. "So, my friend," I huffed. "She wants wine and a good time."

"Adventure. Excitement. A Jedi craves not these things," replied Jedi Mickey.

I sighed. "Yeah, well, I'm about to torch my second career in seven years and fuck up my Jedi training too—"

"PATIENCE YOU MUST HAVE, my severely flawed friend. Learned much you have; now patient you must be."

I pouted. "With no word from the landlord, I'm not feeling it." I shrugged. "But I'll try—"

"NO! Try not. Do or do not; there is no try."

"Hey, settle down, Mickey!" I snapped. "You're not Yoda. You're only wearing his hooded dress."

In Yoda's soothing and trustworthy voice, Jedi Mickey said, *"Hmm, Yoda, I am—"*

My iPhone rang, and my eyes fluttered open. I rubbed my face and noticed it was Christina. *Another dream*, I thought. With a yawn, I answered, "Good morning…" I flipped over my damp pillow.

"I got my Starbucks and am heading north on 95!" said Christina excitedly.

I hesitated. "Yeah, that sounds about right," I muttered.

"I'm going to my friend's house first, and then I'll meet you at Thai Thai," Christina bellowed over her car stereo.

"Don't forget, I have plans with my kids for dinner—"

"I know, relax," she added hurriedly. "We have all afternoon. We'll figure out where to go for a little wine when I get there—"

"Okay—fine," I said awkwardly, cutting her off. "See you soon."

"Bye, ya silly goose!"

Click.

After a quick shower, I started the coffee. With my Tinker Bell mug in my hand, I turned on the news, incapable of discerning what I saw. Another shooting dominated the headlines. This week's catastrophe came during a practice session for the annual Congressional Baseball Game for Charity in Alexandria, Virginia. The Virginia Attorney General concluded it was "an act of terrorism fueled by rage against Republican legislators." I turned it off, wearier of my own personal worries, and scampered out to The Gym.

Once there, my mood brightened with the first positive feedback for our office remodel. It was as pleasant a surprise as my new social media gal pal, Dara. Standing in the office, she gave me a high five and showed me her latest Facebook page improvements. Drawing from that, I mustered the courage to see if anyone from the property management team had emailed me. Scanning my inbox, Wilson startled me. "I'm grabbing a workout before my shift—any news from the landlord?"

I shook my head. "No," I said, not bothering to hide my dismay.

The sides of Wilson's mouth twitched. "Maybe you should think about that backup plan," he said, referring to Cruella Crowley's offer. A wave of doubt passed through me as he walked over to the free weights. Then the ping of a text made me realize Christina was an hour out. Sitting alone and motionless, *The Dark One* whispered, *Cork that last bottle and go fuck her. Tell Lauren and Jerry you got caught up at The Gym and burn it all to the ground. I'll make sure you rise from the ashes to write about it. Just like the last time, Sport!*

With a pounding heart, I stood up shakily and stared at the wine cooler. I noticed the green light went out and touched the wine, caving to curiosity. It was warm. Too warm. Without the slightest hesitation, I yanked the cord out of the wall and whisked it out the back door.

Seconds later, I heaved the last trace of my old wine career into the dumpster and staggered into the outdated bathroom to splash cold water on my face. The green tiles and awful grout lines grated on my frayed nerves as I stared at myself in the mirror, wondering if I was crazy not to take Hook's offer. Or at least hear him out. Fighting a bout of anxiety bubbling up inside me, I called the property manager, yet again. The secretary insisted they would have an answer on Monday. When she rushed to end the call, I feared the worst.

Walking back to the office, I focused on renting the yoga studio out for a private lesson. When the lady showed up an hour later with a credit card, I relaxed a bit. But then Wilson came back in with a shit-eating grin. "Allie told me you have a brunch date on Sunday with someone new..."

"Yes, a teacher named Kim," I said. "Don't look at me like that."

The Dark One shook Allie's pom-poms as Wilson added, "I also heard the girl you're meeting tonight used to be a member who is only a few years older than me."

"This afternoon," I snapped anxiously. "I'm meeting my kids tonight." I continued, attempting to convince myself of it. "And you're nineteen, Christina's eight years older. So, stop being ridiculous."

He rolled his eyes. "So, what time will you be catching fire today?" he asked, checking his watch. "I have errands to run before I can spend another nine hours here."

"Be back at noon, so you'll only work an eight-hour shift."

He laughed, but it did nothing to erase the pit of fear that grew in my stomach. "Hey, I heard your little mermaid, Christina, looks like Halsey with long hair. Pull up her Facebook."

I sighed, knowing I couldn't, and felt both agitated and defensive, so I babbled, "What? She doesn't look like Halsey—"

"Come on," he rubbed his hands together. "Let me see her."

I took a sharp breath. "I can't. Her boyfriend made her unfriend me, and now I'm blocked. He gets uncomfortable with our friendship."

Wilson looked at me for a long moment. "And to you, that's normal?"

From there, it only got darker.

An hour later, Christina inexplicably switched lunch from Thai Thai to The Mansion. At first, I thought it was weird because I had that memorable night there with her old bestie, Maya, but it quickly became a moot point. Two minutes later, she called me back, concerned that her boyfriend would lose it if their friends spotted us together. "Why don't you come to my friend's place? She won't be back until tomorrow."

I swallowed with a tight grip on the steering wheel. "No, I can't," I said, fighting *The Dark One*.

"Oh, relax," she said dramatically. "She wouldn't mind, but The Mansion's fine."

With those words, I noticed the summer sky darken while I was driving north on A1A. Pulling into the 7-11 parking lot, I second-guessed everything. When she turned up the music, I gave myself a skeptical look in the rearview mirror and took a breath, steadfast to pass on it all. Then I heard a cork pop out of a bottle while she sang the lyrics. *"Are you with me, come on baby, get with me—nothing wrong with getting a little tipsy—POP-POP-POP that bottle!* Suddenly there was silence, and I was strangely exhilarated. "So…ya silly goose," she said, stealing my line again. "Are you with me?"

I exhaled all restraint. "I'll meet you at the Mansion in fifteen minutes—"

The music blared. *POP-POP-POP that bottle!*

Click.

I parked my car in front of the restaurant, embarrassed at the little jolt of excitement I felt at the sight of her white jeep and bolted up the stairs to the rooftop bar. It took me a second to recognize her. She was wearing designer ripped jean shorts, a white tank top, and shiny white Miller Sandals. Her dark hair was highlighted and pulled back in a ponytail. I quickly texted her. *Nice tail!* She dropped off the same barstool Maya did in January with her blithe spirit.

Although our recent communication had me uptight, I deduced we'd had many harmlessly flirty occasions during this completely platonic friendship and hugged her, relieved. "I'm sorry I got so silly," she said. "I've been a bit edgy lately."

"You and me both," I replied, scoping out a table. There were a few under the overhang by the side of the bar. With dark clouds circling, I pointed to one in the middle, and the hostess brought over menus.

"I want a bottle of Kim," Christina said, nudging me in the back. Being a fan of *The Show*, she insisted on Wendy's old favorite, Kim Crawford Sauvignon Blanc. After ordering the bottle and two Tortilla Salads, she placed her elbows on the table and leaned forward. "Talk about great material. It's quite ironic that we got close after Maya shared intimate details about you while I was reading your book."

I grinned. "I love a plot with twists and turns and twenty-somethings—"

"Maya's thirty-three." Christina smiled her smug twenty-something smile, then received a text. She looked up deadpan and blank-eyed for a moment before mentioning Cruella Crowley's proposition. I quickly regretted sharing that news when she pushed her opinion to dump The Gym. She glared at me, and I shook my head, feeling certain that I would disagree, but she pressed on. "It's failed for years. Everyone knows the rent is outrageous, and no one cares. Wouldn't you bail if Hook gets you close to what you need?"

"I've thought about it," I said under my breath. "But wasn't it you who was upset with me for looking at the glass half empty?" I paused as she made an exasperated sound and sat back irked when she brought up the landlord, not negotiating with previous owners. She jabbed at me until I added, "I'm most focused when all options are exhausted. And couldn't handle a dream where Jedi Mickey stabbed me in the nuts with his lightsaber because I sold The Gym to Captain Hook."

"Jedi Mickey?" She shifted her gaze to the dark clouds and then back to me. "Take their offer and move on."

I sighed. "Let's think happy thoughts." I made a head gesture to the wine bottle coming our way. "It's been a while since I've had Kim (Crawford)."

She had a distant smile for the waitress. When she poured me a taste, Christina seemed oddly annoyed as her thumbs flew texting someone. By her expression, I assumed it was her boyfriend and then nodded to the waitress to pour our glasses. Christina reached for hers and said, "Okay, we're gonna play a game."

At that moment, I read a text from Linda, who was currently Lucy: *Ricky, I miss you! I want to play the eyelash game.* My gaze shifted to Christina, humored. "Lucille Ball loves the eyelash game. Is that the game you're thinking?"

"No," said Christina, rolling her eyes. "I'm gonna ask some questions from your year at The Gym. Okay?"

With thunder rumbling around us, I gazed out to the ominous sky. "Okay, but try not to upset Mother Nature. I'd like to polish off two bottles this afternoon before getting struck by lightning."

Christina chirped, "My questions will help you put your thoughts in perspective to write that sequel."

"Oh boy," I said while staring at the lovely pale-yellow color of my wine against the dark clouds swirling viciously.

She grinned. "Your best sex was?"

I raised my eyebrows in question and took a long sip. "Mm, that's good," I said. "As was Maya."

"Fuck you," she moaned. "Worst sex?"

My eyes narrowed at her. "I'm not going there in any sequel."

"Come on!" she gushed shamelessly. "The bad experiences are the funniest."

I winced, miffed by my first dating site date. "Beth, the shoe girl," I muttered. "One and done."

Christina breathed in and out for what felt like a minute. "You lost a load and a shoe on your first date?" She wiped her mouth as the wine went down her chin and leaned back aghast.

I shook my head. "No load lost there," I confessed. "We started in one bed, but she moved us to another—in the dark—worried about the time, too drunk to realize I was done."

Christina pulled her glass back up to her mouth to conceal a growing grin. "So, how did it happen?" she squeaked out and took another sip from her glass because she seemingly needed one.

"Well, she was," I cleared my throat, "quite wet." Christina's eyes slowly closed. "So, she slid in what was left of me, but when I looked into her eyes and only saw a clock counting down with a two-minute warning, I scrubbed the launch—"

Christina chuckled giddily. "Maya said your testosterone levels are of a sixteen-year-old. She made it seem like you'd never scrub a launch." Her eyes narrowed at me. "Why was that shoe girl night different?"

"Well, I had this vision of running away with one shoe dodging bullets from her gun-wielding boyfriend, knowing I wasn't wearing my bulletproof bloomers." I smiled. "And that was that." She pulled the napkin over her face as her laughter was startled by another text.

Christina took a few slow breaths. "We should've ordered two bottles at once," she said, reading it. Her body stiffened. "So, there is a picture on Facebook with you, your trainer Fern, and Allie. You guys seemed quite cozy, and Fern had her hand on your leg." She glanced back at the text and then to me. "Is it true you had a threesome with them?"

I blinked. "How did I miss that rumor?" I said, looking at her sideways. "No. Sorry to disappoint you."

She smiled at me, but there was something about her expression that seemed insincere. "Too bad, sex sells," she said unapologetically. "Have you ever had sex in The Gym?"

A text then hit my iPhone. Distracted, I sputtered, "The Ripper has some sick stories from back in the day. You should ask him about the couch—" she interrupted me with a single clap, desperate to get back to her questioning.

"You bent Allie over one of Diane's Pilates balls in the yoga studio!" she chuckled.

I grimaced. "Stop. She's twenty-two."

She furrowed her brow and plowed on. "You fucked your old yoga girl in the massage room!"

My breath caught in my throat. *I guess if you throw enough shit against the wall, something will eventually stick,* I thought, and then said, "I might need to change my first answer."

Christina jumped up as if she was a jack-in-the-box. "I knew this game would help you." She held the back of the chair, a little too tickled.

"It's probably best you go to the bathroom because none of these people can look away, and all of them want to finish their lunch before happy hour." When her hands went to her knees, wheezing, I noticed the text was from Kristen. Before I could read it, Christina dropped back down in the chair with a thud and asked me if I regretted not calling Maya when she suggested I should. Then, with the ping of another text, I realized Kristen was desperate to speak to me.

Christina leaned over the table to recapture my attention and smiled blankly. "Well, Maya liked you more than she could handle—"

"I often miss her," I replied, haunted by that road not taken.

Christina made a face, pink lips wincing above her petite chin. "We don't talk anymore…" she hesitated, scowling at another text, and then became even more flustered.

"Are you okay?" I asked as Christina's eyes erratically scanned it. "Is that your boyfriend blowing you up?"

She gritted her teeth in exasperation. "No, it's work-related," she murmured and slowly pushed herself up. Standing perfectly still, she added, "I'll be right back." She rushed down the stairs.

I exhaled as the waitress dropped off the salads and read Kristen's texts. *I heard you're about to lose The Gym and that Christina works for Hook in Miami! Her new best friend is Michelle Crowley. CALL ME!!*

All my instincts had me rereading it before I took a breath and called her. After the first ring, I put her on speaker with an eye on the stairs. Kristen's voice startled me. "I want to scream at you, but only have a minute." I took her frantic voice off speaker. "Christina has ulterior motives. She came up to dig for information that will ruin your reputation. They want to paint you as a player or worse!"

I exhaled. "Are you watching Lifetime movies while throwing back Yoo-hoos again?"

"You think this is a joke?" she pressed.

"I'm not sure what to think," I said. My voice was irritated. "But Christina knows the truth—"

"They're spinning the truth!" she squealed, cutting me off. "Hook hates you, and Christina's desperate for his money. That trumps her little crush, so check your ego and don't be naïve."

"Where are you?" I asked, feeling queasy.

With a sharp breath, Kristen reminded me she'd been in Miami since Tuesday. She had lunch with a friend who knew Cruella Crowley. Since

Kristen knew Christina was coming up for wine time, she eagerly did some digging when my name came up and found out that Christina had gotten close to Cruella right after Bill ousted her from the law firm. Shortly after that, Cruella offered her a property manager gig for a strip mall Hook owned not far from where she lived. Kristen confirmed pictures of Cruella and Christina partying on her Facebook page, which I then realized was the real reason she had blocked me. I took a shuddering breath, and from the corner of my eye, noticed the waitress. I motioned for another bottle.

Kristen continued, "So, to sum it up, your gal pal, Christina, is now under the spell of guess who?"

"Cruella Crowley."

"Cruella she is, and right you are," she said. "Shit…I have to go—"

"Boy, does this world need more laughter and love," I muttered, noticing the call ended and sighed as I read a text from Wilson. *Christina's profile picture is with Michelle Crowley, and she does look like Halsey. LOL!*

My heart was in my throat when Christina came back to the table. "The storm passed us without a drop, but it's pouring on the beach," she said. "I guess I didn't piss off Mother Nature after all."

No, you just pissed me off, I thought but said, "So, you never told me about your new job. How's it going?" I took a quick forkful of salad as she nervously pulled her hands off the table and placed them on her lap.

Christina looked at me. "It's fine, I suppose," she said solemnly. "It's temporary." Her gaze shifted to the clearing sky when the waitress informed us that we had the last bottle of Kim Crawford. That was my cue to leave, although my heart was pounding in my chest. Hastily, I wiped my mouth and told Christina that I had to pick up my son at his summer play rehearsal unexpectedly.

Racked with anxiety, she sputtered, "I'll buy lunch." Christina shifted to the bar, "I'm going to have another. I thought you'd stay." She tightened her ponytail. "How about brunch on Sunday," she smiled thinly, "before I drive back."

I shook my head. "I'm having brunch with Kim on Sunday." I paused as she looked away, blinking. At that point, she knew I'd heard something and withdrew her shaky hand from the wine glass. She hesitated and then slowly stood up to hug me goodbye. "Trust is hard to find and easy to lose," I said softly. "Take care of yourself." I walked out as she stood speechless with watery eyes.

Racing south on US1, I called Kristen back, but it went to voicemail. I gripped the steering wheel tighter, wondering how many villains I was dealing with. When she finally called me back, I was at dinner with Lauren and Jerry and could only let out a weary sigh watching her call go to voicemail. Kristen's message was chuck full of ambiguity before suggesting we speak in the morning before their flight back to Antigua.

When I arrived home, I captured the day's events on my notepad, took a deep breath, and then flipped through the pages. *What a year*, I thought, and stretched my neck to the left, then to the right, and sighed.

Meanwhile, Wilson texted me that he'd sold an annual membership. Excited to add any totals together, I yanked the sales folder from my knapsack, and a picture startled me as it flew to the floor with a post-it-note. I picked it up and read the note. *I figured you might want to keep this one. Cheers, Wilson!*

It was the picture we found of Allison Tinke from the rusted file cabinet. Ironically, I recalled a conversation with Christina about how weird it had been, repeatedly hearing Allison's name and grinned. *"It's not weird,"* she insisted. *"Our lives are filled with meaningful coincidences or synchronicity. There might be a reason it's happening."* I placed the photo on my notepad, pondering it, and sighed. Suddenly, my eyelids felt heavy, and I headed to bed, hopeful.

At some point after that, I saw another trail of pixie light flash by my window. And then Jedi Mickey said, *Clear your mind must be if you are to save The Gym,"* he drew his lightsaber, *"and find the girl...*

TWENTY-FOUR

ZEN TIME

JUNE 19, 2017
THE GYM

It was Monday morning.

My alarm went off at five o'clock, but I stayed in bed ten minutes longer, basking in the silence of my bedroom. I felt an urge to unplug from a year of noise and distraction and hangovers that blurred the thin line separating laughter and pain. With a fresh cup of coffee, I sat down in a silence that came with an energy I referred to as "Zen Time." It had been too long since I cleared my mind, and it never felt so good.

I wasn't doing any diaphragmatic breathing exercises but took a couple of deep breaths when I received Wilson's text. *I still think you're the coolest boss, even though your storyline as the hero who went on the adventure to find the girl and save The Gym didn't work out.*

Why do you think the story ends here? I texted back.

Because we're about to go out of business, he replied.

An hour later, I thanked Kim for our pleasant Sunday brunch and strolled into The Gym, thrilled I wasn't dehydrated. With a warm smile, I waved at Chuck and his sister-in-law, Jane, on her favorite elliptical, before I said good morning to Bill "Two a Day" Tidden on my way into the office. I slid around Fern, who showed Dara pictures of her son's allergic reactions to pretty much everything any person could be allergic to and checked my emails. Although there was still no news from the landlord, I remained in good spirits. I attributed that to a serene start to the day.

Thirty minutes after that, we received another shipment of Mixtiles with our members smiling faces. The week before, I had found an unused credit card to purchase the twelve-inch squares, which instantly transformed the dreary space. After completing the first wall, I stepped off the ladder, pleased. A woman staying at the Seashells Suites Resort hopped off a spin bike and took a picture of it. "What a great idea," she said to me, taking out her earbuds. "These tiles look great." I thanked her as the club's handsome fit thirty-something, Scott Maki agreed.

Quickly checking the time, I whisked the ladder off the floor before Barbara's Body Sculpt class ended. An attractive older lady wandered in and over to the check-in counter. Immediately, Fern asked her if she was a member. I knew she wasn't and said hastily, "I got her, Fern."

Fern turned to me as old Chet muttered, "He makes them laugh, takes their pictures, and hangs them up, creating the illusion this place isn't going under." He hit the hand sanitizer and rubbed his hands together with a single nod to the lady who glanced back at me humored. "Smoke and mirrors," Chet added quietly, shuffling out. "In all my years, I've never seen anything like it."

I made my way around to the lady. She looked up at me with a pleasant expression and said, "You must be Larry." I nodded. "Can we speak outside?" With a nervous nod, we hurried outside to the bench. She turned to me and lifted her chin. "Walter Clement died of cancer." My jaw dropped, and my shoulders slumped with no idea what to say.

Slowly my gaze shifted to where he stood to say his final goodbye. "Walter recently came to The Gym," I explained. "We spoke right here." I became choked up. "I had no idea…"

She grabbed a tissue from her purse. "He liked you. That's why I came by. We'd have dinner together, and he'd talk about his friends at The Gym. He told me you reminded him of himself," she murmured. "Walter was a special man. Too special to have been alone." Her cheeks were flushed, and a vein in her neck fluttered as she then laughed, reminiscing. "He'd sit on his balcony and listen to the waves sipping his wine. He'd tell me it was his Zen time."

I blinked back tears and stood up straighter as if that would give me strength. "I-I liked him, too," I stammered. "He gave me good advice." I tilted back my head to prevent tears from sliding down my face.

She smiled graciously at me, gave me her tissue, and turned to The Gym. "It was only because of your book that he came back this year. He told me you'd be the one who saves The Gym."

I glanced at her crumpled tissue in my hand and hugged her when she walked into me with her arms out. "Thank you."

Karen patted my back softly and looked up at me with a tired smile. "The tissue was for you," she said before walking away.

Ten minutes later, I sighed back at my desk, grateful I'd met Walter. I couldn't help pondering the parallels in our lives, unable to deny my life was playing out eerily like his. Needing to move my thoughts along, I changed the air filters and noticed a text from Kristen. *I can explain why I couldn't talk on Friday night.* (sad emoji) *Call me.*

Thirty minutes after that, she called me. My shoulders stiffened, contemplating what to do. I was still confused about too much having to do with Friday and sighed, thinking about Christina. Just before the call went to voicemail, I answered: "Hey—"

"I told Steven we had sex." She drew in a shaking breath and let it out slowly as I straightened in the office chair, speechless. After a moment, she continued. Her voice incredulous and insulting: "Are you there? Do you even know who Steven is?"

I frowned. "Why would you wait until now to tell your boyfriend we had sex back in January?"

She coughed. "Because it's been wearing on me for six months and blew up on Friday," she said, getting on with it. "That's why I was edgy when I heard the news about Christina." Kristen took a sharp breath, then segued seamlessly into apology mode before losing it again. "I've been trying to tell you all weekend. I'm sorry. But I can't believe you thought I was in cahoots with Hook." My muscles twitched when I put her on speaker and told her I didn't want to hear Hook's name. "Well, I'm sure you don't want to hear Steven's either, but he suspected something happened between us that night. I mean, he knew about your book and The Gym and that we would chat."

I considered that. "Chat?"

"Shut up. It makes it easier for me if I don't spell everything out."

"Couldn't you have told him we'd gotten too close and not spelled out that we had sex?"

"No. The MS you sent me fucked him up," she proclaimed and blew out what sounded like smoke.

I gazed at my iPhone as if we were Face Timing each other and said, "Are you smoking?"

"I'm stressed out," she answered, blowing out another drag. "He began checking my texts, looking for more of your boyish charm. I couldn't take it anymore. Steven agrees that I was a diversion to the abrupt end of your little yoga girl fling."

"Because we got friendly?" I stammered confusedly.

"And started flirting," she said faintly. "And then that night happened—"

"It wouldn't have if you'd mentioned him before it." I eased myself off the chair in need of fresh air. When I walked out to the bench, she changed the subject back to Christina. My sun-strained eyes stared straight ahead. Kristen wasn't shocked that I hadn't heard a peep from Christina or the landlord and then inquired about The Gym's fate. I could tell she did not think this would end favorably for me, so I looked to end the call. "I am sorry about your boyfriend. But I'm on drama overload and must get going."

She sighed. "Well, keep collecting those notes on your notepad. Soon, you'll realize this girl drama is the foundation of your sequel."

"How so?" I asked.

"These experiences will better prepare you for the day you meet her. The one."

"Well, I hope she finds her way into the storyline before we hit eight-hundred-pages."

"Patience, Larry. Many chapters will close without closure. It's life." A door slammed. "Shit," Kristen breathed out. "It's Steven—"

Click.

TWENTY-FIVE

THE CALL

JUNE 20, 2017
THE GYM

The next morning, right after Allie's Zumba class, Julie, the local representative for the property management company, wandered in. She looked up at the new picture wall, and with her puzzled expression came a prickling of self-doubt and anxiety. Then the office line rang, and she seemed startled. "Good morning, The Gym," I answered, eyeing her curiously while only hearing a bird call. "Whibbles, I can't talk."

"Is this the leader—"

Click.

Julie placed her clipboard on the check-in counter with a raised eyebrow and her iPhone against her ear. She gave me a small smile but still looked annoyed. "Larry, does your office line work?"

I blinked at her befuddled gaze. "Yes, I just answered it," I said, doing my best to leave agitation out of my voice.

She shook her head. "My office said it was disconnected."

"If they don't help me today, it will be," I said, panic rising in my voice. "Can they call me back?" She nodded, and it rang again. It was Whibbles.

Julie said, "Is it my office?"

"No, it's Whibbles." I put the phone back on the charger and turned to the office door.

Allie drifted in, holding her hula hoop. "Are we going to Jake's on Thursday?" she asked and looked up at Julie standing at the check-in counter. They stared at each other with identical expressions of surprise, which tickled me. Then my iPhone rang, and my stomach clenched. It was the call I was waiting for. I informed Julie it was her boss and ran outside to get a better signal.

Julie looked up, languidly. "Oh…good…"

The smell of rain lingered in the air as the gentle breeze soothed my frayed nerves. I could taste the salt of the ocean on my lips as they asked me to explain every significant task and function in my business plan.

It all came down to this moment.

I paced the plaza with my heart pounding in my chest. Serving up answers, I fought for my life, heading back to The Gym as if the bench outside it was the finish line. Twenty minutes later, I delivered my last answer and held my breath. When they laughed, I sensed relief. They confirmed that they would give me the rent subsidy. After thanking them, I collapsed on the bench, and a second later, Allie ran out, fearing the worst. "Lawrence, I saw you were pacing. I'm so sorry."

I took in a slow breath of the moist tropical air, overcome by my emotions. "We did it."

Allie's jaw dropped. "What?" She took a step towards me. "They'll help?" I shushed her and escorted her over to the bicycle rack in front of Fancy Nails to make sure only Wilson would be privy to this news. Afterward, I suggested taking as many pictures of our happy members as possible. She nodded. "Yes, of course, everyone loves the picture tiles." During a collective sigh of relief, my iPhone rang. Allie's green eyes rolled over to it. "Is that Kim?"

I shook my head. "No, it's Linda," I replied. Allie flashed me a look of disappointment, walking inside when I answered. Ironically, Linda was curious about how my date with Kim went. I sensed her becoming increasingly unsettled by my pleasant recap of it and wondered how I could date someone who didn't drink alcohol.

I swallowed hard and stumbled back to the bench. "Well, I had to cut back, and my liver has appreciated it," I said, reading a text from Allie that one of our Mikes—one who is a parrot lover—was looking for me. "I have to get back to The Gym." I jumped up off the bench into an awkward moment of silence. I didn't mention that I was getting a friend-zone vibe from Kim that was a direct result of her interference. She didn't deserve that satisfaction, so I only added, "I have to go."

"I'd like to continue this conversation," said Linda, as my fit grey-haired parrot loving friend opened the door for me. "I'm going to Riverside Café for lunch. Can I call you later?"

I hesitated. "Sure."

Click.

Holding the door, Mike quickly said, "Larry, do you remember me telling you that I chase my parrot, Ollie, with a towel to give her exercise?" I nodded, smiling. "Well, she attacked me last night!" Mike's eyes were wide, and his hand was bandaged. "I had to douse my cut in rubbing alcohol because she also eats her own feces." Just then, another Mike came in with a new office chair to replace the one Bob broke. The timing of his generous donation couldn't have come at a more opportune time. Fading to black, I collapsed on it in need of a sturdy seat. Not to mention the broken chair stuck out like a sore thumb since the office no longer looked like it was furnished from a yard sale. When a third Mike came in—one of our attorneys—Allie ran over and took a picture with him for one of the tiles.

Meanwhile, Wilson strolled in for his shift with yet another Mike. I chuckled, glancing at the check-in screen lit up with his name, and wondered if the universe would explode if another Mike happened to enter the small space. "So, Larry, have the new handles come in?" That Mike was referring to a bad tape job on the handles of a weight machine that looked so ridiculous, I allowed a hotel guest to believe it was a prank. With the other Mikes joining the fun, I emailed the landlord pertinent information they required during the call.

Three hours later, I called Allie and Wilson in for a quick pep talk. Wilson had spoken to Allie before his shift to make sure we were still open, and therefore knew we received the rent relief package. So, with a shit-eating grin, he listened intently as I said, "Well, girl and boy, contrary to popular belief, I know exactly what I'm doing," I winked at Allie, "we live another day…"

"Heeeell yeah, Lawrence," Allie sang while proceeding to strum something on her Ukulele. "Heeeeeeeell yeeah!"

Suddenly it was surreal.

"This is a huge day for us," I continued. "Smile, laugh, and kill them with kindness." I paused when my iPhone pinged with another text from Linda. "We're going to be changing up how we do things. Starting next month, we'll have more membership options. Right now, we need to switch as many members to auto-debit as possible. That's critical—"

Wilson murmured, "Yes, it is—"

"We're also adding a mid-day membership—and we're phasing out the paper towels, but keep that quiet for now. If all goes as planned, we'll transfer over to cloth towels in August."

Allie smiled curiously. "This is awesome, Lawrence."

"I'll have the new pricing tomorrow," I glanced back at Linda's texts. "I have to make a call. Excuse me."

I walked out and called Linda. She answered frantically, "I have thirty seconds. Sheldon showed up early to hang my new ceiling fan."

"I didn't need that update—"

"Listen." She took an erratic breath. "Bill Reed wanted to talk to me when I left Riverside Café. He was with a bearded guy drinking Bud Lights, so I told him I had to run."

"Do you know him?"

"No, but Sheldon told me that Bill knew him from Melbourne Beach. Sheldon knew the bartender who served Bill, the bearded guy, and someone with a goatee yesterday."

"Sounds like Hook and Tillie," I guessed.

I heard a man's voice call her. "Hold on," she whispered. "Shit, I'll call later—"

Click.

Why does this happen to me? I thought and then smiled with a storyline dancing in my head.

TWENTY-SIX

THE NIGHTMARE
THAT WAS A DREAM

JUNE 21, 2017
THE GYM

The next day, Chuck walked by the office with a client and said, "Your long-lost buddy just pulled in." He forced a smile as voices murmured it was The Gym's outspoken liberal, RJ Minelli.

Just as I stood up, he strutted in with the towel he used to rest his elbows on when he'd gab with me at the check-in counter. RJ looked me over for a moment before glancing at another member. "I can't believe Larry's still alive," he said to our retired secret service agent, Randy, before shifting his gaze back to me. "So, how do I look?" Detecting in my eyes that his antics still amused me, he spun around. "Don't be jealous; I'm seventy," he held out his arms. "But someone thought I was in my forties today," he tossed his towel over his shoulder and gently touched the skin on his arm. "It's genetics." He held his arms out again. As I shook my head, they fell to his sides. "What's wrong?"

"Nothing, I'm just envisioning beginning a chapter with your entrance." I smiled. "I'd forgotten how delightfully disturbing it is."

"Stop deflecting," his eyes narrowed at me, "you, smug bastard, and tell me what's wrong?"

I shrugged humoredly. "There are always challenges, but I'm feeling better with everything now."

He shot me a look. "Oh, I know what's wrong with you."

"Please lower your voice," I insisted. "Some people actually come here to work out."

He waved his index finger at me and took a few of his quick little steps around the check-in counter. "A man defined by his penis—which has been in too many vaginas in this tiny town—is bound to slip into a depressed state when it no longer works." His mouth curled into a devious smile when he entered the office. "Am I right?" I stared at him for a few dizzying seconds before we sat down. "Okay, fuck you. One day it won't work, and you'll be devastated."

"I was devastated in *The Show* when Marie said it was shrinking—"

"Oh, did that make my day!" he cried out, seemingly ecstatic. After regaining his composure, he crossed his legs and opened his mouth to speak. A member moaned for Fox News, and he slowly closed it. "It's awful how many racists and bigots are in here," he snarled while gazing up at the new picture wall. "And getting rid of the previous owner's yard sale furniture won't override the Trump stickers on the cars out front." He laughed obnoxiously. "That parking lot alone will prevent anyone with half a brain to walk through your door."

I laughed. "It didn't stop you," I said as Allie texted me. *Are we still on to catch up at Jake's tomorrow?*

RJ looked offended. "I only come here to counsel you."

I cocked an eyebrow and texted Allie back. *Yes, Wilson's coming in at two. And RJ surfaced again and is in rare form!*

RJ tilted his face back to the flickering fluorescent light. "And I'm not just a pretty face. My quick wit stifles the racists." He smirked. "I remember telling your early morning bigot brigade that I don't check in because I deal directly with you." He paused and hit his knee. "That sent Chuck over the edge!" He crossed his arms. "Put your phone down. When I come to see you, I deserve your full attention." I read Allie's reply. *RJ's hilarious and LOVES you.* (smiley face emoji) *Enjoy.*

Cindy peeked her face in the office door. "I hear laughter—"

RJ couldn't spin to her fast enough. "Of course, you do," he jumped up, "I'm counseling him." Cindy grinned curiously. "And it's a daunting challenge considering he lives for only two things."

Cindy's eyebrows arched. "I can't wait to hear this, RJ."

His towel fell to the ground, and as he stepped on it, his index finger rose in the air. "One, wine, preferably red. And two, vagina, preferably under thirty," RJ shot me a sinister stare. "He loves that even more. A reckless fornicator, he is, my dear." Cindy took a few steps in, clapping her hands as if she were gifted a ticket to the circus, and RJ shot me out of a cannon in a clown suit. Her amused state fueled RJ's flame. "Back in October, I used to give him three counseling sessions a week. Through his dark swirling chaos was a yoga instructor who came in with fire in her eyes one day and fuck me eyes the next. But the sick bastard was tickled, not knowing if he was going to be shot or fucked." My eyes slowly closed when Cindy let out a guffaw eating this up. "By December, I ended my counseling sessions with him because he joined a couple of dating sites. It was then I had to douse the place in muriatic acid."

I winced and then jumped up when the expression on a member's face went from being humored to mortified. "Okay, the show's over. Cindy, give me your keys, and I'll pull your fancy sports car up," I said with a smile. "And RJ, go home and moisturize your beautiful oil olive skin—"

"See," RJ shouted, interrupting me. "These damn Republicans always ruin our good time."

At that point, RJ received a call. He took his quick little steps outside, and there was a sense of relief in the atmosphere. I chuckled as Matty pedaled a spin bike, holding her hands up as if her prayers were answered.

Meanwhile, Cindy lingered in the office chatting about her writing project before shocking me with news of her impending move to Vero Beach. "I love this vibe, and the picture walls look great, Larry." I spun my chair and looked up at her expectantly, "I'll pay month to month until it's all finalized," she said as she sighed. After reminiscing for a few more minutes, she added, "I will miss you..." she held out her arms.

"I'll miss you too, Cindy," I said, and we hugged goodbye.

In the summer sunlight streaming through the windows, Matty then pointed out a dusty corner that needed to be cleaned as Patty "Cakes" Miller caught my eye to chat after her spin class. We had discussed adding a Sunday spin class, and she recommended that I interview a younger spin instructor named Gemma Sloan. When she divulged how taxing years of cycling were on her body, I got the impression this year would be the forty-somethings last. "I'll have Gemma reach out to you, Larry," Patty said.

I thanked her and answered the office line. "Good morning, The Gym…" I only heard our notorious bird call. "Hey, Whibbles…"

"Is this the leader?"

I pinched the bridge of my nose. "Yes, Whibbles."

"Well, I just wanted to thank you for saving The Gym."

I tugged at my T-shirt, taken aback by his statement. "I'm starting to think The Gym saved me."

"Odd things happen to us on our way through life, but a good leader stays strong. Even when it gets dark," he said with another bird call. "I'll see you before I go to lunch at the Apron's station at Publix."

I exhaled. "Okay, thanks."

Click.

Minutes later, my favorite nurse, Nicole Tona, checked in. A smile always formed on my face when she'd walk in, gifting The Gym her positive energy. Since the attractive thirty-six-year-old didn't have a member tile up, I grabbed my social media gal pal, Dara, for a photoshoot by the free weights. With that came more laughter as Nicole beamed. "Larry, what do you want me to do?"

"Grab a couple of dumbbells, swing your ponytail, and smile!" With a couple of calming breaths, she did, and we got another adorable shot for the wall.

An hour after that, Marie implored me to cut back on all spending. My overhead had increased steadily while our sales nosedived, which immediately ate into the rent relief package. The only time I smiled was when one of my members checked in.

Amid the clamor of obligations, I felt sentimental regard for The Gym. It took a year to realize how much I cared about these people. Ironically though, it was a double-edged sword, a new beginning with insurmountable odds. I sat there for a long time, lost in that thought.

And then Kristen texted: *Just checking in. Have you heard anything further from Hook? Any other offers for The Gym?*

• • •

That evening darkened quickly. The summer sky grew ominous as I questioned if the rent relief package came too late. Was my debt too high? Should I have taken Hook's offer? Kristen's text had haunted me for the rest of the day…

After closing The Gym, I felt the need to release some stress while also sweating out a year's worth of toxins. I hit the quick-start button on a treadmill. With a deep breath, I began jogging—faster and faster. I ran through the memories of my playlist—songs from The Chainsmokers and Ed Sheeran sparked furious flashbacks before I blinked away a vision of Maya singing the Peter Pan song.

Then the lights flickered. A sudden chill went up my spine. I slowed the treadmill and noticed a car racing across the empty parking lot.

The wind began to howl.

There was danger in the air.

The car turned and sped towards The Gym.

I hit the stop button and flew off the treadmill into the white caps of the beach mural, momentarily blinded by the car's headlights. It screeched to a stop inches from the doors. I swallowed, took a breath, and tried to calm down. My heart pounded in my chest when the engine reeved louder. Sweat poured into my eyes as a text flashed up.

I wiped them and read it. *Hook's lost his mind! Run!!*

The double doors burst open. Through the pounding rain emerged the silhouette of a menacing figure against the car's headlights. It was Captain Hook. His face was dark, and his beard flowed into his black curly hair. He slowly advanced, gripping a Flintlock pistol with his good hand. "Aye," he said. "You could've been freed from The Gym! I gave you an out, but you only laughed at me." A curdling smile lit up his swarthy face as the sinister man brandished his hook threateningly. "Now it's time you die, Pan Man—" his jaw clenched as a trail of pixie light flashed by him and all around me. In an instant, the light vanished, and the rain stopped. A spellbinding hush had fallen over The Gym.

All I could hear was the whisper of my heart. And the loveliest tinkle of bells.

"Allison," Hook called softly. A petite figure came out of the darkness.

My heart skipped a beat.

It was Allison Tinke exquisitely gowned in a green leaf, in which her figure could be seen to the best advantage. Pixie dust fell as the beautiful blonde looked up at me. I leaned forward, took her chin in my hand, and her glistening blue eyes opened to her soul.

The magical dust fell harder. It hadn't fallen like this in seven years.

I caught my breath and smiled. "Jeez, it took you long enough…"

Her bells tinkled with delight.

Our moment of bliss was interrupted by Hook's gravelly voice. "Get your hands off her, Pan Man." I twisted to him. "She was the reason I stopped coming to The Gym. The timing wasn't right for us back then." He pointed the gun at me and gritted his teeth. "But now she needs what I have. Money!" She trembled, shaking her pretty little head. "So, back away from her broke boy—"

I held up my tiny sword that magically appeared on a rope around my waist. "No!" I yelled. "She's coming with me back to my sacred Never Land, Hook." I turned back to her and whispered, "Unfortunately, I am broke. Is that a problem?" She shook her head vigorously. "Good, because I'd love to have wine time with you somewhere between reality and all we've ever dreamed…" her eyes sparkled with delight.

And then Hook pulled the trigger—BANG!

My eyes shot open. It took me a second to realize I was dreaming. I took a deep breath, flipped my damp pillow over, and then grinned when that same trail of pixie light flashed by my window awake.

TWENTY-SEVEN

IT'S TIME FOR A LITTLE PIXIE DUST

JUNE 22, 2017
JAKE'S CRAB SHACK
It was ten hours later.

After a much-needed dip in the warm waters of Melbourne Beach, I collapsed on a towel, unable to get the vision of Allison Tinke out of my head. I checked the time as two teenage girls squeezed suntan lotion onto their fingers singing the lyrics to "Despacito" when Allie called. I answered with wet hands. "Hey, Allie Gi—" and almost dropped the call in the sand.

"Lawrence?"

"Sorry, I almost dropped you."

"I'm heading to Jake's now. Where are you?"

"Across the street at the beach."

"You better not be backing out," she huffed. "We need to catch up on all this drama."

I snickered. "I'll be ordering the wine by two."

"Good. See you in fifteen minutes."

"See you soon, ya silly goose."

Click.

I parked in front of The Gym and walked across the parking lot to Jake's Crab Shack, antsy to hear Allie's take on everything. After ordering a bottle, I answered Wilson's call. "Hey, Wilson."

"I convinced Bud and Linda to sign up for auto-debit," he stated proudly. "They also invited us to a bible study at the airline pilot, Joe's."

"Wilson," I moaned. "Stick to the memberships."

"Sorry, pilot Joe and German Joe will remain annual." He shuffled pages. "And we actually have new memberships to enter onto the ledger."

I smiled. "Imagine that..."

Wilson laughed. "I'll update you later."

Click.

I took a breath and noticed three new messages on POF from the same women I had no interest in talking to the week before. Feeling certain it was time for a break; I decided to delete my last dating site app. When I hit the POF icon, there was newfound inner peace.

Minutes later, I slumped in the chair, frustrated by the degree of difficulty for such a simple objective. I placed my iPhone on the table when a petite-verging-on-emaciated waitress walked over with the wine. She looked familiar but wasn't the waitress I ordered from. My chin lifted to her when she struggled to open the bottle. "You own The Gym. I served you guys the night you came in wasted last month." Her hands were shaking, and she proceeded to destroy the cork while filling my glass in one motion.

I shifted my legs around the chair. "It's good to see you," I said with drops of wine still dripping on the table. "Maybe we should wipe the bottle." I grabbed my iPhone and smiled at her.

The waitress shifted behind me as I went back to the POF app. When I turned to her, she leaned over my shoulder and said, "I went to see Wonder Woman last night and was ruined on some wacky weed." She paused as an older man fell off a barstool, got up, did a jig, and stumbled out. Then she pointed to the app. "So, you found love?"

I blinked slowly and took a long sip because I needed one. "No, why?" I sputtered and pulled a piece of cork off my tongue, wondering if I should go to the bathroom and pull the fire alarm.

"I think they deliberately make it impossible to leave the site," she whispered.

I paused, staring at her. The line between her brows was a deep crevasse. "I agree," I said and leaned back, "I had no idea how daunting a challenge this would be." I raised my glass to her. "So, I'll just concentrate on enjoying this. Cheers."

The waitress raised her eyebrows—or what was left of them, smiled, and stumbled off when Allie strolled in. We clinked glasses to our momentous week, and she got right to it. "Okay, so let's start with Kim," Allie insisted. "I'm thinking you two hang out but only as friends."

I took another sip thoughtfully. "I want to disagree," I confessed. "But can't."

"Moving on, I'm glad you didn't sleep with Christina. Money makes people do desperate things." She paused and shook her head, grinning. "And the Cruella and Hook drama is Kristen's imagination gone wild."

I let out a weary sigh, then tried to explain. "Well, there might be something to it. Linda recently saw Bill Reed with Hook and Tillie." I swirled my wine in the glass. "What do you make of that?"

Her chin lifted from her glass. "Hook's still plotting to kill you, Pan!" she laughed.

"Wait till you hear about my dream—"

"Seriously, Hook's a coward. He sends other people to do his dirty work." Her eyes widened. "But it would be hilarious if Bill found out about you and Linda, knowing about your fling with Maya." I sat back, pondering that, when Allie added, "Is Bill on Facebook with Linda?"

I shook my head, although unsure, and called her. Linda answered as Lucy, "Ricky!"

I took a shuddering breath. "Lucy, are you on Facebook with Bill?" Allie stuck her finger in her mouth, and I took the call off speaker. Within seconds, Linda informed me that she accepted Bill's friend request because she didn't want any issues when she ran into him. She did so in her serious Linda voice. "Okay," I added, mindful I should end the call. "I'll call you later—"

"Why are you asking?" Linda insisted.

"I'm out with Allie," I explained. "I'll call you—" she angrily interrupted me.

"I want to know why you're asking."

"A girl Bill dated reached out to me while they were technically together," I said quickly and held my breath. Then a cabinet door slammed shut on her end of the line.

Allie rolled her eyes.

"Was this one the young crazies you slept with?" Linda snapped as *The Dark One* appeared.

I said, "She isn't crazy—" Linda slammed another cabinet door.

"Sheldon's right. Your life is and will always be wine, women, and chaos—"

Click.

Panicked, I fidgeted in the chair. My inner peace had been disrupted. I lost all patience as *The Dark One* pulled up a chair and whispered in my ear, *Wine, Women, and Chaos would make a great book title, Sport!* I winced, thinking about Lauren and Jerry, my separation, and my new life on this little sandbar. For a year now, I woke up, hungover from too many wine times with nothing but a notepad full of shimmering insanity for a sequel. Where is the girl who saves me? That was my dream—my storyline. What page am I even on? What kind of story am I writing? I wasn't going for scary fucking ugly, but it sure seems to be following me. There were things I figured out and forgot in an instant of doubt. The clock was ticking. Fifty was thirty-eight days away, and I didn't want to be walking in Walter Clément's footsteps. I could feel beads of perspiration forming on my forehead. Allie kicked my Converse under the table. "Lawrence, you're going to the dark side again," she said, clapping once. "Snap out of it." Her head tilted slightly. "Has your publisher been in touch with you about the sequel?"

I took a breath. "Yes, I committed to it, but there's no end to this storyline in sight."

Her eyebrows arched. "Patience. The material from your dating experience is necessary. It's relatable life. Everyone enjoys that."

I shrugged. "True, but I'm a sucker for happy endings…the guy gets the girl, she saves him from himself, and the second star to the right shines bright in the night, again." I raised my glass. "The End."

She smiled at me. "Well then, I guess this is the part of the story that needs a little pixie dust," Allie joked as I leaned back, musing my dream.

I couldn't help but laugh. "Magic happens when you believe, Allie Girl!" I said, feeling better as if that magical golden glitter was falling on us.

We clinked glasses again, and Allie said, "To a little pixie dust." She glanced at my iPhone on the table when I received another POF notification.

I picked it up. "I just tried deleting my profile on here," I murmured and opened it. "It's been the same women for weeks—" my heart skipped a beat. Over the screen, I could see Allie's mouth moving but only heard the whisper of my heart. And the loveliest tinkle of bells. Just like in my dream.

Then Allie kicked my Converse again. "Lawrence, who is it?"

I smiled. "It's Allison...Allison Tinke...r Bell..."

TWENTY-EIGHT

ALLISON TINKE-R BELL

JUNE 23, 2017

THE GYM

The next morning, I was eager to get to The Gym.

With the sun rapidly rising over the dunes, I took a hard right into the parking lot on an animated call with Allie about Allison and noticed the Ripper getting out of his old police car. He was just the guy I was hoping to see. I pulled in next to him as Diane's Friday morning Pilates class began. "Allie Girl," I said, cutting her off. "I have to go—"

She ignored me. "And let's not forget Bill was engaged to Allison. So, think about a plot twist that has Bill finding out that you are dating his true love…after the drama with Maya and Linda."

I drew in a breath and slowly said, "Let me call you back."

"Ugh. You better—"

Click.

I hopped out of my Kia, and the Ripper lumbered over with an odd smile. "I hope you're not hungover because I'm bringing in a guy who can fix your computers." He gave me a fist pump. "His name is Rich Crowley. No relation to Michelle or," he hesitated, thinking, "what's the nickname you came up for her, Cruella?" He chuckled. "I ran into her at Squid Lips. She told me she had a newfound respect for you. I was scared to ask…"

I changed the subject. "Hey, do you know Allison Tinke?"

The Ripper paused with a startled look. "Yeah," he replied while stiffening slightly. "She was a member of The Gym when I helped her through her divorce. Soon after, Bill Reed talked her into moving to Vero," he snickered, nudging me on the shoulder. "Reed won't be back at The Gym, thanks to you. So, how's that Lucy…Linda chick you're on Facebook with?"

I shook my head. "Same sitcom—stuck in reruns."

The Ripper smiled as if he understood. "A writer is the sum of their experiences, and yours are unfuckingreal." His eyes bulged as a more concerned look flashed across his face. "So, why are you asking about Allison?"

I took a breath, unable to wipe the smile off my face. "She reached out to me on POF."

At that moment, Louis and Lenny—two of our favorite old school surfers—were heading to Pilates class and shouted out their approval for the new picture walls. We walked up to the door, and I held it for them. "Morning, guys," I said with great enthusiasm.

"Morning Larry," they said in unison before Louis added, "You should change the name of this place to Larry's Gym. Things are looking up," he patted me on the back. "Just don't raise the prices." We laughed, and the Ripper pointed to Rich. The eighty-year-old was sitting in an office chair with a smile anyone would trust. "Larry, this is Rich," said the Ripper. We shook hands, quickly hitting it off before Rich shifted his gaze to one of the old computers. With determination, he laid out his plan to get us up to speed.

With an undeniable buzz in the air, I noticed another message from Allison. She wanted to talk. The excitement of this moment had me preoccupied. I only looked up when Wilson chuckled. "Allie told me about Allison Tinke-r Bell. I'm happy for you."

"Relax," I said anxiously. "I haven't met her yet."

"You will." He flipped his hair back and lowered his voice. "Oh, I stashed a case of beer in the electric room. We're heading to the beach, but I forgot the chips," he grinned, "I'll be right back."

I nodded as Stacy Storm, another one of our cherished members, wanted to add her son to her membership. "Hey, Larry!" Stacy chirped, checking in. "I'd like to add my son, Blake."

"Hey, Blake." I shook the handsome young surfer's hand. "How's the summer so far?"

Blake beamed. "Good. I'm surfing."

"That's awesome." My gaze shifted to Stacy. "So, Stace...we're adding one student to yours?" When I ran the fit forty-something mom's credit card, I heard a familiar voice shout out to change a channel to WESH TWO. Ironically, it was Allison's old neighbor when she was married and living in Melbourne Beach.

Amused by it all, I walked under the line of TVs reporting on President Trump's Travel Ban and held up the remote. "Mary Ann," I said, changing the channel. "You crack me up."

"Oh, why, Larry?"

"Because I get a million channel requests, but never one for channel two," I admitted, chuckling.

Mary Ann lifted her head. Her fair skin was flushed. "Oh, I know," she breathed out. "I just love WESH TWO!" She kept the elliptical going at a quick rate and somehow added, "And thanks for putting me on a tile. I love them, Larry. What a great idea."

I glanced in the yoga studio and only saw our dance instructor Gary and his wife, Kathleen. I had no recollection of Diane's classes ending and then blinked at the time. It was twelve-thirty. I smiled, still thinking about Allison, and walked over to Joey and Vinny at the free weights. "Boys, can we do another photoshoot for some more tiles?"

Vinny said, "No doubt, Larry..." as Joey said, "Shirts on or off?"

"Off..." I replied, switching to my camera.

"Alright...alright, alright," Joey added, ripping his tank top off in one quick motion.

After that photo op, I had dozed off in the office when I heard the bell ring on the door. I rubbed my face when Rich Crowley walked in with a stack of papers. "Hey boss," he said as if we'd known each other for a lifetime. "I printed out some instructions should the system crash again. And just in case I'm not home, I'm leaving Francis's cell number. Francis is my wife."

I gazed at him and smiled. "Thank you, Rich."

Rich sat down to check one of the computers when my gym friend, Laura Lox, checked in. "I left my review for *The Show* on Goodreads," she said with a warm smile.

"Thank you. I haven't done enough to promote it lately."

Laura nodded. "When's the sequel going to be ready?"

"Well, my notepad is almost full," I said, thinking about Allison. "Hopefully, I'll end up with the story I envisioned soon."

She smiled. "I'm rooting for you, Larry." She pointed to the picture wall in the office. "And The Gym looks great," she said, walking on to her workout.

Three hours later, at just before four o'clock, Allie and Wilson burst through the door suntanned and buzzed. Allie jumped in a chair with her hula hoop when Wilson tossed a Frisbee at me. "Allison Tinke-r Bell!" he shouted. His voice was more animated than it should've been. "Tinker Beeell…"

"You two are hammered," I checked Allie's eyes. "And stoned."

Allie put on her sunglasses and started giggling. "Oh, Lawrence," she pulled her sandy feet up on the chair. "The second star to the right shines in the night for you, to tell you that the dreams you have really can come true…Allison Tinke-r Beeeeell!" she slurred into laughter.

TWENTY-NINE

A DOSE OF REALITY
BRINGS HEARTACHE

JUNE 24, 2017
MY HOUSE

At nine the next morning, Allie called me as I had completed *The Gym's* prologue. With a smile, I answered before the call went to voicemail. "Morning, Allie Girl," I said after a moment.

"Hold on," she replied, sounding irritated.

My nerves shuddered when I pictured her hungover in her bed. "Please tell me you're at The Gym."

"Yes, calm down," said Allie coldly. "I'm walking out to the bench." I heard voices and poured a cup of coffee before she continued, "Thanks for having that big guy, John, with the leaf blower come in and clean."

I frowned, thinking for a few seconds. "John's the old owner and cleans because you don't—"

"We have a bunch of students signing up for our summer special."

"Great," I said. "But if the place is dirty, it takes away from the fresh paint and pictures."

She hesitated. "These old people just love to bitch—"

"Allie," I said, cutting her off. "What's wrong?"

She sighed. "Chuck pulled me aside, sipping his damn Monster Energy drink, and told me I'm wasting my life at The Gym." She paused, and I sat back down at the kitchen table, listening. "The other day, Fern asked me if I ever thought about going back home. I started feeling better about things. Now, I'm hungover and hurt."

I placed up my Tink mug down, feeling vaguely disappointed by this. "People say a lot of things, Allie," I said solemnly. "You have your dreams, and I have a bigger plan for The Gym that includes you."

"I love this place mainly because of you!" she exclaimed. "And everyone knows your bigger plan for The Gym is your sequel to *The Show*."

I envisioned her smiling her smug twenty-something smile and said, "That's part of it. So, please stay positive." I held my breath, awaiting her response.

She signed. "I still prefer working nights," Allie said earnestly as someone began a conversation with her. Her voice was muffled. Seconds later, she continued, "Sorry. So, Donna Richards—the grey-haired lady who takes my Zumba class—is going to ask you to become a Zumba instructor."

Allie seemed shocked that I laughed outright, breaking the tension somewhat. "She already did," I said. "I thought it was a great idea. She has a lot of passion."

"I'm too hungover to argue, but holy shit Lawrence," she giggled, "I'm sorry, I guess I need to laugh. Are you drinking coffee out of your Tinker Bell mug?" I divulged Maya's theory that it was a teaser for the sequel, which continued to lighten the mood. "Maya also brought up a scenario with Allison Tinke if my memory serves me right. One that has begun playing out as your reality." She chortled. "It's the pixie dust and would have anyone believing. So, have you made plans for that wine time with your little Tinker Bell, Allison?"

I waited for a moment, searching for the right words. "Not yet. So, come back to reality for a bit. Tonight, I'm seeing Kim."

"Shit," she gasped. "Someone's at the check-in counter—"
Click.

After mulling that over, I scrambled a couple of eggs. Then I continued writing. Although I hadn't heard from Kristen in nearly a week, her voice was in my head. Checking my notepad, I started the first chapter exactly where she advised me to; on that dark night in January with her. Even though I had my detailed notes, I called Kristen in search of anything I might have missed. I figured there was a good shot she was with her boyfriend, but I willed her to answer, and she did.

Happy to hear from me and able to talk, she ran through the night with dialogue that included—my penis—Wendy having my shadow—and channeling my rage. When I hung up, it all felt right.

A long hour later, I walked out to the pool deck, responding to Lauren and Jerry's text about dinner on Sunday night. I smiled but then took a breath, all at once concerned about Marie, and texted her.

Minutes later, she responded as she had when we'd meet for a glass of wine swearing, she was fine. Happy, in fact. I sat back down, startled when she then called me. "Hey…" I answered. "So, everything's okay?"

"I told you it was," Marie replied hastily. "So, are you taking the kids to dinner tonight?"

I hesitated.

"No, tomorrow."

"So, are you going out with that Linda…Lucy, chick?" she laughed. "Not that I care. Watch the money, though. Your members can't lift weights in the dark…without air."

I sighed. "I know," I said quietly. "I will—"

"How's your drinking been?" she added quickly.

"Much less. I met a girl who doesn't drink."

"Really?" she said. Her voice was full of sarcasm. "Okay, have a great night!"

My heart sank. "You, too."

Click.

When I wandered back inside, there was a new atmosphere of wistfulness about the house that made my heart ache. I splashed cold water on my face at the bathroom sink, thinking I would grow old with her in this house.

Then I crashed on my bed and fell asleep for an hour, only to be awoken by a call from Jerry. He was with Marie finalizing plans to tour some Universities in August while focused on FSU. Once I confirmed I would go with them, Marie began spouting out dates in the background. Jerry quickly informed me he'd call me back in the morning. I hung up and wandered outside. The summer night had a smile of light but no sign of my second star to the right.

I walked back into the house, and Marie texted me again.

Lying in bed, I thought about the year we'd been separated, and the years we tried to make it work. I could've easily said the grass isn't greener on the other side. But I didn't. I processed it all, envisioning a long road ahead, but one I was sure of. Two happy homes for Lauren and Jerry were better than one in emotional unrest. It was time to keep the amazing memories, learn from the ones that weren't, and start anew.

THIRTY

SUNDAY UNFUNDAY

JUNE 25, 2017
MY HOUSE/THE GYM

The next morning, I awoke to *The Dark One* in my ear. *Rise and shine, Sport! You have another POF nymphomaniac who wants to meet up.* I rolled over. *Come on.* I pulled the sheet over my head. *Kim's never going to be more than a friend; Lucy's a tired sitcom stuck in reruns, and you still haven't met Tinker Bell.*

Four hours later, Allison informed me, she had her two girls every Friday night. We had been looking at possible dates to meet up, and I thought that was strange. *Is she making up excuses not to meet?* I wondered. Of course, I had not been subjected to this next phase of the dating process and sought advisement. After explaining my concerns, I relaxed when a divorced member insisted it all depended on their parenting plan. With those words, Allie jumped into the other office chair. "Lawrence, do you really want to get involved with someone who has a seven and nine-year-old?" she asked. Her tone was serious.

"It's way too early to be asked that," I replied and sighed.

"It could be too late if Allison turns out to be who you think she is."

I contemplated that. "If she is, I wouldn't have a problem with her girls."

"Well, if that's the case, are you going to start calling her Allie?"

I blinked, thinking about too much. "What?"

"Allie is short for Allison."

I straightened myself up. "I know," I choked out. "And no…I mean, I haven't even met her yet."

I craved butterflies and goosebumps, but with no actual date set to meet Allison, I began looking backward again. The moments I missed had me flipping the wine-stained pages of my notepad, haunted by the names.

Meanwhile, Kristen was aware I had finished the first chapter of *The Gym* and begged me to read it. An hour after I sent it, she informed me that her boyfriend was furious. *The Dark One* howled, *You do realize you will have to rewrite the prologue and first chapter if this Tinker Bell twist doesn't pan out. Hahaha! Get it, Pan—out! Hahahaha!*

Increasingly irritated, I texted Kristen. When she didn't respond, I broke away from it all to take a shower. Ten minutes after that, I noticed a text from a number I didn't recognize. It was Kristen. *Hey, it's me. I'm using my friend's phone. Don't be upset. Your only take away should be that the chapter worked. It's life! This actually helped my relationship, but I won't be able to text you like I used to, so stay focused.* (heart emoji) *Kristen.*

My thoughts were too scattered to grasp anything. I captured it on my notepad and raced away from it all to meet my kids at Carrabba's.

During dinner, I received a message from my college sweetheart, Meg. *Great timing,* I thought and smiled awkwardly at Jerry. After three more messages, it was obvious Meg wanted to talk.

When I got home, she called me. The conversation sparked memories, which made it seem like yesterday that we were young and in love. Yet, in a way that made it seem like eons ago. Life does not stand still.

I blinked with the realization that this was relevant to *The Gym's* storyline and ran for my notepad. When I returned, Meg was carrying on about not being invited to my wedding. "Marie was not going to have me there. Do you remember—"

"You can't blame Marie," I interrupted her. "Our communication was unexplainable."

Meg hesitated.

"Why do so many songs remind me of you?"

My thoughts flashed back to the night that could have changed our lives forever. "Those mix-tapes were our storyline."

"Our never-ending love story…"

I took a much-needed sip of water. "Indeed."

Seconds later, I got an unexpected tingly feeling when she turned up her stereo. The song playing was "Don't Walk Away" by Rick Springfield. I sang it to her as it blared out of an old boombox the first weekend we met. It was a Sunday night, and her soccer player boyfriend was coming back from a road trip on Monday. "I still see you singing this to me," said Meg in her Cincinnati accent.

"I still see you looking back at me while walking away with him."

She let the lyrics fill my head and then became choked up. "I felt guilt. I didn't expect to meet you—"

"Are we really rehashing this again?"

"I didn't know how to deal with my feelings, I...," she paused, overwhelmed with emotion. "I-I can't believe you said that..."

At that point, I knew something was wrong. "I'm sorry."

Meg took a calming breath. After a long moment, she said, "Where did all the years go, Lars?" Staring at an old picture of us from that memorable night, she admitted that she was sick. I feared the worst when she refused to talk about it while bringing up a friend who had cancer.

I thought about my older sister battling the disease and said, "Mary Ann...my older sister overcame cancer—"

"I know both of your sister's names, Lars."

"Yes. Well, she had a positive mindset and is better—"

"I'm glad," said Meg, ambiguously. "But I called for an escape. I wanted to hear your laugh and these old songs." With those words, I became emotional. In a low voice, she continued, "I never thought once upon a time would mean so much. I often wish I could go back and do things differently."

"Such as?"

"Not walking away..."

Again, the call went quiet.

I cleared my throat. "The last time we spoke, you told me your job takes you all over. You wanted to meet up—"

"I can't." She coughed. "Lars, my goal wasn't to ruin your Sunday."

My mind raced backward as I was clutching at some last hope. "Right after I bought The Gym, you mentioned we could meet up in

Orlando," I choked out. My mouth was still dry, impatiently waiting for her response.

I took another sip of water.

Finally, she said, "Last summer would've worked, but you were busy being an author and a new gym owner."

A chill shot up my spine when I looked at Meg's picture keenly. I vaguely remembered her insisting we meet. She had manipulated her schedule to stay in Orlando overnight, but I couldn't because of a book signing. We didn't speak for six months. And now, six months after that, regretfully, I said, "I had planned on us getting together. This year has been…a lot." I paused, shaking. "Anyway, is it a possibility now?"

"No, lost boy…" a tear fell on our faded pictures as she added, "You're still a hopeless romantic. What you need to remember is that we weren't looking for love; we just found each other and laughed in one hell of a magical moment."

"We did." I took a long breath and wiped my eyes.

"Life's funny," she said solemnly. "Thirty years later, and I'm still hiding from my significant other to steal a moment with you." She sighed. "Try not to fuck up another woman's life…Peter."

I felt myself tense, musing Allison. "I don't plan on saying goodbye to this one—"

"Sometimes, it's not the goodbye that hurts," Meg said softly. "It's the songs that spark the flashbacks and memories that follow…"

Her voice faded off, and I glanced impatiently at my iPhone.

Time stood still for a moment.

Then two hours went by in a flash. I assured her I would call in a few days, but I knew this was it when she didn't respond. When we hung up, I blinked back tears for another hour, but to my relief, I finally drifted off to sleep.

An hour later, I awoke to the ping of another text from her: *They say you spend your whole life rewriting the first poem you ever loved. I believe that to be true.*

Love Meg

THIRTY-ONE

A CHANGE IN PERSPECTIVE

JUNE 26, 2017
THE GYM

Another Monday came too quickly. While still digesting the night before, I ended up in an interesting conversation with an investment banker from Boston. He was vacationing in Melbourne Beach with his much younger girlfriend and seemed to have an eye for the ladies, as they did for him. After joking with two hotel guests, the handsome man shifted his deep blue eyes back to me when his iPhone rang. With what appeared to be a genuine smile, he informed me it was his wife and answered. Nonchalantly, I peeked at his girlfriend on a treadmill. My first thought was that he was having an affair. After he spoke to his wife, I thought differently. "I'm sorry about that," he said to me when the call ended. "We've been separated, and I wanted to wish my kids a happy summer. They just arrived at the Cape (Cod)."

Promptly, he explained his situation as if we were kindred spirits. At any rate, I felt unsettled and then told him mine. When it became difficult to deny our stories were too similar for my liking, he nodded sympathetically. "So, dating here must be quite the experience," he said.

I shrugged. "It's produced some book-worthy material."

His eyes grew wide. "I'll bet," he replied. "We're staying with my girlfriend's mother, and when we took her to church, she pointed out three couples that were having affairs before communion." He looked behind him and lowered his voice. "The blond on the last treadmill looks like one of them. Has she been on vacation recently?"

I glanced at the woman. "She only recently joined The Gym," I said. "Why?"

He laughed. "If it's her, she posted their family vacation on Facebook right after going on a business trip with the boss she's having an affair with." I stared at him, eyes wide, mouth open, picturing this all going down during mass, and bit down on my lip. "I believe divorce should be a last resort option," he continued. "But there are too many people who would rather live a lie while throwing stones from a glass house." His voice tinged with humility. "So, how long have you been married?"

"Twenty-three years," I mumbled, in need of smelling salts.

"And you said you'd been separated for one?"

I replied with a groan.

He pulled his hand through his thick greying hair. "Before it's all over, you'll have material for three books," he said and looked faintly amused. "We enjoyed your first book. When we got here last week, one of your members recommended it." Glancing back at the lady, he added, "Be patient. It's taken me a lot longer than I expected."

I swallowed. "So, when did you start dating in this process?"

"Once we were separated," he replied. His eyes were intent, and his voice was serious. "Hey…you okay?"

"I never thought I'd be divorced," I said, feeling clammy.

He glanced over my shoulder. "Shit," he whispered.

"What—" I paused when he stiffened against a spin bike and caught his girlfriend coming in hot.

"Hi, I'm Kate," she said to me and shook my hand. "I love the boutique feel you've brought to The Gym," she said. "I come every summer when I visit my mother. Hopefully, when we come back next summer, we'll be married." She hit him. "David's wife is the reason we're waiting for the divorce to be final."

David crossed his arms as his eyebrows drew down to stare at the floor. "We need to get going," he mumbled.

Meanwhile, Kate had launched into a full-blown soliloquy. "And don't think I won't wait her out," she said, checking her teeth in her reflection in the dark screen of her iPhone, "I most certainly will." Since she looked like she was in high school, it didn't seem so strange. "Next year, I'll be thirty-five, and that's the age I always said I'd be married." She hit David again.

After an awkward moment of silence, I said, "Good luck to both of you. It was nice meeting you."

"Likewise," she said. Now bright red, he waited for her to take the first steps to the door and patted my shoulder when he passed me, following her out.

Increasingly anxious, I watched them drive away and hurried out to the bench to call Marie. Unsure exactly what I was doing, I looked to confirm we wouldn't be in a similar situation. Within seconds Marie swore she wanted the divorce finalized but needed her name off the mortgage. She reminded me that I wanted to keep the house and take full responsibility for our sizable line of credit. Although I realized her name should be off the mortgage, I was not interested in rehashing everything else. I ended the call and marched back into the office to pull up beachside rentals to make sure I had all my options covered. Quickly, I realized the prices had gone up since the last time I checked them and cursed under my breath as Chuck's voice startled me. "Larry, Rick's out of town again, so I'll open tomorrow," he said, holding the back of the other office chair. "Everything okay?"

I nodded. "Yes," and then shook my head, "no," I laughed gently, "but I'm dealing. Thanks, Chuck. Thanks for everything."

"I'm only glad to see things are coming together here. A few months ago, I was concerned," he said, grabbing his Monster Energy drink before he walked out.

Wiping my brow, I scrolled through the rental listings. At that point, something triggered thoughts about Kristen's text and my call with Meg. I slumped over the computer keypad sullen. Matty's voice startled me from behind. "Son, are you hungover?" she said as I sighed. "You were doing so good."

Curiously, this is precisely what I needed. "I'm not hungover, Ma!" I barked, unable to contain the smile creeping across my face. I spun my chair with narrowed eyes at her. Matty expressed how happy she was that I would reach the milestone, and I said, "My fiftieth birthday?"

She gave me a sideways glance. "No. Your first anniversary at The Gym. You survived a year."

I leaned back in the chair. *It feels like I've been here for ten years*, I thought but said, "I'm reflecting on it now, Ma!"

Her eyes lit up. "Oh really, are you wondering how our yoga girl is?"

"Ma, please stop."

She hit my shoulder, delighted. "Here comes Chet. He'll cheer you up." She was in rare form while switching gears on the fly. "He loves you."

Chet slowly leaned over the check-in counter after hitting the empty hand sanitizer. "Hey, Prince," he mumbled. "This thing has been empty for two days. Do you think you can fill it?"

Matty's hands went to her head. "Don't get him going, Chet. Lord knows what he'll fill it with."

He peered at Matty for a moment. "I'll go wash my hands at Publix," he said, turning to the door. "Nothing but smoke and mirrors. I've never seen anything like it."

We watched him shuffle out.

Matty hopped up on the other chair, looking for a scoop, as I explained my concerns. Listening intently, she said, "It takes time, but you've always been honest with these women. That's the most important thing." She paused to ponder it all. "Can you sell your house?"

"And do what?" I groaned, rubbing my hands over my face as if that might help me think more clearly. "Move into a rental that's twice what my mortgage is and half the house? Not to mention I'd be a business owner who is renting."

Matty shook her head slowly as Gemma Sloan, my new trainer, texted me she would begin teaching the Sunday spin class. And then said, "Can you refinance the house?"

"Yes, realistically, four years from now." I stopped short of saying anything about the rent relief package but knew that was the first step in solving this dilemma. Matty nodded, suddenly preoccupied as her client walked in for her training session.

I became choked up when Meg texted me: *It's hard to turn the page when you know someone won't be in the next chapter, but the story must go on. Please keep writing, knowing that I'll be reading it from Never Land...*

I wiped my tear off the iPhone screen and wrote: *A year ago, everything was different. And now that I look back, I realize that year can do a lot to a person.*

THIRTY-TWO

IT'S ABOUT CAPTAIN HOOK

JULY 10, 2017
THE GYM
It was two weeks later.

Ivan and Betty Ignatius were standing at the check-in counter when Allie scampered into The Gym with a scowl. I was praising Ivan's vocal prowess after watching a video of his latest Karaoke performance. "Allie, you have to see Ivan sing," I boasted. "He's amazing." I paused when she stopped by the spin bikes. "Don't you have a cheer gig?"

She turned her eyes toward us absently. "Yes…"

Prideful of his pipes, Ivan plugged his next performance. "Allie, I do Mustang Sally and Disco Inferno every Friday night at Rooney's. You two should come over."

Allie said little. Her presence said enough.

She dropped her giant hippie bag in the office, wanting to talk to me, but Ivan lingered to pull up another video. Allie grabbed a bottle of water from the old cooler and stared out the window after watching it. Ivan chuckled and lowered his voice. "Is she upset you stopped posting pictures together drunk on the beach?"

I rolled my eyes at him and whispered, "That's not funny."

"But those drunken Lucy and Ricky posts are," he added quickly. "I live through you vicariously. So, you better keep posting your shenanigans on Facebook." He waved his tiny baseball cap at Betty, who shook her head at us from the free weights. Then he turned back to me. His eyebrows arched. "Oh, and from now on, just call me Schultz. Like your sales manager in *The Show.*"

I chuckled. "Why?"

"Because when people ask me about you, it's best I say, I see nothing...I hear nothing...and know NOTHING," he made a head gesture to Allie. "Your princess needs you," he peered at her, "NOTHING!"

As he walked over to the squat machine, Allie collapsed in the other office chair. Quickly the space felt like it was rapidly heating. "Allie, what is wrong with you?" I asked, annoyed.

She kicked off her flip-flops and pulled her bare feet up on the chair with a bleak expression. "Captain Hook was arrested for hitting Cruella last week. His people bailed him out of jail, but she left skid marks."

We sat in silence as I processed that. "What man hits a woman?"

Allie stared at me for a long moment. "A man who is now dating Allison Tinke." A jolt of energy hit me, and I cringed. "I'm sorry, Lawrence. Have you heard from her?"

"Not in a few days." My heart sank. "Who told you this?"

"I ran into Bob at L.A. Fitness. He swore it all to be true."

"Impossible," I insisted. My mouth was suddenly dry. I took a sip of water and peered at her, searching for some trace of a bad joke. When she remained frigid, I babbled, "You know Bob is a pariah who notoriously spins the truth!"

She raised her hand to calm me down. "And envious," she added. "But he knows Hook better than you were led you to believe."

I shook my head. "That might be true, but there is no way Allison Tinke is dating Hook."

She unleashed a torrent of pent-up hostility, having nothing to do with me or this situation. The truth was that little had been going her way, and she was hurting. She had been for weeks. I gave her a minute to vent, and she relaxed. When she looked back at me, I could tell she had to have a solid tryout. She needed this cheer gig. Her feet slid off the edge of the chair. "I wish I could stay," she muttered. Her green eyes dulled as she checked the time. "But I have to go."

I wanted to make sure she was all right. "Allie Girl, are you okay?"

"I'm fine," she lied. "For your information, Bob claims Allison caved because of Hook's money—"

Adamantly shaking my head, I insisted that was not who Allison was and leaned back in the office chair, feeling sorry for both of us. Then Allie pointed out that I did not know Allison like I had hoped I would've by now. Pondering that, I tensed up. Perhaps I was so eager to buy the fairy tale that I had lost sight of reality. Gripping my iPhone,

I went to text Allison about Hook but stopped. I couldn't decide if I did so because I didn't want to spook her or if I didn't want to be spooked by her.

My gaze shifted to Allie.

She was distracted, reading another text. Seconds later, she met my gaze and informed me that Bob wanted to apologize to me. Sighing loudly, I noticed Ivan shaking his head in the distance. Over the past couple of months, we had gotten closer, and I trusted him. Within minutes, Allie went to change, and Ivan walked up, looking concerned. "I couldn't help but hear that bullshit," Ivan said quietly, adjusting his wrist ban. "You shouldn't trust that guy. He is not your friend."

"Bob or Captain Hook?"

"Both, but I was talking about Bob Tillie."

I blinked, with voices at the check-in counter, and smiled when Camilla Stock placed her bag on the counter. She was a worldly widowed Canadian who I enjoyed. When she asked me if I had a moment, I nodded, knowing she'd heard snatches of this conversation. Within seconds, she informed me she did not trust Bob either. She eyed Ivan walking away as if she was my overly protective mother. "I like you," she whispered. "I'll always let you know what I hear." She pulled her bag off the counter with a warm smile and walked over to the ellipticals.

I sighed, relieved, but then winced when Allie rushed back in. She paused, then confessed, "I guess when it's too good to be true, it is."

I took a breath. "I know you still believe, Allie Girl."

She shook her head. "I'm not in the mood to believe today, Lawrence."

I changed the subject. "So, where is your cheer tryout?"

"West Palm," she snapped. She frantically rummaged through her giant hippie bag and looked back at me. "Are you going to be okay?"

I looked into her eyes. "I can't settle for companionship."

She pulled her hair back. "Why? At least that's something. Everyone else is just miserable and cheats, and then raises boys who suck on Tinder."

I wasn't expecting that and took a moment before I said, "Allie, your anxiety levels are through the roof. It's never as bad as it seems—"

"Captain Hook stole your Tinker Bell," she insisted. "That's as bad as it gets."

I crossed my arms. "Said, Bob Tillie?"

"This is perfect for your story —"

"What?" I cried out. "Why?"

"Because it's exactly how things really turn out. Shitty. This is a true modern-day love story. He has the money and gets the girl." She paused and dug back into her bag. "Why can't you settle for companionship?"

It was quiet for several moments. I looked at her and said, "I need the chemistry I felt."

After a long silence, Allie said, "Wendy?"

I caught my breath. "I know it sounds insane, but I've felt it with Allison, too. I mean, I know I haven't met her, but I still feel it. I must meet Allison Tinke."

Allie took on a guarded expression. She started to speak but stopped herself. "What are you going to do? Drive to Hook's mansion on the river and ask Tink for a chat? Maybe you'll get in that sword fight you dreamt about, after all."

I crossed my arms. "I refuse to believe Allison Tinke is with Hook."

She rolled her eyes. "Why? The men with money get the women. I'm going to be late, and I'm sure my car will break down. Wish me luck, Lawrence."

I sighed. "Good luck, Allie Girl."

• • •

Two days later, Allison texted me about meeting up on the following Saturday. The next day she was reminded of her plans for a girl's night out and canceled. I never questioned her or said anything about Hook, and it began eating at me.

And then our communication stopped.

THIRTY-THREE

THE BIG 50!

JULY 30, 2017
OCEAN 302/CARRABAS
It was three weeks later.

On Sunday morning, just as I was heading out to meet Kim for my birthday brunch at Ocean 302, Allison finally texted me back. *I'm sorry I'm just getting back to you, but the truth is that I have some things to work out before I can have that glass of wine.* No emojis. That was it. Short and unsweet. I leaned against the kitchen counter with a feeling the wind was knocked out of me. My heart sank as *The Dark One* whispered, *I guess she settled for Hook's money, Sport.* I inhaled sharply and snatched my keys off the counter, scrambling out. As that door closed, I pretended I was okay and focused on Kim.

But when I hopped in my car, I couldn't deny I would be meeting a friend. Nothing more. I backed up through my cloud of despair, fighting the hollow ache of loneliness, wondering what my next move would be.

Fifteen minutes later, as I drove over the Melbourne Causeway, a text flashed up. When I stopped at the light on Riverside and Fifth Avenue, I noticed a birthday wish. *HAPPY BIG 50!!* It was a highly sexual forty-five-year-old teacher named Tammy. She had some pleasant pictures on POF, and since I could not delete the app, I had remained on the site chatting with her until we exchanged numbers. During our last conversation, I affirmed I wouldn't meet anyone else unless my situation had changed while suddenly overwhelmed it did.

Driving along Riverside Drive, I raised my eyebrows in question to our last call when the ping of Tammy's next text startled me. Slowing to a stop at the Ocean Avenue light, I read it: *We should meet while you wait for those women in your life to get their shit together!*

I took a deep breath and exhaled.

Maybe I need one final, last-ditch, Hail Mary date, I thought and received a Facebook friend request from her. It took me a second to realize it was her. Tammy's profile picture looked different from her dating site pictures, and to this point, I didn't know her last name. I glanced up at the red light and back at her request. The women who came and went on my Facebook page flashed in front of me. When the light turned green, I lowered the windows for some fresh air and pulled into the restaurant's parking lot.

After regaining my composure, I walked into Ocean 302. Kim had flowers, a balloon, and a card on the table and hopped up with a warm smile to hug me. Two hours went by quickly, although much of the conversation revolved around the colleges our kids were interested in. It was clear we both wanted the best for each other as we then strolled next door to Melbourne Beach Market for some Italian bread. When Kim stood up on her tiptoes to grab a loaf from the bakery lady, I confirmed plans to see Lauren and Jerry for an early dinner. Just as I did, I was surprised by another text. This one was from my new/old wine industry acquaintance, Michael. Still not used to needing cheaters, I held it out to read it. *Happy birthday, Larry. I have decided not to self-publish my manuscript. I appreciate you being respectful and am looking forward to reading your sequel. I'm sure you're celebrating your birthday in ways only you would. Cheers Michael.*

After thanking him, I hugged Kim goodbye and drove back to the mainland on the phone with my mother. My spirits lifted when she made plans to come down for a rare summer visit; however, my mind raced on when the call ended at a red light in front of The Mansion. The old restaurant sparked the sudden memories of Maya and Christina. *What if I called Maya when Christina suggested, and she stayed in Florida?* I felt like I blinked and missed another moment that could have changed everything. When a horn moved me along, Wilson called. I made the left onto US1. "Hey, Wilson," I answered.

"How do you feel turning the big five-o?" he asked.

"I feel the same," I replied.

Wilson laughed. "I figured. Hey, how's Allison Tinker Bell?"

I hesitated.

"That turned out to be nothing more than a twisted tease…" I faded out of the conversation as dark clouds formed on the horizon.

Three hours later, after the summer storms rolled through, I met my kids at Carrabba's. The early evening breeze still had a scent of rain when Lauren collapsed in a chair with a new blond streak in her hair, as Jerry confiscated my iPhone to follow Bernie Sanders on Instagram. Lauren took a Snapchat of me giggling with my wine glass up to my face to hide my humored expression. When I placed it down, Jerry brought up his desire to give his high school graduation speech. I leaned back, startled by his ten-month plan, and braced myself when Lauren rolled her eyes. "Jerry," she said. "You're not going to be selected to give that speech. Besides, you're not graduating high school until next May."

Jerry looked at me for help, and I nodded. "I like a man with a plan," I said, cherishing the moment.

"Dad," Lauren snapped. "Stop encouraging him!"

"Jerry's a wonderful writer and has a great stage presence. There's no reason why he won't be selected."

"The chances are so slim, dad. I'm calling mom."

"Everyone, please calm down."

Lauren shook her head. "Dad, Jerry believes what you tell him."

I smiled. "He better, or it'll never happen."

A text hit my iPhone, and Jerry read it. "Matty wishes you a happy birthday and says your life is like the show Californication." He shook his head. "She wants to know when the sequel will be ready."

"Let me have my phone back, please." I grabbed it as Fern then sent her birthday wishes.

"Who keeps texting you?" Lauren asked.

"My trainers at The Gym."

Lauren glared at me. "They even know your life is like that show?"

"She's joking."

"No, she is not," Lauren replied, amused.

Two hours later, I was back at the house, shuffling through my notepad, intoxicated as if I was Hank Moody. With thoughts of watching reruns of the old Showtime series, I answered a call from Allie. "Hey…"

"You home?"

"Yes," I moaned, turning a page of my pad.

"How was your birthday brunch and dinner?" she asked.

Despite my apparent discomfort, I glanced back at my notes and laughed. "They were fine," I said, trying to sound upbeat. "It was a fun day."

"You seem distracted."

"Why is my notepad filled with a woman's name I never met?"

"Allison Tinke?" she said, obviously remembering I had mentioned this before. "Lawrence, it must mean something. You should call her. I'm sorry about the way I spoke about her. I've been in a bad place myself. Call her—" I interrupted her.

"Nah," I groaned. "She finally texted me back this morning. She has things to work out."

Allie gasped, "Captain Hook?"

"Someone!" I snapped, struggling for mental balance. "I'm not going there again."

"What if she started something new but feels good about you and just needs reassurance."

I felt my thoughts drifting from the present to the past and sighed. "It's done," I said, sounding whiny and drunk.

"Lawrence, you sounded like me a few weeks ago. Please stop. I feel partially responsible."

My pulse quickened when a picture of Tammy, the teacher, flashed up. "This teacher keeps texting me. She sent me a bikini shot. I'm going to meet her—"

Allie exhaled slowly. "You're not thinking rational thoughts."

Staring at the enticing picture, I murmured, "Through all of this, I still believe I'll find her."

"You might already have!" Allie protested. "Her name is Allison Tinker Bell."

"Nah, I have to keep moving forward."

"Go to sleep, Peter." She laughed. "Tomorrow's a new day."

I gulped my wine. "Yeees," I slurred, wiping my mouth. "A new day indeed."

"Goodnight, Lawrence."

I hesitated. "Night, Allie Girl."

Click.

THIRTY-FOUR

FATE INTERRUPTED

AUGUST 2017
SQUID LIPS
It was the following Sunday.

I decided it was time to expand my small social sphere and agreed to meet Tammy, the teacher at Squid Lips in Melbourne.

I parked my car, unfastened my seatbelt, and noticed the forty-five-year-old blond leaning on the guardrail going up to the restaurant. Mindful she had seen me, I nervously tugged at my Rolling Stones T-shirt and headed over, wondering what role she played in my life because I hastily concluded it would not be the role of a girlfriend. She looked older than her pictures but still attractive in a weathered Kendra Wilkinson sort of way. I cleared my throat and said hello. My smile felt frozen as she stared at me through pink, mirrored sunglasses. She shook my hand. "Hey, it's nice to meet you." Her voice seemed different than when we spoke on the phone—or at least hesitant.

She brushed a bug off her Cheetah print shirt and waited for me to lead her into the restaurant. We requested a table inside because the live music on the deck was too loud. Minutes later, Tammy pulled her iPhone from the back pocket of her faded jean shorts and placed it on a high-top table, glancing at the hostess.

Tammy waited, looking at me with suppressed eagerness.

"Does this table work?" I asked politely.

With a single nod, she hopped up on the stool across from me with a curious smile. Our attention shifted to the waitress. "What can I getcha?"

Tammy pulled her blond hair back off her face and said, "Just water."

My gaze dropped to the menu. I asked about their wines but then said, "I'll have a Stella, please…" and handed her the menu.

The waitress nodded and strolled off. I smiled at Tammy, attempting to lighten the mood. "Water?"

A sigh was her answer.

I continued, "So, you live up by Lake Washington, right?"

She nodded and finally took off her sunglasses. "It's close to work," she confirmed.

I smiled, running out of things to say. "It's a nice change for me. I've spent the past year around The Gym or down in Vero." I paused, wondering why this outspoken woman was so quiet.

Smiling with her eyes, she seemed to relax a little. When her gaze shifted back to me, she reminded me that she had taken over the lease of an apartment off Lake Washington Road. "I moved in with the guy who I told you couldn't get it up," she said, with an unsubtle twinge of bitterness in her voice. "He cried like a little girl when I ended it."

There she is, I thought but said, "Ah, yes, I remember."

Promptly, she shifted gears to a man who she referred to as Steven the Stallion. Her facial expression was animated, describing their sex life. "His penis felt soooo good!" she gushed, mock fanning herself.

I caught myself tilting slightly on the stool. "Oh." I blinked. "Okay. What happened to him?"

She laughed. "I couldn't stand his scent." She made a face. "I still have pictures of his cock, though. Why haven't you sent me a dick pic?"

My eyebrows arched when she flashed me his penis, and I muttered, "I thought you were joking."

"Yes and no," she said, barely able to speak. "I do get a lot of dick pics, but I knew you only sent your little boy—G-Rated—mirror shots."

My hands felt clammy as I wiped my forehead with the napkin. "Is it warm in here?"

She grinned deviously. "So, what do women send you?"

With visions of too many, I said, "Everything from mirror shots with hands across their nipples to pictures that leave nothing to the imagination." I smirked and read a text from Linda. *Do you remember the night we blacked out in the movies and woke up with no car keys? I want to do that again!*

My gaze lifted to Tammy. "Is that one of the women who don't have their shit together?" she asked.

I nodded. "Yes."

Tammy stared at me as if she were trying to make sense of it all. Then she informed me that she liked the taste of semen. With an erratic breath, I reminded myself that there was a reason this woman unexpectedly came into my life while also realizing I would need some alcohol to make it through her next story to figure out what that reason was. When the waitress approached with my beer, I took a steadying breath and grabbed it from her before she could place it on the coaster. Tammy continued, "I mean, some semen did sting." I spilled some of my beer in shock as I sipped it. "It's wicked in so many ways. All the different types."

"Different types?" I then took a gulp. "Are we still on the semen or back to your penis pictures?"

She chuckled as I tilted the other way and dropped the beer down with a thud. "Are you okay?" she asked.

"Not at all," I sputtered and swiped the table with the same napkin. "But don't stop now."

A small smile lifted from her mouth. "You are good about keeping secrets."

I took another sip of my Stella. "Secrets?"

She quickly added, "Your book! The one that you're a narcissist in."

I gave her a nervous grin as beads of sweat formed on my head, wishing for the quiet Tammy to come back. *Great now, I'm woozy and wet,* I thought, then pleaded, "Please warn before shifting topics; it's a long way to the floor."

She smiled, looking away. Then she looked back at me and said, "Okay, I moved on to your book." She raised an eyebrow. "So, explain yourself, you have a captive audience, and I'm getting a little wet."

"You and me both," I said and patted my forehead again. "Why didn't you tell me you read it?"

Tammy's face had paled and then flushed pink, annoyed. "How could you not tell me you wrote it?"

I sighed. "Because it's been a distraction."

"I'll bet," she said. "So, you drink in excess, act recklessly, and are amused that you're a narcissist?"

I straightened my back. "Well, no. At least not the part about the narcissist." I cleared my throat. "That was an inside joke with a character in the book."

Her eyes glistened, tickled. "Go on." She crossed her arms.

"So, the Molly character who said that line was a fan of a movie during *The Show's* storyline—"

"Iron Man."

I nodded. "Yes. And a fan of Tony Stark—"

"Who was a narcissist," she said, cutting me off amused. "I get the correlation between you and Tony. Tell me something I don't know."

"I'm not a narcissist. I used Tony's exact line—agreed—from the second movie to continue the fun with Molly. Okay?"

Tammy sprung from the stool and took some slow steps to stare into my eyes. "Okay," she chirped and then stood on tiptoes and sniffed my neck. "I had to give you a little shit." She peered at me, eerily for a moment, and added, "I like your scent." I blinked, and she was off to the bathroom. Then as my head spun, I finished my Stella and bribed the waitress to get me another before Tammy got back. When she did, she plowed on. "So, are you excited about the solar eclipse?" she hopped back up on the stool.

I gave her a little shrug. "I bought some nifty glasses for it."

Her lips were motionless for a few seconds before moving us along to a topic that I had pondered walking in. "Life brings people together for various reasons, and I've looked at things differently since speaking with you," Tammy said, and then took her time sipping her water deep in thought. "I mean, after reading your book, I believe your crash and burn was necessary. I found that anguish and emotional suffering were only warning signs that I was living against my own truth," she continued. Her tone was serious. "And I feel you did too."

"That's interesting."

"You can't tell me that you didn't sabotage your career to end the lie. The pain." She paused, seemingly as fascinated as I was. "I'm sorry," she snickered, "I'm talking like I know you because of your book."

I took a breath. "No, it's okay. It is true."

Her face lit up. "Well, on a lighter note, I was fucking with you to see if you did pout," she confessed. "I knew you weren't a narcissist, but you are a bit of an anomaly." She smiled whimsically.

My eyes grew wide as I glanced out at the demographically diverse tables turning to us and said, "How were you sure about the narcissist part?"

"Because I read your book thoroughly," she smiled, "and a friend told me you were a good guy. A caring person."

"Who is your friend?"

"Michelle Crowley."

I winced, stunned. "Cruella?" I said with a halfhearted laugh.

"No, Crowley, Michelle Crowley," she retorted.

My head tilted, musing the Ripper's comment about her newfound self-respect for me. "I called her Cruella, jokingly, but I shouldn't have. I really don't know her."

She placed her elbows on the table. "Michelle said that you're a writer who needs to be in the middle of a mess of your own creation."

I exhaled. "What else did she say?"

"She told me that your cock got you in a lot of trouble." I shushed her, nervously glancing over at the next table. "Don't shush me." She laughed. "And don't tell me good sex isn't important."

I peered at her and smiled. "I wouldn't dare." I paused, humored yet eager to find out if Tammy knew who Hook was dating. Allison had popped into my mind, and my heart thumped in my chest as I casually added, "By chance, do you know who Michelle's currently dating?"

"That's a random question." Her eyes narrowed at me. "Please, don't tell me you have the hots for her."

I shook my head. "No, I was interested in the guy she used to date."

"James Hook." She chuckled. "That name would be great for your sequel. A real-life villain. So, you know him?"

"Yes, he's been my archenemy for a year now and is Captain Hook in the sequel."

She grinned at me for a long moment. "Of course, he is," she said. "How many of his love interests did you take to Never Land?"

"One who attempted suicide coincidently right after," I whispered. "Do you know who he's currently dating?"

She squinted at me. "Nope." She was eager to get back to her questioning. "So, your ex...Marie didn't seem awful in the book."

I gulped my beer. "No, Marie's a wonderful person and a great mother."

Her head tilted slightly. "It's rare a guy doesn't trash his ex. So, was the split caused by irreconcilable differences?"

I said, "Partly." I checked the time. "Unfortunately, we're better apart than together."

With racing thoughts, I refused to get into twenty-three years of life with a woman I knew I was not going to see again. Regardless of my wishes, Tammy's inquiries continued until I convinced her that I did not take divorce lightly. That seemed to be her goal, although what she said next made me wonder why. She frowned. "Your facial expression when we shook hands made me realize I wasn't your type, and I'm now a little disappointed."

I took in a slow breath, unable to deny that but said, "Well, it's more than that—"

"How about a little summer fling?"

I exhaled. "It is tempting."

To appear somewhat nonchalant, Tammy laughed awkwardly. "Right..."

I shook my head. "It would only further complicate my currently complicated situation, which I need answers from."

"Life is a reality to be experienced," she said. "Not a problem to be solved."

With a slow breath, I nodded.

Ten minutes later, we were heading to our cars when we turned to each other simultaneously. "You should call that Allison chick you told me about," she said, two parking spots over. "Women often need reassurance...and she seemed to have piqued your interest." She nodded with a smile. *And that is why Tammy came into my life*, I thought and smiled back at her. As I backed out of the parking spot, Linda called.

On the ride home, she pressed my buttons perfectly.

• • •

The following week, I tagged along with Marie and Jerry to tour FSU. The day after I got home, I began seeing Linda again.

A week after that, I stood outside The Gym with Allie wearing silly solar eclipse glasses to catch a glimpse of this natural phenomenon, still pondering Tammy's advice to call Allison. It had worn on me for two weeks as I only conjured up different excuses not to. As the moon obscured the sun, I felt I had to reassure Allison that I was still interested in having a glass of wine. After passing my silly glasses to Allie, she wished me luck, and I trod over to the bench to make the call. With a racing heart, my eyes focused on Allison's number. I gripped my iPhone with one hand, and as my finger went to hit her name, it rang.

I blinked at Linda's name, flashing over Allison's.

I hesitated, unnerved by her timing, and knew she wouldn't answer as Lucy, and didn't. Finally, Linda's intentions went beyond wine and a good time. Although I got her in a way that most refused to, I also understood our seven months of reruns were unexplainable at four. When Allie startled me, thinking I was talking to Allison, I tensed up. "Lawrence," she whispered. "How's it going?"

I quietly said, "Fine."

Holding her hula hoop, she rummaged through her giant hippie bag while I lowered the volume on my iPhone. Allie said, "Good. I have that cheer tryout in Orlando...but...shit, I can't find the address." She peeked back at me, and I swallowed hard. "I'll talk to you tomorrow, Lawrence."

"Okay, good luck, Allie Girl."

I held my breath until she jumped in her car, convinced I had invested too much time not to finalize this thing with Linda one way or another. I refused to believe I needed closure.

The hour-long conversation wore me out, and as I hung up, I sighed exhaustedly.

THIRTY-FIVE

IRMA

SEPTEMBER 2017
THE GYM

It was two weeks later.

I ran into The Gym, and everyone had their eyes glued to the news reports tracking Hurricane Irma. Everyone except Baby Gaga and Will Burleson. Although I hadn't seen Will much since he attempted to train me, he seemed to have gotten close to Baby Gaga. I smiled, glancing over at the twenty-somethings, thinking love was in the air while wondering why Linda hadn't called. I went to call her and sighed frustratedly when Chuck and Matty texted me their plans to evacuate.

Everyone seemed to be leaving the Barrier Islands. The storm had devastated the US Virgin Islands before battering the Turks and Caicos Islands with Category Five winds. Nerves were frayed, but Linda's were fried. Ten minutes later, she texted me to call her, but she answered as Lucille Ball when I did. "Ricky, my cat food didn't come, and this fucking Irma is pissing me off!"

I wandered outside to the bench so none of the members would hear this and said, "Lucy, relax. The storm's still days away, and the track is uncertain. Are we meeting up at The Patio?"

"You're seriously the only lunatic who's thinking about wine time!" she shouted. "My brand-new house doesn't have its shutters up, and now I have to reorder the cat food, buy bottled water, and get my batteries."

I let out another weary sigh and then tried to explain. "Getting away from the nutty news coverage on this thing would do you good. You're going to have a breakdown if you don't."

"It's a CAT FIVE! I can't turn it off, and I know your reckless prissy ass doesn't put up shutters," she said as I glanced at another text from Chuck: *Rick, Curt, and Joe are evacuating too, so you'll need one of the kids to open tomorrow. When are you closing for the storm?*

"Lucy, I have to call you back."

"RICKY—"

Click.

My gaze shifted to the patrons pouring out of Publix with bottled water, so I made my way over. Since the shelves were empty, I hurried back to The Gym, oblivious that I had missed another call from Linda. Hours later, when I left The Gym, I noticed a voicemail from her after sending me a frantic text: *Ricky, where are you? Check your voicemail.* (angry emoji) *I am really upset!*

I texted her back, but she didn't respond.

Days later, Hurricane Irma made landfall in the Lower Keys as a Category Four storm, and it took another week for everything to get back to normal. Meanwhile, Allison Tinke's old picture from the file cabinet haunted me while I was cooped up in my house. Finally, I went to throw it away but stopped. I walked back to the kitchen table with a tight grip on the picture, and I found the strength to call her. Although the call went straight to voicemail, I left a reassuring message that I still wanted to have a glass of wine. When I hung up, I placed Allison's picture on my notepad, startled by a call from Linda. She was at her parents' house and couldn't talk, so we made plans to meet up the next day on the last Monday of the month. She suggested we pick up where we left off—laughing—at The Patio in Vero.

When I arrived, though, I didn't anticipate our table being occupied and the Rodney Strong Pinot Noir we always ordered being out of stock. Sitting off to the side, I looked over the wine menu and murmured an overpriced bottle to the waitress distracted by a text from Linda.

As predicted, she was running late. My mind raced back to the ugly night she showed up thirty-five minutes late. Thankfully, I received a text from Wilson: *That guy Paul who shoots the shit with you actually had to work out today because you weren't here. (laughing emoji) He wants to know if you will be in tomorrow.*

I texted Wilson back: *Yes.*

Then I checked the time, and Linda made her grand entrance. "I hate hurricanes," she growled. Her voice was as anxious as I felt.

I pushed myself up, and we hugged. "But you made it through."

Fifteen minutes later, we poured our second glass of wine, but things were strained. The emotion heightened when she vaguely brushed over the days around Irma while rewriting the day when I missed her call. She wanted me to believe that I deliberately avoided her but then accidentally mentioned Sheldon's name. "Should we move inside?" she said, desperate to change the subject. "It looks like rain."

I grimaced. "So," I choked out. "You're still speaking to Sheldon?"

Her answer was a slash to my heart. "He put up my storm shutters," she sputtered. I fell back in the chair, nauseous, and she raised her wine glass to me. "Ricky, stop." She held it higher. "To picking up where we left off before Irma."

With racing thoughts, I pressed on. "Who stayed with you during the storm?"

She hesitated for what felt like a minute. "Sheldon," she finally said, just above a whisper.

I looked at her aghast. "Sheldon?" My voice was heavy-hearted.

She shook her head vigorously while pretending he was there as a friend. She began a diatribe about her missed call and how freaked out she was by Irma. Tension shot up my back. I cut her off before she could get rolling and said, "Do you really want to rehash this?"

She stared at me for a beat, and as her hand shook, she took a sip of wine and nodded reluctantly. "I don't care," she snapped defensively. "Why wouldn't I?"

I shook my head and said, "During our call, I found out my trainer who opens The Gym couldn't, so I had to find someone who could. I did not blow you off. I missed your call amidst the storm's chaos, at which point you panicked and called Sheldon." I paused, and as she glared at me speechless, I added, "That's the truth. So, stop spinning it."

"No, you need to stop dwelling on it," she muttered incomprehensibly. "We need to focus on where we were before Irma."

I rubbed my face. "How do you utter those words after eight months of this?"

At that point, she hit the rewind button and went on her rambling tirade about my book and having sex with women in relationships while highlighting her favorite two. "You had to run out of one of their houses with one shoe and jump off another nut job's balcony!" she cried out.

Her lines were so worn out; I recited her last one for her. "It has taken me all of this time to work through all of your shit shows, Ricky!" I said, in my best Lucille Ball voice.

She bit her lip to prevent her from smiling. "Stop. You can sit there and pout, or we can—" I interrupted her again.

"If you were prepared to change anything, we'd be at my house with some candles listening to one of my cheesy jazz CD's from Target while making passionate love," I said with a tired smile.

She laughed obnoxiously. "So, now you're suggesting that I'm not attracted to you?" Linda made a face. "Ya, okay…"

"You can joke and point your finger at everyone else, but this is on you—"

"I'm coming to your house this weekend!" she blurted out, cutting me off.

Before I could answer her, a text hit my iPhone, and my heart skipped a beat.

It was Allison Tinke.

Linda peered at me restlessly as I read it. *Hi, thank you for that voicemail. It was nice. I am ready for that glass of wine now. Does Sunday afternoon at Captain Hiram's work?* I placed my iPhone back on the table. Linda looked at me and narrowed her eyes. "Wow, the sun's coming out. Who texted you?"

With a warm light settling over the patio, I literally had goosebumps, unable to wipe the smile off my face. "A woman whose name I've heard repeatedly since I bought The Gym," I explained.

She hesitated. "Someone, you know?"

"I feel like I do," I glanced back at Allison's text, "it's quite magical."

She rolled her eyes. "Stop with your fairy tale bullshit and explain this." She spilled her wine. "Dammit, Ricky!"

"I've repeatedly heard Allison's name over this past year, and then she reached out to me in June—"

"She had your number?"

"No, she sent me a message on POF. I say quite magical because it was right after I tried to delete the app but couldn't."

Linda made a scoffing sound. "Oh, stop. I'm sorry I pissed you off." She paused, studying my face, and realized I was telling the truth. Her voice rose with frustration. "How come you never told me about her?" she asked, looking worried with her lips remaining apart.

"Because she wasn't ready to meet me—"

"Until now?" she demanded. Her voice was just short of shouting. "So, help me understand this," she pushed the wine bottle to the side of the table, "you have mutual friends who mentioned her name, and then miraculously, she just reached out to you?"

I took a long slow breath. "Yes, she used to go to The Gym," I insisted. "And was Bill Reed's fiancé."

She stared at me in silence, pressing her lips together. "Bill Reed's fiancé?" she echoed, looking genuinely horrified. "Are you serious?"

"Yes, I am."

Linda opened her mouth and shut it before she added, "So, Bill reached out to me," she took a sharp breath, "after his girlfriend reached out to you." She shook her head. "Then you met me after I ran from him, and now his fucking ex-fiancé wants to meet you after you've repeatedly heard her name while at The Gym?"

I swallowed hard in need of more wine. "Yeah, that sounds about right."

"When does she want to meet you?"

I shifted my gaze to the bar, waved for the waitress, and cleared my throat. "Sunday—"

Linda yelped, "And the plot thickens!" She paused, looking pained and panicked and desperate as I forced a smile at the waitress walking up. I rubbed a stab of pain in my chest.

"Would you like another bottle?" the waitress asked, rushing by— scared to slow down—I quickly nodded.

Linda's mind raced on.

Then she anxiously adjusted herself in the chair with a harsh warning that Bill trashed Allison on their date while insisting he ended the engagement as quickly as possible. "There was nothing good about that one. I remember that jackass telling me her name was Allison." With a deep frown on her face, she sighed. "Bill said she was a nightmare."

My pulse quickened. "Bill, the guy you ran from?" I said, with a circumspect look. "The guy you told me lies to women in hopes they'll feel sorry for him?"

Linda said something under her breath. She knew the truth but had to doubt what she'd told me because the enthusiasm radiating out of me since Allison's text was indisputable. After two quick sips of wine, she continued, "So, what does Allison look like?"

I flashed a picture of her on my iPhone and said, "Tinker Bell."

She met my gaze and looked dazed. "Oh God," she murmured. "Well, good luck with this next chapter. It seems to be as scripted as everything else having to do with you." She paused as my iPhone rang. Realizing it was The Gym, I answered. "Hey."

Allie whispered, "This witch wants to talk to you…"

"Hello?" I heard voices.

"Larry, this Victory Pavia, you know my daughter Monique."

I hesitated. "Yes, of course," I replied. "What can I do for you?"

"I would like to sign up, but you're rarely here, and I'm not giving these children my credit card."

I jumped up and walked away from Linda, who reached into her Coach bag for something that could've distracted me even more than I was. "Allie's very trustworthy..." I glanced back at Linda to make sure it wasn't a gun.

The woman lowered her voice. "When can I deal directly with you?"

I sighed. "I'll personally take care of you tomorrow, Victoria. I'm sorry for any inconvenience."

"Fine, but you should know there are pompoms and hula hoops and red cups with lord knows what in them all over the sidewalk in front of The Gym."

"Thank you. I'll handle that now."

"Good-bye—"

Click.

I pinched the bridge of my nose, walking back to the table, and Linda said, "Was that Allison?"

"No." I raised my eyebrows and stared at her pointedly. "I came here today to see about us," I reminded her. "But..."

"But what?" Linda asked anxiously, churning with emotion.

"But honestly, I knew you hadn't ended anything with Sheldon," I said softly. "And maybe you shouldn't."

"Interesting," she deadpanned. "Well, don't tell me I didn't warn you that Allison and Bill's old girlfriend are cray cray."

I placed my wine down and leaned over it. "I've only heard good things about Allison and can personally tell you Maya's actions were more understandable than yours," I said as eight months of frustration burst out of me. "So, I'd take a long look in the mirror before you call anyone else crazy—"

"If Irma didn't hit, we wouldn't even be having this conversation," she spat out furiously. "So, fuck you!"

It took us five days to apologize to each other, and it turned out to be the day before I met Allison. A day Linda texted me that she fell in love with me, right after I walked out of her life.

THIRTY-SIX

I LOOKED IN HER EYES
AND SAW EVERYTHING I NEEDED

OCTOBER 1, 2017
CAPTAIN HIRAM'S SANDBAR

It was the Sunday I had long-awaited.

All the meaningful coincidences and synchronicity and magical moments suddenly left me breathless as I sprung out of bed and into the reality of finally meeting Allison Tinke.

I poured my first cup of coffee into my Tink mug and grinned. After nearly two storylines, drinking out of this mug didn't seem so silly. I concluded that Maya was onto something and took a sip reflecting on that enchanting evening. I felt like a little boy on Christmas Eve, waiting to tear open his presents from Santa. *Five hours and twelve minutes to go!* I chirped to Jedi Mickey.

I added to the T-shirts scattered across my bed, unsure of what to wear. *Maybe a real shirt?* I thought, but then took a call from The Gym. "Hey Wilson," I said enthusiastically.

"So, Allie told me today is the day you're meeting Tinker Bell."

I chuckled. "Yes, it is."

"So, is this your writer's brain willing a love story for the ages?"

I pondered that. "Well, some magical moments led me to today," I surmised. "So, we'll see."

"Cool, enjoy."

"Thanks."

Click.

Five hours later, I pulled into Captain Hiram's and texted Allison that I'd be at the Sandbar. With a hop to my step, I jumped over some puddles as it began to rain again and hurried by an older man in a red shirt and meticulously neat beard. "Ahoy-mate," he said. His raspy voice sent a sudden chill down my spine. As I turned to him, he disappeared into a torrential downpour. The winds picked up, and I staggered off the wooden deck into the sand area under the bar's metal roof. Then it hit me. It was the guy who handed me the booklet of businesses for sale with The Gym circled in red.

Eyeing a row of tables against the river, I decided that it couldn't be the same man if only to avoid looking so bewildered when Allison arrived. I took a seat and a few deep breaths. With rain hitting the table's far edge, I gazed up at the darkened skies and tugged at my damp T-shirt, wondering why this felt like a dream.

A spellbinding hush had fallen over the space.

All I could hear was the whisper of my heart and the loveliest tinkle of bells. I pinched myself as the first ray of sunshine danced off the ominous river to the bar's entrance.

Our gazes met.

Allison stood there, glowing in nature's serene spotlight. Her blue eyes opened to her soul as her blond bob blew in the blustery autumn afternoon's sudden light. She looked just like her pictures, adorably beautiful. I stood up and brushed my sweaty palms on my jeans, with a tingling sensation rushing through my body. We hugged like we knew each other and then quickly agreed we both felt like we did.

With the restaurant being remodeled, we sat down at a booth off to the side of the Sandbar, drinking warm wine out of little plastic cups that somehow tasted fine. In fact, we promptly ordered another round. As the conversation continued to flow, it was as if our masks had fallen to the sand allowing each other to see ourselves as flawed and vulnerable.

Twenty-five minutes later, we again raised our little plastic cups to each other with the next round while admiring this pure connection that momentarily left us speechless. Then Allison smiled and pushed her blond hair behind her ears. "Seeing your profile came to me so unexpectedly," she confessed. "I was hesitant to put this on hold."

I was so excited that I almost shared the first time I had seen her pictures. Thankfully, I caught myself after realizing I would then have to explain Maya. Hastily I said, "I was crushed when you did."

She grinned with a little shrug. "I only did because you told me you'd dealt with those women who reached out to you before ending whatever they were looking to move on from."

I sighed. "So, were you dating someone else?"

"Not exactly."

"Do you want to talk about it?"

She hesitated for a moment. "Yes, with you, I do," she continued. She took an anxious breath. "Right before I reached out to you, I'd gotten closer to a guy who felt that I was the one. It was difficult and tempting. I liked him. He had money, and honestly, I'm struggling to pay bills right now...but in the back of mind," she smiled whimsically, "I just had this feeling about you."

I smiled with more confidence than I felt. But then I couldn't take it anymore and asked, "Was the guy Hook?"

She blinked. "Who?"

"James Hook."

She cringed like a teenager. "Eww, no—"

I exhaled. "Oh, thank God..." and collapsed along the bench, curling up in a fetal position for a split second before springing back up a new man. Then I realized she was right next to me. "Oh hi—"

Allison looked ten years younger as she gazed up at me. "So, you know Hook from The Gym?"

"Sort of," I explained. "He wasn't a member of The Gym when I took over, but his company used to do our advertising. He's been a thorn in my side ever since."

Her eyes narrowed at me. "I'm scared to ask."

We both laughed. "It's a long story," I said. "I'd heard he had quite a crush on you."

With another brief downpour, Allison confirmed what Sarah had told me in January. The two women had lost touch, and Hook was interested in Allison during their days at The Gym. "Right after my divorce, Hook asked me out before a yoga class," she said honestly. "Looking back, he'd asked me out repeatedly, but I blocked it all out. Maybe that's why I was so surprised he tried again in July—"

"This past summer?" I continued to quiz her.

"Yes, I ran into him with friends at Riverside Café." She laughed. "He was drunk and promised me a condo and a car if I'd marry him. He actually called me the next day to see if I'd take him up on it." She turned to me, and we gazed into each other's eyes. Her face lit up like an angel's as our eyes locked. My enchantment was growing as a warm sensation took over me. Our lips touched, and as cheesy as it sounds, I felt every emotion that you ever imagine when you kiss the woman of your dreams. Still lost in each other's eyes, her voice brought me back to earth. "I was so happy to hear your voicemail that I played it over and over."

At that point, words seemed superfluous, so we leaned gently towards each other and kissed again. Chuckling like children, we then said to each other, "That was nice."

"This feels like a dream!" Allison exclaimed. She took a breath to steady herself. "I can't remember ever kissing a man on a first date." She took a quick sip of wine as if that would sober her up. "So, we're both from the northeast, and you're...fifty."

I laughed. "And you're forty-two you. And a teacher...with two little girls."

She sat back in the booth. "Is that a deal-breaker? I realize your kids are in college."

"No." I bit my cheek. Her concerned expression tickled me. "My son, Jerry, is a senior at West Shore."

"Oh, that's a good school," she said, mulling it over. "Their father would've wanted them to go there if we hadn't moved to Vero Beach."

I had to remind myself that the father of her children was not Bill Reed. When I brought up Bill, she didn't mince her words. "Moving in with him was a mistake." It was refreshing to me that she wanted me to know everything. After admitting she was relieved to be out of Melbourne Beach, I wondered if she would move back.

"So, I heard you won't date anyone with ties to Melbourne Beach again," I said teasingly. I couldn't help but smile at her.

She smiled back at me. "That was true," she confirmed. "But things change unexpectedly." We shared a glance and even went to the bathroom at the same time. When we stood up together, Allison added, "I can't get over the comfort factor I have with you."

"Likewise," I said with a smile.

An hour later, she questioned me about my ruined career, and it dawned on me that she had not read my book after all. It was then I realized we never actually discussed it. I adjusted myself awkwardly in the booth. "I'm sorry," I said. "It's been an interesting dating experience with the book. I assumed you read it after you sent me that message about meeting me for a glass of wine."

She raised her eyebrows, confused. "So, it's about wine?"

I sighed. "Well, sort of."

"Oh, wow," she said, startled. "No, I sent that message because I just thought you were cute." She paused, and her eyes widened. "That is a crazy coincidence because I'd never asked any man to have a glass of wine before that."

My heart fluttered.

I felt such relief at that very moment. When I ordered our last round, the waitress chimed in. "You two are adorable together. I see a lot of love birds, but rarely chemistry like this." Her words brought me right back to my days with Wendy. I looked down when Allison grabbed my hand.

Minutes later, we stood in the rain under her giant umbrella and said nothing. But it was that magical moment that meant everything. "I'd like to see you again...soon."

Allison looked up at me and smiled. "Is fifteen minutes back at my apartment too soon?"

I looked into her eyes and saw everything I needed. "No..." was all I could utter.

THIRTY-SEVEN

IT'S MORE THAN A FEELING

OCTOBER 4, 2017
THE GYM
It was three days later.

With Marlene's yoga class filing out, I raised an eyebrow at Allison's emoji-less text. I was chatting in the office with our new trainer and spin instructor, Gemma Sloan, when I scanned it and realized something was wrong. I shifted my gaze back to Gemma and said, "When are you back at The Gym, Gem?"

"Friday," she replied. "Is everything okay?"

Allison called before I could answer her. "Yes." My iPhone rang again. "I'll see you on Friday."

The attractive thirty-something stood up. "See ya, Larry," she said and smiled politely.

Allison's voice was shaky as she spoke. "Bill thinks you're using me to get back at a woman who has a boyfriend. Someone named Linda."

Hearing that Allison still spoke with Bill was a bitter pill to swallow. I was mindful this conversation would be best taken outside and stopped in my tracks to the side of the bench, feeling a wave of disappointment. After that downer, it dawned on me that Bill also had a conversation with Linda. Although Allison rambled on, confused, I steadied my breathing. I wanted to be fully prepared to respond and not overreact to whatever was coming.

I took steps to the edge of the sidewalk and calmly said, "I should have predicted this."

"Predicted what?"

I sighed. "That Bill would call Linda," I said. "He went out with her a couple of times." I paused, pondering it all. "It appears they're spinning the truth to drive us apart."

Allison continued, "Who is this woman?"

I meandered back to the bench, irked, and said, "Someone I hung out with, too."

"So, you want her back?" she said under her breath.

Without the slightest hesitation, I said, "No."

"Well, then what?"

I sensed Allison believed Bill and became flushed with anger. Shortly after that, things deteriorated, and I wondered if I should call Linda. For a moment, I thought it would be best to hear her side of this sham. I was hopeful that Bill was the culprit, but the more Allison shared with me, the more I realized that Linda was painting a distorted picture, too. Part of me couldn't blame her. It was like I had been freefalling from a cliff that she had pushed me off and now raced to the bottom to catch me. I stood there, ruminating everything. Allison sent me reeling when she mentioned Bill would be stopping by her apartment after work. I looked at her name on the screen questionably as she continued. "Wait!" I interrupted helplessly. "Bill still stops by your place?"

"He's a friend," said Allison incredulously. "And he's worried about me."

"You believe that?" I asked Allison, wandering in front of a car that almost hit me. "I'm sorry," I muttered to the driver.

"Bill has known me for years," continued Allison, almost aggressively.

"Well, Bill filled Linda's head with lies about you, Allison—"

"Well, Bill told me that you've slept with half of Melbourne Beach."

My spine stiffened. "I slept with four women since I've been at The Gym. I made some mistakes and learned from them. And now, I met you."

After a long moment of silence, Allison asked, "What am I to you? What is this?"

"It's more than a feeling with you."

I stared up at the clouds, collecting my thoughts, and she kept going. "Charming men have hurt me, and all you've said is that you hung out with Linda."

"Yes." I took a breath, burning up. "But Bill is spinning—" she interrupted me.

"Bill told me Linda's in a relationship. He said you still reach out to her knowing she is with another guy." Her voice was now calm but laced with bitterness. "Is that true?"

With tension shooting up my back, I had to prove myself and frantically pulled up Linda's string of texts. "I texted you a screenshot summing up exactly what happened," I huffed. "I realize the truth always finds its way, but at this point, I see Linda's lost it. Go ahead and read that and call me back—"

"I'm reading it now," Allison pressed. "How did she fall in love with you. How did that happen, Larry?"

All the characters flashed in front of me as I saw my time at The Gym playing out on the pages of different chapters. "After Bill again mysteriously left Melbourne Beach, he went out on a couple of dates with Linda," I said, fighting hard to keep my voice down. "On the second date, he got her drunk at his house because he was too cheap to buy her a glass of wine and creeped her out by undressing as they made out—"

"Just get to where you came into this mess, please," she demanded, seemingly disgusted by Bill.

I wiped my forehead. "Well, ironically, because of Bill, Linda got more comfortable with her current boyfriend, Sheldon. But since she wasn't all that crazy about him, she continued dating and met me."

Allison added, "And then I met you, and Bill and Linda lost it."

"Yes." I rubbed my temple with my free hand because I knew I had to tell her about Maya. "Can you be strong? There's something else—"

"How?" she said aghast. "I will call Bill and tell him not to come to my apartment after work. That I promise you. Just know that I won't be able to handle getting hurt by you."

"I don't want to get hurt either," I said cautiously. "But I don't want you to think I'm keeping anything else from you. Not when shit like this happens days after we met."

At just above a whisper, she said, "Larry, I believe you, but I can't handle anything else right now."

"Okay," I breathed out. "I understand."

Click.

I walked back into the office, and one of The Gym's beloved music enthusiasts, Mel Stevens, popped his head in as "More Than a Feeling" came on. "La, what year was the album Boston released?"

I couldn't help but laugh. "I believe it was 1976, Mel."

We were roughly the same age and enjoyed our daily strolls down memory lane. "Crank it up!" Mel shouted. After a tug on his DEVO T-shirt, he pointed at me and started singing. *It's more than a feeling—when I hear that old song they used to play—I begin dreaming...* Mel was a talented musician with a strong singing voice who played in a local band with one of the surgeons who happened to be in a picture tile under him on the wall.

The MD and long-time member, Milan Malkovich, pointed to the tiles and said, "Larry, our tiles are in a perfect position," he grinned, "as a drummer, I always had to lift Mel and the band."

I glanced back at the tile. Milan had his arms up to a bar, and it did appear that he was lifting Mel. "Is that how you remember it, Milan?" Mel joked. As the two old bandmates continued having fun, my iPhone pinged with another text from Allison. *I'm sorry for doubting you. It's more than a feeling for me too. I'll call you during my lunch break.*

Mel strolled back by singing. *It's more than a feeling—I begin dreaming...* I smiled with sudden chills.

Throughout the rest of the morning, I chewed on everything. I was anxious to speak to Allison again. When the clock struck noon, I walked back out to the bench. The vibrant autumn sun blazed across a bright-blue canvas. There was no humidity, and the high hovered in the low eighties. *Welcome to paradise,* I said to myself and sat down.

Seconds later, Allison called, and I quickly answered. "Hey..."

"Hi," she said softly. "My past relationships have caused me to have doubts. I'm not used to feeling what I do with you, and there's something else that happened. I wanted to tell you at Captain Hiram's but didn't want to scare you."

"Okay," I said slowly. "What is it?"

My heart beat faster and faster.

"When did your father pass?"

I hesitated. Beads of sweat broke out on my forehead. My hands were suddenly clammy. "How did you know he did?"

"During our first call, he came to me," she confided. "I felt your father in my apartment with me. He smiled and was gone."

The weight of her statement stunned me into silence. I blinked away tears and then cleared my throat, trying to compose myself. "Does...does this sort of thing happen to you?"

"It has," she admitted. "But it's been a while. It's more than a feeling for me, too. Can I see you on Friday?"

I let out a breath. "Don't you have the girls?"

"I got a babysitter."

I became choked with emotion. "Oh, good—"

"Lunch is about to end," she whispered, as children's voices called her name. *Miss Tinke...Miss Tinke*, "I'll call you tonight."

"Okay, bye."

"Bye."

Click.

THIRTY-EIGHT

LAUGH AT THE CONFUSION,
LIVE FOR THE MOMENT

OCTOBER 5, 2017
THE GYM

"Hey, Sam Drucker, some guy just loaded one of your dumbbells into his trunk!"

I whipped my head around to see The Gym's prominent doctor at the check-in counter. "Dr. Linder, what a pleasant surprise."

The sixty-year-old doctor was a strong-willed woman, gifted with intelligence and a keen sense of humor. "Matty told me you finally found love, so I booked a flight to check on the house and get the scoop." She was speaking loudly, in the sort of voice I imagined her using on her lecturing circuit. "The place looks great, but where's your wine cooler?"

I winced and quickly waved her into the office. Her husband, a scratch golfer named Mark, glanced over at us and shook his head on his way to the treadmills. Dr. Linder was blessed with many gifts, but height was not one of them. She sat down, pointing to her new gym shoes as her legs swung in front of me, like a child on a swing at the playground. "Do you like my new sneaks?" she asked, raising her gaze to me.

Something about her was absolutely refreshing. "When was the last time I saw you?"

Her face was thoughtful as she sought to remember. "January," she said. "Right after one of your adventures with a girl you called Maya the Mermaid." She clapped once gleefully, pointing at me. "How's that for a memory?"

"Not so loud. That mermaid bit never sounds the same sober."

She leaned forward, lowering her voice. "I wasn't kidding about the guy who stole your dumbbell. He slammed his trunk and left skid marks."

I smirked. "That sounds about right."

She laughed lightly. "You know him?"

"Yes, it's Fred," I nodded. "He steals dumbbells because I refuse to freeze his membership when he plays golf instead."

Dr. Linder's jaw dropped, her eyebrows raised, and she muttered, "You better be taking notes for the sequel because that is priceless." She paused as the office line rang. "Are you going to get that?"

"No, it's old man, Whibbles." I leaned back in the chair as her eyes widened, amused. "It's funny," I continued. "I bought this place hoping it would inspire a sequel, but when I found my notepad from *The Show*, I started using it as a journal for *The Gym*, and it ended up changing my perspective on everything."

"Perhaps Peter Pan's finally growing up?" She smiled her sunny, good-natured smile at me. "Dr. Seuss said that you'll never know the value of a moment until it becomes a memory."

A new member stuck her head in the office, moving her gaze over us. "Larry, can you show me how that weight machine works?" she said, pointing across The Gym.

"Sure," I said, jumping up. "I only hope you have a sense of humor."

With a reluctant backward glance, she smiled, walking over to it, and flipped her ponytail. "It's the one in the corner..."

Dr. Linder shook her head. "This ought to be good."

With the doctor chuckling bright red, I thought twice about that and yelled, "Matty, can you assist on the...um," I lowered my voice, "hip flexing...bicep curl thingy in the corner?"

Matty shot me a look as the young lady stood at the machine. "Thanks again, Larry," she shouted back to me, taunting me with another flip of her tail.

Dr. Linder fanned herself, attempting to regain her composure. Her gaze shifted to the office line when it rang again. "Whibbles?" I nodded. "So, tell me about this loony toon who steals your weights?"

"He's a few cards short of a full deck, so his wife brings them back wrapped in her yoga mat to keep the peace." The office rang yet again, and my jaw firmly clenched. I snatched the phone off the charger. "Good morning," I moaned. "The Gym."

"Is this the leader?"

I cringed. "Whibbles, if the voicemail doesn't pick up, please just come in." I heard a thud and felt a tiny swell of panic when I spun to the doctor, who was wheezing. She had tipped backward in the chair and gotten wedged against the wall. "Got to go, Whibbles…"

Whibbles repeated himself, "Is this the leader—"

Click.

With Dr. Linder's little legs flailing in the air, I dropped the phone and pulled her back down. Mark was still shaking his head at us from afar as voices of concerned members shrieked in unison, "Is she having a heart attack?" Her eyes were slits, so I gave her a quick mist of spray from our new organic cleaner.

I stood back. "Dr. Linder," I said urgently. "Can you see me?" I held up three fingers. "How many fingers do you see?"

A collective sigh went out when she smacked my hand away from her face, which was now a brighter shade of red. "I'm not having a heart attack," she choked out. "I can't stop laughing!"

I took several deep breaths and then said in a far calmer tone, "Well, you might want to start incorporating our organic cleaner into your daily beauty regimen because your skin's looking radiant." I resprayed her. "My gift to you."

I handed her the bottle.

A hoarse groan escaped her throat. "Stop—" She took an erratic breath. "I started cracking up because this place is Petticoat Junction, and you are Sam Drucker!"

Laughter bubbled up in the back of my throat. "I'm stealing that line."

She took a sip of water. "It's true."

I said, "That's why I'm stealing it."

She then took another sip of water, relaxed enough to ask for a picture of Allison. "Okay, let me see her," she insisted, placing the bottle down. "Show me your new leading lady." She rubbed her hands together. "Matty said she's adorable."

I lunged for my iPhone like a lost boy. "Okay, who does she look like?" I asked her and held up Allison's picture.

She wiped her eyelids, cursing me under her breath while staring at it for a long moment. And then gasped, "Tinker Bell!"

I smiled at the serious depth of her wonderment but nodded cautiously. "Dr. Linder, please don't lean backward," I pleaded when she started wheezing again. "What now?"

"I just finished reading about Wendy in *The Show,* and you hand me a picture of Tinker Bell for the sequel," she exclaimed incredulously. "And do it with a straight face?"

I tried to smile. "I realize how it sounds, but it was in the stars—"

"What?" she said quickly, her eyes flashing.

"I've heard the name Allison Tinke from the time I bought this place. She reached out to me, and then—"

"STOP!" shouted the doctor, cutting me off. "Don't ruin the story because I'm really looking forward to reading it."

Perhaps she had a point, I thought and rose to my feet as my eyes fell on her when she asked me who the villain in the sequel was. After I told her to guess, I hinted that she did business with him, and her eyes lit up as if I flipped a switch. "Of course, Hook…Captain Hook!" she said knowingly. "He couldn't stand you, which means one thing." She paused for effect. "His girlfriend somehow found her way into your storyline, too."

My chest tightened with anxiety. "I only asked for his name. And for the record, I had no idea she was with the Captain." I cleared my throat. "You're putting me in a fragile state. Let's move on."

Her girlish glee tickled me. "Hold on, I better be in it, too!"

I smiled. "I'm visualizing a chapter with you now." I started scribbling notes. "Give me a second."

Without a moment's hesitation, she asked, "What happens?"

"Picture this," I said eagerly. "You surprise me at The Gym, then proceed to laugh so hard that you fall back to the wall with your little legs flailing about, wheezing uncontrollably—"

"I will shoot you!" she shouted ecstatically. "And how about Matty?" I nodded again, as she then hollered across The Gym. "Matty, Larry's sequel stars Tinker Bell, and he battles the evil Captain Hook, and we're both in it!"

With raised eyebrows all around us, I quickly shoved the notes in my backpack and sank into the chair as Matty marched in with her Mighty Mouse persona on ten. "Of course, we're in it," said Matty excitedly. "You're the doctor, and I'm his gym mom." The fit trainer took a breath. "And you have no idea how taxing it's been on me," she turned to me with a burst of laughter, "right, son?"

Just then, the ponytail girl came back. "Hi, again," she said and shifted her gaze to Matty. "You showed me how to use the leg press yesterday, but I want to know how many reps I should be doing?"

Matty shot me a look while handing me Fern and Gemma's business cards. Placing them in my back pocket, I whisked the young lady by the spin bikes. "Would you like to hire a trainer?" I asked. She shook her head and skipped on into the yoga studio.

When I turned back towards the office, Dr. Linder shouted, "I'll bet you wish you still had your wine cooler now."

Matty was scolding her when I walked back in. "Don't tempt him, doctor. He's met a nice girl and changed his wayward ways," she said with a smile, as our voices rose into a perky prattle.

Just minutes later, my social media guru, Dara, strolled into the merriment and said, "Lar, I can hear you guys laughing outside."

"Come on in and join the fun, Dara," I said, glancing at where my wine cooler once sat. "I only wish I had a glass of red to raise to you."

Comprehension registered on Dara's face as she pulled her T-shirt out and stuffed her iPhone in her bra to give me a high-five. "We should be toasting to The Gym. I haven't lost an ounce since I've been a member, but I always leave laughing and feeling great."

I gave her a quick sympathetic look when Allison's name flashed up on my iPhone and said, "Keep it down to a low roar, ladies. It's Tink!"

I hurried by Dara as she gave me another high-five before racing out the door.

After pacing with nervous energy for a minute of small talk, I finally sat down on the bench when Allison got to the point of her call. "Bill knows your publisher wants a sequel, and he's concerned," she said. "He'd like to take you to lunch, but you didn't respond."

I took a deep breath that came out in a weary sigh. "I'm not having lunch with Bill," I said. "But before he spins anything else, I need to tell you something."

"About Linda?"

I adjusted myself uncomfortably on the bench. "No," I said solemnly. "Before Linda, I went out with Bill's ex, Maya—"

Allison heaved an even deeper sigh. "Maya?"

"Yes," I confessed. "But I want to tell you something she said—"

"Bill only used Maya to make me jealous," Allison huffed. "What did she say?"

"She came up with this incredible scenario for a sequel, and it's turning out to be true. With you—"

"With me?" she blurted out, cutting me off.

The sea breeze picked up, and I shot to my feet, energized. "Yes. Maya suggested the Tinker Bell coffee mug I drank from in *The Show* was some mystical sign you'd come into my life during the storyline of *The Gym*."

I could hardly breathe for a moment.

Allison continued. "Bill told Maya they called me Tink at The Gym."

My stomach dropped. "And therefore, Maya had this dream while reading *The Show* that we met. She viewed the mug as a terrific tease because obviously there was no mention of Tink—of you—in *The Show*."

"I'm starting to think I should call you, Peter." With a sharp breath, Allison exhaled. "Larry, this is scary…"

"It's magical."

My pulse quickened.

"I feel like a little girl with you," she said slowly. "So, this is a happily ever after for us. And Karma coming back to kill Bill."

"Kill Bill," I laughed, "that's a good one—"

"Now I know why Bill's losing it," she said, just above a whisper while abruptly moving us along. "How about The Kilted Mermaid Friday at seven?"

Mindful, it was time to move on from my story's imaginary backdrops, I quickly added, "Great. Should I pick you up?"

"Yes," she responded enthusiastically.

At that moment, I realized I was happy to be on that bench, talking to her, and smiled. "I'm excited."

"I wish it were Friday," she giggled like a girl, "oh, and Peter, I like this storyline…"

My mouth was dry and my hands clammy, but I felt exhilarated.

"Bye, Tink."

"Bye, Peter."

Click.

THIRTY-NINE

AND THE SECOND STAR TO THE RIGHT BURNED BRIGHT AGAIN

OCTOBER 6, 2017
THE KILTED MERMAID
It was Friday evening.

At 6:47, I glanced at my iPhone, took a deep breath, and knocked on Allison's apartment door. Immediately, it was thrust open. Josie, Allison's adorable youngest daughter, first introduced herself along with their dog, Biscuit. The rambunctious Chihuahua jumped and yapped as wildly as she did when Allison showed me her place on Sunday night. My heart pounded in my chest, unable to move around the dog, snipping at my hands. Then with a sudden tug on my shirt, Josie pulled me into the apartment.

We stopped at the side of the kitchen.

My gaze ran over the quaint candlelit space when their babysitter's head abruptly turned to avoid eye contact. With another step forward, I saw Allison's beautiful, more reserved older daughter, Amelia, watching TV. She didn't say a peep. When her gaze shifted to the bedroom door, Allison stepped out, looking as pretty and perfect to me as she did on Sunday. She smiled wide, not thinking twice about the chaotic scene playing out in front of us, and placed her wine glass down when the teenage sitter whispered something in her ear.

Minutes later, we were on our way.

"I'm sorry about having the kids see me," I said as we walked to my car.

Allison grinned. "I thought you'd wait in the hall," she said unconvincingly. "But it's fine."

"So, Josie's seven, and Amelia is nine?"

Her blue eyes darted up to catch my reaction. "Soon to be eight and ten," she answered and chuckled. "And my babysitter approves of you."

We stood still for a moment, mirroring each other's smiles.

Ten minutes later, we sat a high-top at the Kilted Mermaid, picking up right where we left off. It was as if we were gambling all our chips at once, only with the realization we'd already won. The happiness we felt together was comforting, yet constantly pinpointing that moment of freefall. "Do you believe in love at first sight?" I asked, exhilarated.

Allison was thoughtful as the waitress brought over our bottle of wine and said, "I'm not a hopeless romantic." She paused as I tasted it and gestured to the waitress to pour our glasses. "But as I've stated, there is something about you. Something I was willing to get a babysitter to explore." She leaned back as the waitress poured her glass and added, "So, thanks for leaving me that voicemail."

We raised our glasses to each other.

"Thanks for sending me that message," I replied with a smile.

She beamed. "I guess this has been quite the love story already."

"To further exploring us."

We clinked glasses.

I gestured to the menu and asked her what she was in the mood to eat. As I lifted my gaze to her, she told me that she didn't typically have heavy meals at night. She planned on getting a small plate, possibly the seared tuna. While pondering that, Allison explained that she had struggled with an eating disorder. "Have you dated anyone with one?" she asked. Her tone was serious. Suddenly, I wondered what size her petite sleeveless top was.

I took another sip of wine. "I don't think so," I said. "But I'm sure you can enlighten me."

As Allison did, I realized she had suffered through a surprising amount of emotional and physical abuse, which she more easily spoke about since the "Me Too" movement had blown up. But then she brought up her depression, and my expression startled her. She shook her head with a flash of concern. "I'm sorry," she said. A look of embarrassment came over her face. "That's too much for a second date."

"No. I appreciate you speaking so candidly—" she interrupted me.

"I see a woman's baggage overwhelming you."

I leaned back, concerned; however, I wanted to be reassuring. "It used to," I admitted. "My perspective has changed over the past year. Ironically, the notepad I kept for *The Gym* helped me immensely."

She hesitated. "You mentioned it became a journal, right?"

"Yes. One that played into me leaving you that voicemail."

"Really?"

I nodded, relieved she was smiling, and continued, "There was this teacher who I went out with once last summer. It wasn't a love connection, but she seemed fascinated by the women I talked to and suggested I call you. I stared at those notes for weeks and believed that was the reason I met her. Crazy stuff like that..." my voice trailed off.

An amused expression flashed across her face. "It sounds like a story within a story."

"I guess it is. Anyway, it was necessary. And I'm grateful."

She smiled. "It's refreshing that I don't need my walls up around you. I guess that's why I'm sharing so much. That is rare for me. Trusting a man is not something I easily do." She paused thoughtfully. "So, did you come here with Linda?"

I took a sip of wine and almost spat it out. "Yes," I wiped my mouth, "I'm sorry. I wasn't expecting that—"

"Any good stories from that night?"

I blinked, thinking. "There was always something with Linda. That's why I called her Lucy." Allison rolled her eyes. "We sat on the deck one-night last summer and posted a picture of us on Facebook." I shook my head. "Shortly after that, she lost it when Schultz went off on her."

"Schultz?" she said with a puzzled expression.

"My sales manager in *The Show*. The guy who saw nothing heard nothing and knew nothing having to do with me." I paused as her eyes narrowed at me. "You didn't get to Schultz?" She shook her head and placed her wine glass down.

"No. I just started your book," Allison admitted. "So, what happened?"

"Well, Schultz enjoyed pressing Linda's buttons, and it all blew up on that hot summer night. I'll have to show you." I scrolled my Facebook searching for the post and realized Linda was gone. "She unfriended me." Then I noticed the teacher did as well. The only one who hadn't was Kim. I held her profile picture up to Allison and added, "She's the only one left." I laughed awkwardly. "Too many women have come and gone this past year."

"It's life in the dating world." She paused, and her head tilted slightly. "Why are you smiling?"

"Because I'm happy sitting across from you."

The pixie dust began to fall.

Allison lifted her glass over her smile and took a sip. She placed it down gently. "I don't have my girls this weekend," she said, looking irresistible. "Spend the weekend with me so we can be happy together."

Two hours later, we walked out under the stars. Allison trembled as I kissed her parted lips. A cluster of stars palely glowed above us, and then one suddenly flickered brighter, and I kissed her again.

"Is that your second star to the right, Peter?" she whispered with a whimsical expression.

I gazed up at it, inspired by her enthusiasm, and continued the fun. "It's been a long time since I've seen it. This weekend we'll take it…and go straight on til morning, Tink…"

Allison looked up at me. "I can't wait," she breathed out, as the second star to the right burned bright again.

FORTY

A SAUCY & SEXY KINDA SATURDAY

OCTOBER 7, 2017
ALLISON'S APARTMENT
I opened The Gym the next morning.

The ocean kissed the shoreline as a sunrise of promise lifted in front of me. I leaned back on the bench, thinking about Allison, and drew in a slow breath of the beach air, feeling energized. Wilson texted me. *I'll be there shortly, but you should call Allie. She seems upset that we don't hang out anymore. That wrestler guy who lifts weights wearing the Santa hat is getting close with her.*

I sighed and went to call Allie when Allison then texted me. *I want to go to Waldo's first and take a walk on the beach. The girls will be picked up in thirty minutes, so hurry up!*

And that was the end of that.

An hour later, I was at Allison's apartment. She answered the door with her blue eyes glistening and her left leg out behind her to hold back Biscuit. We hugged with an eye on the rambunctious Chihuahua, who was yapping and springing in the air. "Biscuit," she yelled, abruptly shutting the door. "Stop!" When Allison noticed me swaying with beads of sweat forming on my forehead, she scooped the dog up, and I scurried by them as if my overnight bag were a football, and I was going in for a touchdown. I set it down on an odd armchair with a quickened pulse and turned to her. She was singing the Swedish reggae band Ace of Base's song "The Sign." When it ended, she added, "I hope you like nineties music. I'm a bit younger than you. You were the eighties, right?"

She looked adorable, and I couldn't help but smile. "Is seven years that big a difference?"

She turned up the next song, "No Scrubs" by TLC while dancing up to me, shaking her head. *No, I don't want to meet you nowhere*—she pointed at me and sang the lyrics, *No, I don't want none of your time - No, I don't want no scrub - a scrub is a guy who can't get no love from me...*

I wiped my forehead with the boxer briefs that I had pulled out of my bag and planned on asking for a cup of coffee but grabbed the bottle of Josh Cabernet under them. "Would you mind if I open this?" I asked, envisioning a sexy, saucy kinda Saturday.

Her eyes lit up, pleased as punch. "Great idea!" she chirped and grabbed two wine glasses. "I'm going to change into a sundress I bought." I tore the cork out of the bottle. "I'll be right back." She pulled her shirt off and danced into her bedroom. "You're going to *love* it..."

After watching the shirt land on her bed, I filled the glasses she left on the counter. Instantly aroused, my gaze shifted back to her bedroom, and I noticed my book on her nightstand. With a racing heart, I took a giant gulp of wine, listening to her beautiful voice as she sang in her closet. When she came out, she looked so irresistible I only wanted to tear it off. "I don't like wearing bras," she said with a smile. "Does it work?"

"Uh, huh," I muttered, adjusting my jeans.

She held her arms out as House of Pain's song "Jump Around" blared out of the little TV speakers. Before I knew it, I was refilling my glass, and she was jumping up and down with her hands in the air as if she didn't care. *JUMP—JUMP—JUMP...*

Two hours later, we were at Waldo's in Vero Beach. We kicked back at an outdoor table with the stiff breeze blowing off the glistening Treasure Coast waters. Allison continually pushed her blond hair behind her ear as it blew in her face while I answered her questions about Wendy. She leaned over her Chardonnay and asked, "So, where is Wendy now?"

"Still in Tampa."

She smiled. "So, you let life play out and then write about the experience?"

Feeling a flutter in my stomach, I said, "I tried to write the sequel as more of a novel, but real life became stranger than fiction. Besides, my publisher insisted on a continuation with my inspired character—"

"Peter Pan Man." She grinned mischievously.

I raised the wine glass to my lips. "Yes." I smiled and took a sip.

"Imagine that," she said. "Does he grow up in the sequel?"

I reluctantly nodded. "He is trying."

She tilted her head up at me teasingly. "So, this is another love story?"

I shrugged. "Hopefully."

"Hopefully?" she continued. "From what I see, it's like life gifted you a romantic comedy with some colorful characters and a beachside gym. I mean Bill and Maya and Linda and Hook and your notepad and your father coming to me and you hearing my name from the beginning of the storyline...and now, here we sit," she shrugged her shoulders. "How do you get better than that?"

I swirled my wine in the glass, thinking I shouldn't get ahead of myself. "I mean, hopefully, it will have a happy ending."

Her blue eyes rolled into mine. "Last night, when you told me you were happy to be sitting across from me, it summed up how I feel with you," she breathed out, relieved. "I'm happy. I've never felt this comfortable or compatible with anyone."

Our gazes shifted to my iPhone when Wilson called. "What's up, Wilson?" I put the call on speaker.

"Those two ladies who complain about everything want their money back because they found out the old owner uses Pine-Sol when he cleans The Gym," he replied.

I sighed. "How would they know that?" I asked and shook my head.

"Chuck told them."

I pinched the bridge of my nose. "Say goodbye, Wilson."

"Bye, boss—"

Click.

Allison shot me a confused look and said, "So, how did you end up at my favorite beachside gym?"

I took a longer sip of wine. "After signing the publishing contract for *The Show*, I received a list of businesses for sale, and it was the only one circled." I shrugged as her jaw dropped. "I didn't want to freak you out, but I could've sworn I saw the same guy the day I met you at Captain Hiram's."

Her eyes flashed. "I just got chills."

"I did too."

Three hours later, after a long walk on the beach, we had to go back to Allison's apartment to walk the dog. "My neighbor Donny loves dogs and walks Biscuit during the day, but I do at night," Allison explained, as we walked the dog around her apartment complex.

"What happens when Donny's no longer there for you?"

She paused and tugged on the leash when Biscuit started chasing a squirrel. "I don't know, but when I eventually move out, I'll be fined for the damage she's done to the place."

I shook my head. "The dog seems to be a lot to deal with—"

She quickly cut me off, "We love her."

I left the conversation there, and when we got back in the apartment, Allison turned up her nineties music and lit some candles. Meanwhile, Biscuit ate dinner in the kitchen and yapped at something under the stove as I opened a bottle of Bonterra Cabernet. I was feeling quite buzzed, and it wasn't from the wine.

I sat down on the couch and gazed around the apartment.

Allison grabbed her wine and kicked off her flip flops, sending them under the coffee table. We clinked glasses yet again and stared into each other's eyes for a moment before we kissed. After placing our wine down, I gently grabbed her cheeks and kissed her again. Then my shirt was on the ground, and her sundress landed on our wine glasses. I throbbed with desire staring at her. Her beautiful breasts were calling my name when I cupped them, moving us into her bedroom. At the foot of her bed, I blinked back to our trail of clothes while kissing her neck, and with a sudden breath, we were on it. I swept my fingers between her legs as cool air from a ceiling fan hardened her nipples even more. Her body shuddered. Her face was glowing. The veins in her neck fluttered wildly with every beat of her heart, and I was right there with her. The strength of what was building was staggering. She shuddered against me, her legs trembled, and then I collapsed to the side of her as if I had taken a bullet.

Biscuit snipped at my ass, which was facing the side of the bed. I heard myself scream, "MAN DOWN!" and she raced out of the room. Allison jumped up with an expression of amusement and exasperation as the dog ran around the tiny living room like she was possessed. The scene was indescribably chaotically erotic. I stared admiringly at the back of Allison's perfect little body as she kicked my jeans out of the door frame and slammed her bedroom door. I shook my head, humored after she locked it feeling for blood. She turned to me with wide eyes. "Stay like that," she warned me in a lusty whisper. "Just. Like. That."

"How much blood did I lose?"

Staring at my stiffy, Allison beamed. "Not much—"

"The dog bit my ass, not my Sicilian saaausich (sausage)."

Her cheeks puffed as she huffed, "You're not from Sicily, you're from Long Island, you freak!" She jumped back on the bed, glowing. "But I love your saaausich—" she ignored the dog bouncing off the door—THUD—yapping piercingly.

I winced and wiped my forehead. "Please, tell me this Biscuit of yours came with a tranquilizer gun."

She straddled me. "Make love to me." We kissed, then tensed when there was another—THUD—even louder.

With the door shaking, I sputtered, "I doubt MMMBop can drown out Cujo, but can you at least raise the volume?"

She murmured, "Shush...I want to drink in your scent." She lowered her head and kissed me again. My head throbbed with excitement.

I couldn't hear anything but my pounding heart. Our bodies were on fire as Allison slid, effortlessly, over me. "Fuuuck..." I breathed out blissfully and heard that lovely tinkle of bells, again.

FORTY-ONE

THE PROMISE

OCTOBER 8, 2017
ALLISON'S APARTMENT

My eyes fluttered open to Allison's fairy face, asleep with a magical smile on it. With waves of warm energy radiating from my chest, I visualized her as my girlfriend and dozed off again, mirroring her smile.

Thirty minutes later, I awoke to take a piss and winced when Biscuit scratched on the bedroom door. I must have still been drunk coming back through the bedroom because I tiptoed around the bed as her obnoxious whining could be heard in the apartment across the hall. With a quick peek at sleeping beauty, I climbed back under the covers wondering why Biscuit was now bouncing off the door—*THUD*—*THUD*—*THUD!*

My head pounded from the wine and racket, and finally, I whispered, "Allison." She smiled wider. "I'm no dog whisperer, but I believe Cujo wants a walk." She backed her bare ass into me, and I tried again. "Allison…" I paused, suddenly aroused. "The sun is up…and so is my…" I shifted myself in bed while lifting the covers to blow on it.

That made it worse.

She pushed herself back against me, and that was that. "A-Allison," I softly sputtered. "I need to take you deep. Again." Her eyes snapped open. I gazed into them and felt something else. The forthright intimacy between us produced this absolute bliss.

She moved closer, and we began again.

Just as that fantastical energy washed over us, we were shaken back to reality, breathing heavily with the dog barking and most of the covers on the floor. We calmed our breathing, and Allison jumped out of bed.

"Are you really fifty?" she asked with a curious grin. I only smiled at her as she grabbed a shirt from her drawer and continued, "That was nice. I have to walk, Biscuit. I'll make you a cup of coffee and turn on CNN."

I wiped my forehead. "I'm happy."

She turned to me with a sleepy smile. "I'm happy, too."

After putting on her adorable Lilly Pulitzer shorts, she kissed me again. I rolled over and waited for the dog to be harnessed up with this funky leash thingy they walked her in before I pushed myself out of bed. I stretched out with a yawn and then meandered into the kitchen for my caffeine fix, timing it in sync with the door shutting behind them. With a quick sip, I sat down on the couch, eyeing all the organic shit in her kitchen, when her iPhone pinged on the coffee table in front of me. I leaned over the text, and tension shot up my back. It was Bill Reed. *Allison, call me!* I swallowed hard. Ten seconds after that, he texted her again. *Larry's a talker. He's been with many women.* And then, *I will always look out for you.*

A sick feeling balled up in my stomach as I paced the space before sitting back on her couch with racing thoughts. *Three texts on a Sunday morning. How often do they communicate? Why do they still talk? What the hell is going on here?*

Ten minutes later, I stood up and brushed dog hair off my briefs as Allison walked back in, elated. "How's the coffee?" I nodded, sitting back down with my best pouty face when Biscuit immediately curled up next to me on the couch. "Oh, how cute is that? She loves you!" I waited for a beat, then met her gaze. It was then she read Bill's texts. I took a breath, realizing I should relax.

Meanwhile, I checked my iPhone, and she strolled back into the kitchen without saying a word. With a raised eyebrow, I was curious as to why she seemed as annoyed as I was. She glared at me and said, "What's going on in the news?"

"Harvey Weinstein was fired from his company after allegations of sexual abuse," I said as my right foot tapped the carpet anxiously. "What's going on with Bill?"

She grimaced at his texts for a moment. "I wish you would've responded to his Facebook message, Larry."

I exhaled with doubt, then placed my coffee on the table. The air was thick with discomfort. "Why wouldn't you tell me he texted you?"

She stared unblinkingly at me. "Because I now know the truth," she said. Her voice grew angry. "I refuse to get caught up in Bill or Linda's bullshit. But it's you who have provided them enough ammunition to scare anyone interested in you off." She paused, and I knew that was the reason she was annoyed. "Your book is a lot to handle, and for the record, I'm not interested in reading about Wendy."

"It's a book to entertain, Allison," I said, increasingly irritated.

She continued, "It's accurate. But I know the guy behind the pixie dust is not a player, regardless of how many people swear he is."

She shot me a look.

There was a short, uncomfortable silence.

"So, what is it that you see in me?" I asked, feeling vulnerable.

With sincerity in her eyes, she said, "A flawed, good guy determined to get this next chapter of your life right. I know you don't want to hear about another man, but—"

"No buts," I said, cutting her off.

She quickly added, "Well, as I told you, I walked away from someone this summer who promised me the world." She paused and shrugged. "I did it because of this feeling I have about you."

I suddenly realized some jealousy was necessary to maintain the idea that I could fall in love with Allison and sighed. "Okay, I got jealous." I held up my hand, "I'm sorry, although it dawned on me, this could be a good thing."

She crossed her arms. "Go on..."

"I had sat down with my coffee, feeling fantastic about you, and Bill's crap flashed in front of me. It's been a long road full of potholes to get here, and suddenly it's real."

She exhaled. "Well, your storyline calls for a strong leading lady to endure all that is you."

I worked hard to keep the hysteria out of my voice. "All that is me? I've heard your name since I purchased The Gym, and now, you're about to star in the story of my life while still receiving texts from your ex-fiancé?"

Allison took a deep breath to compose herself. "An ex who left The Gym because a girl he dated ended up with you."

"A girl he dated to make you jealous!"

A spark of humor flitted across Allison's gaze, causing me to brace myself. "A girl who was seventeen years younger than you. Like your little Wendy!"

I moaned obnoxiously, "Wendy was...okay, whatever. You're putting me in a fragile state."

Allison's lips lifted in a little half-smile. "Let's not forget about Linda," she said and rolled her eyes. "Lucille fucking Ball—"

"Okay," I cried out.

"I'll give you a fragile state."

I stood up, and the dog jumped off the couch as our eyes met in mutual understanding of our unique situation. "Shit," I muttered softly. "This is ridiculous. I really like you and was freaked out."

She echoed, "I really like you. So much so I wanted to cross off everything on my checklist this weekend. I've never had a man stay the weekend after two dates, so consider yourself special." She tilted her head slightly with a lusty smile.

I leaned back on the couch. "I get it," I smiled as Biscuit came right back to me, "sex is important."

She nodded. "So, does your penis like my vagina as much as my vagina likes your penis?"

I could've sworn Maya used the same line and laughed awkwardly but then began getting aroused again. "Oh, yes, they belong together like peanut butter and jelly," I said, while even pretending to pet Biscuit, who now had her head nuzzled on my thigh.

Allison beamed. "And by the way, everyone knows you end up with Tinker Bell, not Wendy." She took a steadying breath as her facial expression turned serious. "So, if I'm going to star in the story of your life, you have to promise to be strong with me, too." A look of hope crossed her face. "Promise me..."

"I promise."

FORTY-TWO

LOVE IS A GAME THAT TWO
CAN PLAY AND BOTH CAN WIN

OCTOBER 18, 2017
THE GYM
It was ten days later.

Every new day had us focused on the next time we'd see each other. We were like little kids for whom the best amusement was just being together. I searched for seven years for this.

I lowered the windows driving south on A1A, besotted with "love hormones," awaiting Allison's first text. On this beautiful autumn morning, it flashed up as I swung into a parking space in front of The Gym: *I miss you!* (heart face emoji)

Grateful for every goosebump she gifted me, I typed: *I miss you too!*

It was just before eight o'clock, fifteen minutes before Patty's spin class, when I pulled a load of fresh gym towels from my dark trunk and into a brighter day. Waving at my gym family calling out to me, I approached the door greeted by Chris Aron, a new member I befriended. He was a realtor roughly my age who moved into the empty office space next door. "I have to make a call, but I need to talk to you," Chris whispered. "I'll be back in a bit."

I nodded and rushed into the office ahead of a woman from D.C. She purchased a week pass and my book while visiting her mother in Melbourne Beach. "Good morning, Caroline," I said to the forty-something pharmaceutical rep, anxious for her recap of *The Show*. "Were you able to finish?"

The Lisa Kudrow look-alike appeared anxious. "Yes," she said hastily. "I left a review on Goodreads for you." Her gaze shifted to the parking lot and then back to me. "So, Peter Pan Man, how do you find true love?"

I grinned at her. "It's written in the stars. But you must believe."

Caroline stared at me for a long moment. "Seriously, you're not jaded after that crash and burn?"

I opened my mouth, but no words came out. Then sputtered, "I…well, no." I paused as the door opened.

Her boyfriend stumbled in. "You forgot your earbuds," he yelled out. I marveled at how much he resembled George Costanza from Seinfeld. When he turned to stretch out, I blinked away from the curly chest hair coming out of his V-neck and bit down on my lip when he started doing squats. "Okay, sweetie, are you ready to sweat?"

She nodded at him, unenthused. Then her gaze fell to the floor. "Why are you wearing different socks?"

"What?" he pulled his earbuds out.

"Never mind," she moaned.

He looked down. "Oh, it was the way they came out of the wash," he muttered. His voice was as flat as his personality.

She rolled her eyes at him, and I smiled. "Enjoy your workout."

I sat down and read a post-it-note from a member who enjoyed our yoga classes. *I heard you're dating Allison. Congrats, you should get her to teach yoga here. She's terrific!* I placed the note on the desk next to a stack of bills and still managed to smile, even after Patty sent me a text that she was sick. When Patty suggested Gemma sub for her, I answered the office line without checking the caller I.D. "Good morning, The Gym."

"Is this the leader?"

I chuckled. "Whibbles, I can't talk. I thought you were Patty—"
Click.

Since Gemma was training a client, I ran over to confirm she could teach the spin class and then heard a loud thud. It was Caroline's boyfriend against the odd beach mural by the treadmills. He sat against the wall, bright red, as Caroline waved me back, embarrassed. "He dropped his cell and almost ended up in the nail salon but is fine," said Caroline as the Ripper strolled in.

I took a shuddering breath. "Please be careful." I turned to the Ripper, who shook his head en route to the office. Once in there, he looked at me, startled before he dropped into his favorite chair.

"I heard you're dating Allison Tinke now."

A smile erupted on my face. "It was written in the stars..."

His brow furrowed. "Don't give me your Never Land nonsense. How did you pull that one off? She's down in Vero."

I crossed my arms. "I-it's a long story," I stammered.

Relentlessly he continued, "Didn't you tell me you knew Allison?"

"No, she reached out to me over the summer on a dating site."

The Ripper recalled the conversation and grinned mischievously. "Her nickname was Tinker Bell when she was a member of The Gym," he said quietly as if he didn't want to hear what he was saying. "Wasn't the leading lady in your book, Wendy?"

Thankfully, my iPhone rang. His smile was so eerie; I stared at it ringing. "It's my son," I finally choked out. "I'll talk to you after your workout..." the Ripper gave me another fist pump, and I ran out to the bench. "Hey, Jerry."

"Daddaay (daddy), don't forget my play!" said Jerry excitedly. "I have two tickets for the matinee. Not this Saturday, but next."

"Yes, of course," I replied, waving at Matty, marching up. "I can't wait."

Jerry continued, "Lauren told me you're bringing your new girlfriend, Allison. I'm looking forward to meeting her."

I hesitated. "Yes, she can't wait to meet you too—"

"Awesome," he said. "I have to run."

With a quick glance at the screen, the call ended, and I spun to a voice behind me. It was my new realtor buddy, Chris, trudging back over. "I heard you're dating Allison Tinke."

I smiled. "Word does spread fast in this tiny town."

Chris lowered his voice. "It was Bob Tillie who told me. I ran into him at Sands on The Beach. He has issues with you. It was unsettling." Chris turned to an associate who called to him. "He said you guys used to be close."

I stood speechless for a moment. "We were never close," I said with a rush of emotion. "He used to be a member."

"Well, he wants to talk to you. He claims he's left messages and even had members leave post-it-notes for you." Chris shook his head. "He also knows I'm next door and wanted me to tell you." His associate called to him again. "We'll talk later."

I nodded, biting my tongue.

Flustered, my eyes darted nervously from him to our hippest couple from the land down under. Rocky and Paul were morning regulars with the coolest Aussie accents. Walking in with them, I knew Rocky needed her HGTV fix and smiled, knowing she'd be asking for the remote. "You know what I need, Larry," said Rocky, sounding as cool as Cate Blanchett.

"Love that accent, Rocky," I said and handed her the remote.

"I'm here for you, Larry."

Agitated about the Bob Tillie update, I forced a smile at Caroline on a treadmill and wandered back into the office.

Ten minutes later, Caroline popped her head in, glistening from her workout. "My forty-one-year-old friend is pregnant!" she blurted out and looked up from a text, shocked. "Sorry, I just heard." She paused, took her earbuds out, and lowered her voice. "Is it weird that I feel like I know you after only a few conversations because of your book?"

I shook my head. "No, I get that a lot."

She sighed, relieved. "Can I pick your brain? It has to do with *The Show*."

I invited her in, scrutinizing her. She pulled her blond hair back and sat down as her brown eyes perused my picture tiles. "It looks like this book's been an awesome experience for you." She took a breath as I nodded. "So, I brought my boyfriend," she rolled her eyes, "Mr. Athletic, with me to introduce him to my mother, but lately, I'm sure. I turned forty-one in September and can't afford to make any more mistakes." She stopped as I nodded quizzically, waiting for her to get to her point. "So, Pan Man," she smirked, "should I wait for that guy who causes me to lose all control or push through with someone stable?"

I gazed out into The Gym. "Where is your boyfriend?"

"He's in the rental car on a conference call." She crossed her legs, seemingly relieved.

"I don't miss those," I commented, as her mind raced on.

It was obvious she wanted to say something. And then whispered, "I was an executive's Wendy," her eyes widened, "although the guy I was involved with was nothing like you."

With a raised eyebrow, I said, "So that's why you were so interested in *The Show*..."

"It hit home for me."

"What was the guy like?"

With a deep breath, she explained that he held a prominent position, but the experience was more of a sexual release than the connection that I had with Wendy. That was what she really *craved*. When she insisted it was nothing like *The Show's* love story, I reiterated the book was fictionalized. And then, with an eye roll, she sneered, "Come on, the connection you had was real. What I had was sleazy."

"And now you want the love story?"

She nodded. "Yes."

After a calming breath, I felt like Dr. Phil. "Well, at least you're not married while looking this time," I shrugged, "but you are in a relationship, and he is into you."

Her shoulders caved. "God, is there something wrong with me?"

"No, I felt the same way during parts of my marriage. It sucks. But it is common—"

"In the book, you could sell ice to an Eskimo but couldn't communicate with your wife. How accurate was that?"

I paused, pondering it all. "Quite accurate, and a major problem."

Without a breath, she added, "You felt trapped?"

"I handled it wrong. I was not raised to get divorced. I thought I could fix everything."

"So, your book is quite accurate."

I nodded solemnly. "I isolated myself in a sports memorabilia room with expensive wine thinking everything would be fine."

She laughed. "But instead of fixing it, you met Wendy."

"Yes."

She grinned. "Isn't it ironic that Bud Fox—your supposed buddy, stuck the knife in your back? I screamed out a few times during those chapters." Caroline paused and touched my knee. I was lost in thought about what Chris had said about Bob. "Are you okay?" she asked. I took a breath and nodded again. She pursed her lips for a moment, then continued, "I think it's best to wait for that person I'm passionate about. I would have a better chance of surviving these crazy stages of love if I did," she rambled on. "I just doubt I'll ever find him."

I shrugged; suddenly, cognizant love is a powerful drug that makes grown-ups act like children. "You must believe in yourself and then actually believe you'll find him…or you won't."

She said nothing for a moment. "Do you believe you'll find another connection like Wendy?"

I smiled. "Yes, I recently found Tinker Bell." I paused as her eyes popped forward alarmingly.

She sat there, motionless, for a couple of seconds. Finally, she laughed. "Now that would be a great sequel," she shook her head, "totally outlandish, but fantastic fantasy!" she gushed like a girl before sighing exaggeratedly. "Seriously, do you?"

"Allison's nickname is Tinker Bell. I was just having fun because I'm not well, but yes, I do believe. And I did find her."

She took a deep breath, seeming to relish the moment. "I need a glass of wine." She sighed, fanning herself with her hand. "Sometimes, I think love is a cruel game."

I shook my head slowly. "Love is a game that two can play and both can win."

She fell back in the chair, grinning, and then read a text.

Her crossed legs uncrossed quickly, and she sat up straight as her tickled grin flatlined. "Shit," she sputtered, looking up. "John's done with his call." She started cracking up. "I can't believe I'm showing you this, but this is what he sent me while reading your book."

"Your boyfriend read my—" I lost all words when she passed me a shirtless picture of him pulling his shorts down to his pubic hairs— hairy belly hanging out—smiling into a bathroom mirror.

She quietly said, "Oh my God, your expression is priceless!"

I blinked hard and handed it back to her. She was now sideways on the chair with her hand over her mouth, giggling. "Why is he pulling his shorts down—never mind—"

Caroline's face lit up, instantly elevating from plain to pretty. "Has anyone told you, you remind them of *Californication's* hopeless romantic writer, Hank Moody?"

I pushed myself up, and my knees buckled. Averting her eyes, I lied, "I don't recall that. No—"

"I'm shocked." She stood up and hugged me. "I enjoyed your book and chats." She took a step back. "You've reminded me I should laugh more, Larry."

Oddly, she then shook my hand. "It's the best medicine for life," I said and walked her out.

Caroline took a few steps and turned back to me. "Love is a game that two can play and both can win." She smiled warmly at me. "I like that."

I smiled back at her as her boyfriend pulled up. "Safe travels home."

"Thank you, Peter Pan Man."

FORTY-THREE

OLIVER TWIST

OCTOBER 28, 2017
WEST SHORE HIGH SCHOOL
It was the following Saturday.

"Allison, we can't be late!" I said in my pseudo actor voice. "The play starts at two."

"Ra-rry, (Larry) rits (it's) ren, (ten)," she mumbled, with toothpaste in her mouth.

With a wry grin, I lowered my voice. "But I miss you."

She started cracking up. "So, you want to have sex before the play?"

"I need you."

"You need my vagina."

"It's delightful. Please hurry."

Two hours later, we pulled into the West Shore High School parking lot. Still feeling high, we jumped out of the car childlike, excited to see Jerry play Bill Sikes, the main antagonist in their fall production of Oliver Twist. With overcast skies, I convinced Allison to leave her giant umbrella in the car. "Allison, that umbrella's bigger than you," I pointed out with an anxious laugh. "Please, leave it in the car."

She tossed it in the backseat with a serene smile.

Suddenly, it hit me how big a deal it was to be walking into this play with my new girlfriend. I stared at the school in consternation, and she squeezed my hand. "Am I really the first woman you've taken to Jerry's plays since you separated from Marie?"

I unclenched my jaw. "Yes."

"Well, I'm honored." She smiled proudly. "Oh, and Bill unfriended me on Facebook. He told me he couldn't stand watching us together. Last Sunday's picture of us at the Lemon Tree killed him."

I ignored her, glancing at the time. "We made good time."

She looked up at me adorably. "Bill could only have sex once every three days."

My eyes narrowed at her. "I don't want to hear his name right now."

"I'm sorry, but I had to kiss a lot of frogs to get to you, Prince Pan."

I sighed. "Okay, but I don't need to be briefed on your sex life with those frogs, Princess Tink."

"Well, it's a compliment!" she chirped, amused. "Mr. Twice a Day."

"I'm sorry." I squeezed Allison's hand. "I'm nervous. This is a big deal. I feel like every eye is on us."

Her gaze shifted to one of Marie's friends. "They are. Who is that lady staring at us?"

"Okay, that's Christina," I muttered quietly to Allison as Christina watched us walk in.

Allison looked up at me. "Not the Christina you told me about from The Gym?"

I blinked. "No—no, not her," I babbled. "She has the son, Gianni. Do you remember?" Allison nodded, and I squeezed her hand. "Here she comes—"

It was time to greet the group. My heart pounded in my chest when she strolled over to us with amusement flickering across her features. After a quick introduction, we shifted to another cluster of people and then sat down with more eyes darting our way.

Minutes later, the lights dimmed. Allison leaned into me and whispered, "The blond who keeps looking over lives in Melbourne Beach."

"Which one? Three heads have been on swivels since we sat down." The music started, "Shush…"

I had goosebumps with Jerry's first scene. The moment he came out, my mouth broke out in a prideful smile. He was wearing a black trench coat and hat. He nailed the Sikes character, and the audience loved it as much as we did.

"Hi, Jerry's dad, Jerry was great!" one parent commented.

I turned to another parent as their gazes were shifting from me to Allison. "Jerry was wonderful!"

"Thank you," I said, walking outside. "Your daughter was great too…"

Ten minutes later, Jerry and Allison hit it off instantly. We took some cute pictures, and off to dinner, we went. Halfway through it, Allison informed me we had to get back to her apartment to walk Biscuit. I placed my wine glass down. "What happened to Donny?"

"He won't be back in time," she muttered.

I took a slow breath. "We'll have to go back to my house and get your car."

"I'm sorry I didn't expect this to happen."

Just as we finished dinner, it started drizzling. By the time we pulled into my driveway, it was a steady rain. I grabbed my overnight bag, wondering how we would walk the dog in a downpour, and hurried out irritated. "We better get going. The forecast only gets worse—"

"Please, don't stress me out, Larry!" Allison cried out with an expression I had not seen yet.

I hesitated. "Okay, I'll wait for you at the stop sign," I said and backed out of the driveway. Driving slowly, I glanced back but didn't see her.

The rain came down harder.

With my windows fogging up, I called her. After it went to voicemail, I started backing up but stopped the car when I saw her little blond bob coming up the street. Panicked, I threw my door open. "What happened?"

She was soaking wet. "Your driveway is so long, and the rain was coming down so hard, and those trees on that side—"

"Allison, what happened?" I snapped, cutting her off, drenched.

Her eyes were wide with worry. "Don't yell at me," she pleaded. "I drove into the swale, and it's filling with water!"

I sprinted back to her car with its headlights shining upwards to the darkened sky. *Holy fuck*, I thought, *I have one shot at getting this out.* I turned to Allison. "Stand back—"

"Stop yelling at me!" she cried out, as anguish flooded her face.

The water was rising fast.

I shouted, "ALLISON, PLEASE STAND BACK!"

My breath was quick and ragged when I climbed into her car. I put it in drive. Slowly and steadily, I pushed the accelerator. The vehicle sank slightly, and I hit it harder to catch the back wheels. It shot up and out of the water as I spun the steering wheel and landed back on the driveway. "Allison, get in."

Thirty minutes later, we were at her apartment. After letting Biscuit out for a few minutes, mainly under the hallway overhang, we dried off. With the scent of lavender wafting out of her bedroom, I opened a bottle of Hess Select Cabernet and noticed Allison had a steady gaze into her laptop. When her fingers began typing frantically, she informed me she was answering emails from the girls' father. Privy to more of her personal life with each passing week, I handed her a glass of wine and made my way to the couch. I shifted uncomfortably on it as anger bubbled up inside her. One email led to another as I listened to her vent. Frantically she typed and shouted out, and after finishing my second glass, I noticed Biscuit eating my Converse and jumped up to snatch it out of her mouth. Allison turned to the commotion, shut her laptop, and then settled on the couch next to me. I put my arm around her attempting to change the subject. "So, you're not such a good driver," I said, cracking a smile.

She scowled, trying to catch her breath. "I used to be," she insisted. Her tone was defensive. "But that was back in New Jersey." I immediately realized that was a mistake, and when she received a text, I quickly moved on.

"Did you give any thought to doing a yoga class at The Gym—"

She didn't let me finish. "Do you remember I told you I ran into Barbie from The Gym?"

I nodded. "Yes."

With her eyes fixated on the text, she continued, "Well, the word's spreading that I'm dating you." She paused reading on and then added, "I heard from another old friend who wants me to do a yoga class at The Gym."

"Wow!" I commented, lifting an eyebrow, realizing she didn't hear a word I said. "You should do one in November. One of those

Brewalicious classes," I took a sip of wine when her eyes slowly closed. "As long as they bring their own beer."

Her eyes shot back open as her face contorted. "Wha-What? It's BrewAsanas," she stammered. "And I don't do that."

My eyebrows were high and mocking when I continued, "How about one of those get fit and stay lit classes, my little yogallini—"

"It's Yogini!" she insisted. "You don't have a clue about yoga, so if you want me to do a class, stop giving me shit about Biscuit."

My eyebrows shot up as the dog destroyed one of the girl's shoes. "Allison, the dog is eating another shoe," I sputtered. "The carpet is trashed, and the furniture's chewed up—" I stopped mid-sentence as she flashed a pained smile staring at Biscuit. "Fine, I'll stop."

Her eyes darted nervously from the dog to me. "I'm not done," she huffed, desperate to move us away from anything having to do with their beloved Biscuit. "I'm only doing the yoga class if you stop making fun of my essential oils and Lifetime movies—"

I stood up. "Whoa!" I sat back down. "Hold that thought. I'll need more wine to continue this negotiation."

"I'm the one who needs more wine." she barked with a sparkle in her eyes and a smile curling on her lips. "Let's talk about the giant Jedi Mickey Mouse on your nightstand."

I raised my index finger and said, "Mickey doesn't chew on that nightstand, though, Allison."

"Larry, grow up!"

One conversation quickly led to another, and as life exposed some of our shortcomings, we were both humbled. It seemed life had a way of doing that to us as we age. It also confirmed our desire to commit to each other. She snuggled up next to me, and all I could think about was how right she felt sitting next to me during Jerry's play.

"So, did you like Oliver Twist?"

"I did very much."

FORTY-FOUR

PLEASE DON'T JINX THE STORYLINE

NOVEMBER 2017
THE GYM
The Snowbirds were coming back.

Just as Barbara's Body Sculpt Class ended, I heard a voice cut through the laughter. "I can't believe you're still alive." I spun around to see Nick Weathers, standing at the check-in counter. Nick was a gregarious Snowbird who had read my book, quite confident I would go off another cliff.

"Hello, Nick," I said with a curious smile. "You're early this season."

He nodded wide-eyed. "I thought I'd be shopping for a new gym," he responded smartly. "But the place looks great. Towels," he picked up one of the spray bottles, "and the picture tiles…wow!" His head was on a swivel. "I am shocked."

"We're redoing the tile in the bathrooms, too," I chirped enthusiastically.

He waved his index finger at me. "The last time I saw you, you were hungover and caught up in some girl drama outside on the bench."

My face flushed with embarrassment. "Yeah, that sounds about right," I said softly while abruptly turning to raised voices.

"He knows nothing about foreign policy and is flying to Asia?" Tensions rose over a news report about President Trump boarding Air Force One for a trip to Asia. *"That buffoon is going to start a war."*

"Really?" our morning regular, Mike, retorted from a treadmill. "We're in a better place now than under Obama." He adjusted his Italia hat as other voices chimed in.

No doubt about that!

A wave of startled uneasiness broke over us. Then there was silence. Snickering at the outburst, Nick inched his way dubiously towards me and into the office. He looked me in the eyes. "You met a girl—another Wendy, perhaps?" he crossed his arms and peered at me, "and you're writing again. I can smell the storyline here." He rubbed his hands together. "Come on, tell me I didn't nail it."

I laughed. "You got me—"

"I knew it." Nick was an avid reader who spoke about life as if it were a storyline. "So, you chased stars while masking your pain, collecting these moments for a new book, unaware they were shaping your destiny. Who's the girl?"

Knowing Nick knew her—because he knew everyone—I muttered, "Allison Tinke."

His head slumped slightly. "TINKER BELL?!" I shushed him. With heads turned to us, I motioned him to have a seat. "Are you kidding?"

I threw up my hands. "I know how it sounds."

He continued, "Tink? We called her Tink back in the day."

My pulse quickened. "I know," I said. "It's been an adventure—"

"Second star to the right and straight on 'til morning!" he exclaimed without taking a breath. "When is the sequel going to be ready?"

"I'm still writing," I said and shrugged. "I'm hoping for a happy ending."

Nick sat down and stood back up, gesturing all around him. "You found Tinker Bell," he smiled eerily, "and beat Hook at his own game." He paused with wide eyes. "Is that miserable bastard still around?"

I could feel the grin on my lips. "He's regrouping on the Jolly Roger."

He chuckled. "Excellent. And you saved The Gym!"

"No, The Gym saved me."

He stood perfectly still for a moment. "Jesus. Pan has grown up." He nodded slowly. "I like that ending even more." Nick paused with a sly smirk and added, "How's Fern and Matty and good ole Chuck?"

"The team's coming together nicely. And we've added a new trainer named Gemma." I pointed to her picture tile.

He peeked at it and shot me a thumbs up, and then made a face. "I heard you had a falling out with Bob Tillie."

I sighed. "Yes, he had a problem for every solution."

Nick flashed me a triumphant smile. "Well said. I wanted to tell you that back in January, but he never left your office. He was not a friend." Nick read the check-in screen. "Is Ohio State Steve back yet?"

I shook my head. "Not yet, but Jack's back."

His gaze shifted to the free weights, and his eyes narrowed at him. "Is he still taking your little cheerleader's Zumba class?"

"He is."

Two days later, Jack, a slightly vain yet fit Snowbird, raced into the yoga studio to take Allie's Zumba Class, not knowing Donna Richards—a grey-haired lady much closer to his age—was now teaching it. This awkward moment created an instant classic. The next day, Jack stormed into my office with a bewildered look on his face. "Larry, where's Allie?"

By this point, the story had circulated through The Gym like pollen, and I couldn't help but laugh. "I'm sorry, Jack. Donna's taking over her class during the week, but Allie's still teaching the Saturday class. She's been busy with her cheer gigs."

He hesitated. "Well, holy shit, Larry. You have to warn me when you do something like that. You almost did me in."

His expression of shock and anger tickled me as I excused myself distracted when Marie texted me. *October makes three months with a sales increase. Keep it up. You might somehow pull this one off!* My heart began pounding in my chest as I stared at the text, suddenly overwhelmed. My new life was being struck in the rear by my old one, and the change was unnerving. When I glanced back at the text, another one flashed up. It was from my college roommate, Mark: *Did you see Meg died? It's all over Facebook. She had been sick. Cancer? Shit. We are officially old. Call me.*

I felt like I was going to hyperventilate and stumbled out to the bench for some fresh air. Sitting there, I hit my Facebook app with watery eyes. Minutes later, I went to call Allison but realized she was teaching and called my daughter instead. "Hey, dad," Lauren answered.

"How's your mom doing?" I said with a sharp breath.

She hesitated. "I mean, she knows Allison's probably going to turn into something serious."

"I want your mom to be happy, too. That's why I'm calling."

"Mom's stubborn," said Lauren. "She does things the way she does them. Didn't we discuss this at Carrabba's?"

My head fell between my knees. For a moment, I listened to the rough surf. "The ocean sounds as angry as you."

She continued, "I'm not angry. I'm happy you found Allison, and mom is fine. She has moved on in her own way. Okay?"

I looked up over the dunes and said, "Meg—my first love died."

"I'm sorry."

"Am I going to see you and Jerry for dinner this weekend?"

"Of course. I think Friday works better." With those words, the breath that had seemed stuck in my chest loosened.

"Okay, good, I love you."

"I love you too, dad."

Click.

In the coming days, I felt better. I realized this was the beginning of what would be a lengthy transition period. So much would be different. On a positive note, I was encouraged that Allison understood my feelings, and we grew closer because of it. She taught a yoga class on the Saturday before Thanksgiving, with another one planned for the second week in December. She was genuinely excited to be back at The Gym as my girlfriend.

One night, as we were getting ready for bed, she had informed me an old member sent her a Facebook friend request while inquiring about her yoga classes. As she carried on about it, I asked her who it was. Thinking I didn't know him, she casually mentioned he was no longer a member but someone who knew Bill and Hook. I sat up in bed. "What's his name?"

While washing her face at the bathroom sink, she bellowed, "Bob Tillie. Do you know him?"

I winced, stunned. "Yes, I do."

She continued, "He heard about my last yoga class and is interested in taking the next one."

I frowned and then took a breath and, as calmly as possible, said, "Allison, he doesn't care about your yoga class."

Holding a towel, she stuck her head out of the bathroom. "Ouch!"

I straightened against the headboard. "I'm sorry. This is about me."

She threw her hands up in frustration and returned to the bathroom. "Everything isn't about you, Larry," she shouted back at me. "So, check your ego—"

"Allison," I said. My voice began to rise. "I'm exhausted, and it's too long a story, so please trust me."

She stuck her head back out and gave me a skeptical look. "Tell me what's going on."

I looked up at the ceiling fan, trying to articulate this. "I'm not on Facebook with Bob anymore, so if you accept his friend request, it's going to be a problem—"

"I'm asking why?" replied Allison in exasperation.

I swallowed the lump in my throat that was always there when we argued. "I don't trust the guy and don't want him to see what we're doing," I said. My tone was sharp.

For an awkward moment, we eyed each other without speaking. "You've shared the names of so many during your adventure at The Gym. Why haven't you mentioned him?"

I looked at her for several long seconds, then said, "Probably because I blocked him out of my mind." I paused for a moment as her eyes begged me to fill her in. "Okay, well, last November, he started hanging out in my office. He was fascinated by the rumors he had heard about me—"

"Me...me...me!" she interrupted. "My God, do you hear yourself?"

I stared at her, my heart racing. "I'm done with this conversation."

She shook her head, adamant. "The truth is the guy had the hots for me years ago." She sighed. "I never liked him that way, and now he's interested in yoga at your gym. You should be happy."

I clamped my lips into a razor-cut line and took a breath. "Allison, Bob can't touch his kneecaps. He has no desire to take any yoga class," I tried to assure her. I slid under the covers, frustrated.

Allison stood there, watching me. She was suddenly amused. "Oh, the little boy's feelings are hurt," she scoffed with the hint of a smile. "Are you okay, Peter Pan? How's your golden penis? Do you want me to kiss it?"

"Go to sleep, Allison."

Her eyes softened. "Pouty little mama's boy."

"Please go to sleep," I murmured as my eyes drifted closed.

The next morning, I left her apartment at five o'clock and raced home to shower before heading to The Gym. During my first break of the day, around eleven o'clock, I sent Allison a lengthy text explaining everything that happened with Bob. An hour later, at lunch, she texted me back. *I'm sorry, I hate it when we fight. I did accept Bob's friend request and invited him back to The Gym. If you want me to unfriend him, I will.*

I felt uneasy but let it go.

Later that night, I found out that Allie ran into Bob at L.A. Fitness, again. Allie now thought Bob was obsessed with Allison. With a sigh, I read through some old notes and called Allie. After she brought me up to speed on how much weight he had gained, she surmised from their conversation that Bob was obsessed with Allison.

When she repeated herself, I said, "I think you're a bit overly dramatic."

"I'm not. Bob rambled on about both of you with slurred speech. It was like he was on something. I'll warn Allison."

I raised my brows, thinking about the notes I had read, and realized Allie might have a point. "That won't help. Allison still doesn't understand us, and you explaining this before meeting her would sound crazier than what I sounded like last night."

"It is crazy, Lawrence. But unfortunately, it is true. You might have escaped his envious assaults in the past, but now you're dating a woman he is obsessed with. When I spoke to him, all I saw was Bud Fox spinning out of control at the end of *The Show*—"

"Please don't jinx the storyline of *The Gym*," I said and paused for a breath. "Maybe Bob will go back to New York—"

She sighed loudly. "Maybe you should reread *The Show*."

I hesitated. "Maybe, I will."

Click.

FORTY-FIVE

WICKED WARNINGS

DECEMBER 4, 2017
THE GYM

It was three days later.

"Lawrence," Allie whispered. "Who's the handsome dark-haired man who runs like the wind on our treadmills?"

I laughed. "That's Gary Yates. He was our fifteenth new member since Thanksgiving."

"I'm so proud of you, Lawrence."

"Us," I insisted. "This is a group effort, Allie Girl."

"Awww, thanks, Lawrence."

"I'll be there in about twenty minutes. What am I walking into?"

I gripped the steering wheel tighter. "Um, Gemma's training Karen in the yoga studio," she said. "Matty keeps pestering me to clean something…Chuck's wife, Jean, is joining The Gym, and Fern's son missed the bus again and is pacing outside on her phone." She giggled. "Oh, yeah, and your buddy, who wears the Cubs hat, wants to talk to you."

"Paul Abruzzo?"

"Yes."

"I'll call him. Anything else?"

"There's a letter from Captain Hook's advertising company."

I smiled grimly. "So, the Jolly Roger's back at port."

"What?" she replied, puzzled.

"Nothing. I'll see you soon."

Click.

I strolled in The Gym with Barbara's Body Sculpt Class and opened the letter from Hook's advertising company, R.H. Marketing Solutions. Hook was billing me for the direct mailers that never went out when he returned my check during my drama ridden days with Sarah. Dumbfounded, I fired off an email to his billing department. After a brief back and forth, they ended all communication when I pointed out that they missed the cut-off date to print the mailers.

An hour later, my buddy Paul Abruzzo scurried back into The Gym, out of breath. The sixty-five-year-old die-hard Cub fan looked like he walked right off the set of the Godfather. He joined The Gym in August, and we became close after he read *The Show*. Lately, he had been sharing the story of his career demise. Members who lived in his neighborhood would notoriously send pictures of us laughing to his wife with captions: *Paul's workouts at The Gym!*

On this day, Paul was not laughing, though. He snatched a fresh gym towel off the stack and rushed into the office. "Your old advertising nemesis, Hook, was talking about you at Sunny Side Café this morning," said Paul as he sat in the other office chair.

My mind was clouded. "What's Hook up to now?" I asked myself out loud. I felt instinctive that this had significance, but part of me didn't want to know what that significance could be. I contemplated shrugging it off but was unable to stifle my curiosity. "Did you hear anything else?"

Paul took his Cubs hat off and wiped his buzzed head with the towel. "Yeah, some woman left the guy he was talking to, and Hook insisted he takes something for his depression."

Bob Tillie, I thought. For reasons that I couldn't comprehend at that moment, I only wanted to confirm it. "Was his name Bob?"

"I don't recall hearing a name."

I sat forward, then said, "What did he look like?"

Rasping his fingers over his scalp, he said, "Heavy-set guy with greying hair—Italian looking..." the office lights flickered.

My jaw dropped a little. "Did he have a goatee?" I asked intently.

He wiped his mouth with the towel. "Yes." He paused, thinking. "I've never seen him at The Gym, though." He blinked at me. "What are you doing to your shirt?"

I looked down and saw my fingers grasping it, and mumbled incredulously, "He used to be a member. His name is Bob Tillie."

His nostrils flared, sniffing for a scoop. "He reminded me of myself after my career meltdown; moody, quick to anger, and desperate. He looked like he is on the verge of a breakdown. What's his deal?"

The look I shot him was equal parts of anger and resignation. "He's a pariah." I smoothed out my T-shirt and shifted uneasily in the chair. "A guy who ultimately was used by Hook, too."

Paul swiveled in the chair with his greying eyebrows raised above his brown eyes. "This is unbelievable."

I nodded. "And I don't know what the correlation is, but I received an invoice from Hook for a direct mail job they were supposed to do nearly a year ago."

"You told me you don't use Hook's company anymore."

"I don't. Hook canceled that deal. That's why this is weird." I took a sip of water. "What else happened?"

Paul thought for a moment. "Well, the other guy...Tillie left. But Hook stayed texting on his phone, annoyed."

I nodded thoughtfully and thanked Paul before hurrying out to take a call from Allison. "Hey," I answered distractedly.

She excitedly said, "Hey, sweetie, when can we get the straps and blocks for my yoga class?"

I sat down on the bench. "Allison, we're not buying anything right now—"

"Larry, we have to," she whined.

"This is a business," I replied sharply. "I'm asking you to trust me."

After an awkward moment of silence, she said, "Fine. But you really need to practice some yoga, Larry. It would do you good."

I hesitated. "I'm sorry, I've heard things, and I don't know what to think. Has Bob Tillie reached back out to you?"

She sighed. "Larry, he's harmless."

Even though Allison was testing my patience, I took a breath and felt relaxed. At that moment, I had a profound sense that we'd be together for a long time. In a calmer voice, I said, "So, he's going to your class?"

"Quite a few people are. Why?"

With storm clouds rolling across the sky, I only assured Allison that I was proud of her and noticed Allie walking out of The Gym. She gave me a quick look that I couldn't quite read. "Allison," I stood up, "let me call you back."

"Okay, bye."

Click.

When I told Allie about Paul's message, a faint look of alarm passed across her face before she tossed her giant hippie bag in the back seat and exclaimed, "When you first hired me, you told me to be kind to everyone. People don't like you because you're the author of a book or a gym owner. They like you because you are a sincerely nice guy. You seemed to have lost sight that that's the real reason The Gym has a new life." She paused with her point and shifted her gaze to the waves crashing against the shoreline. With the breeze picking up, she pulled her hair off her face and looked up at me. There was a steely glint in her eyes, and her voice grated harshly. "Bob sincerely misses you—"

"Allie," I said, cutting her off. "When he was a member, you couldn't understand why I allowed him in the office."

"Well, I've grown a little over this year, too," she insisted. "Bob has deep-rooted envy issues, but he realizes you did care about him. Even if I'm wrong about his sincerity, you'll be keeping your enemy closer."

I glared at her, startled.

The late morning sun had disappeared. When I explained I couldn't allow negative energy back in The Gym, a few large drops of rain began to fall. "At some point, you must let the bad apples go, Allie."

"I agree, but you can smooth over a situation that can turn ugly in a hurry. After *The Show*, I figured you would never forget that."

More stunned than sensible, I said, "This is a different story, don't get caught up in an old one."

"Life stories always have similarities," she sighed deeply. She sounded almost grief-stricken. "After everything you endured to get to this point, I thought you'd do more to ensure you don't have another not so happily-ever-after…"

I stood there as she drove off, suddenly chilled by fear.

FORTY-SIX

HE'S COMING TO MY YOGA CLASS AFTER ALL

DECEMBER 6, 2017
THE OLD FISH HOUSE
For the past two nights, I had been restlessly rereading *The Show*, desperate to collect my final notes for *The Gym*.

Although Kristen urged me to give the story a full year to play out, I agreed without regard to the last twenty-five days having any consequence.

In short, Paul and Allie spooked me.

Contemplating too much, I opened a Josh Cabernet while deeply absorbed in my notepad, which I separated by month on the kitchen table. I gave those thoughts free rein as my fingertips caressed one of the rough corners of a wine-stained page from January.

Notes:

JANUARY 19, 2017
THE GYM
After the Ripper's warning about Captain Hook, I surmised Bob Tillie had spun stories to him. Ironically, before this news about Hook, Bob's fabrications had done nothing but helped promote my next book.

On the one hand, I want to thank the guy for being a cagey character most readers will love to loathe. On the other hand, I know the dangers of keeping someone like that close to me. But there is something else going on here. Ultimately, I've allowed this to continue because I'm as lonely as he is. I hope he hasn't given up trying to find that special someone, even though he insists I'm naïve for believing I will.

I swallowed hard. So much had happened since I wrote those notes that I did feel naïve. Rubbing my face in disbelief, I couldn't deny Allie had a point. Maybe Bob slid down the same rabbit hole Bud Fox had. *Should I call Bob and clear the air?* I asked myself, glancing at *The Show.*

My iPhone rang. "Hey, Allie Girl," I answered, welcoming the distraction.

"Hey, Lawrence, Dr. Linder wants to meet Tinker Bell." She laughed. "She mentioned dinner at Yellow Dog Café next week."

I smiled. "Tell her I got her text. I'll ask Allison what day works."

"Okay, Lawrence. Bye."

Click.

I took a long sip of wine and checked the time.

I was meeting Allison for an early dinner at The Old Fish House down the street from my house and placed my wine glass down, too high strung to continue. *A nice dinner on the river will relax me;* I thought as Allison called right on cue. "I'm ready to go now," I answered and let a slight smile come to my lips.

"It's too early," said Allison cheerfully. "Did you send the finished chapters to your publisher?"

I sighed, resigned, a deep silence surrounding me. "Not yet," I muttered. "I'm struggling a bit."

"I thought everything was coming together?"

"Allison, this story won't be in book form for a couple of years," I snapped defensively. "It's a long process to complete a manuscript."

"I get that," she replied. "But something is bothering you…"

I hesitated.

"I want the story to end now," I said softly. "Happily."

"So, do it!" she insisted emphatically.

"I can't," I said after a moment. "I'll explain why at the restaurant."

She sighed. "Is your buddy, Chris, bringing his boat over?"

"No, he's showing a house tonight. When can you get there?"

"I'll be there in forty minutes, right around five."

"Okay, bye."

"Bye, sweetie."

Click.

It was an unseasonably warm day, so I finished my glass of wine on the lanai while talking to Paul Abruzzo. After explaining this dilemma to him, my anxiety levels rose when he said, "Time with you should be measured in dog years. Your twenty-five days is like eight months for anyone else."

I poured another glass.

Thirty minutes after that, I pulled into The Old Fish House. I parked next to Allison as Paul texted me: *DOG YEARS. SO TRUE WITH YOU...LMFAO!!*

Chuckling apprehensively, I deleted the text and hurried in. Allison was sitting at a high-top on the back deck overlooking the water in an irresistible Lilly Pulitzer short outfit. She looked like a tiny pixie princess as her blue eyes sparkled and blond bob blew in the breeze. "What a gorgeous evening," I said with a smile and kissed her.

"I can't believe I'm wearing shorts in December." She raised her wine to me.

We clinked glasses to a beautiful sunset as sailboats drifted by, admiring the Christmas lights on the houses along the Indian River. After Allison briefed me about her day at school, she got back to our earlier conversation and asked why I couldn't end the story. With a slow breath, I mulled over how to bring up Kristen Bircher, aware the only other time I had, Allison was focused on the night we shared and not the importance of her message. So, I tried again. "Kristen had a keen sense for a storyline and insisted that I give the story a full year to play out—"

"Kristen was the really young one you had a one-night stand with, right?" Allison interrupted. Her gaze grew distant.

I nodded once. "Yes, but her advice made sense since the story plays out in diary form by each month of the year," I said, with a little smirk of a smile.

She kept her face steady. "So, January to January," I nodded, "which gives you...what, three weeks. What's the big deal?"

I answered without hesitation. "In my life, it's like dog years." My tone said clearly that that had been a silly question, but she didn't get it.

Her brow rose as the waitress dropped off our seared tuna. "What?"

"I've been reading the end of *The Show* because Allie and Paul spooked me."

Allison teased, crossing her arms. "Is this about Bob Tillie?"

I took a bite. "Mm…yes," I said. "But you can't get this, so forget it."

"Calm down. I don't need a crisis to bring me to my senses. I mean, I get the dim manager in *The Show*, losing his shit at the end of that story, but Bob is older than you. From what I remember, he is nothing like you. Or your flunky protégé, Bud Fox."

I sighed. "I realize that—"

"So, this is about Bob's secret infatuation with me," she murmured, arching one eyebrow.

No less absurd was his hidden agenda with her. "It plays into it, Allison," I said as calmly as I could, wanting to scream. "The notes I have and what I heard and what you told me, make it difficult to deny his fascination with both of us. He's had people even leave post-it-notes at The Gym." I paused as her expression caused deep fatigue-generated hopelessness. "Let's talk about something else, please."

Her lips curled into a flirtatious smile. "Okay, I'm picturing us in your bed."

My eyes widened, aroused. I swirled my wine glass, with a sudden desire to bend her over the high-top. I swallowed. "I need to write—"

"I know you," she wailed, cutting me off with an eye roll. "You're not going to be able to write without a release. You're Italian."

Boy, did I sell that one, I thought but said, "You know me so well."

She raised her glass. "Yes, and our sex is too yummy to pass on."

We clinked glasses again.

Our gazes held. Allison looked adorable in that moonlit moment as sensual anticipation overwhelmed us. "I need you," I whispered desperately to her, with a wry smile.

"You're still that sixteen-year-old Italian boy you felt like in *The Show*…" she giggled with her wine glass to her lips, attempting to conceal her giddiness enough to spit out the rest of her statement. "Only now, you're fifty."

I inwardly laughed. "I think there's something wrong with me."

She placed her glass down and leaned over it. "I'm not complaining," said Allison with a whimsical smile. "I love Italy!"

"Where the hell is our waitress?" I replied as she grabbed her iPhone with purpose.

Her eyes grew mischievous. "Bald men are known to have higher testosterone levels," she held up the article, "see…read this…"

"Please don't bring up my bald bean," I whined pathetically. "It puts me in a fragile state." I tipped back my wine and then spilled some. "Shit…" I rubbed my shirt.

"I'm complimenting you," she pleaded, eyeing the mess I made. "Dab some water on that, so it doesn't stain." Increasingly amused, she then tipped back her wine.

I waited for her to place the glass back on the table and said, "It's not nice to make fun of me."

There was a pause as she kicked off her flip flop, then a magnanimous, "I'm not. I just love it when you look like a little boy!"

Heads turned, and I suppressed a wince. With Allison's barefoot running up my leg, the waitress walked up with our Mahi and fish tacos. Her eyes flew from me to Allison. "I'll bring the check, enjoy."

I almost laughed. "Thanks…"

We ate our meals as if we were competing in one of those Nathan's hot dog eating contests and raced back to my house.

Twenty minutes after that, while lying naked on our backs still breathing heavily, Allison's Facebook messenger pinged alarmingly loud from my nightstand. She jumped off the bed and whirled to it as her gaze shifted from Jedi Mickey to the message. "It's Bob Tillie." She shot a frantic glance at me. "He's coming to my yoga class after all."

I closed my eyes and saw nothing but flames.

FORTY-SEVEN

SOMEWHERE BETWEEN REALITY AND ALL WE'VE EVER DREAMED

DECEMBER 27, 2017
THE GYM

It was the day of Allison's yoga class. She had moved it to the open timeslot after Diane's Pilates class on the last Wednesday night of the year, and I was edgy. I still hadn't sent the chapters I owed my publisher, and we'd been arguing about it for days.

Pacing outside The Gym, I texted her again and fell back on the bench, looking for solace. Typically, I would find it in the ocean's breeze. But today was different.

Time passed with no response from Allison. I had no idea what was going on, but something was up, something big. Something bad. Minutes later, I had my arms crossed in an instinctive gesture of self-protection when Allie came in for her shift. "There's a storm coming!" she exclaimed. "Hurry home and send those chapters to your publisher. And send me one, too," she smiled, "I loved the last one." Her smile turned a little grim when we glanced out to the ominous clouds on the horizon.

"Okay," I moaned, sounding like Eeyore.

Allie was quiet for a moment. "What's wrong?"

Despite the growing darkness, I took steps towards my car and said, "Nothing…" while craving the courage not to need all the answers.

Forty minutes later, I was in front of my laptop to send chapters of *The Gym* to my publisher but stopped. Instead, I reread the third chapter and rubbed my face, annoyed. *Bob played into too much of what was wrong,*

I thought. Standing at my wine rack, Allie confirmed that Bob showed up for Allison's yoga class. "Since you didn't heed my warning," she said snippily. "What do I charge, Bob?"

I scowled, trying to catch my breath. "Charge him the price of a day pass," I croaked. "Actually, let me talk to him."

"He stepped outside."

I took a breath to press for more. "For what, his yoga pants?" I tried to sound calm, even amused, but my heart was beating too fast, glancing back at my manuscript.

She laughed. "No, I think Allison pulled in."

"What?" I snapped irritably. "She hasn't called me all day."

"That's weird," said Allie with a snort of laughter. "Did you know Bob has the same political views as your Tink and loves Chihuahuas?"

"What?"

"He just told me that. He seems to be on something again."

I let out my breath in a long sigh. "Please tell Allison to call me," I said, my words laced with anguish.

As if sensing my restlessness, she ended the call abruptly, "I'll call you back—"

Click.

My thoughts turned as dark as the sky.

I tore the cork out of the bottle and heard a familiar voice behind me. *Long time no see, Sport!* It was *The Dark One.*

He looked well-rested as he leaned back on the kitchen counter. *Did you really think you were going to feel stars exploding inside of you forever?* He trilled with his spine-chilling laugh.

I wavered a moment with a heavy sigh. "We love each other—"

I don't recall either of you saying that The Dark One reminded me with a blunt cut off. *And men still text her...*

My lips compressed briefly. "We love each other," I repeated, eyes flicking nervously.

Come on, Sport, your little Tink was a nice twist to your fucked-up fairy tale. That's it. You got your dick wet and pretended you were normal. But let's be real, you're not. He filled my wine glass. *So, drink up and continue writing—*

"I'm not caving to your bullshit anymore!"

Bullshit? If you loved her, you would've told her. Like Wendy before, Tink has served her purpose. She'll end up with some rich guy she doesn't like, and you'll fly on to a hot brunette who you'll rename Tiger Lilly for our next shit show! The Dark One howled with delight. *Tomorrow and the few days left in this storyline will be different. Indeed, another unhappily ever after, Sport...*

I took a deep breath. The house was eerily quiet. Each room seemed to be holding its breath, waiting for me to scream out. And then *The Dark One* continued taunting me. Songs played over in my head, reminding me of the women from earlier in the story. I questioned too much. *Why is this happening again? Why haven't I told Allison I love her?*

I tried hard to dismiss this chaos of thoughts, this mixture of sadness and anger, but I couldn't. All the life lessons I learned over this past year seemed to be fading fast. It was as if *The Dark One* had banished it all from my heart and mind as the wind howled in the torrential downpour.

When I closed my eyes and took in a reflective breath, the songs in my head stopped. *This is all me*, I reminded myself. *When anger invades my insides, life shifts on the outside.* With the tightness easing from my neck and shoulders, I smiled, more relaxed.

Then I received a text, and the lights flickered. The ping sounded different, dark, and threatening. I walked over to my iPhone, and tension pulled my shoulders tight again when I read it.

Call 911. Bob Tillie has a gun!

The house went dark.

Staring at it in disbelief, it fell from my hand. My heart pounded out of my chest. The security cameras went dark, too. *Breathe...just breathe!* I repeated to myself and called Allie. Immediately it went to voicemail. The lights flickered back on with the cameras. I hit camera four, which was the yoga studio, and it enlarged. Bob waved a gun at Allison as she had her hands up to him, begging him not to pull the trigger. Fear shifted to anger. I struggled for a breath in this panic-stricken state.

Holy fuck, breathe!

With a pained determination, I took short breaths and called 911. I snatched my keys off the counter and squeezed them tightly, running into the dark and stormy night. My wet hands slipped off the wheel, backing out of the driveway. With the wipers swooshing heavily back and forth across the windshield, I punched it in drive and sped off.

I tried Allie again.

Again, it went to voicemail.

The rain was hitting the car sideways. The wind made it difficult to stay in a lane. Racing over the Front Street train tracks, I skidded to a stop at US1 and wiped the wetness from my eyes. With a frantic breath, I took a left, racing through the puddles while peeking at my screen. Bob was standing in the middle of the yoga studio. His self-loathing settled upon his shoulders just as it did when he'd sit in my office. My eyes darted to Allison as the car slid into the left lane. Gripping the wheel, I hydroplaned on a sheet of standing water when a lightning bolt struck the river.

The screen went black.

In that single flashing, throbbing moment, I knew my relationship with Allison was written in the stars and drawn into our destiny. I could see her smile at me. We had fallen in love with each other. I didn't care how hard being together would be; nothing was worse than being apart. I couldn't let anything happen to her.

I took another slow breath and hit the screen again.

All the cameras were still dark. Minutes later, I took a hard right off US1 and sped over the causeway as this feeling welled up in me. Adrenaline rushed through my veins. Then, in quick succession, I tried Allie again. Police cars raced by me as the call went to voicemail.

I tried to keep my eyes fixed ahead but began looking back with the overwhelming feeling that this was my fault. Anger bubbled up inside me. I hammered my fist against the dashboard. *It had been years since Allison had even seen Bob. She had no idea how troubled he was. I should've never allowed him to get that close to me,* I thought sourly, *just like with Bud Fox. It was all fun and games until all I saw were flames.* My heart was pounding, fit to burst out of my chest, unable to fathom how much worse this could be.

I gripped the steering wheel more tightly, sweat collected at the base of my neck. First, Second and Third Avenues flashed by my passenger window, with no recollection of taking the turn off Ocean Avenue.

When I passed the Breakers Condos, a SWAT team came off Oak Street ahead of me.

Following closely behind their taillights, I hydroplaned again. I overcompensated and spun out into the oncoming lane, just missing a Budweiser truck. Spinning out of the wet sand, I made it back on the right side of A1A.

The cameras on my iPhone came back on.

Bob raised the gun to Allison and pressed it against her forehead. In an instant, I was doing ninety. Tears poured down her face. I strained my eyes to see, to believe this horror. With mounting panic, I lowered the windows because I was hyperventilating. It was like the air was being squeezed from my lungs as street signs blurred by me with the rain pouring in. I could not catch my breath. Bob put both hands on the gun, and the screen went dark. I hit it with such force, it cracked. Gasping for air, I pulled back too hard on the wheel and crashed into the curb at the entrance of The Gym.

Police were everywhere.

With another flash of lightning, there was a blitzkrieg of voices, noises. I staggered towards them, disoriented as the rain pelted my face. *I need to get in there*, I thought to myself. Police officers motioned me back, but then the rain stopped, and everyone shifted on their ready. I snuck behind the line, and the skies suddenly cleared. This darkest of nights had the second star to the right shining brighter than ever.

Illuminating The Gym, I sprinted into it with a feeling of hope.

One startled police officer lunged for me and missed but couldn't scream out either. After a moment of chaos, I advanced to the yoga studio, my senses on alert. Inching against the odd wall of mirrors, I heard Allison pleading with Bob to drop the gun. Thankfully, she didn't seem to be hurt. Then the SWAT team leader whispered into his radio. "We have to go now!"

He was right.

A red laser flashed up on the door, and I thrust it open. Without the slightest hesitation, I shouted, "I love Allison, Bob!" His body convulsed as if my words were bullets. "Put the gun down."

He staggered to the side, releasing his hold on the gun. His jaw was firmly clenched, and his brimming eyes stared straight ahead as the officers dropped him to the floor.

Allison rushed into my arms, and as I squeezed her tight, there was a fantastic light. It was the second star to the right, and we took it straight on 'til morning. Holding my hand, she looked over at me and said, *I believe this dream is forever...*

My eyes fluttered open. "Hey, sweetie," said Allison. She turned on the bedroom lamp. "You were dreaming."

I slowly lifted my head off the damp pillow with a stiff, awkward smile. "Wow," I sputtered, amused and enlightened. "That was an interesting one."

Her eyes narrowed at me. "Your eyes have a light..."

I had a moment of revelation. "Because I caught the moments that changed everything."

She looked curiously and carefully at me. "What do you mean?" she asked thoughtfully.

"Life," I assured her. "The Gym has changed my perspective on it." I smiled at her, reflecting on it all. "What an adventure. All the meaningful coincidences and synchronicity and magical moments from the beginning blurred into now," I shook my head and sighed. "I guess I'm babbling—"

"No, I understand," she said softly. "I get we were meant to meet. I get what you have done for The Gym. And what The Gym has done for you." She paused with a gleam in her eye. "And can I tell you something else?"

With a grateful nod, I muttered, "How about what you've done for me?"

Her face flushed, and as her eyes opened to her soul, the pixie dust began to fall as we simultaneously said, "I love you." Our lips touched with a magical kiss, and we fell back on our pillows.

The air in the room tingled.

"I love breathing you in," Allison added with her adorable smile.

"I love it when I look at you, and you're already smiling back."

She snuggled her face against my neck as my gaze shifted to the sunlight that crept through the plantation shutters. I followed it onto the last page of my notepad and grabbed it off the nightstand inspired.

Only one-page left, I thought.

Allison pushed herself off the bed to read another Facebook message. "You were right," she confessed; expression was wary. "Bob is not coming back to The Gym." Slowly, she made her way around the bed when her eyes rose to squint at me in the dim lamplight. "This guy is toxic. I'm not even going to respond to this." She opened the plantation shutters and stood there for a moment. Turning towards me, she smiled with an expression of utter tranquility on her face. "I'm going to make our coffee." She gazed at Jedi Mickey, walking back around the bed, and added, "I know you like yours black and your morning's bright, so enjoy that beautiful sunrise before you pick up all your little boy clothes and move that ridiculous Mickey Mouse to the garage. This place looks like a frat house…"

I shook my head and felt an unpleasant smile curl my lips. "Listen, here, Tink, I don't complain about your asinine Lifetime movies or essential oils and diffusers," I huffed, suddenly tickled. "Besides, Jedi Mickey guards my sacred Never Land."

Allison looked at me, amused. "Um, Peter," she mocked. "I'm the new pixie who'll be guarding your little fantasy land now—"

"It's Never Land, Tink…" I sighed and looked impatiently at her. "Don't you know where I live?"

She smiled at me. "Yes, somewhere between reality and all we've ever dreamed! Now get dressed, you freak."

I smiled back at her. "Oh, can you grab me a new notepad from your classroom?" I glanced down at my old one. "I'm using the last page to finish this magical adventure of ours at our beloved gym."

She was gone.

For a long moment, all I heard was the whisper of my heart and the loveliest tinkle of bells. Then a kitchen cabinet slammed shut, and her teacher's voice echoed over me. "*The Gym* will be your last book for a while, so there is no need for any new notepads—"

"What happens if Captain Hook comes back to The Gym, and we have another adventure?"

"I need a break from your adventures," she answered quickly.

With a nervous chuckle, I put the pen to the last page of my old notepad as scintillating birds chirped outside my window with sweet voices and wrote:

So, as a new day dawned on our beloved little gym, our magical fairy tale played out with all the blissful insanity that comes after the "I love you" kiss. You know, life...

THE END

EPILOGUE

THE INTERVIEW

JANUARY 11, 2020
THE GYM
It was two years later.

The editing and production stage for the manuscript was underway. I was being interviewed at The Gym by Carla Kimbrel, a Gator alum who worked for *Florida Book Buzz Magazine*. *The Gym's* release date was only months away, and it went without saying that I was excited. Ironically, our paths crossed when Carla, who was friends with none other than Michelle "Cruella" Crowley, suggested she interviewed me after Carla mentioned she was looking to do a piece on a local author. It felt like another serendipitous encounter when the date we chose to meet was exactly three years after I was inspired to write the story.

It was a breezy Saturday afternoon. The Gym closed at three o'clock, and Carla scheduled the interview for four. At three-thirty, I opened the doors to air out the faint musty smell from our busy morning and set up two chairs in the yoga studio for the interview. Ten minutes later, I heard a woman's voice. "Hello, anyone here?"

I strolled out and into Carla's firm handshake. "Hi Larry, I'm Carla," she said with a smile that had a hint of anxiety. "Am I too early?"

I smiled at her. "No. You're fine."

She nervously tugged on her Gator T-shirt. "Good," she replied, rubbing her hand in a circle on her faded jeans. "I wanted to check out the pictures." Her blond shoulder-length hair blew across her face. "This story has undeniable energy. It is quite special."

"Amazing people have inspired me," I assured her, en route to close the doors with a glance back to her. "Please, thank Michelle for me."

"I will," said Carla, squinting at a picture full of intrigue. "I bet I can pick out some of the characters from these tiles." She whirled to me with an amused expression on her face. "That's Allie Girl!"

I nodded. "Yes, I miss her."

"So, she finally left The Gym?" she asked. Her voice was delicate and light.

"Yes, it's been over a year now," I murmured. I was shocked; it had been so long.

She shifted to look at me with raised eyebrows. "Where is Allie now?"

I blinked. "She went home. To Ohio with her fiancé."

Determined to get updates on as many characters as she could, Carla hastily sputtered, "So, Allie found love—and Wilson?"

"He's back in school. I'm proud of him."

Carla continued, "And this is Lauren. Your daughter's beautiful." She tapped her finger on the next tile. "And your son...Jerry." Staring at a picture of him playing Bill Sykes from the Oliver Twist chapter, she added, "I heard he was chosen to give his graduation speech, after all."

I nodded. "It was impressive."

Gleefully, Carla bent down to view some newer tiles. "And these kids are the new Allie Girl and Wilson," she said, again referring to *The Gym's* storyline.

I laughed. "Yes, that's Anthony, Max, and Sammie. She's Barbara's daughter—"

"Body Sculpt, Barbara?" she exclaimed, cutting me off.

"Yes, do you know her?"

"Only from the story," she confessed, eyeing me with a wide smile. "I enjoyed all the characters." Standing on her tiptoes, the shortish journalist gestured to a picture of Allison. "And that's Tinker Bell!" she added with a tight smile. "She's adorable."

"Indeed," I agreed, watching her process everything.

Her warm blue eyes narrowed at me. "So, what's the secret to your happily-ever-after?" she asked.

"When life gets dark, we always end up seeing the light in each other's eyes," I replied, slowly pondering our recent struggles.

Carla's smile flatlined when her eyes widened, focused on a text. "Well, now it's official." She looked over at me. "Captain Hook is my new boss." She laughed awkwardly.

"Excuse me," I said, thinking I misunderstood her. When she explained that Hook purchased her magazine, I sighed, startled. "So, much for this interview."

Her eyes averted mine while ignoring my comment. After regaining her composure, she changed the subject. "That mural is just as you described; ocean caps and birds...1990s," she said, shaking her head. "I'm sorry, I feel like I stepped into the story. Maybe I'll be in the next book—"

"Be careful of what you wish for."

A mischievous smile curled on her face. "Would you mind if I record the interview?"

"No, I have chairs set up in the yoga studio."

Walking in, the interview ahead appeared to me in a series of inspiring images. This, I knew, would refocus my perspective as I now envisioned an epilogue. Carla pulled up her questions and leaned back, thoughtful. Her voice perked up when she suggested I turn the stories into a book series under the name Peter Pan Man. I grinned, intrigued. "*The Show* would be *Peter Pan Man Book One*," she continued. Her eyes had a light. "*The Gym*—"

"*Peter Pan Man Book Two*," I said, finishing her sentence with a nod. "That could work."

With a warm smile, she chirped, "I believe! I believe it will."

It was then I realized the end of this story was just the beginning of this next chapter of my life. Musing that, she took a sip of water and crossed her legs. "Would you say everything having to do with this book has been a bit serendipitous?"

Reflecting on it all, I nodded. "Yes."

Her eyes narrowed at me. "I have my take on individuals who elicit magical moments which I'll circle back to," she said, wonder in her voice.

I shrugged, like a lost boy. "Can't wait."

After rattling off questions about the challenges of completing both manuscripts, she mentioned how much she enjoyed reading about my notepad. Her gaze lifted from her own notes. "Let's talk about the topics you covered in *The Gym*, like fate and destiny," she insisted. "I'll only use certain answers for my summary of the book without spoiling the end." I nodded and felt a shortness of breath as she added, "How would you describe your notepad changing your destiny?"

"It became a journal which gradually provided me clarity," I said as my shoulders relaxed. "Honestly, it allowed me to begin this next chapter of my life."

Carla leaned forward, instantly curious. "I found that fascinating. Can you elaborate on that?"

"In short, I slipped into a rather dark time of my life, not realizing I was overthinking everything. We can't live a healthy life when the past consumes us. The notepad helped me see that."

"Were those early chapters as dark as you wrote?"

"Yes, I was reckless," I admitted. "Lucky to be alive."

Carla caught a glimpse of my tense expression and shot me a genuine smile. "It was refreshing to read how the characters you were emotionally involved with were more than entertaining dates. Which woman provided the most impactful message to the storyline?"

"Both Maya and Kristen," I breathed out. "After reading *The Show*, they convinced me just to be me and believe—"

"Beginning with Chapter One," Carla gushed. "Just Be You...And Believe!"

I nodded. "Yes. Kristen saw the love story I had envisioned. Ironically, I stood on her balcony with a vision for the cover of *The Gym*."

"So, you were destined to go," Carla said, looking ten years younger. "I felt these young ladies kept you true to who you really are. Do you agree?"

I held her gaze, mirroring her smile, then nodded. "I let life play out and then write. With each passing month and chapter, the experience changed my perception. It sounds corny, but life tests you, and even their emoji-filled texts were like messages from the universe leading me on."

Carla looked up from the next question and broke into a huge smile. "Would you say the magical moments in the story happened to you because you did believe?"

Her question hung in the balance. "Yes," I said finally. "Things weren't exactly going my way when I didn't. You must believe in yourself first, and then believe that that special someone is out there. And you must keep living, loving, and laughing along the way."

My words seemed to comfort her as her blue eyes gleamed. "Living, loving, and laughing seem to be your motto. Would you say *The Gym* is also a story of hope?"

With humility, I nodded slowly. "Most definitely."

"So, as the story goes, you found the girl and saved the gym. Why did you insist it saved you?"

"Ultimately, The Gym has taught me that life is a reality to be experienced," I said, suddenly emotional. She stared at me, intently listening. "It's humbled me to take chances, make mistakes, and laugh as I grow."

Carla held my gaze for a long moment and then smiled. "Last question."

I glanced at a text from Allison: *I opened the wine, hurry up.* (heart face emoji) *I love you!* And then said to Carla, "Perfect timing," I held up Allison's text. "It's wine time!"

With a whimsical stare, Carla concluded, "All endings are also beginnings. I see this story with an ending that really is a beginning for you. Did you see that writing it?"

I smiled as warm light from the setting sun shone through the window and said, "Not as much as I do now."

ACKNOWLEDGMENTS

I would like to thank:

My mother, Jo Ann Sola, for believing.

My kiddos and their mom, Lauren, Jerry, and Marie, for supporting my creative energy over the years.

My sisters, Mary Ann Colucci and Christine Sola/Rizzo, for doing the same growing up.

Everyone who inspired characters in *The Gym*.

Everyone who has supported both books with pictures and reviews.

Everyone at Black Rose Writing, but particularly, Reagan Rothe for this opportunity.

My father, Jerry Sola, who is behind all of this from up above.

Allison Pojanowski for getting me and loving me.

NOTE FROM THE AUTHOR

Word-of-mouth is crucial for any author to succeed. If you enjoyed *The Gym*, please leave a review online—anywhere you are able. Even if it's just a sentence or two. It would make all the difference and would be very much appreciated.

Thanks!
Larry

ABOUT THE AUTHOR

After a climbing the corporate ladder in the wine industry, Lawrence H. Sola received a publishing contract for the story of his career rise and fall aptly titled, *The Show*. Shortly after that novel was released, he began a new career in the fitness industry, which inspired a sequel titled, *The Gym*. He is currently enjoying his time on the beach with his sights set on his next writing project.

Thank you so much for reading one of Lawrence H. Sola's novels.
If you enjoyed the experience, please check out our recommended
title for your next great read!

The Show by Lawrence H. Sola

He worked hard, played hard, and was referred to as the Peter
Pan Man, set to be a star in the industry he adored. After his third
promotion in four years, he was granted a rare bright future tag
that only two executives, with very different agendas, were
aware of. The company relocated him to run a new selling
division and his seemingly scripted life appeared to be a dream,
until the warnings he ignored caused it to have traits of a
nightmare.

With pixie dust bathing the scene in magic, the Peter Pan Man
met his Wendy, and the curtain rose on *The Show.*